Valentina

by

Fern Michaels

Copyright © 1978 by Roberta Anderson and Mary Kuczkir

All Rights Reserved under International and Pan-American Copyright Conventions. Published in the United States by Ballantine Books, a division of Random House, Inc., New York, and simultaneously in Canada by Random House of Canada Limited, Toronto, Canada.

Library of Congress Catalog Card Number: 78-51757

ISBN 0-345-29580-3

Manufactured in the United States of America

BALLANTINE BOOKS • NEW YORK

Library of Congress Catalog Card Number: 78-51875

ISBN 0-345-29580-3

Manufactured in the United States of America

First Edition: May 1978
Fourth Printing: July 1981

To Roberta

Prologue

Soft night sounds and cool, whispering breezes at last persuaded her thickly lashed eyes to close in slumber. Stars shone in the black sky, and a mellow sliver of moon watched over the earth like a lonely sentry, protecting the lovers in the magic hush of the desert darkness.

Valentina lay quietly, listening to the slow, even breathing of the dark-eyed, raven-haired man beside her. From time to time she gently touched his cool skin to reassure herself that he was real. He was hers, totally hers, for now, forever, for all eternity. Nothing save death could take him from her.

He stirred and reached out a muscular arm to bring her closer. She sighed contentedly as she laid her dark head on his broad chest, feeling the thicket of fine fur soft against her cheek. Imperceptibly his arm tightened and Valentina nestled closer, whispering soft words of endearment. She felt warm lips caress her bare shoulder and then heard her husband's soft murmur as he breathed her name. "Valentina . . . Valentina . . ."

"Hush." She placed gentle fingers upon his face, and he turned his head to press his mouth against her sweetly scented wrist. Her skin was smooth and warm, and even in sleep he was drawn to that place where her pulse drummed in a contented rhythm. "I am here, I'll always be here," she whispered. "Sleep, my love." He too shared her anxieties. The soft moan of her name on his lips drew her back to their love-making of a few hours past. . . .

"Valentina," he had whispered huskily, "come to

me, let me love you," as his mouth closed hungrily over hers. His sun-darkened hands had swept her long silky hair into a knot, drawing her still closer, closer, always closer.

He caressed her neck, her smooth, womanly shoulders as his lips clung greedily to hers. She wrapped her arms about his neck to bring him closer, to make them as one. He drew his mouth from hers and looked down into her shining eyes. His gaze covered her, devoured her. He loosened the satiny belt of her robe, which clung to her slim feminine curves. His dark eyes expressed his hunger. Her breasts became taut, their rosy crests stiffening beneath the heat of his gaze.

A warm glow of yearning danced up her spine and spread through her long, slender haunches. He stroked her skin with tender, teasing touches, stirring her to the heights of her passion. Gently he circled her hips and drew her to him, smothering her mouth with smoldering kisses. Valentina was totally aware of him, her senses drowning as his sinewy, muscular legs locked with hers. His husky murmurings sent rivers of passion flooding through her as she felt herself being lowered to the bed.

Her arms encircled him more tightly, feeling the light, rippling muscles beneath the broad expanse of his back as she drew him to her again, this time whispering his name over and over in a tone low and throaty, a sound, she knew, that pressed his desire for her into an erupting urgency.

Desire coursed through her as his hands explored her intimately; her breasts were alive with a hunger of their own; her mouth searched his as her passion mounted.

Her body demanded release as she strained toward him and felt his surge of manhood within her. A low moan of ecstasy was born of her passion and stirred and excited the man atop her to heighten her pleasure still more. She felt herself drown in his passion, only to rise to the surface as they soared to become as one. The soft cries of her name, repeated over and over, beckoned her to join him in the dizzying heights as she surrendered to her love.

Spent, they rested in each other's arms. They whispered quiet words, their bodies entwined. . . .

Even now as he slept he whispered her name, and the sound drew her back . . . back . . . to the first time she had seen him: in the arena; his smoldering black eyes, his gleaming white teeth, his powerful body as he sat atop the stallion; his superb show of strength in the jousting match.

Had she known, had she perhaps suspected, that one day she would belong to him? That she would pledge her love to him for all time? Had she ever dared to think that she would lie in his arms as she did now? To know that his love matched hers?

While he slept, Valentina relived the incredible adventure that had played with fate as if it were a pawn upon a chessboard and had brought her here to rest at the side of her one true love, for all time.

Chapter One

The city was buzzing with excitement. Knights and soldiers of the realm had all gathered in Messina to take part in the tourney to celebrate the wedding of Berengaria of Navarre and King Richard of England. They had halted their Crusade to the Holy Land to join the festivities.

From her tower window Valentina could see the arena where the tourney would take place later that afternoon. Banners and bunting in vibrant colors had been hung around the perimeters and the pavilions for the royal spectators. She had attended tourneys and jousting matches before, but always as a child and never as a woman. She was thrilled that today she would take her place in the center pavilion, the king's pavilion!

Valentina had taken the most exciting journey of her young life; halfway across the world from Navarre to the Eastern city of Messina. She had come as a lady-in-waiting to Berengaria, who was now the queen of England. An adventurous journey, a royal marriage, and now a tourney!

Valentina's excitement grew; her smooth ivory cheeks were flushed a becoming pink, and her mysterious blue-green eyes were bright and luminous. She was wearing the gown she had worn to the wedding, a soft hyacinth-blue, and she had artfully woven a matching ribbon through her dark, gleaming waist-length hair.

This was a day that would be forever in her memory. There was something intoxicating in the air, and she was keenly aware of it. A vibrancy, a feeling, a sensation she could not name. Without knowing why, Valentina felt that somehow today was going to be the beginning of an enormous change in her life. Smiling to herself, she thought, Whatever today has to offer, I'm ready to meet it!

In the hills above the arena the sun blazed upon the late, lush spring foliage creating dappled shadows upon a lean masculine figure reclining in the shade. He settled himself in the dense undergrowth, his long, doeskin-clad legs stretched out before him, and nibbled lazily on a blade of sweet grass. His sharp dark eyes narrowed as a rider raced up the road, a trail of red dust in his wake. Grinning, he rose and watched the solitary rider whose black Arabian steed cautiously picked its way off the road into the wild, uncultivated rocky field. His grin widened in a show of flashing white teeth, but he remained in the shadows.

Paxon had the eye of a hawk; it would be interesting to see if he could spot him here in the dense undergrowth. Suddenly he heard the whiz of a spear and saw the shaft come to rest in the rocky earth near

4

his feet. Throwing back his head, he roared with laughter as he stepped into the open. Paxon, sultan of Jakard, slid from the black stallion and shared his laughter.

"I expected you a full hour ago."

Paxon continued to laugh. "The horse was in no hurry. We have time before the tournament begins. I see you ride the white Arabian. Is she as fleet of foot as this stallion? Don't answer me; we shall see how he rides in the tourney," he said, running his hands over the horse's sweating flanks. "You look well, my brother; the years have been good to you."

Menghis laughed, his white teeth gleaming, the dark hair falling over his wide forehead. "And you also appear well, Pax. It's been a long time," he said, extending a welcome toward Paxon. The brothers clasped hands, looking into each other's eyes.

"I could not have been more surprised when I received your missive telling me to meet you here, Menghis. What brings you down from your Eagle's Nest in the mountains?" Paxon laughed, a devilish glint flashing from beneath dark, heavy brows.

A haunted expression flickered in the depths of Menghis's black eyes, and the muscles in his lean jaw bunched and knotted. "The time has not yet come for me to take my place on the throne of Alamut. I wished to see more of the world before that day came," he said grimly. "I have traveled the length of Europe as well as England; soon enough it will be time to embrace my duties."

Paxon laid a hand on his brother's shoulder, regretting his words. "You belong down here with the living, the throne of Alamut be damned!"

Menghis laughed again. "Ah, but you are of noble birth, and I am but the product of our father's infatuations with a harem girl."

"You were also our father's favorite son, and we were born mere hours apart."

"I am not bitter, Pax. Destiny cannot be changed. We both agreed. For you the province of Jakard, for me the eagle's aerie of Alamut."

"We were boys then and we are men *now*. Saracens, sons of an Islamic leader," Paxon said harshly. "Come back with me to Jakard," he added impulsively. "I'll make you Grand Wizer. Help me rule our father's kingdom."

"No! Destiny cannot be altered, only forestalled. When I return to Islam I leave all things behind me. My destiny is to become *Sheikh al Jebal,* Old Man of the Mountain. The time and the place of my birth declare it. I have already been recognized by the *fedawi,* and my predecessor prepares for his death."

Menghis was so vital, so life-loving. Paxon's heart constricted in his chest as he saw his brother now subdued and resolved to meet his obligations. "Our father was wrong to offer you, to sacrifice you!"

"He did as he thought right," Menghis defended. "To his legitimate son the kingdom of Jakard; to me, the son of a harem girl, a kingdom of the underworld, the third world, where there is neither good nor evil, only the will of *Sheikh al Jebal.* Take heart, Pax, I do not sit on the throne today." He clapped his brother on the back. "Today is the tourney and I mean to enter it."

"Then you read the notice and heard the crier announce that the tournament is open to all in celebration of the marriage between King Richard the Lionheart and the beautiful Princess Berengaria of Navarre."

"Yes, Brother." Menghis winked wickedly. "And it is also said that once winning her, he doesn't know how to pluck that fair flower. He sleeps not in her bed but among his soldiers."

Paxon laughed. "I have heard about this worshipping of women. Christians have a name for their uncertain manhood; they call it 'Chivalry.' Pray that Allah never deems it fit to strike the men of Islam with that malady!"

Down the rocky hillside and through the dusty, travel-worn city of Messina rode the two brothers. They arrived at the tourney gates and entered them. Equally matched in height and coloring, they created

6

a striking picture; both tall and lean of limb astride their magnificent Arabian mounts, one black as the desert night sky, the other bleached a dazzling white, like desert sands beneath a relentless sun. Dark blue, tightly knit chausses clung to Paxon's legs, revealing their strength; the pale blue tunic rode high on his thighs, displaying the firm grip of his knees pressed authoritatively into the black flanks of his Arabian. His hauberk, edged with silver threads and bearing the insignia of a fire-breathing, three-toed dragon embroidered across the back, fit snugly. It was obviously tailored to emphasize his broad shoulders and powerful arms, yet was trimly cut over his flat belly and lean torso. From beneath the wide, flaring sleeves the cuffs of a snowy-white shirt were exposed. His panther's head was bared to the bright sunlight, and blue-black highlights glinted in his cropped, tousled mane.

Paxon viewed the masses that were gathered to witness the grandiose tourney, and a reckless expression lifted the corners of his mouth in a grin rife with deviltry as he noticed the glances pass over himself to rest curiously upon his brother. Paxon's dark gaze fell proudly on Menghis. The remarkable doeskin breeches were full length to the tops of his soft, low, flat-heeled boots. The pliant skins cleaved sleekly to the firm weightiness of his thighs and the rounded bulge of calves. The short tunic of the same skins ended just above the narrow line of his hips and was laced loosely across his chest with leather thongs. The journey into England's colder climate had not diminished the coppery effects of the southern sun, and the whiteness of his teeth and the sootiness of his hair showed in stark relief.

Menghis sat his mount with casual grace, and the fabric of his costume made him appear to be almost an extension of the animal. If he was aware of the stir he created among the spectators, his expression gave no hint of it. His generous mouth was fixed in a grin and his wary, dark gaze was fixed in the distance. Here was a man Paxon was proud to name brother. They drew many curious glances from the armored

7

knights and their squires as they strode over to the tourney master's tent to sign in.

"Paxon, sultan of Jakard, and Menghis, brother of Paxon," the tourney master read aloud to quell the curious onlookers who surrounded his tent. "Your names will be called when it is your turn."

"Tell us," Paxon asked craftily, "is it true the Lionheart will take to the field to unseat the winner?"

"True," the tourney master said curtly, "but you need have no fear of the king of England." He laughed mockingly. "Neither of you will win the chance to meet the Lionheart on the field."

"A small personal wager." Paxon grinned as he tossed the tourney master a small purse of gold coins. "I say that one of us will win the field to joust with your king. I go further and say that we will unseat Richard and win the prize!" Menghis added a similar pouch of coins, his dark, sun-gilded face laughing at the nervous tourney master.

"It would be unwise to unseat the king," he said fearfully. "It could mean your life."

Paxon pretended alarm. "Are you saying the Lionheart is a dishonest man beset by pride?"

Menghis glanced about and saw that the once-curious faces of the Christian contenders were now set in grim lines. The presence of these Saracens was intolerable enough without listening to them mock their King Richard. "Have no fear," Menghis laughed somewhat uneasily. "We Saracens are a clumsy lot. Richard will live to lead his Crusaders into the Holy Land. We are here only for the sport."

Paxon hastened to agree, the light of the devil shining in his eyes. Menghis could barely control a smirk as he marched along beside his brother into the stalls surrounding the tourney field, their horses' reins held loosely in their hands.

The perimeter of the field was awesome with its gay hangings and banners. Small square pavilions, draped with colorful bunting that could be lifted to the side, lined one edge of the jousting field. Knights of valor loafed about these pavilions for a glimpse of a favored lady, and perhaps to induce that lady to bestow upon them some article to bring them luck on the field. At the lower end of the plain, peasants sold their wares and hastily made souvenirs of King Richard's wedding and the coronation of his queen, Berengaria.

King Richard's pavilion was still draped with bunting as Menghis and Paxon watched the archers entering the field, long bows in hand. Trumpets blared, announcing the arrival of Richard and his party. Not to be outdone, Philip of France was announced by a still greater blare of horns, as was King Tancred of Sicily.

"What a day for your faithful ones," Paxon whispered to his brother. "What havoc could be wreaked upon the countries of Europe if their kings should be assassinated where they sit."

Menghis's face darkened as he watched the parade of monarchs. "The title of *Sheikh al Jebal* is not to be taken lightly, Brother. True, I am to be the next Old Man of the Mountain, as these Christian dogs refer to it, and the *fedawi* are not merely faithful, but devoted as well. A world of difference, would you not say?"

Paxon regretted his words. Menghis, although he decried his fate, nevertheless took the title of *Sheikh al Jebal* seriously. It was what he had been trained for, and it was his destiny. He recalled how Menghis had referred to the society of *fedawi* as a third world, the underworld, and he knew this to be true. Soon, after the death of the present *Sheikh al Jebal,* Menghis would step into that title, and the world would continue to think that the Old Man of the Mountain was ageless, beyond the grasp of death, immortal. Only a select and trusted few knew the secret behind the legend of *Sheikh al Jebal* and how the assassins managed to appear to be all things to all men. Like many of the mysteries of Islam, where the straight path went roundabout and the prophets spoke in parables, the imperium of *Sheikh al Jebal* could strike fear into the heart of a fearless man. Only once, as a boy, had Paxon been to the Eagle's Nest, Alamut, and above the entrance gate was written:

9

AIDED BY GOD,
THE MASTER OF THE WORLD
BREAKS THE CHAINS OF THE LAW.
SALUTE TO HIS NAME!

The master of the world, the legend said, *Sheikh al Jebal!* Paxon turned his eyes to his brother. Menghis was heir to that title of power and wealth, and yet there was an unfathomable sadness in the depths of his eyes.

"You look at me strangely, Brother," Menghis said. "Is it so difficult to understand that I have no desire to step into that place on the mountain? That I would rather serve in the armies of Saladin than look down upon the world from my mountaintop? When I told you it was a third world, you must take me literally. The laws which bind the men of Islam do not bind me. The society is a law unto itself for the betterment of itself. I am not the supreme power, I am but one among a council of men who make the decisions. If the society reasoned that it would profit by the assassination of these European leaders, they would have already felt the stab of a *fedawi* blade. Since there is no profit to reap, these monarchs sit upon their pavilions waiting to be amused by the spectacle of the tourney."

As they watched, the draperies of bunting were lifted, and in the center pavilion sat the powerful figure of Richard the Lionheart, English king sworn to recapture the Holy Land from the hands of the Infidels. Even from this distance his proud head of red-gold hair was obvious beneath a circlet crown of hammered gold. On the dais behind Richard sat two ladies, their silken gowns of jewel colors sparkling in the sunlight. Both had dark hair; it was impossible to distinguish Richard's queen from the lady-in-waiting.

"By the Prophet's beard!" Paxon whistled. "Would that I could gain a closer look at this fair flower they sing of. Which one is she, Menghis?"

"I am as ignorant as you, Brother. From this end of

10

the field, that could well be my own mother sitting with the Lionheart."

"Menghis, do you remember the time we snatched Father's favorite woman from the harem? I got the whipping and you got the woman," he said, his black eyes glinting with mirth.

Menghis laughed. "Unfortunately I was so in awe of our daring that when I had her in my clutches, I was beyond doing anything. You received a sound whipping for naught."

"Are you telling me . . ."

"Would I lie to my brother?" Menghis grinned. "Look, the archers are about to demonstrate their accuracy."

Paxon's attention was turned back to the field, but from time to time his glance peered through the blazing sun into the shade of Richard's pavilion, his eyes straining to see Berengaria, deemed the most beautiful queen in all Christendom.

The archers displayed their skill and met with a rousing cheer from the audience. Next came the ax and mace experts, battling each other in matched sets. Down through the ranks the competitors battled, until at last Paxon and Menghis heard their names being shouted by the tourney master's croaking voice.

"Listen, it is time, they call our names. May the best man win, Brother," Menghis said softly.

"I always do," Paxon laughed as he raced his charger toward the reviewing stands, his eyes eager for a look at the famed Berengaria. Menghis kept pace alongside, his stallion sensing his master's anticipation. Before Richard's pavilion Menghis and Paxon awaited the king's approval and signal to begin.

Paxon's eyes delved the shadows within the pavilion and rested upon the slim figure of a young woman who sat behind the Lionheart. She raised her eyes and he saw they were the color of sapphires. Her hair was gleaming jet and rested softly against the smooth buffed ivory of her face. She lowered her thick, sooty lashes, which cast a deeper shadow upon her cheeks, and Paxon realized the impertinence of his stare.

11

Would he never get used to seeing these Christian women go about with their faces bared of the protective yashmak that all Moslem women wore in public?

King Richard eyed these two Saracens who were audacious enough to meet on the jousting field devoid of armor. His curious glance swept over the tall, muscular forms of the combatants, and smiling, he gave the signal for the play to begin. Richard himself was known for his daring upon the tourney field, and it was common knowledge that nothing pleased him more than a show of gallantry and bravado upon the field. It would be interesting to watch these two equally matched Saracens in battle.

Paxon and Menghis took their positions at opposite ends of the field. The sun in his eyes, Paxon had the disadvantage as he spurred his black stallion out, his lance poised. Just as Paxon came abreast of the white Arabian, his lance poised to throw, Menghis in one fluid movement was atop the horse, his stance secure on the fast-moving Arabian, his arm extended high above his head. The crowd roared its approval as they prepared for the second charge. This time it was Menghis who had the sun in his eyes. The steeds plowed up clumps of sod as they raced toward the center, and it was Paxon who avoided the lance by slipping beneath his horse's belly.

Menghis laughed as he reached the far corner of the field. Paxon had not changed at all! The trumpeter sounded for another charge, and both horses raced down the field. At what should have been the moment of impact, both men leaped to their feet atop the fast-moving steeds and spun about, their lances clashing. Slipping to the ground, they held their positions until the tourney master called a halt. The crowds cheered their approval at this daring horsemanship, and Richard acceded to the crowd's demands. Signaling to the tourney master, he indicated that the match was a draw.

Menghis and Paxon threw their lances to the scarred ground and went to rein in their horses. "What do you suppose will be our prize?" Paxon asked breath-lessly.

"A jewel. Perhaps a ruby or a sapphire," Menghis answered.

"I have seen the sapphires I wish to claim." Paxon's eyes drifted back to Richard's pavilion.

"Pax," Menghis said, deviltry lighting his eyes, "I can think of a more worthy prize, if you're willing." Paxon tilted his head to one side. Almost before Menghis spoke, he knew what he was going to say. "When we go forward to claim our prizes, attract their attention to give me enough time to circle the arena and capture the prize which should be ours. The queen of England!"

Paxon choked and Menghis slapped his back. "What of the matter of unseating the Lionheart?" Paxon asked.

"The devil take the Lionheart! Berengaria would make much better sport. What say you, Brother, are you game?"

"Menghis," Paxon said slyly, "which of us gets the prize?"

"Foolish question. As you are the eldest brother by two hours, you shall have the prize. I only mean to capture it for you. I will take your undying gratitude back to my throne on the mountain. Agreed?"

"And how long do you think we will be allowed to live, after we abduct Richard's queen?"

"Many long years. Tell me, Pax, are you man enough for this Anglo queen?"

"I'm man enough," Paxon said confidently. "Remember, Menghis, there will be no laughing, indulgent father to face when this is over."

"Look!" Menghis directed. "The Lionheart takes to the field. It is a small wonder he can walk with all his armor weighing him down. Shall we take him on the first charge, or shall we have our sport?"

"Do it quickly," Paxon instructed. "I wish to have as much time with my prize as possible."

"Your wish is my command." Menghis grinned, bowing low. "You know what to do." Paxon nodded.

13

The trumpeter blared his horn and raced back to his position in the stands. Richard bowed to his audience and held his lance erect in his hand in a show of coming victory. Not to be outdone, Menghis and Paxon leaped atop their steeds and prepared for the charge.

From out of the stalls a squire led a huge golden destrier. "That will be Flavel," Menghis whispered. "The Lionheart's charger is already a legend. It is said that once, when Richard was unseated, Flavel stood nearby and fended off the Lionheart's attackers with a brave show of hooves and teeth."

Although a tall man, Richard's head came merely to Flavel's withers. The great golden steed stood waiting for his master to take his position in the saddle. The muscles trembled beneath the destrier's golden hide, and his hooves pawed the earth in an impatient gesture to begin the charge. Once in the saddle, Richard waited for the signal from the tourney master. On the count of three, the horses raced down the field. At the last second, Menghis transferred the lance from his left hand to his right. Richard rode fearlessly toward them, Flavel instinctively swerving to avoid being outflanked by the Saracen steeds. Again the men took their positions for a return bout. Again Richard rode unswervingly toward the Saracens, but this time Flavel's maneuver was anticipated and Richard found himself outflanked.

Flavel snorted, his eyes round with rage as he turned and returned the attack. Richard spurred the great animal again, and again found himself between the Saracens. This time Menghis and Paxon stayed true to the attack and dodged Richard's lance, grasping him by the arms and lifting him out of the saddle. The Lionheart went sailing through the air, his armor clanking in the hushed arena.

There was no applause, voices were stilled, and the audience waited breathlessly for Richard's next move.

Paxon was the first to Richard's side, and Menghis watched from atop his steed. The king's face was deadly in its fury.

"Smile," Paxon goaded. "Your knights will think you a poor loser. Were we on a field of battle, your life would be lost."

Regaining his stance, Richard shouted to be heard. "I claim the right to challenge my victors at a later date in another tourney. The tourney I will elect to have to celebrate the taking of the Holy Land!"

The crowd roared its approval, and Richard clapped Menghis and Paxon on the back in a show of good sportsmanship before he allowed himself to be led off the field by his squires.

"Claim my prize and be quick about it," Paxon muttered to Menghis.

"Go to claim your purse. When you see I am abreast of the queen, throw it into the air and spear it with your lance. That should take their eyes away from the pavilion. Then ride as if the furies were after your soul! I will hold your prize just so long, and no longer." Menghis smirked.

"Just don't use it," Paxon snarled. "Not even King Richard has done that, if rumor is to be believed."

Paxon strode slowly over the tourney master's pavilion, the hackles on his neck rising. The pronouncement was made, and he was handed two purses which jingled with gold dinars. Estimating their worth, he hefted their weight in his hands. Satisfied, he spoke to the tourney master and walked back to the center of the field. Menghis was leading the black stallion to Paxon, and then he rode off to start his wide circle of the arena. Paxon tossed one of the purses into the air and threw his lance, neatly spearing the leather purse and spilling out the gold coins. The crowd was on its feet clamoring for more, shouting and waving, cheering its approval. Where was that devil Menghis? Spotting him out of the corner of his eye, Paxon threw the second purse as high as he could.

Menghis was almost abreast of the queen, and he turned his head to look back at Paxon. The moment the purse sailed into the air he reached for the queen. In his arms, atop his white stallion, he held the girl who had sat beside the queen. A better choice, he

15

commended his miscalculation. The queen is too plump for my liking.

Menghis laughed as he held the squirming young woman on his lap. Her eyes were flashing pinpoints of green amid the sapphire-blue. "So these were the sapphires which caught my brother's attention," he said to her, noticing her smooth ivory skin and raven hair. "Could it be that my brother thinks you are Berengaria? Well, young mistress, what my brother does not know cannot hurt." Spurring onward toward the gates, Menghis saw Paxon take a running leap and mount his black Arabian to follow him out. It was only a few moments before they heard the thudding of hooves charging after them down the road.

Time was suddenly meaningless as Valentina was swept away atop a speeding horse in the strong arms of the handsome Saracen. His steed far outpaced their pursuers, and he slowed the stallion to a walk. His breath was warm on her cheek, and his gaze demanded that Valentina look at him. Her breath quickened and her heart fluttered madly in her breast. His eyes were dark and fathomless, but there was humor in them, a smile. It was a moment, a brief taste of eternity for the startled young woman resting in strong arms.

His arms tightened about her, pressing her closer to his chest, crushing her breasts against him. His body was hard and muscular, and Valentina's arms encircled his neck. Unreasonably, she felt safe and secure in his embrace, and she stared into his laughing dark eyes without a trace of coquettishness. She was aware that she could drown in those incredible eyes and emerge as an extension of this man. His gaze sobered and fell upon her mouth, seeing her moist lips part and offer themselves to him. He lowered his mouth to hers, touching her lips, tasting their sweetness, drawing from them a kiss gentle yet passionate. He robbed her of her senses. Searing flames licked her body, and the pulsating beat of her heart thundered in her ears.

When he released her, his jet eyes searched hers for an instant, and again time was eternal for Valentina. From somewhere deep within her a desire to stay forever in this man's arms, to feel the touch of his mouth upon hers, began to build, to crescendo, threatening to erupt like a riot of fireworks. Her thickly fringed eyelids closed over her sparkling jewel-blue eyes, and her breath came in small pants as she brought her lips to his once again, offering her mouth, kissing him deeply, searchingly, searing this moment upon her memory. She knew, in that endless moment of time, that this man, this Saracen, belonged to her in a way no other man could.

Menghis's sun-darkened hand touched her cheek softly. He stared deeply into her eyes and nodded to show he understood what she was feeling. "If it's not meant to be in this world, then in eternity," he whispered huskily.

Something in his voice saddened her, and her eyes filled with tears. Seeing her tears and regretting them, the Saracen's mood changed to a lighthearted one. He looked down at Valentina and smiled, his black eyes flashing and triumphant. "I actually captured you for Paxon; a purse of dinars was an unfitting prize. It was the queen that I reached for back there in the arena, but you are a better prize than the one I intended. Down you go," he said lightly, lifting her from his lap and steadying her until her feet touched the ground. "Wait here for your captor, and whatever you do, don't tell him you are not Berengaria. I wouldn't want him to feel cheated," Menghis laughed.

Valentina laughed with him. "I would not think to reveal your secret." Her eyes were blue and merry as she looked up at this daring Saracen. "I will allow you to take your leave of me. Richard's men are in pursuit by now."

Menghis laughed again just as Paxon's horse raced up behind them. "It's a shame you won't be able to enjoy your prize. The king's men are on the way. Travel eastward; my men will watch for your safety."

"Menghis . . . Allah's blessing."

Menghis neither looked back nor acknowledged Paxon's words but rode into the forest.

Paxon redirected his attentions to the dark-haired

17

girl in the hyacinth-blue gown. Her eyes danced with mirth and he was struck by the beauty of her smile. "It would seem, your Majesty, that being abducted by a savage Saracen is an everyday occurrence for you." He dramatized the "savage Saracen" by a snarling show of teeth, making her laugh again.

"At least once a day," Valentina teased. "It is quite an annoyance and sadly interferes with my needle-work."

"It would also seem that the Lionheart's queen has a delightful sense of humor." Paxon was entranced by her, and his eyes boldly gazed down the long, slender length of her. "No matter," he said, dismounting and coming to wrap a muscular arm about her waist. He drew her closer and pointedly surveyed her full, luscious mouth. "A woman without a flair for humor can quickly become a nag." His lips closed over hers in a lingering kiss which suddenly became demanding.

Valentina was aware of his body bending over hers, crushing her to him, of his broad chest and powerful arms. Her resistance ebbed, and she realized that she was secretly comparing him with the Saracen whose dark eyes held laughter. They were so much alike. Tall, muscular, virile, handsome . . . and yet there was a difference. There was no gentleness in this Saracen called Paxon. There was instead a demand, an aggressiveness, a passion, that any woman would find hard to resist. And Valentina was no exception. An answering response was ignited within her.

He released her and she felt a flush stain her cheeks. "By the Prophet's beard, you are a fair flower!" His eyes lingered hungrily on her heaving breasts, which revealed themselves as high and proud beneath the thin silk of her gown. "Would that I could stay to further taste your delights, madame, but your husband's men would see to it that I not live to ever taste the lips of another woman." Seizing her once again, he covered her mouth in a last searching kiss, released her, and leaped atop his stallion.

Before Valentina could catch her breath, he was gone from her sight into the dense woods. She was breathless, and a flurry of emotions whirled through her. She still could not grasp the events of the past few moments, so quickly had they occurred. One moment she was sitting next to Berengaria, marveling at the skill of the two striking Saracens, and the next she was swept out of her seat and held tightly in powerful masculine arms atop a fiery stallion racing out of the arena. The daring of the escapade left her tingling. Everyone had been so intent on the Saracen's skill in lancing his purse of winnings, they hardly noticed what was transpiring in the king's pavilion until it had already happened.

Valentina could hear the steady beat of hooves and knew the king's men were coming to rescue her. She wondered what they would think if they knew that the last thing she wanted was rescuing. In fact, she wished she had had a few more moments with the most exciting men she had ever laid eyes upon.

Valentina smiled to herself, her full lips parting and her aqua eyes shining. She had known this would be an exciting day. She had sensed it and she had been proved right. As she waited for her rescuers her thoughts were lost to the two Saracens. Which did she like better? The Saracen who had spirited her away under the eyes of the king himself, and who had a mysterious sadness in his eyes in spite of his laughter? Or the Saracen who thought she was Berengaria, the one who had kissed her so soundly that her knees still threatened to give out from under her?

Chapter Two

Beneath the first rosy glow of daybreak, the city of Acre awakened from its deep desert night's sleep. Before the sun climbed its fiery ladder in the heavens to burn the sands and glance blindingly off the white stone walls of the city's houses, merchants began to set up their stalls. Soldiers carrying their helmets in the crooks of their arms noisily greeted one another as they left or arrived at their posts. Kurdish goatherds dressed in long, rusty black robes led their bleating flocks along the narrow alleys, enjoying their privilege of entering the city unmolested. Although Acre was under Christian rule, the Saracen merchants were valuable to the city's economy. The masses must be fed. Fruits, wine, meats, cheeses, and even breads were brought into the marketplace daily by the dark-skinned followers of Mohammed.

In the midst of the war, they alone were free to come and go and conduct business as usual. They were unchallenged by Christian soldiers, who greedily sought their wares, and they were sanctioned by the Islamic leaders who, like themselves, possessed an inborn appreciation for the art of bartering.

Within the hour the labyrinth of the bazaar would be filled with a multitude of buyers and sellers. Outside the pillared arches of the mosques, carpets would be piled high, their brilliant jewel colors dazzling the eye; bales of hemp would surround precious jars of olive oil; coffers of spices and pearls, guarded by armed servants, would sit in the glow of colored lamps that had burned through the night. Gold and silver would gleam amid the debris as Jews, wearing blue robes and bells around their necks to show that they were Nazarenes, would bargain shrilly for the highest prices.

In the palace at the far end of the city, in a bower room overlooking the expansive gardens, the first light of day touched Valentina's soft ivory cheek. Her thickly lashed blue-green eyes fluttered open, narrowing slightly against the sun's glare. Turning on her side to face away from the narrow window, Valentina pressed herself into her pillow, determined to ignore the arrival of another day and the sounds of stirring filtering up to her room from the courtyard. She stretched her long, slim body beneath the silken coverlet and was resurrendering herself to the arms of Morpheus when she heard the lifting of her door latch and recognized the heavy, musky scent of Berengaria's perfume.

"Wake up, you lazy slugabed! Have you forgotten what day this is?" The queen's light, childish voice held a note of anticipation. Excitement widened her doelike eyes, lighting their deep brown color with golden glints. "Valentina, wake up, it will take simply *hours* for us to dress. It isn't every day we get to see the king of Islam!" Berengaria's soft, dimpled hand shook Valentina's shoulder.

As always, Valentina was struck by the strength of that plump, velvety grasp. Beneath Berengaria's diminutive, childishly rounded, girlishly pink exterior lurked an unsuspected iron will. Her stubbornness of nature was known only to her most intimate consorts and would have astonished those around her who viewed her as a sweet, guileless child whose tastes were simple and whose wants were few.

"Valentina," Berengaria persisted, her voice edged with a note of command, "get up! There's so much to do! Sena must wash my hair and it will take hours to dry—"

Not wishing to hear any more of Berengaria's plans, Valentina threw back the coverlet and climbed out of bed. "Somehow I don't believe my liege, Richard, will take kindly to your appearance at his meeting with Saladin this afternoon. The exchange of prisoners is

21

serious business. I'm certain neither your husband nor Saladin will wish to suffer the presence of women."

"I'm not going to listen to you, Valentina," the queen pouted. "Suffer the women, indeed! I'm the queen of England, or have you forgotten! Besides, Richard wouldn't even notice us. When does he ever take notice of a woman?" Her tone was bitter and snide.

"My queen hints at treason," Valentina cautioned.

"Treason! Hardly. When I see the smiles that pass between Richard and Philip of France, it sickens me. I find it more difficult each day to hold my head up. The entire Christian army knows Richard doesn't sleep in my bed. They call him Lionheart. 'Faint of heart' is a more apt description. The brave warrior is afraid to bed a woman."

" 'Garia, hush. Someone might hear you. The walls have ears."

"And would they hear something they haven't heard before? Minstrels sing of his liking for men; gibes and jokes fill the courtyard. But Saladin! That's a horse of a different color. The noble Saracen warrior, king of Islam, defender of his faith . . . I could go on for hours. They say he has sixty wives, imagine!" Berengaria danced and twirled about the room; her nightdress billowed out, revealing her tiny slippered feet.

Valentina watched her queen and lifelong companion with a prickling of fear. From the time they were children Valentina had learned to be wary of Berengaria's wide mood swings. When she was like this, excited and elated over some planned mischief, nothing could stop her. No amount of reasoning could sway her. For the past three days, since learning of Saladin's proposed arrival, Berengaria had plotted to be present at this historic conference.

" 'Garia," Valentina said softly, using the name she had adopted for the princess of Navarre. "No one would dare to stop you from entering the conference room, but after the introductions are made, the king will excuse you. If you still persist, I've no doubt your husband will have you lifted off your feet and carried

22

out. Spare yourself this insult," Valentina entreated, thinking of the embarrassment she herself would suffer as the queen's companion. But she could see it was useless to continue along these lines. With tact and connivance, she had learned that, in order to live with Berengaria's erratic personality, one must endeavor to play the role of conspirator. "If you must see this Saracen for yourself, 'Garia, I know a way you can spy and witness the entire council meeting."

"You do? Oh, Valentina, tell me, please! Your little schemes are always so clever. I must see Saladin for myself."

Valentina's face lit with a secret smile. There were times that Berengaria could be played like the strings of a lute. "The servants have been readying the large vestibule that opens onto the gardens. There is a side entrance to the gallery, and just inside the door is an ornate grille hung with draperies. The gallery looks down onto the floor of the chamber. You would be able to see and hear everything without making the king angry."

"Yes, yes," Berengaria exulted. "It's perfect! Not that I care if Richard is angry or not, mind you," she added petulantly, her little, pointed white teeth biting into her lip.

Valentina knew that the king's excuses for neglecting his queen were feeble and rife with rejection. This created a volatile reaction in Berengaria, a headstrong and willful woman lacking in patience or discretion. It would take all of Valentina's wits to save the queen from bringing destruction down about her head.

The sun had climbed higher in the sky and was spilling through the long, narrow window which faced the east. "Look, we are wasting the morning. You said you wanted Sena to wash your hair; shall I call her for you?"

"No, I'll find her myself. She's most likely waiting outside my chamber door like a faithful dog, eager to do my bidding. Valentina, I'm breathless. Imagine, I'm going to see Saladin with my own two eyes! By God's toenails, won't my pious sister Blanche fly off her roost when I inform her that my sanctified eyes have beheld the Infidel of Infidels?" Laughing excitedly as she pictured Blanche's face white with shock, the diminutive queen danced out of the circular bower room.

Valentina's blue-green gaze watched Berengaria take her leave. Immediately she began to calculate how many gold coins it would cost her for bribes to gain possession of the key to the gallery door. Like most royalty, Berengaria had no sense of how dependent common folk were upon the power of the coin. Even if Valentina were to complain that this little adventure cost her half a month's allowance, Berengaria would never think to repay her. To the queen, a royal smile was payment enough. Not that she was penurious. It was simply that she had no concept of the value of money. She lived in perpetual comfort, her every desire fulfilled, and never gave a thought to the fact that someone was paying for it.

So often Berengaria would order something from the bazaars and marketplaces, then turn her back, leaving the poor servant standing there terrified to remind the queen that her purchase would cost several dinars. How could they carry out her bidding if they hadn't the money? At these times Valentina would dig into the small embroidered pouch which hung from her girdle and press a coin or two into the servant's open palm. She found it comical when, at times, she ceremoniously jingled her coins or went to great lengths to instruct the servant to bring back correct change. Berengaria would take no notice. She would continue to pluck at her embroidery or strum on the lute strings lethargically.

At home in Navarre, King Sancho saw to it that money was provided for his daughter's wants. When dealing directly with the peddlers who visited the queen's tower, Berengaria merely made her selections, and the merchants presented their bills to the king's chancellor.

But since she left Navarre, all of Berengaria's little purchases had been paid for either by Lady Eleanor, Richard's mother, or by his sister, Queen Joanna.

More often than not, it was Valentina who settled what was owed.

Several times Queen Joanna would remind Berengaria of her financial obligations. The sprinkling of freckles on Joanna's nose would be heightened by the embarrassed flush staining her cheeks. Berengaria's response to these reminders would be to race to her room and bring forth handfuls of gold dinars from her coffer and press them on her ladies with an air of holiday, as though it were a gift instead of a debt owed.

Valentina shook her head to clear it of thoughts of Navarre and the familiar creeping of homesickness. Stripping off her nightdress, she emptied the ewer of water into the basin. Shuddering slightly at the chill air against her nakedness, she began her morning ablutions. Toweling herself dry, Valentina moved into the golden shaft of sunlight streaming through the window. Hearing a sound behind her, she turned to find Berengaria standing in the doorway with a strange expression in her eyes.

Suddenly Valentina was conscious of her nudity and the inadequacy of her scanty towel to cover her long, slim legs and narrow hips. For a long moment the two women looked at each other. Valentina grew increasingly uncomfortable. She was aware of the picture she created with the sun glancing off her body and turning her fair skin to a rich gold; the droplets of water gleaming like little jewels; her thick, heavy black hair hanging straight almost to her waist, covering her shoulder and one firm, pink-tipped breast like a capelet.

"I just came back to show you the frock I intend to wear." Berengaria's voice was husky, halting, and her gaze never left Valentina's body. Her eyes were bright, her face flushed. She displayed the same uninhibited curiosity as when she first encountered a new and attractive man, before launching her campaign which would lure him into her bed.

Valentina stripped the coverlet off the bed and draped it about herself. Berengaria's open scrutiny had passed the point of making her uncomfortable; she was beginning to feel unclean. Through the door old Sena's voice called, "Majesty, the water is ready for your hair. It mustn't get cold."

"Coming, Sena." Before turning to leave, Berengaria cast a look at Valentina, a wicked gleam dancing in her eyes. "Poor Valentina, I shouldn't have barged in on you. But you mustn't be embarrassed," she intoned in the falsely sweet voice Valentina knew so well. "We are both women, you know." Laughing lightly, she turned and left the room, the barren corridor echoing her sarcastic laughter.

In two long strides Valentina reached the door and slammed it shut. Berengaria had gone too far this time! For want of a man to warm her bed she was seeking out other fields of pleasure. She was insufferable!

Valentina wished that the popular Christian image of the flesh-eating, blood-drinking Saracen were true. Perhaps if it were, Saladin would fall upon Berengaria and gobble her up!

Shortly after midday a great commotion occurred outside the city gates. A long, twisting caravan of camels and horses appeared on the horizon, makings its slow plodding way toward the entrance to Acre. Throughout the city shouts were heard: "Saladin is coming! He brings the Holy Cross of Jerusalem!" A month had elapsed since Richard's capture of Acre, and the Crusaders were eagerly awaiting the sight of the "True Cross," which had been captured eternities ago at the battle of Hattin.

The caravan snaked through the narrow city streets. Camel drivers in wine-colored robes whipped at their ornery beasts' flanks, pushing them onward. Dervish warriors, cloaked in bright yellow and black, Saladin's colors, rode proudly on their spirited Arabian steeds. Huge black eunuchs, wearing bright red pantaloons and little jeweled fezzes atop their kinky black heads, marched alongside the camels. The parade seemed endless as the Crusaders watched, their eyes alert for

26

the gold-encased relic of the true cross. But the cross did not come.

The Hospitalers and Templars, those brave, beknighted warrior monks, wept openly. Though anger and disappointment charged through the ranks, not one soldier made an overt action. King Richard had commanded it. Under no circumstances, he had ordered, was anyone to jeopardize the outcome of the council meeting. There was none among the men, no matter how great their anger, who would disobey the king, Richard the Lionheart.

Valentina and Berengaria were in the gardens when the Islamic leaders arrived. Berengaria searched the dark, swarthy faces beneath the jeweled turbans for Saladin. Amidst the crowd she noticed a tall, lean rider atop a graceful, long-legged black stallion, and her heart missed a beat. Unlike the others, he was clean-shaven, his strong, handsome jaw accented by a black headcloth wrapped with a white turban. He wore a black robe with wide sleeves trimmed with gold thread. A long, curved Arab scimitar was thrust into his bright yellow girdle, its long tasseled ends meeting the tops of his tall, black kid boots. Even more remarkable than him here in Acre was the sleek black hunting panther that kept apace with his horse. The cat's jewel-studded collar caught and reflected the sunlight, and its thick gold link chain was attached to the stirrup.

"Look, Valentina," she said, pointing to the handsome rider, "see his panther—have you ever seen anything so beautiful? His collar must be worth a king's ransom."

Valentina kept her eyes on the handsome horseman. She admired his easy seat in the saddle, his tall, lean, muscular movements as he dismounted and took hold of his panther's leash. She was struck by the similarity between man and beast. Sleek of build, loose-jointed movements, proud head . . . the feeling of carefully reined power, that any moment his easy, swaggering elegance could coil into the strong, fleet spring of a cat.

27

Berengaría was studying Valentina and saw her aquamarine eyes deepen to the rich luster of sapphires. "I see you've already recognized him. Is that not the Saracen who sported you away at the tourney in Messina?" Berengaria watched Valentina slyly, waiting for her answer.

"No, 'Garia, it was the other Saracen, known as Menghis. Who you see here was in the copse . . ." Too late, Valentina realized she had stumbled into Berengaria's trap.

"So you *did* have more than a fleeting glance! What did you say his name is, Paxon? A sultan!" Her fingers bit viciously into Valentina's arm. "And when you were alone with him, did he ravage you? Did you let him taste your lips and touch your breasts? What right had you to enjoy an adventure that was meant for me! It was clear to everyone present that it was *me* the Saracen reached out for when you pushed me aside and *leaped* into his arms! Was it not humiliating enough that on my wedding night the proud and manly Lionheart kissed my hand and bid me a peaceful night's rest and went to sleep in his own bed, and this before the jeering eyes of the wedding guests! Then you, my traitorous friend, you robbed me of my chance to prick my husband's heart with jealousy."

Valentina closed her eyes and gritted her teeth. She had been listening to these same accusations for several months, and each time she had wanted to close her fingers around Berengaria's neck and strangle her. At first she had been able to mark Berengaria's injustice to disappointment in Richard, the man whom Berengaria had pined for almost to the point of death. But now the accusations were wearisome and placing a heavy strain on their relationship.

" 'Garia, I have told you nothing happened with the Saracen. As for your disappointment in the king, surely you cannot blame me. You are too quick to judge my lord. He is facing a war and is preoccupied with his duties in the military. I beg you not to measure his worth by the minstrel's rhymes."

"The rhymes speak the truth! My bed has been

28

empty of my husband since the day of our wedding! You are always so defensive of Richard, and I cannot believe you when you say it is because he is now your king. *I* am your lifelong friend and your queen— where is your loyalty to me?" Berengaria leaned closer, her face only inches away from Valentina's. "Perhaps it is lost to me because you have stolen the Lionheart's love from me as cleverly as you threw yourself at the Saracen and robbed me of my adventure. Is this the reason my bed is empty of my husband?"

Valentina's desire was to push the queen into the hedges and leave her sprawling on her royal backside. It was true Berengaria's bed was empty of her husband, but not of a myriad of other masculine figures who spent the night in the queen's service. "Spare yourself, 'Garia. My feelings for King Richard are those of fealty and loyalty for a great leader. As for the Saracen . . ."

"Yes, Valentina, tell me, what do you think of the Saracen?" Berengaria asked cynically.

Valentina stiffened; she resented Berengaria's ability to read her emotions so easily. "The Saracen is so . . ."

"Young! Handsome! Yes, I see your point, Valentina." The queen's eyes swung back to the horseman as he entered the door of the council chamber. If she had to move heaven and earth, Berengaria swore she would have him in her bed before the negotiations were completed.

From behind the grille on the gallery, Valentina and the queen could look down at the floor of the council. In deference to his Moslem guests, Richard had equipped the room with thick, intricately patterned Oriental carpets and pillows. The tables were low to the mosaic floor in the Eastern tradition, and carafes of fruit juices were provided to wash the dust out of their mouths, as wine was prohibited by the Moslem religion.

Richard, king of England, was resplendent in a royal purple robe over his fine-tooled mail. His flaming red hair gleamed beneath the thin circlet of gold that he wore to denote his position. Before negotiations took place, the Moslem visitors turned to the east, bowed their turbaned heads, and chanted a prayer in unison.

There were murmurings and a shocked response. King Richard was clearly upset, his face flamed to match his hair. Listening carefully, Valentina and Berengaria learned that Saladin was not present. Instead, he had sent his brother, Saif ad Din, and a retinue of generals. Saif ad Din would speak for his brother, and all contracts would be binding. The Moslem generals showed their deference to Saif ad Din, whom they knew also by the worthy name of Al Adil.

Richard took the lead. "I've spoken with Philip Augustus, and we've decided that the surrender terms must be put in writing. All Islamic citizens are to vacate Acre, and we demand a sum of two hundred thousand dinars. Conrad of Montserrat will act as our representative. Do you find this agreeable?"

Saif ad Din nodded, his eyes traveling to the Crusaders raising their banners in the garden. "I shall advise my brother of this. Malik en Nasr, my brother whom you refer to as Saladin, has bid me read you these requests." With great ceremony, the Moslem opened a scroll and began to read: "Greetings, mighty kings. Of two things, do one. Send us back our fellow believers who are captives in your garrison, and we will send to you the hostages under our care. Or, accept the payment we make to you today and give us hostages whom we will keep until our comrades, held by you, are sent out to us."

The bargaining continued; the air resounded with argument.

Valentina's eyes searched for the tall sultan with whom she had shared that brief moment of passion in the copse. He was seated on a high cushion at the far end of the room, the huge black cat asleep at his feet. Berengaria had been correct; he was magnificent. Even from this distance she could see his muscular arms, and she remembered how they had held her

30

captive in a warm embrace. She knew that once his muscles were flexed, a lance would find its target dead center. The panther stirred and he laid a gentle hand on its head, and immediately the cat quieted.

Berengaria, greedy for a closer look, lifted the silken hangings away from the grille. The movement caught the sultan's eye. In a quick, fluid motion his dark hand flew to the scimitar at his side. "In the gallery, Meshtub, what do you see?" he asked quietly of his attendant.

Meshtub swung to the left, his arm poised on the hilt of his sword. "I see two women, Paxon. What do you see?"

Paxon smiled, his white teeth flashing in his dark face. "I also see two women. For a moment I suspected a Christian trap."

"Or a trick of *Sheikh al Jebal*—the Old Man of the Mountain. Think of the havoc he could wreak if his assassins could somehow infiltrate the council."

"These are no emissaries of that old scoundrel," Paxon said, his eyes intent on the gallery.

Meshtub laughed mirthfully at the expression on his friend's face. The Saracen blood was hot in Paxon's veins. "One brief look at a woman and your thoughts turn from war to lovemaking," the burly Meshtub goaded.

"She's beautiful," Paxon said softly, eyeing Valentina boldly.

"Paxon," Meshtub whispered in warning, "I have seen with these own two eyes the lady you desire ride into Acre seated next to the Lionheart. Would you lust for King Richard's queen? An unbeliever?"

Paxon's face fell into a scowl. Meshtub was too knowledgeable of the workings of his mind. "I have a first-hand knowledge of the queen. We became quite —er—friendly in Messina."

Meshtub quirked a quizzical brow. "Do you mean to tell me that you were intimate with her? Berengaria? Queen of England?" Meshtub asked in disbelief.

"Do you hope to lessen her desirability by reminding

31

me she is a Christian?" Paxon continued his scrutiny of Valentina.

"I only hope to warn you. I see by the look in your eye that you should like to bed her. I also see an answer in her eyes. By the Prophet's beard, you play with fire!"

Paxon smiled at his friend and attendant. "Tell me, Meshtub, do you suppose these Engleyses bed differently from a Moslem?"

"You ask the wrong man, Pax. Perhaps the old fox, Saladin, can help you. I've heard tales that he once loved an Anglo, and she was such a wild one she almost killed him in the end. When he disposed of her, he took instead sixty wives and claimed they were less demanding than the one Christian."

"Perhaps I'm more fond of the sport of bedding than our honorable Malik en Nasr."

Meshtub scowled. "If you are caught, it will mean death," he cautioned.

"I might be willing to die for one so beautiful," Paxon said softly, gentling the head of his panther as though it were the smooth, rounded curve of a woman's breast.

"You're a Saracen and a sultan. You must not endanger your life for a few fleeting moments of pleasure. She is a Christian, an unbeliever. Mohammed proclaims her unclean!"

"Did Saladin sully himself? Did his love for an Anglo prohibit his rise to king?"

Knowing when to give over, Meshtub hoped to divert Paxon's attentions. "Look to Al Adil. The negotiations are coming to an end for today."

The question of hostages brought about the heated bitterness that was to affect the destinies of all those present. "We will have no further bargaining on behalf of the hostages," Richard roared. "Pay the ransom and penalties now and accept our solemn oath that your people will be returned to you. We shall discuss the terms concerning the return of the Holy Cross tomorrow." Signaling to his aides, Richard left the chamber.

Valentina and Berengaria hurried out the gallery

door, down the steps, and across the courtyard to the queen's private entrance to the bower. Stopping just outside the entrance, Berengaria gripped Valentina's arm. "Valentina, did you ever see a more handsome man? I want him,-I must have him! Arrange for him to come to my rooms this evening."

" 'Garia, have you lost your senses? He is our enemy! You mustn't—"

"Arrange it! Your queen commands you!"

"The queen is often foolish!" Valentina snapped back. "If you insist on placing your head on the chopping block, then do so. Leave me be! If I should die alongside you, who would mourn you, who would pray for your soul?"

"If it should ever come to that, your life is already lost. You've been my accomplice in treason before this. Arrange it!" Berengaria's face twisted into ugly, scornful lines. Valentina had to admit that the queen was correct. If the truth be known, her life was already lost.

"How can you be so sure he would come? The Moslems consider unbelievers unclean. If he doesn't come because of his principles, he would hold your name up for ridicule. And he would have proof, your message to him. 'Garia, you can't—"

"Arrange it. For this evening. Sign your own name if you wish, or don't sign it at all. Didn't you see the way he looked at me? Didn't you see the desire in his eyes? Let your note make mention that the lady who caught his interest in the gallery today wishes to meet with him this evening. What harm can that do? He'll know it was from me, and there will be no proof of my treason. Why are you standing there? I command you to arrange it!"

"I will send him the message, although it is against my better instincts."

"Everything is against your better instincts, Valentina. That's why your bed is cold and lonely. I must have him, Valentina, I mean to have him!" Berengaria's face softened, and her smile was sweet as she cajoled, "Do this for me, Valentina, and I, as your queen, will confer a new title on you."

"I wish no title, 'Garia. I only wish to save you from yourself."

"But you would like this title, Valentina. It fits you most aptly." Making a pantomime of the royal knighting ceremony, Berengaria lifted her handkerchief and lightly touched each of Valentina's shoulders. "I dub thee Valentina, queen's procurer!"

As Valentina's face flushed scarlet, Berengaria turned her back and proceeded to climb the stairs to her chambers, the echo of her laughter a knife piercing Valentina's heart.

Valentina wrote the note to Paxon, sultan of Jakard, and paid a little city urchin to deliver it to the section of the city quartered off for the visiting Saracens.

If the black-haired Saracen was interested, he would arrive at the gates to the garden and she would lead him in to Berengaria. No, no, her mind screamed, I don't want to sit outside the queen's door and listen to the sounds of lovemaking within. Her heart fluttered madly at the thought that she was jealous. She didn't want the dark Saracen to make love to the queen. She wanted him to make love to her. She wanted to feel Paxon's arms about her, his lips pressing against hers, her mouth yielding to his. Cheeks flaming, she flew up the circular stone steps to her room in the bower, her heart racing faster than her feet could carry her.

Berengaria, clad in a diaphanous gold metallic gown, literally danced around the room, her eyes sparkling with excitement. She was scented and perfumed from head to toe. Valentina found it difficult to breathe, so heavy was the air with the smell of smoldering incense.

"It is time to go to the gates, Valentina."

Valentina shuddered. She too knew it was time to meet the Saracen. Pray God he didn't come! She would explain it somehow. She knew she would be accused of failing to send the message, or worse, that she intended to try for him herself.

It was a still night, black as velvet, with only the stars to light the way along the footpath in the gardens. Would he come? If he did, would he ride on his great stallion?

Quietly Valentina unfastened the chain bolting the gate and stepped behind a Judas tree to wait. Within moments a tall, dark form emerged from out of the black night and entered the gate. Valentina stepped from behind the tree and stood looking up into the face of the Saracen. She looked into Paxon's eyes and felt her heart begin to pound. What was this strange look in his eyes?

Suddenly she was gathered close in a powerful embrace. Fire raged through her as his lips crushed hers. He cradled her head in strong hands as his lips became more demanding. For a long moment she surrendered, answering his demands with her lips, with the soft press of her body.

Someone was calling her name, whispering, "Valentina, Valentina . . ." It was Berengaria. Suddenly she was standing erect, her breathing coming in ragged gasps. She tried to blink the misty film from her eyes to see clearly. Mother of God . . . he didn't, he couldn't . . . She tried to speak, but he forestalled her with a light, mocking laugh.

"Tell me, Berengaria, do the Christians stir your blood as I do?" he asked mockingly.

Valentina struggled to find the words, but her throat was dry, and the best she could manage was a hoarse croak. "I'm . . . not . . . the one you came to see. I'm not Berengaria. I'm her lady-in-waiting." Her cheeks flamed at the incredulous look on Paxon's face. She cleared her throat, her hands trembling as she noticed his eyes narrowed to slits. "I'm to take you to the queen." Gathering the last shreds of her dignity about her, she murmured softly, "I have never had anyone stir my blood, Christian or Saracen."

Paxon laughed in delight. "Then we shall have to remedy that matter in the near future, won't we?"

The whispers persisted. "Valentina, are you there?

35

What are you doing out there in the dark? Is someone with you?"

"That is Berengaria," Valentina said. "You'll find her at the end of the footpath."

"And I mustn't disappoint her, or it will go hard with you." The look he bestowed upon Valentina was hot and smoldering. He gave her a heavy-lidded wink and stepped down the footpath.

Valentina wet her dry lips and leaned against the Judas tree. She forced her imagination away from the scene within the queen's chambers. A tinkle of laughter wafted through the garden. Valentina clenched her teeth and squeezed her eyes shut. Over and over she repeated to herself, He is the enemy, he is the enemy!

Chapter Three

Paxon bit into the hard line of his mouth as another whining whisper wafted through the shadows. His footsteps faltered before the ornate grilled door, and he fought the urge to turn and leave. Treason was a crime he didn't take lightly, and he already regretted his involvement in this crime against the English Crown. Still, how many men could boast that they had pleasured a queen? He smiled, lights dancing in his night-dark eyes. If the tales Paxon had heard were true, even King Richard couldn't boast that he had bedded Berengaria. England's king was said to prefer the pimply, pockmarked face of Philip of France! The humor of the situation made him quicken his step.

Thrusting the heavy unguarded door open, he followed a dim pool of light spilling from beneath a door bearing the queen's crest. For a brief moment he feared a trap but he remembered the hungry look in Berengaria's eyes when she had peered down at him from the gallery, and his caution abated. Pushing open the door, he stepped into an atmosphere heavy with musk and incense. The circular stone walls were hung with tapestries and silks, the floor strewn with thick carpets, and in the center of the room stood a silken hung bedstead lighted with tall flickering candles. From out of a shadow stepped the diminutive figure of the queen. Her dark, shining hair hung loosely down her back and over her shoulders. Her fine pink skin glowed in the candlelight; her soft doelike eyes were large and luminous. For an instant he wondered if indeed some trick were being played on him. Berengaria's expression was innocent, almost chaste. It seemed unlikely that this pure, virtuous girl could be waiting for a lover. Then he noticed the sensual smile playing about the corners of her full, petulant mouth.

"Do you neglect to pay homage to a queen?" Berengaria asked, her voice light and teasing, yet holding a sharp edge. "Down on your knee, Saracen!"

Paxon remained standing, a dangerous glitter in his narrowed eyes. "It is not the queen I have come to see, but the woman." His tone matched her own and beneath the lightness challenged the ring of iron. His smile mocked her, dared her, excited her.

"I have been waiting most patiently," Berengaria whispered. "I know that my patience will be rewarded." Her soft eyes measured him, taunted him.

"Patience is always rewarded," he answered, taking a step toward her.

Berengaria retreated into the shadows and loosened the ties of her dressing gown. "I have heard many things concerning you Saracens." Her voice was unsteady; her breath came in tremulous little gasps.

"And have you heard that we Saracens are artful lovers?" He undid the wide belt he wore and carelessly dropped it to the floor.

"It would also appear that Saracens are also artful talkers. Actions," she whispered, "speak louder than any words."

Paxon threw back his head and laughed. Berengaria's first instinct was to turn and run. This man, she knew, was dangerous! She had had other lovers, scores of lovers, and each had come to her to comfort her, to do her bidding, and to be grateful for her favors. They had been safe distractions, wooing her with words of love, professing their undying loyalty. But this man, this Saracen, dared to mock her! Presumed to treat her like a wanton! Challenged her with his eyes and mocked her with his lips! Suddenly she was frightened and knew she was out of her depth. With a show of bravado she commanded, "To your knees, Saracen! I am a queen and you are only a common soldier, and an enemy at that! I could call my guard, and in the morning I would cheerfully watch your head roll!"

Paxon eyed her dangerously, his dark, powerful hands resting lightly on his narrow hips, the long, muscular length of him restive, like a panther readying for the kill. "The common soldier for the common whore!" he taunted from between tight lips.

Berengaria's heart thudded within her breast; her pulses raced; she wanted him more than she had wanted any man, including Richard. Gazing into his eyes, watching him, she loosened her dressing gown and shrugged it off her shoulders in one graceful movement. Standing naked before him in the flickering light, she said boldly, "Then have me."

Her skin was smooth and unblemished, her round, full breasts stood high on her torso, and her magnificent hips tapered into the firm-fleshed line of her thighs. Slowly she reached out to him, entreating him.

The perfumed, musky air was provocative, and the dancing light on her silken skin aroused him. Slowly, mockingly, he undid his tunic.

Berengaria watched him, passion flooding her veins, as he discarded his clothing and stood before her in all his manly splendor. His expression was menacing, the candlelight glinted off his jet-dark eyes, the clean square line of his jaw was tight and threatening, but his body told her he was as filled with desire as she. Her breasts heaved with excitement, waiting for him to spring. Waiting for him to come to her, praying he wouldn't.

An unspoken command in his eyes, he raised his arm, beckoning her to him. Slowly she obeyed him, moving dreamlike toward him, fearful of his touch yet hungering for it. He drew her close to him, her rosy-tipped breasts grazing the black furring on his massive chest. He cradled her face in his powerful hands as his mouth crushed hers.

Her knees were weak; the blood boiled and coursed through her veins. She had never wanted a man the way she wanted this Saracen, needed him. His touches on her buttocks, his tongue searching out the warm recesses of her ripe, full mouth. The pressure of his body against hers, the demands of his passion, the hard muscular feel of his back, his raven eyes peering into hers, boring through her, experiencing the delights her body offered. Each movement he made was created to excite her, to drive her to the brink of madness.

Valentina paced nervously back and forth along the footpath. It would soon be daybreak. Surely Berengaria wasn't fool enough to keep Paxon past dawn! Within the hour the kitchen servants would begin to prepare the morning meal for the queen and her entourage. At dawn the changing of the guard would take place; merchants selling fresh eggs and milk would be making their daily procession to the huge kitchens. In the stable yard the grooms would be rubbing sleep from their eyes and scratching their flea bites as they acceded to the demands of their charges. What could Berengaria be thinking of? If the Saracen was to leave the bower undetected, he must leave now!

The small sound of a lifting latch echoed in the approaching dawn. Valentina looked up and emitted a sigh. "Hurry," she whispered. "It is but minutes before the guards change."

This was the first time Valentina noticed Paxon's head was bare of his head cloth and turban. His head was well-shaped, with close-set ears and a crop of crisp dark waves. He noticed her glance and read her thoughts. "So, it is true," he laughed, mirth dancing in his eyes. "All Christians believe we Saracens are as bald as eggs beneath our headgear." His firm, well-defined lips parted, showing an even line of startlingly white teeth.

Valentina was not amused and hurried down the path to the walled gate. Quickly she fitted the long key into the rusty lock and pushed against the groaning gate. "You must leave quickly," she urged. "There are only minutes left."

"A minute can be an eternity. Are you the one the queen calls Valentina?" he asked boldly.

Valentina ignored his question and tried to push him through the gate as voices from the other end of the garden reached her. "Go now!" she breathed fearfully, glancing over her shoulder.

"I refuse to leave until you answer my question," he insisted. "What is your name?"

The voices were coming nearer. "Very well," Valentina answered hastily. "I am Valentina." She hesitated a second and added, ". . . queen's procurer." Her tone was bitter, her expresssion grim.

Paxon's eyes widened at what he considered a feeble attempt at humor. Her eyes were a stormy green, and her full, sensitive mouth trembled as she fought to hold back the tears. He sobered instantly, realizing she was not making a jest. "Good night, Valentina, queen's procurer," he whispered as he sprung into the saddle of his waiting stallion. The black hunting panther stretched luxuriously and strained at the leash that was secured to the saddle. The cat fixed its yellow stare on Valentina.

"Lady Valentina," old Sena's voice croaked from inside. "My queen wishes to speak with you."

Valentina chose to ignore Sena's entreaty as she watched Paxon ride out toward the marketplace, his panther keeping pace alongside.

"Lady Valentina!" Sena croaked again, a shrill note of hysteria rising in her throat.

Valentina groaned. What would Berengaria want now? It had been a long, sleepless night on the stone bench in the garden, and she was tired. More than tired, exhausted. Through the long, cold desert night she had listened nervously for the sound of the Saracen's footsteps coming out of the queen's bower. During the endless hours she had agonized over the perfidy being enacted against King Richard, a treachery in which she played an active role. The disgust she felt for Berengaria had ripened to loathing. The girlhood secrets and nursery intrigues had evolved into arcane schemes to provide the immoral Berengaria with the object of her desires. From stableboy to nobleman, Berengaria had beguiled them all with her pink nubile beauty and inveigling innocence. It seemed as if it were only yesterday that Berengaria had first set her wide liquid eyes on Richard, heir to England's throne, and decided she *must* have him.

King Sancho had moved heaven and earth to acquire Richard for his best-loved daughter, but to no avail. Richard had been betrothed since boyhood to Alys, sister of Philip of France. All of King Sancho's maneuverings were useless, a royal betrothal was as binding as a marriage . . . until Richard discovered that his betrothed, the golden-haired Alys, had taken a lover, Richard's father himself, King Henry. Then Sancho's offer of a generous dowry and men and arms for Richard's campaign to regain the Holy Land became most persuasive.

Philip of France had been furious. He berated Richard for being a tardy lover. "Marry her," he had said, "it can be no worse than marriage with a widow." But though Richard made no move to take Alys as his wife, he didn't publicly denounce her, as was his right. For this alone Philip was grateful, and united himself with Richard to take up the sword to defeat Saladin's army for Jerusalem. King Henry, proud ruler who had never known shame, took to his bed and refused food or drink and medical attention and so died, leaving the flame-haired son he detested to sit on England's throne.

Berengaria had achieved her desire: Richard was her husband and she was queen of England. A queen who had never set foot upon England's soil, with a husband who had never shared her bed. The desire she felt for Richard had fermented to revulsion, a repugnance that deepened with each successive lover.

Whenever Valentina thought of King Richard, she died a little inside. Berengaria hadn't been the only one to become enamored of the dashing warrior. Valentina had also come under the spell of his charm.

"Lady Valentina!" Sena's harsh croak brought Valentina back to the present. She hurried to the bower door, where the old woman waited as she wrung her work-reddened hands in distress. Judging from the dark rings beneath Sena's eyes, Valentina knew that the old nursemaid had also spent a sleepless night.

"Lady Valentina, the queen awaits you. Hurry, child, she's in a rare mood this morning."

Pushing past Sena's formidable bulk, Valentina entered Berengaria's chamber. The air held the faint aroma of incense mingled with the charred tallow of the gutted candles. The bed was in complete disarray, the coverlets trailing across the floor. Berengaria was perched on an embroidered footstool, brushing her thick, dark hair. Her skin glowed pinkly and was as fresh as an early spring rose. Her eyes were bright, her mouth full and slightly swollen from the Saracen's kisses.

"You wished to see me, your Grace?" Valentina asked softly.

"Yes, and dispense with the formalities, they bore me." Berengaria sighed. "I wish to be bathed, and my bed requires fresh linen. See to it."

"I'll see that it is taken care of—"

"No, Valentina, I want you to do it. And while you're about it, I wish my personal belongings brought down here to this room. If anyone should inquire, tell them your queen enjoys the proximity of the gardens. Say anything . . . that I've been stricken with plague, that I've the symptoms of leprosy—anything! Paxon will come to me again tonight, and this chamber is so convenient." Berengaria ran the tip of her tongue over her lips, and her eyes became sultry as she remembered the past hours in the Saracen's embrace.

42

" 'Garia," Valentina cried, "I must sleep . . ."

The queen snapped to attention, her gaze sharp and angry. "What do you mean, you are in need of sleep? What kept you awake last night?" she asked craftily.

"The stone bench near the footpath," Valentina answered hotly. "You didn't tell me the Saracen would stay the night with you. If I had known, I would have spent the night in my own bed," she added accusingly.

Berengaria went back to brushing her hair. "Is it my fault the Saracen found himself so enamored he refused to leave? These Moslems are a lusty lot. I found it almost impossible to quiet him. He lusted for me time and again. I would no sooner gain my breath when he was atop me again," she said slyly, watching for Valentina's reaction.

Valentina's gaze was steady and level, but Berengaria took note of a tinge of murky green. Since childhood Valentina's eyes were the mirrors of her emotions. In anger they deepened to the ominous green of moat water; in joy they became as blue as the sky on a summer's day. Berengaria continued to bait her. "Paxon is a magnificent lover. Daring, aggressive, ardent—magnificent!"

"Please, 'Garia, I don't care to listen. You must stop and think what you are doing! The danger!"

"Is it my neck for which you fear, Valentina, or your own? Or are your scruples so acute because of your . . . affection for my husband?"

Valentina drew back in shock. " 'Garia!"

"My deductions are correct, are they not?" Berengaria persisted, a sly, wicked smile baring her teeth. "Do you think me a fool? You accompanied me to that long-ago tourney, where we both saw Richard Plantagenet for the first time. You were as captured by his brilliance and flaming good looks as I was myself, along with every woman present that day. You loved him then and you *still* love him. You defend him," Berengaria spit scornfully, "even though you know he is a lover of men!"

"This is what *you* say, my queen! It is *you* who have slandered the king! Until you propagated these

43

vicious rumors with sly whispers, no hint of scandal touched my lord, Richard. With the gold he gave you to run your household, you bribed your lute players and troubadors to mock him in song! The Lionheart has dedicated himself to a holy cause, and you scorn him for neglecting his marital duties! You are a fool, Berengaria!"

"Nay, Valentina, you are the fool. You cannot see the writing on the wall. My liege, Richard, is not so dedicated to the taking of the Holy Land that he is too busy to exchange fond smiles with Philip," Berengaria accused.

"The king of France is a boyhood friend," Valentina said defensively.

"And that foppish musician?" Berengaria retorted.

"A matter of similar interests. My lord, Richard, is a remarkable musician himself!"

"And does my lord cook and spin and sew a fine seam? Open your eyes to the truth, Valentina. My husband has no taste for women."

"I won't believe that," Valentina shot back, her eyes flashing. "And even if it were so, your conduct is treasonous! Your cravings of the flesh jeopardize not only yourself but Sena and me and your entire entourage!"

"Enough! You overstep your bounds, Lady Valentina. I remind you it is to your queen you speak. You speak so often of treason, what do you consider your behavior to me? I could have you drawn and quartered!" Berengaria threw down her hairbrush and advanced threateningly on Valentina. "Your queen suggests you hold your tongue and prepare her bath."

There was no mistaking the look in Berengaria' eyes. Valentina shuddered and set about stripping the linens from the bedstead. "Your Highness forgets I am a lady-in-waiting, not a handmaiden. I will pass on the orders for the bath."

"Valentina," Berengaria cooed softly, "I have an idea. Remember how Sena used to bathe us when we were children? You say you are in need of sleep." Her gaze was hot and searing as she remembered Val-

44

entina's loveliness when the sun had glanced off her slim naked body.

"Your Highness will have her bath, but not with me," Valentina said firmly, a shiver of repugnance causing her to break out in goose flesh. "The queen forgets we are no longer children."

Berengaria was about to protest, then thought better of it. She would wait and bide her time. There was no doubt in her mind that Valentina would comply sooner or later. After all, she was a vital young woman ripe for the awakening of her passions. There was no doubt that Valentina was still a virgin. As her lady-in-waiting, Valentina's whole life came under Berengaria's scrutiny. Life in the queen's court was cloistered, and no man could woo a lady without the queen's knowledge and approval. "I have no desire for Sena's rough hands this morning. Since you refuse me your company, send me Tarsa, that silly young girl who joined us in Cyprus."

Valentina threw Berengaria a barely disguised look of disgust. Tarsa was the daughter of Isaac, former ruler of Cyprus who was deposed by Richard the Lionheart just before the latter's arrival in Acre. Guy de Lusignon now sat upon the Cypriot throne with the promise from King Richard that one day the crown of Jerusalem would be his. "Does your Highness refer to the princess of Cyprus?" Valentina asked innocently, knowing that it irked Berengaria to hear Tarsa referred to by her Royal title.

"Yes," the queen answered hotly. "What do you think of the unexpected addition to our entourage?" Berengaria was testing Valentina's reaction.

"I regret to say I cannot make a judgment. I have been in her company so rarely." Actually, Valentina had formed a very definite opinion of Tarsa. Small, swarthy, and voluptuously built, the Cypriot was a maid of many talents. She was an accomplished musician; she played the lute, the harp, and the dulcimer, and her songs rivaled the birds for their sweetness. Two full days before her father, King Isaac, was captured, Tarsa gave herself up and threw herself on Richard's mercy. Always chivalrous, England's king welcomed her and directed that she be placed with Berengaria's attendants. To Valentina, Tarsa was a conspiring, conniving vulture ready to profit from any opportunity.

"I will send for Tarsa and call for your bath water. I will see to the fresh bed linen myself," Valentina said as she walked out the door, carrying the mound of soiled bedding.

Valentina returned to the bower chamber to find Berengaria immersed in a huge copper tub of scented water. Tarsa, the dark, voluptuous Cypriot, was attending the queen by lathering a fragrant soap over the pink expanse of Berengaria's back. When Valentina entered without knocking, Tarsa had jumped to her feet, a startled expression contorting her face and staining her skin with red blotches.

" 'Tis only my Lady Valentina," Berengaria soothed as she grasped the Cypriot's hand and pulled her once more toward the tub.

As Valentina went about making the bed, Berengaria and Tarsa giggled like children, splashing one another and playing with the slippery soap. The front of Tarsa's gown was water-splotched and clung wetly to her body, revealing her voluptuous breasts. Berengaria seized the soft cloth and pressed it into Tarsa's hand.

Valentina watched the women covertly as she went about making the bedstead. The Cypriot was gently sponging Berengaria's back, moving upward to the graceful arch of her neck. Slowly, methodically, she lathered the queen's soft pink shoulders. Valentina looked away, embarrassed, when she saw Tarsa lick her lips as though she were tasting a sweet delicacy while the soft, soapy cloth moved slowly across Berengaria's taut, quivering breasts.

Hurriedly finishing the chore of changing the linen on the divan, Valentina turned to leave. Berengaria had slid down into the warm, fragrant water and was resting her head on the curved rim of the copper bath. Her eyes were on Valentina in a long, languid look;

46

her full, moist lips parted, showing her small white teeth. Locking Valentina in a meaningful stare, Berengaria grasped Tarsa's hand and plunged it beneath the water between her thighs. She emitted a little groan of delight, and Valentina saw her hips rise and begin to undulate. Totally shaken and humiliated, Valentina rushed from the room, Berengaria's derisive laughter ringing in her ears.

Paxon rode from the city to the outskirts, where his corpulent friend, Meshtub, waited. "You've had a long wait, my friend," Paxon laughed.

"So I have," Meshtub grumbled good-naturedly, glad to see Paxon return safe and sound. "I was certain the Engleysi had you beheaded!" Meshtub's relief turned to inquisitiveness, his dark round eyes shining with curiosity. "Tell me, Pax, how does an Engleysi bed? Is she different from our women?"

Paxon laughed. "The body is the same, only the spirit is different. I have told you before, Meshtub, each woman possesses a different soul. Smooth skin, soft curves, this is all the same. It is the spirit which makes every woman unique unto herself."

This Meshtub had heard before. Paxon saw the disappointment in his friend's face. "So, nothing less than a detailed report will satisfy you, eh, Meshtub? Very well; this Engleysi is perhaps a little different. She has unquenchable appetites, appetites I thought only men possessed. She is fair of skin and her flesh is soft and yielding, but there is an unsuspected strength about her. The touch of her hands is soft, like the petals of a rose, but one always senses the presence of the thorn. Her thighs, so lusciously plump and prettily rounded, yet their grip is strong and muscular. And that, Meshtub, is enough information for one day. When will you find a woman of your own?"

"Soon, Pax, soon! There is a little Bedouin who camps at the well of El Ribar. If Allah wills it, I will have her."

"There are some things Allah cannot do, and this is

one of them," Paxon roared. "Meshtub, you must do it yourself. Afterward you can thank Allah!"

As they rode, the panther keeping pace, Paxon's thoughts were on the queen's lady-in-waiting. She had seemed troubled, as though she were carrying a heavy burden. Even as the thought occurred to him, he understood the reason for Valentina's anxieties. Her implication in Berengaria's activities made her as guilty of treason as the queen. Paxon was saddened that he had become part of Valentina's distress. He wished she could once again be as happy and carefree as when he had first seen her in Cyprus at the tourney celebrating the royal marriage. When Menghis had miscalculated his stride and swept her out of the reviewing pavilion in place of Berengaria, Valentina's eyes had been lighted with excitement, her cheeks flushed pink, her laugh deep and merry. She was beautiful, tall and slim, her long shining hair gleaming in the sunlight, her eyes a deep sapphire-blue. So beautiful, in fact, that he had never doubted for a moment that she was the newly crowned queen of England whom the minstrels had already begun to praise in their songs.

Meshtub sidled up to Paxon and slapped him on the knee. "Were the demands of the Engleysi so rigorous that you sleep in the saddle? Where are your thoughts, good friend?"

Paxon laughed and spurred on his stallion. "My thoughts, Meshtub, are on eyes the color of the great sea and on long, sweetly shaped limbs."

Meshtub shook his head in wonderment. Allah alone knew where Paxon got his strength!

Chapter Four

The council meetings between Christians and Moslems concerning the exchange and ransoming of prisoners continued for the next six days. This had been a hectic time for Valentina, whose nerves were stretched as tightly as a lute string. The strain was beginning to show by the violet smudges beneath her eyes, giving her a wan appearance.

Her days were spent with Berengaria, witnessing the council meetings from the grilled balcony or listening to Tarsa, the Cypriot princess, amuse the queen with her songs. The relationship between Tarsa and Valentina had rapidly smoldered from a casual dislike to a barely concealed hatred. Valentina was disgusted by the Cypriot's unnatural inclinations, and Tarsa, in turn, was jealous of Valentina's long-standing relationship with Berengaria and the respect she commanded as the queen's confidante.

Adding to Valentina's fatigue were the long, chilly nights spent on the stone bench near the footpath in the garden. Since the first night when the Saracen had slipped through the gate to the bower, Valentina had had little sleep. On five successive nights the sultan of Jakard had arrived sporting a foolish smile and an intimate manner. In the first rays of dawn he would leave his tryst and meet Valentina on the garden path. Each night he tried to embrace her and press his lips to hers. Each time she eluded him and was able to quell his advances by complaining that he reeked of Berengaria's perfume. It had become a ritual as, tight-lipped and silent, she led the dashing Saracen to and from Berengaria's hungry embraces.

"Valentina!" came a harsh command. The past two nights had come and gone without a sign of the Saracen, and the queen was in a murderous frame of mind. "Valentina!" Berengaria commanded again.

Stepping into the queen's chamber, Valentina replied, "Your Majesty."

Berengaria was reclining on the low divan, contemplating her rosy toes. The high leaded paned window was open, allowing the sweet fragrance of blossoms to drift into the circular room. "I want you to find Paxon and determine why he has neglected me these past two nights. Seek him out and convey my wish to see him." Her voice was barely a whisper and edged with desperation.

"My queen," Valentina sympathized, "perhaps he is on an official mission."

"If that were so, I would know it. He would have told me!" Berengaria sprang up from the divan and paced the room, wringing her hands nervously. Her eyes suddenly darkened. "Where have you been these past two nights? Why do you appear so haggard?"

"Has your Majesty forgotten I was ordered to stand by the gate in the event the Saracen arrived?"

Berengaria's eyes narrowed still further. "I think," she said slyly, "that you have intercepted my handsome sultan and lain in bed with him, and that's why you're so tired. Is this true, Valentina?" she demanded.

"Of course it's not true. How could you think such a thing of me?"

"I'm no fool, Valentina. Of late the sultan's lovemaking has been less than . . . enthusiastic. Perhaps his eyes travel in another direction. If I ever find that you've stolen him from me, your head will be severed from your body. He's mine! Mine, do you hear?"

" 'Garia, you make much ado over nothing." Valentina's voice was soothing, as it always was when Berengaria worked herself into an anxious state. At times like this Valentina acknowledged her fear that 'Garia was becoming mentally unbalanced. It was a well-known fact that the queen's mother had conceived her in a rare moment of sanity but had birthed her in the

50

grips of lunacy. Everyone closely connected with the royal household of Navarre kept a cautious eye on the comely Berengaria's erratic moods.

"It's most likely just as I said," Valentina said comfortingly. "He is on a mission. If you don't need me any more, then I would like to bathe and sleep for a while. Then I shall do as you ask and send out a message for the sultan. With your leave, my queen," Valentina said, bowing low.

"Dearest Valentina, perhaps I have been a trifle hasty. You do look wan and tired. I've been beastly to you, and I'm sorry," she crooned, her eyes round and guileless. "To show you how generous I am, you will sleep here in my bed. No one shall bother you, I shall see to it personally. Say you forgive me, dearest Valentina, friend of friends. Say you forgive your queen." The round guileless eyes were now openly speculative, and the small pink tongue was being nibbled on as the queen clenched and unclenched her plump hands.

Seeing the expression on her queen's face, Valentina no longer felt tired; in fact, she felt the blood surge through her with such force that her legs propelled her into a run in spite of their leaden feeling. She was out the door and racing down the footpath. "Valentina," came the shrill command. "Valentina!"

"Valentina be damned!" Valentina muttered as she sped down the length of the footpath. A dungeon was better than this. She would never succumb to those soft pink hands. "Never," she muttered as she continued to run. She found herself out of breath and outside the palace walls, and still she ran. Her thick raven hair had come loose of its bindings and was trailing down her back. Her breathing was ragged, and tears streaked her cheeks as she slowed and leaned against a tree. She rubbed at the tears with the back of her hand as she again vowed to herself that never would those pink hands touch her. Where *was* that bedamned sultan, the man who had captured her queen's heart and her body? It was his fault that she was now being placed in this position. If he had continued his visits, 'Garia would not have eyes for her.

As if in answer to her pleas, a horseman rode up to her and stopped. "So the queen's procurer is out for a stroll. Are you walking or . . . procuring?" Paxon asked huskily as he leaned over the flanks of his steed. Valentina ignored him and continued her long-legged stride down the dusty road, her chin held high. What did she care if he saw the tears on her cheeks?

"Valentina," Paxon called sharply. "Stop! I wish to speak with you." Valentina continued to ignore him. Paxon dismounted and in a moment had her in his arms. Then he noticed her tears. "What is it?" he asked softly. "Who has made you cry?" His fingertip caught one glistening tear as it coursed down her smooth cheek. "Tell me and I'll carve the manhood from his body! Look at me!" he demanded.

Valentina looked unwillingly into his dark eyes and felt herself drowning in their depths. Her arms felt weak and her legs trembled. In that moment of time she knew without a doubt that Paxon was a warrior, with a warrior's sense of borders and boundaries. A woman was something to be won, just like a plot of land or a city or a crown. Having won her, he would regard her as his possession and would fight to defend her, not for any injustices done to her, but for a simpler, more basic reason: that of someone's encroachment upon his property.

Valentina rebelled against the idea of becoming Paxon's possession. She didn't want to belong to anyone. Since her earliest memories she was first a father's daughter, a tutor's pupil, a king's subject, a queen's lady; always her identity was founded upon someone else. She realized in a sudden flash of truth that she harbored a deep desire to be her own person, to be answerable to herself—to be Valentina. And there in Paxon's eyes was the demand that she become *his*. If she were careless he would consume her, own her, her mind, her body, her spirit, her soul. Her reason recoiled, yet she was inexplicably drawn to him as she gazed into the mesmerizing depths of his jet eyes. She swallowed and swayed slightly, only to find hard arms crushing her.

Valentina was so tired, so weary, she could have closed her eyes and rested forever in the safe, warm circle of his arms. She made no move to extricate herself and remained quiet, nestling closer to him, hearing the steady beat of his heart beneath her head.

Paxon gazed down at the soft tangle of dark hair against his chest and felt stirrings of protectiveness. She was so warm, so soft. He cupped her face in his hand and looked down into a sapphire sea fringed with thick dark lashes that still held a small glistening tear. His mouth moved against her lips, at first gently, then increasing in demand. Hesitantly he freed her. "Valentina, I asked you a question and you gave me no answer." Tenderly he led her to an outcropping of rocks and sat beside her.

"Tell me why you are crying. Perhaps I can help." Paxon was shaken by the effect of her kiss and felt he must say something, anything, to break the spell. No woman had ever stirred him this way. The sleek black cat that was always at Paxon's side nuzzled Valentina's hand. She lifted her fingertips and gently scratched the big cat's ears. The panther immediately quieted and lay down beside her.

"Now, tell me why you cry. You must tell me! All things become more simple when discussed. Allah proclaims it," he said, smiling.

Still Valentina made no move to speak. "Is it your queen?" Paxon asked at last. Valentina nodded. "Is she angry because I haven't been to see her? Is she making you suffer for my lack of attention? Is this why there are tears in your eyes?" Again Valentina nodded.

"I see," he said thoughtfully. "I was hoping I was wrong. If I fail to return this evening, then it will go against you."

Valentina, unable to control herself, blurted, "I hate the feel of her hands, those soft pink hands. She makes my flesh crawl. I would rather die," she sobbed.

Paxon cradled her dark head against his chest and

53

stared off into the hills. "You can tell your queen that I will visit her this evening. Dry your tears and push this from your mind. I'll have a talk with Berengaria, and you have my word that she will never lay a hand on you. My word on the Prophet Mohammed. Look at me, Valentina. Believe what I tell you," he said, gazing deeply into her eyes. "Believe me."

If he allowed himself, he could drown in those sapphire pools, he thought recklessly. With a supreme effort he broke his thoughts away and helped Valentina to her feet. "Come, I will take you back to the palace. It is unsafe for you to be about the city without proper escort. Don't worry about the Christians seeing me; as a member of the council, I have the authority to ride about safely in the city." His hard muscles erupted on his arm as he lifted her to ride across his thighs on the black Arabian. Cat, the panther, paced alongside, his golden eyes on Valentina.

She leaned her head against the broad expanse of Paxon's chest and closed her weary eyes. Her lashes cast dark, sooty smudges on her ivory cheeks. Something stirred within Paxon as he peered down at her beautiful face. It wasn't lust and it wasn't . . . it could not be. The panther snarled and swung his head from side to side. "So, Cat, you sense it, too," Paxon said softly.

Queen Berengaria was visiting Tarsa in her tower room, discussing Valentina. Berengaria was careful not to disclose the true cause of her anger. It would be most unwise to reveal her infidelity to Richard regardless of how close her relationship with the dark Cypriot had become.

Tarsa sat on a low stool, idly plucking the strings of her lute. From time to time she made small noises of sympathy as Berengaria angrily paced the floor complaining of Valentina's behavior. The Cypriot princess was wise enough not to join in or add to the queen's disparaging remarks. Although Tarsa hated Valentina's haughty, ladylike manner, she would refrain from making any comments until Berengaria took positive action against her.

"It is time Valentina was taught a lesson," Berengaria said hotly. Her flush of anger was emphasized by the pale mauve of her modest, high-necked gown. "Despite our long-standing friendship, Valentina has overstepped her bounds! She must be punished!" Berengaria said determinedly.

"How will your Majesty accomplish this?" Tarsa asked casually, while an inner excitement held her in its grip. Then Berengaria said the words Tarsa longed to hear.

"She shall be whipped! I myself will see to it. Ten lashes at sundown! And you, dear heart, will bear witness to her humiliation." The queen's plump, beringed hand caressed Tarsa's curly dark head.

A smile on her lips, Berengaria ambled to the high window and gazed down at the road, which ran just outside the perimeter of the palace walls. Paxon! And was that Valentina with him? She shaded her eyes against the sun's glare and watched the scene below.

Her heart hammered in her breast as she saw the handsome turbaned man lean over to kiss Valentina's mouth. Valentina raised her head and smiled up at Paxon. It was a beautiful smile, Berengaria could see that even from this distance. And Paxon! Paxon was smiling down at her. A tender, gentle smile, the likes of which he had never bestowed on her, the queen! Suddenly Paxon embraced Valentina and was kissing her—again! A long, lingering kiss! "Fifteen lashes!" Berengaria called to Tarsa. She continued to stare as Paxon dismounted and lifted Valentina down from the saddle. He placed a hand on her shoulder and lowered his face to hers. He was saying something that made Valentina smile. "Twenty lashes!" Berengaria called to Tarsa, her voice dripping venom.

The tone of Berengaria's voice caused Tarsa to glance up from her lute. Ignorant of the scene the queen was witnessing, she wondered at the sudden hatred Berengaria was displaying. She had thought the queen was making idle threats to whip Valentina, but now she wasn't sure.

Outside, beyond the palace walls, Paxon had remounted and was now leaning down from his high mount, speaking to Valentina. They could not know that Berengaria's vengeful eyes were burning across space to the scene they created.

"Tell your queen I shall not disappoint her. And, Valentina, bathe your eyes before you go to her. Remember what I told you: you will never have to submit to those soft hands. You see," Paxon said lightly, "we Moslems do have hearts. Just as the Christians. Only"—he grinned—"our hearts are in the right place."

Valentina smiled as she watched man, steed, and panther disappear down the dusty road.

Hurrying through the garden and up the stairs to her room, Valentina took the time to make the necessary repairs to her person. She splashed cool water on her face, rinsing away the dust of the city. Quickly she brushed her hair and redid the ornate bindings that held the heavy tresses in a thick coil at the back of her head. A final inspection of her gown proving satisfactory, Valentina skipped lightly down the stairs to the queen's chamber.

Her step lighter than it had been in days, a smile lingering on her face, Valentina found Berengaria waiting for her. "I have good news, 'Garia. The Saracen will be here this evening. I met him on the road, and he begs your forgiveness and said he will be here as early as possible. He very graciously gave me a ride home atop his steed."

"You're a bold-faced liar, Valentina," Berengaria said harshly. "And from this moment on you will address me by my royal title." Astonished by this sudden attack, Valentina stepped backward, looking to the wall behind her for support. "I saw the Saracen kiss you! I warned you this very morning that he was mine and mine alone! Yet at the first opportunity you sneak to his side. I knew I was right. He's been with you these past two nights. Don't bother to lie to me,

Valentina. I can see it in your eyes. From now on Sena will let him in at the gates. I forbid you to ever see him again. Is that understood?"

"Yes, my queen," Valentina said quietly, instinctively knowing that this was not the time for denials. "It is understood."

"Since you seem to be so tired, perhaps you should sleep now. Later your back will be too painful for sleep. I have decided your actions warrant twenty lashes. You brought this on yourself, Valentina," Berengaria said spitefully.

Valentina was silent. Explanations would be useless. Berengaria seethed inwardly, hating Valentina's composure. How could Paxon, a lusty, virile man, be attracted to this dull-witted creature? Valentina lacked the fire and passion that Berengaria knew Paxon found exciting in a woman.

When the door closed behind Valentina, Berengaria sat down on the divan and let her mind race. It was time to get rid of Valentina. But how? Think, 'Garia, she commanded herself. There must be a way. And the sooner the better. Perhaps Richard would be of help tonight at the evening meal. She would seek him out and perhaps come up with a solution. She would have to be skillful, for no one must know, and least of all suspect, that it was because of a Saracen. Her flesh began to tingle as she envisioned the dark-haired sultan standing over her naked body. She would make him forget he ever laid eyes on the placid Valentina. She was confident she could keep him in her bed. One way or another, she would have him for herself, forever if she so desired it!

Chapter Five

As the sun was spewing its last rosy glows over the white walls surrounding the city of Acre, Valentina stepped into the queen's chamber, ready to face the unjustified whipping. Tarsa was reposed on the divan and seemed genuinely surprised to see her. It was clear the Cypriot expected that an armed guard would be needed to drag Valentina before the queen to meet her punishment.

Berengaria appeared nervous and white-lipped. "I am most glad you understood I was serious about your twenty lashes, Valentina. It would have been very unpleasant if I had been forced to send the guard for you."

"My queen speaks of the guard, yet none are in evidence," Valentina said softly, her voice a throaty whisper.

"I have decided to spare you that humiliation. The princess and I will see that you suffer the consequences of your actions." Turning to Tarsa, Berengaria said in a commanding tone, "Princess, will you see that my errant lady is prepared?"

Tarsa moistened her lips with the tip of her tongue and loosened the bodice of Valentina's gown, stripping her to the waist. Berengaria watched silently, a flicker of interest lighting the depths of her brown eyes when she viewed the perfection of Valentina's breasts. Tarsa, jealous of the admiring look in Berengaria's eyes, viciously pulled Valentina across the room to an iron candle sconce that was firmly implanted in the stone wall. Removing her own girdle, Tarsa used the woven belt to secure Valentina's wrists to the sconce.

"I regret that this is necessary, Valentina," Berengaria said. "Your insolence has far exceeded my tolerance."

Her tone was frigid, but Valentina perceived a tinge of excitement in it and shrank against the wall, the rough stone biting into her soft flesh.

Tarsa swept aside Valentina's long black hair. Her fingertips grazed Valentina's silken skin and she frowned.

"Yes, Princess, she is lovely, is she not? 'Tis a shame to mark that tender flesh." Berengaria came close and ran her plump pink hand down the length of Valentina's back.

The blue-green eyes darkened to a murky green, and Valentina shuddered more from the unwanted contact of Berengaria's hand than from the expected fall of the whip.

Berengaria mistook Valentina's involuntary shudder as a pleasurable response to her touch. She stepped before her trussed victim and reached forward boldly to fondle Valentina's rosy-tipped breasts.

"Don't do that! Don't touch me!" Valentina cried harshly. "I abhor you! I loathe your touch! Save your evil inclinations for your Cypriot bedmate!"

Berengaria's hand shot up and she slapped Valentina in the face. "Your queen silences you! Had I been so inclined to spare you, my generosity has abated. Princess, begin!"

Tarsa took her position behind Valentina. A whip, such as the type drovers used, was held tightly in her upraised hand. At the queen's silent nod Tarsa brought the short, thick length of braided leather down across Valentina's back, raising an angry red welt.

A shock of pain coursed through Valentina, and she stiffened in anticipation of the next blow. Stubbornly she bit into her lip, refusing to cry out. Berengaria signaled again, and Tarsa brought the whip down a second time. Again Valentina flattened herself against the wall in response to the pain. Still she uttered no sound.

Tarsa's black eyes locked with Berengaria's. The

queen's breathing was heavy, as though she herself had been struck. Tarsa was quick to recognize the signs: Berengaria was enjoying the novelty of the sadistic beating. Her lips were moist and parted, her eyes half closed and languid. Watching Berengaria closely, Tarsa brought the instrument of punishment down for the third time.

Valentina's body convulsed with pain. Her knees buckled and she hung heavily by her wrists from the sconce. The snakelike length licked through the air once again, slicing into Valentina's tender flesh. Still she was silent; no outcry escaped her. Berengaria was leaning against a chair back for support. Her breathing was steady and rapid, her hips swaying slightly with an internal rhythm.

Tarsa was responding to the sensualism Berengaria was communicating. Excitement impelled her to lash Valentina's inert form again. A sound whizzed through the room for the eternity before the tip bit once again. Valentina was totally unresponsive; she hung limply by her bound wrists. Tarsa became alarmed and looked to the queen in askance.

Berengaria was gripping the chair back, her knuckles shining whitely in the gray dusk. Shudder after shudder coursed through her as she sank, breathless, to her knees.

The Cypriot raised her arm again, her eyes wild, her pulses throbbing. "No!" Berengaria cried. "No more!"

Tarsa stood frozen, her arm in midair. "My queen ordered twenty lashes, and twenty she shall have!" She brought down her arm and snapped the lash into contact with Valentina's back.

"No more, I say! I command you to stop!" Berengaria's voice was shrill with horror. Valentina was so still, so quiet, it frightened her. It would be a simple matter to hide the fact that she had exercised her royal powers and ordered the whipping, however bizarre the procedure, but murder was something that would not be tolerated, even for a queen. "Cease! Before you kill her!"

60

"I would stripe her back for each contemptuous sneer she has thrown in my direction," Tarsa cried. "Pray you let me finish her to teach her not to be scornful of her betters!"

"Nay, Tarsa." Berengaria laid a gentle hand on the princess's dark arm. "I am not wont to killing her. Consider the lesson taught. Cut her down and beckon Sena to see to her."

Tarsa moved to do Berengaria's bidding, her black eyes glowing with unquenched revenge. "Another time, my haughty lady," she muttered as she cut Valentina's bindings with the dainty jeweled dagger she wore in her girdle. "Another time I will finish this."

Old Sena gasped with horror when she saw Valentina's condition. Tarsa had flung the semiconscious form face down across the divan, the long, bleeding gashes swelling and oozing across Valentina's graceful back.

"What have you done?" Sena turned on Berengaria accusingly, exercising the privilege of a nursemaid scolding her young charge.

"No more than she deserves," Berengaria defended. "She has proved herself to be conniving and deceitful. As queen, I need less reason than that to see her whipped!"

"Foolish girl," Sena chastised. "You have allowed this heathen to turn your heart from the truest friend you will ever know!" Sena's sharp blue eyes pierced the Cypriot princess. "Look for yourself!" she ordered the petulant queen. "See how her skin shines with her lustful sweat! Bah! What see you in this swarthy Cypriot? The black fur on her arms and upper lip brings my mind to monkeys!"

"Monkey! You old hag! I'll pluck your eyeballs from your head!" Tarsa screeched, lunging for Sena.

Berengaria threw herself between the women. "Cease, I say! Get about clearing my chamber," she instructed. "Remove that piece of baggage," indicating Valentina. "Both of you!"

Tarsa tossed Berengaria a resentful look. It was old

Sena who gathered Valentina to her fat breast, clicking her tongue and crooning sympathy.

"Shut your mouth, old woman! Take her to her bed and do your crooning there. Even when we were children you always preferred her to me! You always thought her more comely, more intelligent, better with the needle! Admit it, crone, you have always loved her best!" Berengaria's eyes were bright with unshed tears of self-pity.

"Nay! Always I preferred my princess to the lady. Valentina is neither more comely in my eyes nor sparked with more wisdom. But yea, her nature is more loving. And yet you smite her for a Cypriot monkey with female breasts!"

Tarsa bristled and rose to the attack, her hands bent into claws and red nails gleaming like lethal talons. "Miserable hag!" she hissed, baring her teeth like a feral animal.

"Enough!" Berengaria commanded. "Bend your back to helping Sena get my lady to her chamber. Now!" Tarsa shot Berengaria a look which bespoke a threat. It was clear the Cypriot would bear watching.

Valentina was half dragged, half carried up the circular stone steps and laid on her bed. Tarsa wiped the palms of her hands on her gown as if rubbing away filth. "Begone with you!" Sena scolded. "If you ever touch this child again, the events of this night will fall on King Richard's ears. He will not take kindly to the abuse of a noblewoman. Begone!"

The Cypriot made a threatening move and old Sena stumbled backward. Tarsa rewarded her with a sinister smile and pranced out the door. The raucous sound of her laughter echoed off the bare stone walls in a hideous shriek, confirming Sena's impression of a dark monkey.

After reviving Valentina with cold water from the pewter ewer, Sena set about to tend the girl's back. She crooned and clucked like a mother hen as Valentina sobbed with her gentle touch.

"It will be many days before you will be up and about, my little chick. Old Sena will bring you something to make you sleep and ease the pain. Rest now."

Exhausted, Valentina slept, soft cries of pain escaping her as she dreamed of strong arms about her and dark eyes reflecting hers and an infuriating, mocking smile.

Sena's shoulders slumped as she prepared to sit with Valentina through the long night. How could Berengaria believe she loved Valentina more? Loved her, yea, but never more than her love for the doe-eyed Berengaria. Wasn't it old Sena who had brought the newly crowned queen of England into the world? Even as she thought this, an icy hand of terror clutched at her heart and she shivered. Had what Sena always feared come to pass? Was Berengaria following her mother into the agonies of insanity?

In the queen's chamber, Berengaria changed her gown for one of pale yellow silk worn over a kirtle of deep bronze. She had barred the door when Sena and Tarsa left, and it had been only a few minutes before the princess returned, scratching at the door and begging admittance. When Berengaria heartlessly ignored her, Tarsa had slunk off to brood alone.

Working slowly and deliberately, Berengaria brushed her long dark hair to gleaming perfection and adorned her head with a gossamer veil and golden rail. Slipping a girdle of gold cloth about her womanly hips, she breathed deeply to compose herself and stepped out into the hall. Head held high in regal bearing, she went to meet with Queen Joanna and the other ladies to assemble for dinner and make Valentina's excuses.

The heavy doors embellished with bronze plates swung open to admit the ladies. Within, the dining hall was lit by hundreds of blazing torches placed along the high stone walls. The tables were festooned with silver flatware and chalices of matching design. Trenchers of fresh fruit and sweetmeats stood ready for the greedy hand. The delicious aroma of roast boar, charred to a succulent brown and heavily spiced, greeted their nostrils. Servants were pouring wine and distributing salters. Musicians were readying their instruments in an unobtrusive corner. Richard had placed himself at the head table, and in the seat for his queen Philip of France lolled casually, engaging Richard in a ribald conversation.

Berengaria's eyes fell on the thin, boyishly pimpled face of Philip. Taking care to keep her expression from revealing her inner feelings, she examined him yet again. Dark hair, which no amount of oil would coax into style; short, spindly legs that were bowed from being placed in the saddle at too young an age; the slightly hawkish look of his face, with brows too thin and eyes too small. The mean, tight set of his mouth and the long sweep of his nose did nothing to enhance him. To think that Richard could prefer this spindly form to her softer, rounder, more promising curves set Berengaria's pulses throbbing with insult.

Richard himself was resplendent in robes of purple and gold cut to display the thick column of his neck and the wide, muscular breadth of his shoulders. On his arms, just below the elbow, he wore the armlets that were presented to him by Saladin's entourage. On any other man they would have fit on the upper arm, but on Richard they fit snugly on his lower arm. The bunched muscles of his forearms were bronzed and powerful, and Berengaria felt weak when she thought of them crushing her in a close embrace. An embrace she had never experienced.

If Richard would but come to her, love her, take her as his wife, she would never have need for the Saracen. For any man. Within Berengaria beat the heart of the young girl who had fallen in love with Richard Plantagenet. The same young girl who had denied herself nourishment and would have pined until death, had not the fates and her abundant dowry interceded on her behalf. Even now, knowing the twist in Richard's character, Berengaria would rescind her crown and lower her status to that of the stable master's daughter if Richard would find her desirable.

The trumpeter sounded a short note to announce the arrival of the court's ladies, and the hall was astir with

the scraping of chairs and hearty greetings as the officers of Richard's army stood to receive the lady who
would grace their table. Richard also stood in deference to his queen's arrival, although he continued his
conversation with Philip.

Berengaria fixed her stare on the French monarch
until he felt it pierce him. Turning slowly, he met her
gaze with a glare of his own. Berengaria lifted her
head triumphantly. King or no, Philip would have to
allow her to take her place next to her husband.

As Berengaria approached she heard Richard murmur to Philip, "If you are not more careful in your
homage to my wife, I fear she will set the Old Man
of the Mountain upon you." Philip's answer was a
loud guffaw, until something in Berengaria's eyes
strangled the sound in his throat. Hastily he moved to
his place among his own captains on the other side of
Richard.

"How lovely you look tonight, my love," Richard
said courteously as he noted Berengaria's pale yellow
gown and the decorative rail she wore on her head.

"Your kindness flatters me, my liege," she answered
coyly. Settling herself beside Richard so that the Knight
of the Templar could lead them in grace, Berengaria
turned to Richard and asked, "Who is this Old Man
of the Mountain of whom I heard you speak?"

Richard laughed. "So, you would set *Sheikh al Jebal*
on my Gallic friend's neck!"

Berengaria allowed him his moment of mirth before
she pressed on for more information.

"*Sheikh al Jebal,* my love, is known to the Christian
world as the Old Man of the Mountain. Christian and
Moslem fear him alike. I will regale you with tales of
this old assassin after grace, when we will be more at
our leisure."

Berengaria preened under Richard's attention and
could hardly wait for the meal to begin so that he
could once again turn his flaming head toward her
and look deeply into her eyes.

The Knight of the Templar finished his intonation
of thanks to God for the bountiful tables, and the

servants began at once to carve and serve the feast. True to his word, Richard ignored those who would press him into conversation and turned to face his queen.

"So, my pretty, you would have me tell you blood-curdling tales of the ancient assassin. Let me begin by saying that no man has looked upon his face, or so it is said. He rules a kingdom which stretches from Samarkand to Cairo, wherever stand the mountains. His followers are known as *fedawi,* faithful ones. No one is safe from that far-reaching blade of death. He has no God, only his own supreme rule. Because he has erected or sought out sites of castles which look down upon the cities, the Islamites named him Old Man of the Mountain. Few cities in Persia and Syria do not have a castle of the assassins to reckon with. But the one which is most often on men's lips is called Alamut, Eagle's Nest. It is the headquarters of the order. It is said that it rests on the top of an un-climbable mountain, and within its gates are the de-lights of heaven and the agonies of hell."

Richard went on to tell Berengaria of killings which had been attributed to *Sheikh al Jebal* and of the fear that was struck in the hearts of men when his name was whispered. "One never knows when or for what reasons he may strike. I have heard it said that at times the assassins give fair warning. It can be in the sudden death of a trusted servant or on awakening to find a dagger implanted in one's pillow. I have even heard a tale of a certain caliph of Cairo who was so sapped of courage when he repeatedly found these warnings from the assassins that he threw himself upon his own dagger, rather than live under the dread of overhanging peril from these godless creatures."

Berengaria punctuated these statements with little gasps and a widening of eyes and encouraged him to tell her more of *Sheikh al Jebal* and his *fedawi.* "But I must be frightening you out of your night's rest!" Richard protested.

"Nay, my liege," was her answer, "not if I knew you would be close at hand to protect me." Her eyes lowered in feigned coyness, and a slight blush tinged her cheeks.

Richard did not miss the thinly veiled invitation to share her bed, and his annoyance showed in the gruffness of his speech. "I have provided a heavy guard about the castle, my love. Have no fear, your sleep will go undisturbed."

Berengaria was sorry she had spoken so rashly. Richard was obviously not a man to be chased. Trying to regain his favor once again, she asked, "And these *fedawi,* how does one know them?"

"One never knows, my love. Perhaps they are even here among us, even as we speak about them. Who knows where they will strike next?" He enjoyed watching her face lose color and her full lower lip tremble with emotion. But within her eyes, somewhere in their fathomless depths, he saw a spark ignite. Could it be that it would take more than the threat of assassins to frighten this plump and rosy wife of his?

Berengaria turned back to her meal and daintily picked at the roast boar. In her head whirled thoughts of the assassins and the threat of their presence. If what Richard said was true, the Old Man of the Mountain usually sent a warning. It could even be in the form of a dead servant. Valentina was a servant . . . of sorts.

Sounds of an ensuing argument took Berengaria out of her reverie. Philip had opened up the one subject of conversation that could spoil Richard's good temper. Richard was openly hostile and infuriated, his face flushing a deep scarlet that clashed with the purple of his robe. One glance at the French monarch told Berengaria that Philip had purposely directed the talk to gain Richard's attention away from her.

"The negotiations for the prisoners of war have fallen through," Richard exhorted. "I need no reminder of that fact. We may have captured Acre, but that is all we have accomplished. These prisoners are a clog around my foot! I can neither feed them nor afford the men to transport them, nor can I set them free to rejoin Saladin's army. And the Islamic warrior has neglected my demands to release those knights whose names I have listed. Even my ransom goes ignored. I won't be made the fool. I will not tolerate it!" Richard banged his fist on the table and proceeded to sweep everything within his reach onto the floor. He settled back in his chair, clutching a silver chalice of wine. His knuckles stood out starkly white against the brown of his skin. A black mood descended on him as he glowered into space.

Berengaria leaned close so that her words could be heard only by her husband. Her deep brown, doelike eyes measured him for a reaction as she spoke. "My liege, is it possible that the Saracen, Saladin, cannot release the prisoners of your choice because they are already dead? We Christians know what a bloodthirsty lot they are. If the knights you would ransom have been executed, those who enlisted your influence to seek their release would most probably accept a like retribution in return for their gold."

Richard lifted his piercing blue eyes and smiled at his wife. "My dear Berengaria, your wisdom in the ways of war startles the senses. Your reasoning pleases me. Why else would the Saracen break his word? We must assume that our selected men have already met with their end. I would feel it safe to assume that in requesting these certain men, as I was pressed to do by their friends and family, it was, in a sense, signing their death warrants. Nay! There is naught else to do but seek just retribution, one for one—nay, twenty for one! Is not one Christian life worth twenty Moslems?"

Richard sat back, satisfied that he had come to a decision that would save his honor, allow him to keep the ransom monies paid, and rid him of over two thousand Islamic prisoners of war whom he was hard pressed to feed. "Jacko!" he called to a passing man-servant. "See that my lady has the sweetest of the grape! Fill my goblet also. I would drink to the gentle wisdom of my wife!"

Berengaria glowed with happiness. Philip peered in her direction, wondering what event could make

Richard crow like a jubilant lover. As he watched, Richard placed his arm about Berengaria's shoulder and pulled her toward him, placing a great smacking kiss on her flushing cheek. Jealousy, hatred, and the desire to kill boiled within Philip's frail, youthful body. "And what words of wisdom did our fair queen impart, sire? Perhaps a remedy for the ills which beset our armies? The fevers rage into epidemic proportions." Philip purposely introduced the subject of the fevers and dysentery that plagued the Christian army, knowing Richard's concern.

"The fever I speak of is the fever of revenge!" Richard roared angrily. "What think you? That I am a nursemaid and taken to talk of women's business? Leave the nursing of the sick to women and lackeys!"

Philip blanched beneath the Lionheart's anger. Berengaria cast the French monarch a victorious look. Her eyes shone and her full lips parted seductively as she looked back at Richard, who was rejoicing in the solution to his problem.

"What revenge do you speak of, sire?" one of Richard's captains asked. "What new plan have you conceived to make the Infidel turn tail and run, leaving Jerusalem for God's children?"

Richard stood, his towering height looming above the assembly. "This is my plan. All the Moslem prisoners will be led outside the walls of the city. They will be chained and lashed into tight groups. And you, my noble warriors," he said magnanimously, lifting his chalice in a toast, "will ride about them slicing their heathen heads from their heathen bodies!"

An immediate hush settled over the dining hall. Richard's last words seemed to reverberate off the stone walls. The officers glanced at one another with somber faces. Richard was quick to note the effect his words had achieved and hastened to clear up the matter.

"It is safe to assume that the reason Saladin has not moved to honor our request for ransoming those selected knights back into our protection is because he has already seen to their execution. Are we to stand by and allow this? Is not one Christian head worth at least twenty of the Infidel's? Are we, the victors who took this city of Acre, going to allow the defeated Saladin to issue mandates to us? Have you not sworn to uphold the Holy Cross and slay the Infidel? The accountings show there are twenty-seven hundred prisoners in our hands. When Saladin beholds their fate, he will become quicker to accede to our demands in the future."

Berengaria watched as each man and woman looked about themselves, their eyes falling upon the servants. She understood. It was the general consensus that Saladin's spies would run to the Islamic general and warn him of the slaughter.

The talk quickly turned to feats of war and revenge, and the ladies were finding themselves sorely neglected. Pleading a headache, Berengaria made her apologies to Richard and Philip and proceeded to leave the banquet hall. Taking their cue, the ladies of her retinue also followed, leaving the men to their glories of war. As Berengaria was making her good-nights, the talk again focused on the fever that was laying low much of the army.

Richard pounded on the table and called for order. "In the queen's retinue is a fair maid with whom I have had occasion to discuss this illness. The Lady Valentina's father enjoyed the position of King Sancho's physician and rode many times onto the battlefield with the King of Navarre and knew much of the plagues which can beset an army. Lady Valentina has pointed out to me the wide ring of filth and ruin which lies between the white walls of the city and the camps of the Crusaders. The rotting bodies of the dead, which only the vultures pick, and those damned rack-ribbed dogs, which plague us. The dung heaps are high and rife, and the stench causes a strong stomach to retch. The good lady told me that her father often noted that the amount of camp fever was directly proportional to the degree of filth in which an army lives. Hence, on the good advice of that lady, I order wide trenches to be dug. A company of men is to see to the setting fire

70

of that filth and the burying of the ashes. Henceforth, all latrines will be kept outside the camp and promptly covered over. The drinking booths and the dregs and the doxies, those filth-carrying women, will be banned from the camp. If the men don't catch their death by sleeping with them, they are sure to catch it by a dagger between the ribs. Harlots have no place in a war camp!"

Groans of complaint were heard, though no one had the courage to speak out. It would be useless. Richard would mete out severe punishments unless his orders were carried out to the fullest.

Richard concluded his speech with the words, "Lift high your cups, men, and toast to the fair Lady Valentina! She may be the saving of your necks!"

Berengaria fled the hall before she had to witness the toasting. Paxon had fallen beneath Valentina's spell, and now Richard, calling her fair, good, and wise. Soon, if Richard's orders concerning sanitation were heeded, every man in the Christian army would have her name on his lips. Hate was too mild a word for the emotions that coursed through England's queen. Valentina! Always Valentina! I could kill her! Bah! May *Sheikh al Jebal's fedawi* sink their daggers into her soft flesh!

Even as she thought this a thrill tingled through her. *Fedawi* no, but Richard's solution to his problem of prisoners could well be *her* solution to getting rid of Valentina. All she had to do was to get Valentina to the dungeons beneath the city walls before the prisoners were led out beyond the gates . . .

The matter settled to her satisfaction, she climbed the circular stone steps to Valentina's chamber. After sending Sena on a trumped-up errand, Berengaria felt a vague sense of pity as she gazed down at her childhood friend's raw and still-bleeding back. Thank the stars that she had held Tarsa from laying on the lash again. It would be torture for the girl to walk after the lashes she had received, let alone after the twenty promised.

71

Leaning over her, Berengaria compressed her lips and whispered, "Valentina, can you hear me?"

Valentina groaned and moved slightly; her eyes opened, and when she saw Berengaria, she cringed.

"Be not afraid, Valentina. I have come to beg your forgiveness. At times I think I must be as mad as my mother was. Say you forgive your friend, Valentina."

Emitting a whimper, Valentina managed to nod her head. Forgiveness was not forthcoming, but Valentina wanted to be left to herself, and she knew Berengaria would not leave until she had her way. What difference would it make to lie? Withholding forgiveness would not better her own condition. Berengaria would abuse her again whenever the whim possessed her.

"Ah, Valentina, good friend. You have lightened my guilt. But more important still is the message I bring you from the Lionheart."

At the reference to Richard, Valentina opened her eyes wide and struggled through the effects of the light drug Sena had given her. "King Richard has a message for me?"

"Yes. It seems he is most grateful for the advice you gave him about clearing the filth to cut down the camp fever."

Valentina brightened. The golden god, the brilliant-haired warrior, was grateful! She knew Berengaria was telling the truth, for how else could the queen know of her conversation with the king? "What is the message my liege sends me?" Valentina whispered through her pain. Her eyes closed as she listened to Berengaria's soft voice, and so she missed the glint in the depths of those doelike eyes.

"An hour before dawn tomorrow, you are to go to the compound where the prisoners are kept. You are to wear a simple dress and wait there until the prisoners are brought out. One of them will slip you a message, and you are to bring it here to me so I can give it to the king. Do you understand what I am telling you? Richard needs you; you are the only one he can trust. Richard is sending a guardsman to accompany you, but you are not to reveal your mission to him. He is merely there for your protection."

Valentina moaned. What need could the king have for her? There were many others eager to do his bidding. Why her? She would have to refuse him. Her back was painful, and she was certain she would never be able to walk the distance to the prison.

Berengaria understood. "Valentina, listen to me. You must do it! King Richard is counting on you; you must not disappoint him. There is no one else he can trust. Regardless of your pain, you must obey him! Remember, one hour before dawn. The guardsman will come to you."

Valentina shook her head in affirmation. Berengaria leaned over and placed a kiss on the girl's brow. "I told the king you would keep his trust. Good night, sweet Valentina."

Long after Berengaria left, the cloying, musky scent of her perfume remained and brought to Valentina's mind the times she had let the Saracen out the garden gates and the scent of the queen's perfume had mingled with the scent of lust. As Valentina closed her eyes to sleep, she remembered that Paxon was again visiting the queen tonight.

Going down the long, winding stair, Berengaria called shrilly to her old nursemaid: "Sena, where are you? Come to my chamber on the first floor immediately."

Sena, who had taken the opportunity to fetch her embroidery on a new silk kirtle for the queen, listened to Berengaria's commands and nodded her wizened old head. So she was right. It was a man. The Saracen was the reason for Valentina's lashing, the cause of her pain. Sena had always been aware of the streak of cruelty in Berengaria, her best loved. Yet of late the childhood pranks and jealousies had taken a more sadistic turn. Not so long ago, when Berengaria had her mind set on marrying Richard of England, Sena had feared for the young princess's life. When news had come to Navarre that Richard was already betrothed to Alys, Philip of France's sister, Berengaria had been brokenhearted. She had seen the dashing red-haired Goliath and meant to have him. When it did not seem possible, the girl had simply lain down and announced she meant to die.

And die she would have, Sena was sure of it, and King Sancho had also been convinced. No food nor drink passed her lips. Indeed, if such were forced upon her, Berengaria was seized by a fit of retching so violent that many times blood was spilled. For weeks the princess had lingered on in this state. Never a word was uttered by her; her eyes seemed closed by death itself. She never stirred, and simply wasted away before her father's and Sena's anxious eyes. It was only when a chance visitor from the north paid court to King Sancho and made mention that the Lionheart's betrothal to the French princess had been negated, and the desperate Sancho had run to his daughter with this hopeful news, that Berengaria showed the first signs of the will to live.

It was her love for Richard that had nearly killed her, and now it was because of Richard that she had nearly killed. Sena was convinced that if the king paid the attention to his queen that every wife was entitled to expect, Berengaria would never resort to taking lovers, be they male or female, and Lady Valentina would not be sleeping on a bed of pain.

"Sena, you old crone, where the devil are you?"

"I am here," Sena croaked as she stepped into the queen's chamber.

"Because my Lady Valentina is indisposed this evening, I have an errand for you," Berengaria said sharply.

Indisposed! What a clever turn of words, Sena thought. Berengaria always did possess a talent for twisting the truth to her own advantage. Indisposed! "Beaten" was more the truth. At that moment Sena viewed the queen with clear, critical eyes. The child she had loved had become a woman whose precocious ways bordered on the deadly and the sinister.

Before Sena could explore her emotions further, Berengaria ordered, "You will go to the gate in the garden and let in the visitor. After you admit him, you will wait at the bench on the footpath and see him out when it is time. Go now and wait. Bring him to me immediately."

As she watched old Sena take her leave, it occurred to Berengaria that if Richard had been amenable to accompanying her to bed this night, she wouldn't have been able to keep her appointment with the Saracen. Her eyes glowed hotly as she changed her gown for a shimmering blue robe trimmed with silver. All the Saracens in the world would mean nothing to her if only Richard would take it into his head to act as her husband. There was nothing she wouldn't do to feel those strong arms crush her in an embrace and to see his red-gold head bend to hers. Why must he discard her so lightly? Why was he the one man who was impervious to her charms? "Richard, Richard," she cried softly, "why do you make me do the things I do?"

Sena waited patiently for an hour, then two hours. As she sat on the stone bench she became unsettled by her turn of mind. When thinking proved too much and drowsiness took hold, Sena dozed the light sleep of the aged. It seemed that she had just closed her eyes in the dark of the garden when she was aware of the sound of hooves and a scratching upon the gate.

Scuttling to the entrance, she swung open the gate and admitted the tall, black-eyed Saracen swathed in a black tunic and turban. His eyes narrowed when he saw that it was not Valentina who answered his knock.

"Where is Lady Valentina?" he demanded, his eyes blazing as he grasped her arms fiercely.

Sena looked into his jet eyes and smiled. Now she knew why Valentina had been beaten. Never had she seen such a man. Tall, broad, and strikingly handsome. She found herself wishing she were forty years younger. And what was that she saw in those night-dark orbs? Was it concern for Valentina? And his tone —had he some inkling that Valentina was in danger?

"Lady Valentina is . . . Lady Valentina was . . ."

"Lady Valentina was what? Tell me, you old crone! What has happened to Valentina?"

Could he be the answer Sena was looking for? Could this handsome Saracen be Valentina's salvation? Could his help be enlisted to wrest Valentina from Berengaria's deadly grasp?

"Tell me!" he demanded as he shook Sena so violently she imagined she heard her brains rattle.

"The queen has had Lady Valentina flogged," Sena said curtly, watching for his expression to reveal his feelings for the girl.

"Take me to her," he demanded.

"My queen said . . ."

"The devil take your queen, he already possesses her soul! Take me to Valentina."

Such a man! Sena grinned as she minced her way down the footpath and up the spiral stairs to Valentina's room.

Paxon stood in the doorway, a tall dark shadow against the smoking lamps behind him. His eyes went to the deep ridges on the girl's back. Stepping closer, he bent down on one knee and gently touched her cheek. The long, sooty lashes opened slowly and Valentina gazed into his ebony eyes.

She found herself comforted by his presence and smiled weakly. "You should not be here." Her eyes clouded over, and worry for old Sena flooded her thoughts. "If Berengaria discovers you here, it will go hard on Sena."

"Not to worry, little one. I will be careful." Gently he brushed back the long tresses which had fallen over her cheek, veiling her face. He felt a yearning to put his lips to that silky softness and breathe in the fresh, dewy scent of her skin. "Why was this done to you?" he asked, his voice husky and filled with emotion.

"It matters not," Valentina said quietly.

"It matters to me. It was because of me." His voice held a harsh edge.

"It matters not," was her answer. "You must go now. Sena will take you. Worry not for me; the flesh heals."

"But not the spirit, eh, little one? I will come back

for you," Paxon said shortly, his eyes dark and smoldering.

"No," came her soft answer, "never come back . . ."

"Shhh," Sena directed him, no longer in awe of this powerful man, but once again the loving nursemaid looking toward her charge's welfare. "She is sleeping; it is the draft I gave her. She is free of the pain for now."

Leading the Saracen out into the hall, Sena turned expectant eyes upon the man who was so visibly moved by the injustice done.

"What would you have me say, old woman? That I am the reason why Lady Valentina was nearly laid open by a vicious bitch? By the eyes of Allah, I would have no harm come to her!"

Sena continued her penetrating stare, her ancient blue eyes holding his in a challenge.

"Speak your heart, old woman, I have business to attend. What would you have me do for the maid?"

"It is because of you, Saracen, that my lady is in these dangerous straits. What would you do to save her?"

"I can see in your eyes that you feel this is not yet finished. The queen's angers and jealousies know no bounds, is that it?"

"Yea," Sena answered sorrowfully. "Berengaria will make my Lady Valentina's life a hell on earth."

Paxon glanced back into the softly lit room, to the narrow bed where the sleeping girl lay. So slight was she, the covers barely revealed her long, slim length. Her arms were extended above her head, and her long dark hair had fallen back across her lovely face. "Have Lady Valentina's belongings ready for the morning."

Suddenly Sena was frightened. She had heard vile tales of how these Infidels treated their women. "What will become of her?"

Paxon's face hardened, his eyes glowing coals. He had no desire to be saddled with a woman, yet Valentina's fate seemed to be in his hands, and he was honor bound to secure her safety. "Whatever is the lady's pleasure is what I will do."

"The Lady Valentina has family back in Navarre. Perhaps . . ."

"Yes, this will be done. I will see to it that she is put aboard a ship leaving for her homeland. Does your mind rest easy now, old woman?" Not waiting for her answer, he turned and fled down the stairs to the waiting Berengaria.

Sena stepped back into Valentina's room and tenderly brushed the hair away from the girl's face.

"Why did you bring him here, Sena? It is too dangerous!" Valentina whispered sleepily. "If Berengaria discovers this, she will have you whipped or your tongue cut out."

"Hush, child," Sena crooned. "After the morn, all will be well." It was on the tip of the old woman's tongue to tell Valentina that the sultan would return for her in the morning, but she was concerned that the news would excite the girl and she would be deprived of her sleep. Laying a work-roughened hand on Valentina's silky head, she bent and kissed her. Already a great loneliness was building in her heart for the girl. "Hush now, sweet one, the morning will find you in better hands." Glancing back to the door, Sena thought of the scene taking place below the stairs. This would not be a night of lovemaking for the queen.

Berengaria turned and saw him standing there, the door closed and bolted behind him. "How did you . . ." Gathering her composure, she said in a throaty whisper, "I did not hear you enter."

Paxon observed her, the loose black hair hanging over one shoulder, the pink flush of her skin, the blue and silver robe clinging to her full woman's curves.

"Paxon, why do you look at me so? Do I displease you?" she asked, her voice soft and taunting. "I have waited for this moment, to feel your arms about me." She extended her arms, waiting for him to step into her embrace. "Say you have yearned for me; let me hear the words." She took a step toward him, and the

78

front hem of her gown gaped, revealing a smooth, rounded thigh.

Paxon's expression was grim, his black eyes smoldering beneath his heavy dark brows. The set of his jaw disclosed his disgust. Shrinking backward, Berengaria stumbled against the low divan and sprawled down upon it.

Paxon closed the distance between them with a giant stride. Roughly seizing her by the arm, he pulled her to her feet. His eyes locked with hers in a determined stare. "I want to see you! All of you!" Viciously he ripped the robe from her body, leaving her completely naked.

Excitement raced through Berengaria. "I knew you longed for me . . . I knew it!" Exultantly she threw her arms about his neck and pulled his head down for her kiss.

Grasping hold of her shoulders, Paxon firmly put her from him. "Stand near the light," he breathed, his voice heavy with an emotion which she mistook for desire. "Stand near the light!" he ordered, his voice now harsh.

Berengaria knew the first fingers of fright when she felt herself being roughly tossed closer to the flickering flame of the lamp.

Paxon's eyes raked the room and fell on the drover's whip which had been used on Valentina. The sight of that leather so infuriated him that he snatched it up and, with a dangerous light in his eyes, advanced on Berengaria.

"Have I displeased you? Answer me! In what way have I displeased you?"

Still Paxon advanced, the lamplight glinting off the black of his eyes, making them unreadable.

"Come to me, dearest, let us make this a night to remember." The strong hand holding the drover's whip fell to his side. His mouth suggested a smile. "I beg of you, Paxon, a night of love, a night to remember."

"It will be a night you will remember," Paxon said coolly, his sun-bronzed hand flexing the short whip. The long tendrils of leather snaked out and made a

79

snapping sound as it made contact with her flesh. Berengaria lowered her eyes to the floor and the tip of the whip, which slithered about her ankles. Before she could raise her eyes, the whip snicked again, this time holding her leg prisoner.

"Ooh." She pretended alarm. So the Saracen wanted to play. "Dearest," she said, holding out her arms, her breasts quivering, "come to me."

Paxon raised his arm again and the clawing tips of the whip snaked about her thighs. Tears stung her eyes. Again the whip assaulted. This time the thongs curled about her back, the ends stinging into the tender flesh of her breasts. Berengaria gasped with pain, her eyes widening in fright. "Paxon! Gently, you hurt me!"

Again his arm lifted, his expression cold and unreadable. She felt the skin across her buttocks split and swell, and a vision of Valentina's back after the lashes had done their work swam before her eyes. "Paxon! No marks! Please, enough of this play!" Her voice had become a whimper. "I love you, truly I do, but I have no wish to be branded."

Again the whip crack, and again. Paxon held himself in tight binds of control. He would have cheerfully killed her, but he had no taste for a woman's blood on his hands. Instead, he would teach her a lesson. His expertise with the whip told him that the lash marks would heal and fade in a few weeks' time, except, perhaps, the blow he had dealt to her buttocks.

Berengaria was whimpering, dry sobs of fright shaking her body. "Stop, please stop, I beg you!"

"Is that how Valentina cried when you had her whipped? Did she plead with you? Nay, I think not. It is not in her nature."

"Is that why you treat me so? Because I had an errant subject whipped?" she sobbed. "Or did you do this to me because it was Valentina? Yes, I can see it in your eyes!" She laughed triumphantly, thinking of what the morning would bring when Valentina went to the prisoners' compound. "You'll never have her in your bed! Do you hear me? Never!"

80

Paxon smiled mockingly. "My queen, I thought you loved me. How many times have I heard from your own lips that you would do anything for me? Give me anything I desired? Where has your love flown?"

Berengaria forgot her pain and seethed with hatred. "You lay in my arms, you loved me! Admit it!"

"Love?" Paxon laughed harshly. "Never love, but lust! Animal lust!"

"You lay in my arms, you loved me," she whined, refusing to accept what she knew to be true.

"I lusted for you. It was no more, no less," Paxon said, his voice edged with steel. "I have never loved, as you have never loved. We met on common ground . . . lust."

"I have nothing left," Berengaria cried pitifully as she crumpled to the floor in a sobbing heap. "Nothing!"

Paxon tossed the drover's whip to the floor near her feet. "No, madame. Here is something for you, a memento of your night to remember." His laughter was harsh and brutal as he strode from the room, the sound of her whimpering ringing in his ears.

Chapter Six

An hour before dawn Sena went breathlessly into Valentina's chamber.

"Child, child," she whispered as she shook Valentina's shoulder. "Wake up!"

Valentina dragged herself to consciousness and blearily looked into Sena's worried face.

"Child, there is a guardsman here. He says his instructions are to escort you on an errand. What know you of this?"

Valentina's eyes snapped open and became alert. "Oh, Sena, help me. There is something I must do! What time is it?"

"Not dawn yet," Sena told her as she helped her sit up in her narrow bed. "What is this errand you have? You must not go!"

"I am aching, but it is not painful," Valentina assured her old nursemaid. "I will be fine if only you will help me dress."

"I smell a trick!" Sena said adamantly. "What is this errand?"

"It is a secret, Sena, and I am forbidden to share it with you. Let it be said only that it is for the king." Valentina struggled to her feet. Her back felt as tight and stiff as an oiled skin that covered the window in winter.

"How know you this is for the Lionheart? When did you first learn of it?" Sena asked, suspecting Berengaria's hand somewhere in this.

"I cannot tell you, Sena. You must be satisfied with that."

"Wait. I did not tell you last night for fear of spoiling your sleep, but the Saracen comes for you this morning. He will be here anytime now."

"For me?" Valentina's expression portrayed her astonishment.

"Aye! The queen is not finished with you yet. Have sense, child! Your life here will be hell. I have told the Saracen of your family in Navarre; he will see that you find a ship sailing for home. Home, child! Safety!"

"But I cannot! I have an errand for the king!" She reached for a fresh kirtle to wear beneath her soft woolen gown.

"Leave war to men," Sena scolded. "What use can a frail child such as yourself be to the great Lionheart? Look at you, so sadly used you can hardly walk or lift an arm."

"I would crawl on my belly if it were for the good of peace! I am not certain of the full nature of my errand, but I have been called upon by the king. I pray, whatever the mission, it will in some way hasten the council meetings and perhaps be useful in naming a truce."

"As if the Lionheart would have use for a woman. War is a man's game, and women have no place in it."

Valentina held the old woman in a long, meaningful stare. "But peace, Sena, peace and treaty are the duty of women. Help me dress, the hour grows late."

Passing through the gates and down the dusty road in the pink before dawn, Valentina questioned the guardsman who accompanied her. The young man seemed to know nothing of her mission, except that he was to escort her to the prison compound and leave her there.

An uneasy feeling settled over Valentina. So many questions were unanswered. How would a prisoner manage to deliver a message to her? How would she know what she was to do? Pushing back her trepidations, she reminded herself that Richard was counting on her. She could see his reasoning: a woman would not appear suspicious near the compound. She had seen women there before, waiting for a glimpse of a loved one. Purposely she had had Sena select a drab gown of dark brown wool, one she usually wore when doing chores. The fine kirtle she wore beneath it saved her back from the abrasiveness of the gown. Yet she knew that because of her movements, her back had broken open again. She was conscious of a warm, wet trickle of blood.

As they neared the high white walls where the compound had been erected, the foul stench of unwashed bodies and human waste assaulted her nostrils. There seemed to be a great deal of activity in the area this morning. Richard's men were everywhere, but this did not cause her any concern. What could she possibly have to fear from Richard's army?

The young guardsman left her standing in an archway, well into the shadows. As she watched him leave she felt the urge to call him to take her back. Prickles of fear rose on her neck. From within the compound she could hear a great deal of movement and the wailing of humanity. Even as she listened, the wide, stout doors were opened and the unfortunate prisoners emerged, held at bay by armed guards. Some wailed and cried, and others, their arms outstretched and praying to Allah, passed by her. The area beneath the city wall soon swarmed with prisoners—men, women, children—and herding them on horseback were Richard's men. As the massive gates to the city opened, a rousing cheer went up among the Saracens. Through the babble of confusion Valentina understood that they interpreted this unusual circumstance as an announcement of their freedom.

Soldiers moved about the throng, clamping manacles together and tying others into groups of five or ten. Several prisoners questioned the soldiers about why they were being shackled when their freedom was so near at hand, and the stony-faced guards gave no answer. Valentina also questioned the reason behind this but gave up the thought when she noticed a company of men riding toward the compound. As they drew nearer she recognized the powerful golden destrier, Flavel, Richard's war horse. Closer they came, and from the shadows beneath the arch Valentina strained for a glimpse of the flame-haired king.

Saladin, chief general of the Islamic army, rode to the top of the hill. From here he could look down upon the city of Acre. He rode well ahead of his contingent of soldiers, impatient with their pace. Something was in the wind; he could smell it. The white turban he wore above his swarthy brow accentuated the distinguishing gray streaks that salted his carefully trimmed black beard. His eyes looking down upon the city of Acre were somber and sad. War was not to Saladin's liking. His heart was the heart of a poet and a scholar, and the fates that had brought him to lead and command the Islamic armies had been unkind.

Dawn's pink streaks glanced off the gray roofs, and a precocious wind from off the desert beat at the stone walls. In its dry caress was a sensation of restlessness. By birth Saladin was a Kurd, a man of the northern hills where patriarchs still led the clans. His people knew the laws of the sword and loyalty. They were part of the Arab nation, yet they were apart from them. Their word was their bond, and anyone who shared their salt was safe from harm at the hand of the giver of the salt. All Kurds were devout Muhammadans by tradition and fearless soldiers by inclination. Saladin stood apart from his people in that he had no love of fighting merely for the sake of fighting. Courteous and self-restrained, he avoided quarrels and lent his passions instead to fine horses and the study of the written word.

It was because of this knowledge that Saladin, who had been proved a successful leader in many skirmishes against opposing caliphs and their armies, was appointed El Malik en Nasr, the Conquering King. To uphold the faith of his people and to unite the factions of the Near East, Saladin planned the jihad, the holy war. Turkoman, Kurd, and Arab would follow his standard to war against the invaders, the unbelievers, the Christians. All Moslems harkened to the word of the Prophet.

War, to Saladin, was a chore which he knew every ruler must bend himself to, but there was no pleasure in such destruction. Instead, Malik en Nasr dreamed of a lasting peace among the rulers of Islam. However, in order to gain this, Saladin knew he must gather all his strength and rise, united, against the Christian Crusaders and defeat them.

The errant wind lifted the bright yellow cloak draped over his shoulders, and the tails of his turban whipped against his back. Alone there, atop a hill overlooking Acre, Saladin saw a scene that chilled his blood. His people were being led through the immense gates into the desert. He watched helplessly, mesmerized by the scene taking place below him, and turned sharply in the saddle to view his army. Because he had ridden so far in advance, the dust rising from their steeds' hooves was not even visible on the horizon. He was helpless; worse, useless. Surely Malik Ric, King Richard, could not be so barbaric as to forgo negotiations and slaughter the prisoners. He had come here today, to Acre, to meet the English king's demands and more. If slaughter was not in the Lionheart's mind, then what was the reason behind this?

King Richard, mounted upon Flavel, rode past the archway where Valentina strained for a glimpse of her sovereign. From behind her a hand sheathed in a rough-palmed gauntlet reached out, seizing her by her hair.

"Look what I have here!" her assailant called in a thick, heavy voice to his partner. "By the Prophet's beard, this one looks too comely to be a doxie. What say you?" He tightened his grip on her hair, shaking her head till her teeth rattled. "Whose company do you seek this morn?" He spoke French, a soldier of Philip's army, and therefore she would more than likely be unknown to him as a member of Richard's entourage.

"Let me go, please!" she implored. The soldier relaxed his grip and turned her about to face him. "I am a lady-in-waiting to Queen Berengaria! Release me at once and King Richard will never know of your rough treatment of me. At once, I say!"

"Oh-ho! So the doxie has dreams of being a high-born lady!" the soldier snarled. "You speak the language of France with a definite flair, your ladyship," he mocked. "You must have spent a great deal of time servicing the men in the French camps."

Valentina's cheeks flamed as she stammered once again to explain herself without revealing the reason for her being in the compound. "I have business here this day. Release me and get about your own duties."

The man's rough features changed from malicious humor to a cold, suspicious anger. By the inflection of his speech and by his uniform, it was obvious that he was a common foot soldier and not a gentle-born knight. "Who are you ordering about, slut? Think you that I don't know a camp follower when I meet one?" His grip tightened again as he called to his partner,

"Jean, see what I've found for you. Was it only last eve when you complained of the lack of females?"

The soldier called Jean stepped into the shadow of the arch. "What have we here?" he said in slurred tones.

Valentina gasped as she turned her head to see the tallest man she had ever laid eyes on. His bulk was accentuated by the leather vest, shoulder epaulets, and short hauberk that revealed legs and thighs as thick as a horse's flanks. As he stepped deeper into the archway, the first slow rays of daylight lit his features. The word "idiot" flashed through Valentina's mind. His tongue seemed too large for his mouth, and his jaw was heavy and square, making his face appear unbalanced and evil-looking. His nose looked as if it had been broken many times, for it seemed without shape, wide and flat and too high in his face. But his eyes frightened her the most as they bore into her, lustful and menacing and vacant of intelligence.

"What do you think of her, Jean?" the first soldier asked. "Here she was waiting for you."

"For me," the giant rumbled, not a question but a statement.

The first soldier released Valentina to his partner, and with a look that betrayed his own fears, hurried away.

"Yves is Jean's friend," the giant's voice rumbled again. "Pretty, very pretty," he said as he lifted a long curl which rested on Valentina's breast.

"Your friend made a grave mistake," Valentina hastened to explain. "I came here today on an errand for my queen. If I don't return soon, she will send out the guard looking for me." The giant seemed not to hear as he pressed the lock of hair to his nostrils and drank in its sweet fragrance.

"Jean likes you," he said thickly, ignoring her terror and pulling her closer to him. The metal clasps fastening the leather vest over his midsection bit into her face as she struggled to escape his embrace.

"Let me go!"

87

"Yves said you waited for me. Jean likes you, be nice to Jean."

Fleetingly Valentina wondered how a man of such low intelligence managed to be part of the French army, when she noticed the insignia of an anvil and hammer etched into a medallion he wore about his neck. Blacksmiths and weapon forgers were invaluable to an army. Her eyes traveled upward and froze upon the thick iron collar fastened about his neck. Stamped directly into the metal were a skull and crossbones, denoting that the man was a convict found guilty of murder.

"You see what Jean wears about his neck?" He grinned toothily. "They like to say that Jean killed a girl. Not so!" he roared. "Jean never kill a woman, Jean only cover her mouth so she not scream! Jean a good iron man, too good to kill."

Valentina understood this. Even in Richard's army there were countless convicts and prisoners, who because of their skills were more valuable to the army alive than dead. "Jean," she said shakily, "you must let me be about my business. I come from the English queen and I must go back to her. Now!"

"No, stay with Jean," he cajoled in his thick, rumbling voice. To her horror he pressed her against the cool rough stone of the inner arch, searching her with his mammoth hands and tearing her gown away from her shoulders with one strong motion.

Eyes wide and glazed with terror, Valentina saw his mouth descend to cover her own. His teeth bit wetly into her lips and his huge hands pawed her. "No!" she screamed. "No! Let me go!"

Still he persisted, his mouth searching, his hands finding her breasts, her haunches, her thighs. Valentina was paralyzed with terror as he pressed against her, his intent clear as he lifted the hem of her gown. The stone wall bit into her unhealed back, tearing open the wounds and drawing fresh blood.

"No, no!" she pleaded. He covered her mouth with his powerful hand, crushing her lips against her teeth until she tasted her own salty blood. Struggling, she wrested her face away from his grip, and a scream tore from her throat and echoed in her ears.

Regaining control, the giant covered her face and pressed her head hard against the wall in a grip so powerful that she imagined she could hear the bones of her skull cracking. His free hand groped her bared flesh, testing the fullness of her breasts, punishing her yielding softness with his brutal strength.

Straining to breathe, Valentina struggled against his assault, shrinking away from him, writhing and twisting until at last his fingers separated over her mouth. Gasping, she filled her lungs with a burst of air and experienced a searing shock of pain.

He dragged her upward, his sour mouth searching for hers, and so huge was he that Valentina's toes barely grazed the ground. In vicious, painful contact, his mouth clamped over hers; his teeth bit into the delicate flesh of her cheeks and chin in his gaping-mouthed attack.

Even through her vain attempts to protect herself, Valentina was aware of the brute's movements to free his loins of his restricting garments. Terror took its toll in a paroxysm of shudders so violent she wondered that her spine did not snap.

Groaning with the excitement of his lust, he groped for the hem of her gown, pulling it and her kirtle high above her hips. Higher and higher he lifted her, forcing her knees to open, wrapping her limbs around his middle.

Sensibility returned. Filling her lungs with air, Valentina opened her mouth to scream. Someone, anyone, *must* help her! Anticipating his intent to impale her upon his swollen sex, Valentina, in a last frenzied effort, clung fiercely to his thick neck and hoisted herself upward, fighting frantically to deny him that which he most wanted.

Her nails dug, her teeth bit, but to no avail. He overpowered her. Her struggles seemed to incense him. From out of her throat was borne a cry almost inhuman in its savagery. With a swiftness which belied his size, the Frenchman covered her face again. This time his intent was not to stifle her cries; he meant to kill her!

Struggling for air, fighting for release, Valentina felt herself slipping into the thresholds of darkness and oblivion. Her own hands pressed against him in useless effort. She kicked out, but her soft kid slippers did little to dissuade the giant. It was then that she found the hilt of his dagger protruding from his belt. Ripping the dagger from its sheath, she pressed it against the giant's ribs, the point delving through his coarse hauberk into his flesh. She felt him stiffen as his reflexes grasped her intent, and she sensed, rather than felt, that he was about to bring up his hand and capture his dagger. Not allowing herself a second thought, she plunged the thin blade between his ribs.

The giant staggered backward in disbelief. With a roar of rage he reached for her again, his long hairy arms extended, the fingers curled and grasping. Through the whirling vortex of his pain he saw her blanch, her eyes pools of green fire, her bleeding lips staining her mouth a hideous red against the whiteness of her skin. Again and again she slashed out, shredding the flesh of his forearms. The Goliath stumbled backward, shrinking from her savage resolution to protect herself. Dark hair wild about her face, she flew at him, dagger upraised, torn and bleeding lips drawn back from her teeth. Her gown hung in tatters, baring the perfection of her breasts, the lissome smoothness of her shoulders. The cords in her neck were engorged and pulsating as she shrieked a blood-curdling war cry. She advanced on him, an errant ray of sunlight glinting off the dagger's point. The giant knew fear. More to stop her wild shrieks than to defend himself, he wrapped his treelike fingers about her throat, choking off her screams, deadening her vocal cords, squeezing off her air.

Again the dagger found its mark, plunging deep into his gullet and searing his innards in a blazing spear of death. The giant's grip loosened, but in a last effort he brought up his arm and crashed it against Valentina's skull, knocking her into the stone abutment. Sinking to the ground, her eyes closed, blackness engulfing her, she never saw his hands fall to his side and his bulk crumble heavily to the blood-soaked sand.

Saladin looked down upon the perfidy enacted by Richard. His scholar's mind and poet's heart were clenched in the throes of agony. The Christian soldiers had led the Moslem prisoners out onto the open plain, where they were bound by the hands and slain by the sword. The wind carried the metallic stench of spilled blood to his nostrils, the same wind that dried the tears upon his cheeks and stung his eyes with grit. The Christian executioners were riding on horseback among the hapless prisoners and swinging their swords in slaughterous arches. Screams of terror and futile prayers to Allah were carried on the wind. Saladin looked back toward the horizon, but there was still no sign of his cavalry.

A careless job was being made of the massacre. The half dead and dying lay in their brothers' blood, escape impossible because of the shackles binding them to the dead.

A lonely sentry upon the hill, Saladin witnessed the slaughter of twenty-seven hundred of his people.

At long last the Islamic cavalry appeared upon the horizon. Paxon rode beside his friend Meshtub, his thoughts on sending word to Valentina to meet him in the city. He had told Meshtub of his plan and the events of the previous night during the long ride through the desert back to Saladin's encampment. After listening to Meshtub voice his opinion on what a fool Paxon was to become involved in women's affairs, an uneasy silence had settled between the two men. Now glancing at Meshtub's, Paxon saw that his old friend's eyes were skyward. Following the burly man's gaze, Paxon was aware of a stirring overhead. Dark forms swept the sky, soaring and circling over the city of Acre. Vultures!

Several of the officers riding along with Paxon raised their eyes, and a soft rumble of speculation rose among the men. Spurring their steeds, they hastened their pace. The soldiers were caught between an inexplicable feeling of dread and expectancy. They cropped their mounts and raced across the expanse of desert, at last ascending the hill where their beloved and respected general kept his lonely vigil.

The cries of the scavenger birds rang harshly in their ears and mingled with the screams of terror from the scene below. In a frenzy of anger, the entire Moslem cavalry rode down to the Crusaders, and before the execution was complete, swords were clashing over the plain.

Attacker lay beside defender and executioner beside victim, and still the battle raged. Archers stood along the walls of Acre picking their targets. Arrows hissed overhead, scimitar rang against longsword, lances met shields, and horses brayed in pain and terror as they stumbled over the dead.

From out of the hills rode Saladin's select men, cavalry officers wearing the bright yellow cloak that stamped them as Malik en Nasr's guard. In the forefront rode Saladin himself. As though a trumpet heralded their arrival, the fighting ceased, and through the gates of Acre rode the Lionheart, Philip of France at his side holding his gauntlet to his nose.

Moslems and Christians rejoined ranks as they watched the spectacle of their leaders in conference amid the hideous gore. Richard held his head high and proudly, the midday sun glinting off his red-gold hair. Saladin, wrapped in his yellow cloak, sat erect in the saddle. Philip of France was leaning over in his saddle, silent heaves shaking his thin body.

Paxon and his men were alert for treachery and entrapment. The sultan observed the Lionheart gesticulating wildly, his bearing defensive and hostile, while Saladin sat erect and motionless. After several moments the English king, accompanied by the white-faced Philip, turned his notorious golden steed and retreated behind the walls of Acre. A trumpeter then sounded the signal for retreat, and the ranks of the Crusaders made their grumbling way back into the city as they collected their dead and wounded. The cavalry of Islam continued their watch. The gates to

Acre were left open, and Saladin signaled to his officers to join him.

"The Lionheart has disgraced himself this day." Saladin's rich voice was tight with constraint. "No one knows this better than Malik Ric himself. In the sight of his God he is godless; in the name of his Holy Cross he is nameless." The general's eyes were black pools of sorrow. "I would have my officers know that I will not disgrace myself in kind. No retribution will be taken against our Christian prisoners! To bathe in a like disgrace would blacken the name of Islam, but to abstain from retribution will enhance Malik Ric's own disgrace." Saladin's jaw tightened, and a light of fervor was shining in his eyes. "Go and collect our people. The dead, the half dead, and those upon whom Allah has shown his mercy. Leave no one behind! See to it that those who have died in the name of Allah have a decent burial according to the laws of the Prophet." Gathering his windblown cloak about him, Saladin turned and rode off into the desert, his back straight and invulnerable, his heart crushed by the blow of what he had witnessed on the day Richard had placed his name in the annals of infamy.

Chapter Seven

Valentina dragged her eyes open, a searing pain in her head. She became aware of ministering hands smoothing her brow and of something cool and wet being pressed against her lips. Gratefully she opened her mouth and allowed the droplets to caress her tongue, easing the parchedness. Greedily she sought for more, when a woman's soft voice admonished her to drink slowly. The language the woman spoke was a dialect of Arabic, and Valentina snapped her eyes into focus.

"Poor little pigeon, rest easy now. You are safe now, and I will take care of you."

Valentina looked into the dark eyes of a girl not much older than herself.

"Who are you? Where am I?" Valentina whispered, her voice husky with alarm as her eyes darted from the girl to the unfamiliar surroundings.

"Hush, do not be afraid. My name is Rosalan, and you are here in Saladin's camp. No harm will come to you, my word on it. Hush, little pigeon, you must have your rest. Sleep now. I will watch over you."

Rosalan's gentle ministerings and soothing voice brought about the required effect, and Valentina closed her eyes, too weary to wonder how she had come to be in a desert camp with a Bedouin girl as her nursemaid.

Hours later, when she again awakened, Rosalan was still there, looking down at Valentina with concern on her face. Valentina smiled weakly and attempted to sit up. Rosalan pushed her down again and Valentina willingly obeyed her. Her head pained her and her vision was blurred and her stomach felt queasy. Still, her strength was regained enough for her to ask how she had come to be in this dark tent with Rosalan.

Rosalan's eyes sparkled with tears as she related the story of the massacre to Valentina.

"The Christians"—she spat into the sand to show her hatred—"shackled our people and led them out beyond the city walls. There they rode among the faithful, severing heads and slaughtering them. Saladin rode fearlessly into the city," she exaggerated, "and demanded that Malik Ric release the survivors to his care."

Rosalan's eyes shone with the light of adoration as she spoke of the great Islamic general. " 'Leave none of our people,' our honored general said. And Malik Ric allowed our cavalry to ride freely into the city and search the prisoners' compound. That is where they found you! I myself was among the few whom Allah chose to spare. Two officers found you and brought you to me. They ordered me to see to you and warned they would curse me by the Prophet's beard if anything should happen to you. You are a brave girl, they told me. They found you near the dead body of a Christian soldier. The dagger was still clutched tightly in your hand."

As Valentina listened, a shudder of revulsion gripped her. Suddenly she remembered it all. The huge giant of a man who had touched her, reviled her, bathed her with his wet, searching mouth, and fondled her roughly with his calloused hands. She imagined she could still smell the animal stench of him and hear his grunts of lust as he pressed his body against hers and searched between her thighs.

Extending her hand before her, Valentina imagined she could see the dried brown stain of the soldier's blood crusted on her white skin. Jean! He had told her his name was Jean! He wasn't merely a faceless, nameless enemy met on a battlefield, he had a name!

Valentina covered her face with her hands and wept great heaving sobs that slowly turned to hiccups of hysterical laughter. She had done it! She had protected herself! How many times had she wanted to choke the breath from Berengaria's body? She suddenly decided that the Goliath-like soldier's death was brought on by himself. She had been protecting herself, and it felt good.

Rosalan watched the play of emotions that Valentina suffered, and supposed that the girl's gentle nature was upset by the horror of the massacre.

"Weep, my little pigeon, let your tears bathe your soul," Rosalan consoled. "There is great mourning in Saladin's camp this night. Never fear, our great general will wreak out his retribution in kind. Matters will go very hard for the Christians, even though Malik en Nasr has sworn that he will not stain his name the way King Richard has. Nevertheless, woe be to the Christian who finds himself within the grasp of a Saracen! Weep, little pigeon."

Valentina lifted her head, the light of determination

shining in her face. "No!" she whispered in a lifeless tone. "The dead cannot weep for the dead!"

A perplexed Rosalan watched Valentina turn over on her side, her face to the black tent wall, while outside in the camp sounds of keening rose in the still desert night as the people of Islam mourned the victims of Malik Ric's abomination.

Valentina awakened to find herself wrapped in several covers to shield her from the cold desert night. Within the tent it was dark, but she could see the blazing sun creeping beneath an open tent flap and knew it was morning. Outside the tent she heard the voices of people and could smell food cooking. She turned over to see if the girl Rosalan was still sleeping, and emitted a grunt because the skin of her back was tight and painful. The pallet on which Rosalan had slept was empty, and Valentina noticed that, save for a goatskin, the girl had slept without blankets. Rosalan had given up her own covers for Valentina.

Valentina's limbs were stiff and sore and she tried to stretch her muscles, but her back issued another painful protest, a reminder of Berengaria's jealousy. Her eyes narrowed as she realized that she had been a pawn of Berengaria's hatred. She had been sent to her death just as surely as if Berengaria had plunged a dagger into her breast. There had been no errand for Richard; she had been tricked into going to the prison compound. Berengaria must have known Richard's plan to slaughter the Moslem prisoners and had contrived for Valentina to be caught up in the fray.

The extent of Berengaria's treachery was so incredible that Valentina found it impossible to grasp the full impact of her situation. What was to become of her? She couldn't live here among Saladin's people! How long would it be before they discovered that she was not one of them and that she was a Christian? Merely speaking their language was not defense enough against being discovered; there were many things she did not know about them, their customs and habits, that would reveal her to be an impostor. She must

96

somehow manage to get back to Acre, to her own people! She thought of Berengaria's reaction when the queen learned that she had survived her treachery after all, and the thought gave her a deep satisfaction.

Valentina groaned with the pain and stumbled to her feet. She was just about to lift the tent flap when Rosalan stepped through the opening.

"Poor little pigeon!" Rosalan exclaimed, reaching out a steadying hand to Valentina. "You should not be up and about; you still need your rest!"

Valentina's head throbbed and her stomach lurched. She gripped Rosalan's arm to keep from falling and allowed herself to be led back to the pallet. She lay down, her eyes closing as she fought back the nausea that overcame her. "You are right, Rosalan. I don't think I can take two steps without falling on my face."

"Poor pigeon, you will soon be better. I have seen this many times since I have followed Saladin's cavalry. It is the bump on your head, it shook your brain. A few days of quiet and you will feel yourself again."

Valentina looked inquiringly at the desert girl. She herself, a daughter of King Sancho's physician, should have known the symptoms of a concussion. As she lay back, she wished she were a little girl again and could be with her father and his two Islamic assistants, Hassan and Medjuel, those learned men who had taught her the ways of healing as well as their own language.

Rosalan busied herself with straightening and storing away her pallet. She left the tent and returned a few moments later with a basin of water and several large cloths. "You will feel much better after we have washed the grime and dirt away. Poor pigeon," she clucked, much like old Sena.

Sena! The old woman had known Berengaria was up to her tricks. Hadn't the nursemaid had a strange light in her eyes when she had spoken of the Saracen? Paxon. He had arranged with Sena to come and take Valentina away. To save her from Berengaria. Oh, why hadn't she listened to Sena and gone with the Saracen? Paxon. Dark, dancing eyes whose glance could make her feel beautiful, and his hard, demanding body that could elicit such strange feelings within her.

The water was warm and comforting and soothed her aches. Rosalan's ministerings were gentle and efficient as she stripped Valentina of her clothes and tenderly sponged her bruised body. As Rosalan worked she kept up a steady, casual banter.

"I cannot go on calling you 'poor pigeon.' You must have a name. What is it?"

"Valentina."

"Valentina? I'm not familiar with that name. Where do you come from? Where is your home?"

Valentina was at a loss for words. What could she say? Any answer might reveal her.

Rosalan looked deeply into Valentina's eyes. "You can tell me. I promise not to tell anyone, I think I have already guessed the truth." Reaching into her black garment, she withdrew a delicate golden chain from which hung a crucifix. Valentina gasped, and her hand flew to her throat. "I took it from you last night when you were sleeping. If Malik en Nasr's men had found it on you, you would have been executed. I know you are a Christian."

Wearily Valentina explained how she had come to be outside the prisoners' compound, omitting Berengaria's treachery. Rosalan looked at her sorrowfully. Her dark, piquant face held such pity that Valentina could not bear to see it and turned her face away.

"How is it you speak my language?" Rosalan asked, resuming with Valentina's bath.

"My father was physician to King Sancho of Navarre. When he was younger he had traveled to the Holy Land, and while here he befriended two Moslems, Hassan and Medjuel. They had been marked for death by the Old Man of the Mountain for their assistance to an Egyptian emir. With my father's help, they managed to escape and left for Navarre under my father's protection. They were still young men when they made their escape and were very lonely in a strange new land. Trusting them implicitly, my father allowed me to spend many hours in their company and under their tutelage. They, too, were men devoted to the healing of the sick and wounded. During the hours we spent together they taught me the language of Islam."

"It was because Allah willed it, Valentina. The fates cannot be changed, and you were being prepared for this moment. Your secret is safe with me, never fear. I can see by your back that you also met with Christian justice."

Valentina stiffened and turned on Rosalan. "This was not the result of Christian justice, but of the jealous whim of a woman."

Rosalan's eyes danced with curiosity. "Did the woman find you in bed with her husband?"

Shocked at such candidness, Valentina gasped, "No! It was merely because of suspicions. I would never . . ."

"You may have to, little pigeon," Rosalan laughed. Valentina's blushings told her that this strange Christian girl was still a virgin. "You are rather old to be so protective of your chastity. The women of the desert take their first man by the time they are twelve!"

"What do you mean, I may have to? Have to what?" Valentina questioned, her face flooded with color, her voice husky and breathless.

"Sleep with a man, of course," Rosalan laughed. "How do you think I was able to bring water for your bath, and where did you think the food came from? I trade for it. I fulfill the soldiers' need for a woman and they fulfill my need for food and water. It is as simple as that! We all do it; there are many soldiers to be serviced. Some of us are widows who have lost their men in battle, and this is the way they support their families."

Valentina glanced toward Rosalan's pallet.

"No, little pigeon, I did not entertain in this tent last night. Else do you think you would have slept beneath all my covers? No, Valentina, I am not that generous. It was only because I had the company of a brave soldier to keep me warm."

Rosalan misinterpreted Valentina's worried look. "I would never have left you, but I had only finished with my monthly bleeding and it was nearly a week since I had been gifted with food and water. But you were safe enough. I covered the tent flap with a scarlet cloth, which announced that it was your bleeding time. Moslem men never seek favors when the woman is unclean."

Valentina's face flushed even brighter. Announced that it was her bleeding time! What was she doing here in the enemy's camp, sleeping in the tent of a camp follower?

"We women know how to put by enough food and water for those times, but there was not enough for the both of us. I wish I could get myself with child," Rosalan moaned. "Then I would not have to worry about my monthly bleeding, and the soldiers think it lucky to sleep with a woman carrying a child. They are more generous with their payments."

Valentina could not believe what she was hearing. And yet who was she to censor the lives of these desert women? She who had been a procurer for Berengaria. At least these women were honest. They paid for their living with their bodies; they did what they had to do to survive. She glanced at Rosalan as the girl stood in the basin and washed. Her skin was the color of burnt sienna and glowed with vibrant health. She was much shorter than Valentina, but her limbs were in perfect proportion and were muscular and sinewy. Her lean body was denuded of hair, except for the dark, downy patch where her thighs met.

Rosalan donned a fresh gown of drab brown and draped her head with a short mantle. Then she proceeded to use the same water to wash out several garments and took them outside to dry in the sun. When she stepped out of the tent, she left the flap up, and from her pallet Valentina could see some of the other women of the camp and heard them inquire after her health.

Rosalan assumed an air of importance as she related the condition of her patient. Valentina stiffened and listened carefully, fearful that Rosalan, in her garrulous mood, would reveal her true identity.

"And the knock on the head has stolen her memory," she heard Rosalan announce. "I have seen it happen before. There was a soldier in the camp of Taki ad Din who suffered the same fate. Even when his friends told him who he was, he could not remember. It was many months before he found his memory. This one under my care does not even know her name, so I call her Valentina." The women who had gathered about Rosalan oohed their approval and commented upon Rosalan's choice. "Yes, it is a pretty name. I heard it once in a marketplace near Jerusalem," Rosalan boasted, preening beneath the women's admiration for one who was so widely traveled.

In the shade of an overhang that was part of the goatskin tent, Rosalan prepared the midday meal over an open fire. The aroma was tantalizing to Valentina, who was up and about for the first time in three days. Her appetite had returned and the flesh on her back was healing remarkably well, thanks to an evil-smelling ointment which Rosalan had prepared and applied to Valentina's back four times each day.

Each night Rosalan had gone out of the tent to meet one of Saladin's officers. Once Valentina inquired if there was anyone special with whom she spent her time. Rosalan's answer had been to laugh and say, "Does a seller in the bazaars make friends with his patrons? I am a businesswoman; there is no place in my life for anyone 'special.' Do you think one man could support me in all this luxury? No, it takes many men."

All this luxury! Valentina looked about her and suppressed a smile. A dirty, wind-torn goatskin tent, ample water, just enough food, and an assembly of garments that would not have been used for rags back in Navarre. Valentina would never say these things aloud to Rosalan, who was proud of her "wealth" and considered her life most comfortable. As long as she had a roof above her head, rags on her back, and enough food and water, Rosalan's imagination did not seek further horizons.

Stepping near the fire, Valentina asked if she could help in any way. Rosalan smiled her thanks, her white teeth startling against her brown dimpled chin. "Have you ever prepared flour for bread?"

Valentina looked at her helplessly, and Rosalan directed her to sit in the shade while she brought her a small sack of grain and two flat rocks. "This is how it is done," she said, dropping a small amount of grain upon one flat rock and placing the second rock on top. She rubbed the grain between the stones until it became a coarse flour. "Be careful not to bring any moisture from your hands to the grain, or you will make glue."

Valentina made herself busy, a feeling of satisfaction creeping over her at being useful once again. While they worked, Valentina discovered more about her newfound friend. "Rosalan, does it ever disturb you to give yourself to so many different men?"

"Should it?" Rosalan asked without raising her eyes.

"I only meant, well, does it ever make you feel used? You have admitted to me that you have no feeling for these men. They use you! Have you never thought of another way to support yourself, some way that would give you more self-respect?"

Rosalan stopped her chores by the fire and came to sit near Valentina. "Do you think I would be more respectable if I were dead? What could I possibly do to put bread in my mouth? I am merely a woman. My mother was a member of Taki ad Din's camp, and her mother a follower of Nur ad Din. There was no dowry to tempt a man to take them to wife, just as I have no dowry to tempt any man to take me to wife. Without a husband, Valentina, the way of a woman of the desert is hard. I have a profession and I am successful with it. Perhaps in your land it is shameful to lie with a man, but not here in the desert where men are supreme, and it is in Allah's will that women shall serve him."

"Is it so easy, then, to be passed from man to man?" Valentina's eyes were troubled, her voice a quiet whisper.

"I have never thought of it as easy or hard. I am who I am. Within me I am Rosalan, and I am a fine girl, no?" she said frankly, without any of the false modesty of European women, which made her all the more dear in Valentina's eyes. "No one can reach within me and touch that secret place which is *me*. My body, my breasts, my femaleness, that which is visible to the world is all that can be touched. My soul is my own, as is my heart. What are flesh and bones except something which demands food and comfort and freedom from sickness? Ah, but my soul, my secret core, that thing which makes me unique unto myself, that is never for the taking but only for the asking."

"Have you ever been in love, Rosalan?"

The girl's dark, luminous eyes became murky with reverie, and her full, ripe mouth became pinched at the corners. "I thought I was . . . once. And that is how I learned about this secret core within myself. I learned that this is the part of me which can know deep happiness and devastating sorrow. When you give that part of yourself to a man, you are his slave and he owns you, consumes you. If the fates smile upon you, he takes it and cherishes it more than life itself. But if you give it to a man who cannot or will not prize it, above all else you are damned to the torments of the fiery eternity. Before this ever happens to you, Valentina, think well on it."

The fire spit and Rosalan hurried to stir her stew. Valentina pulverized the grain to flour, her thoughts on the wisdom of Rosalan's words. In spite of herself, her thoughts turned to Paxon and she knew that of all the men she had met, he was the one who could reach within her to touch that secret core. But could he cherish it? Would he ask for it, or would he demand it?

Suddenly visualizing his black eyes and mocking smile, Valentina knew that Paxon could never prize her love above all else. He would never ask to be loved; he would demand it, and once having it, he would cast her aside and go on to new triumphs.

Paxon was a warrior, a sultan, a man who placed little value on the heart of a woman.

After their meal, Rosalan and Valentina cleaned their campsite. Saladin enforced strict rules of hygiene in his camp, and woe be to the one who carelessly threw his trash beside his tent.

Everywhere Valentina's senses were assailed by the sights and smells of the camp. It was an endless cacophony of noise. Beggars strode about the tents beseeching alms and imploring the occupants for the mercy of Allah. Rosalan had warned Valentina never to donate anything to the beggars. "Even the scraps from the meals are to be thrown to the dogs. To feed a beggar is to become burdened with a lifetime responsibility! Scraps to the dogs!"

Amid the tents hawkers praised their wares, and their melodic voices enticed the children to follow them about in the hope of receiving a sweetmeat or a fresh fruit. Water carriers, struggling with their burdens, roved between the narrow alleys proclaiming the sweetness of their water and stopped from time to time to dip a carved wooden ladle into their goatskin bottles to fill a customer's ewer.

The chaos of daily living was pierced by the thin, commanding voice of the muezzin, perched high atop his hastily erected minaret, calling the faithful to prayer. At the sound of his call, beggar, peddler, and citizen gathered and dropped to their knees in prayer. Rosalan dragged Valentina to her feet. "They will believe you do not remember who you are, but never that you forgot how to pray. Hurry!"

Valentina followed Rosalan into the clearing beyond the tents. She fell to her knees along with thousands of the faithful, and facing south to that distant city of Mecca, she pretended to recite the ninety-nine sacred titles of Allah along with the others.

Several weeks passed and Valentina's strength returned. The flesh on her back had healed, and in place of the gouging whiplashes there now remained thin pink stripes that would soon fade away. Almost every night Rosalan left the tent to meet with a cavalryman, and Valentina was left alone with her thoughts. Utmost in her mind was her desire to get back to her own people.

Gossip in the camp told her that the Lionheart still camped outside Acre, sending out parties of soldiers to raid caravans and outposts. If only she could find her way back. It would be unfair to ask Rosalan's assistance and thereby put the girl in jeopardy. This was something Valentina must do for herself. Rosalan's generosity in sharing her tent and providing Valentina with food must not be repaid by implicating her in the escape.

While Valentina was not actually a prisoner, the camp was heavily guarded by sentries. Anyone leaving or coming into the camp was thoroughly questioned. Rosalan had told her that the camp was forty miles outside the city of Acre; how could she hope to cover that distance without a horse and water?

A sound outside her tent stiffened her to attention. This was not the sound of a scavenging dog, but a stealthy footfall. All of a sudden the tent flap was thrown aside, and in stumbled two soldiers clad in the yellow and black robes of Saladin's cavalry. They stood for a long, dreadful moment looking down at her in the yellow light of the lamp. Their smiles were leers as their eyes penetrated her drab gown as if they could see her nakedness beneath.

"Out!" Valentina commanded. "Did you not see the cloth of scarlet hung above my tent flap? Out!"

One soldier, the taller of the two, jeered, "We have been watching for the flag to be lowered. Too many weeks have passed for it to have much meaning now."

"Believe it," Valentina sneered. "There is nothing for you in this tent tonight."

The other soldier had been watching her, lust flaming in his eyes. "Prove it; show us and we will leave." Stretching out his arm, he dragged her from her pallet and thrust her to his companion. "Show us!" he commanded.

Valentina's heart pounded; her eyes glared at him

105

as she snarled, "Leave me be, sons of dogs! Would you make yourselves unclean?"

The cavalryman seized the neck of her garment and ripped it to the hem. "We would see! Too long have we waited for the flag to be lowered."

Valentina gasped with the violence of his action, and she lowered her eyes in shame as she was bared to their eyes. "The brave killer of Christians is also a liar," her captor spit, his voice ringing with menace.

"She is as pure as the jasmine petal," said his companion as he touched the smooth skin of her belly. He grabbed a mighty handful of her hair, shaking her head cruelly. "Is it perhaps that you put yourself above the men of your leader, Saladin? Is your skin too fair and are your breasts too firm?" He touched her again, his fingers grazing the erect tip of her breast and sliding down over her taut, flat belly. "Is your woman's place too tender for the common soldier?"

Valentina whimpered in fear as his fingers probed her downy mound. "Hold her, Kamil," the soldier ordered his companion, whose hands were like bands of iron as they dug into the soft flesh of her upper arms. "I will show this one that she is not good enough for the men of Islam." His voice was heavy and thick with animal lust.

She shrank before his sight. His eyes perused her leisurely and his hands explored her intimately. She was by far the most beautiful woman he had ever seen. Her limbs were lean and long, and her breasts, while not large, were firm and high upon her torso.

Valentina's eyes widened and she fought for escape. Her rage had dissolved into strangling terror. She tried to pull away, but the arms that held her were too strong. Her long black hair entwined about them, and she sought her assailant's hand with her teeth. He laughed and stripped her completely of her garment, and she looked down at her nakedness in horror while his eyes feasted upon her. She gasped for breath, and her breasts heaved tauntingly between the silky strands of her hair. His arms closed about her and he tripped her, bringing her down to the floor of the tent,

106

the grit of sand biting into her as she lay sprawled on her back.

She flung her arms to ward him off, and the soldier named Kamil, who had been holding her, fought to regain his control. "Leave her!" her assailant ordered. "I mean to have her in spite of her protests."

He caught her flailing arms and bent them backward to pin them beneath her. He thrust his knee between her thighs and lay heavily atop her, her frantic struggles heightening his pleasure. She recoiled her head to spit at him, but he had crushed his mouth to hers and forced her head back. Her breasts were crushed against his chest while his lips smothered hers in a deep, searching kiss, suffocating her. She writhed beneath him, her movements sharpening his lust as he gained his place between her thighs.

Grunting, he thrust himself upon her, and she saw his eyes widen with surprise at having found her a virgin. This wasn't happening, this couldn't be happening, she thought wildly as a piercing pain raced through her.

The turbaned soldier pressed his weight against her with a force that expelled the breath from her slim body. Valentina's fingers curved into talons seeking his eyes as she twisted her face away from his. The second soldier, the one her attacker called Kamil, seized her hands and held them locked above her head, uncovering her breasts to receive a lustful onslaught of rough tongue and sharp teeth.

Kamil locked his hand around one of Valentina's tightly clenched fists and pressed her other hand to his groin, manipulating it against his aroused sex. Realizing his actions, Valentina looked up into Kamil's face and read there an intent more frightening than the assault of the man already atop her. The man who had penetrated her virginity demanded only his own satisfaction, while this man Kamil would demand much more. Kamil would clamor for response. Kamil's features flooded her gaze; his lean, swarthy face and burning black eyes filtered in and out of focus. Persistently rubbing the back of her hand over his eager sex, Kamil was waiting his turn.

Groaning with release, the soldier atop her moaned with self-satisfaction as he collapsed over her, his weight pressing her into the gritty sand, making breathing very difficult. Paralyzed with dread, Valentina watched Kamil bend over her, his thick growth of chin whiskers prickling the already ravaged skin of her breasts and belly. Wet tracks of warm saliva trailed his seeking mouth, and the horror of her situation nearly drove Valentina beyond the bounds of sanity.

Struggling, kicking, and writhing, Valentina was easily overpowered by Kamil's strength. When his companion attempted to subdue her, Kamil grunted, "Leave her, you've had your turn. I like a woman to be a challenge. Leave her!"

Kamil had a wiry strength which belied his leanness. He handled Valentina roughly, turning her slimness easily in his arms and forcing her onto her belly. He straddled her hips and slipped his hands beneath her to avail himself of the softness of her breasts. "Look here," Kamil called to his friend, "this one has already known the bite of the lash. For her stubbornness, no doubt. Her former master must have grown weary of her cold nature." He laughed coarsely as his hand smoothed over the pink stripes crisscrossing Valentina's back.

Terror stiffened Valentina's spine as his bulk moved over her, and she felt his mouth press forcefully against the back of her neck. She was also aware of his movements to discard his wide-legged breeches. Sensing her opportunity, Valentina freed herself from him when he lifted his weight off her to remove his garments. Quick as a cat, she staggered to her feet, unconscious of her nudity.

Kamil staved off his companion's intervention with a wave of his hand and crouched for the attack. He circled her like a wolf measuring its prey. His dark skin shone with a film of sweat and the black hairs of his lean body stood erect, like the fur of a cat when rubbed the wrong way. Arms extended, knees bent, Kamil closed the distance between Valentina and himself. Frightened beyond her wits, Valentina stood immobile, feeling like a rabbit with the dogs closing in.

"Careful, Kamil, she has the look of a trapped animal, and her claws can take their toll on a man's flesh."

Discounting the advice of his friend, Kamil ranged closer. "The wrath of a virgin, eh?" Kamil grunted.

"A virgin no longer. I had the pleasure of changing that condition," the other soldier laughed.

"A woman can be a virgin in more ways than one," Kamil stated as his eyes pierced Valentina, taking pleasure in the slim beauty of her.

Valentina had no chance to puzzle out Kamil's statement. He sprang on her, knocking her off balance, and dragged her down to the floor of the tent. The force of his attack stunned her; his hand lashed out to crash against her head. Spitting and snarling his fury, he wrestled her onto her belly, imprisoning her arms beneath her. Holding her fast, Kamil tested the firmness of her flesh with his hand. After reaching between her thighs and probing the warm depths of her sex, he withdrew his hand and saw that it bore traces of blood and the lost vestiges of her virginity. He took delight in her vainly fought struggles and raked the lovely expanse of her flesh with his greedy eyes. Delving further into his delights, he spread the plumpness of her buttocks, pinching the firm globes of her flesh cruelly. Tensing her muscles, Valentina strained against his fingers, deep, hoarse groans of despair coursing through her as she realized his intent.

Fiercely he mounted her, forcing himself against her, hurting her, piercing her with unspeakable pain in his crude attempt to sodomize.

Her body rebelled and her muscles tightened as he drove into her unprepared flesh. Screaming with pain and horror, Valentina felt herself filled with him. Hot, searing torments shuddered through her as he lacerated her flesh and plunged himself further into her.

Still screaming, eyes dry and tearless with terror,

Valentina was aware of a flush of hot wetness and was certain that he had ripped her asunder in a frenzy called lust.

An eternity passed before he was through with her. He left her heaving with sobs at his feet as he stood to arrange his clothing. Kamil spoke to his companion, but their words were lost amid her agony. Their laughs and jeers were muddled and stifled and seemed to come from somewhere far away.

When her senses rejoined her, Valentina realized they were both standing at the back of the tent, partaking of the drinking water in the ewer to quench their thirst. The low sound of their masculine voices droned through her inertia, and from deep within her came a slow yet fierce desire to punish them, to whip them, to kill them for what they had done to her. The mania for revenge far outweighed her bodily suffering.

Valentina scrambled to her feet and draped a cover from the pallet about her nakedness. Her heart was a stone within her breast and her eyes were tinged with madness. All thought escaped her, save that of revenge. Her glance fell upon Rosalan's cooking knife, and before she knew it, the hilt was firmly grasped in her fingers. "Cur! Sons of dogs!" she screamed, falling between them. The taller soldier was quick and agile and struck her wrist, knocking the weapon to the floor. Hysteria mounting, she flung herself to the floor, searching the shadows for the glinting blade. Kamil fell on her, his knee pressing into her chest and making breathing very difficult. His hands closed about her throat, choking her, strangling her, until she felt that her lungs would explode and death was inevitable.

Suddenly she felt his fingers lose their grip as he was flung backward, leaving her free to gasp for air. "She is mad! She would kill us!" she heard Kamil stutter to his friend. "Why did you stop me?"

"I have no wish for Malik en Nasr's wrath, Kamil! Many saw us enter this tent and no doubt heard what was taking place within. Leave her now!"

Kamil rose, and as he left to follow his friend out of the tent, he directed a well-aimed kick into her ribs, knocking the wind out of her and leaving her writhing in pain upon the sandy floor.

Alone again, Valentina dragged herself to her pallet and fell upon it, tears of shame and outrage flooding her eyes.

When Rosalan returned a few hours before dawn, this was how she found Valentina. Taking the girl into her arms, she held her close and waited for the sobbing explanations to pour forth.

"Valentina, little pigeon, remember what I told you," Rosalan said as she placed a cool cloth upon Valentina's brow and another about her throat, which was bruised and swollen. "He took your body, not your soul. You are still Valentina and you always will be."

Valentina raised her eyes to look upon this girl who had taken her into her tent with such unselfishness. "You are so wise, Rosalan," she croaked, for it was difficult to talk. "I am ashamed for my body, for the humiliation, but I am still Valentina, I am still me!"

"Little pigeon," Rosalan soothed, "what is to become of you?"

"I cannot imagine," Valentina whispered hoarsely, "but I cannot stay here! I must leave! But how?"

Her question would be answered by Saladin himself when the sun rose in the sky and he called his officers to council.

Chapter Eight

Paxon, sultan of Jakard, rode through the camp to attend Saladin's council. The tragedy of the massacre he had witnessed still weighed heavily on his heart. But foremost on his mind was the girl from

Navarre, whom he had last seen in her dark little room in the queen's bower, her tender flesh displaying the apparent effects of Berengaria's evil whip. That he was the reason behind Valentina's suffering shamed him. If he hadn't been so eager for a bit of adventure with Menghis at the tourney in Messina; if he hadn't become so taken by the sapphire-eyed Valentina; if he hadn't assumed she was the English queen; if he hadn't been so eager to be in her company again that he accepted the invitation to slip through the garden seeking a rendezvous; if, when he discovered Valentina's identity, he hadn't kept the appointment with a woman he cared nothing for, could never care for; if—if—if!

And what could Valentina think of him now? How much had he endangered her by his rash actions? By whipping the queen! Did she understand why he hadn't come for her? That, because of the massacre, the city of Acre was heavily patrolled because the Lionheart feared retribution for the thousands he had slaughtered, and all Moslems had been cast out into the desert? The present situation made it impossible to rescue her.

Paxon spurred his horse to a faster pace; the wind whipped his headgear back from his face, which was set in grim lines. Why should he care if Valentina understood? She was only a Christian woman! And too thin for his tastes. A lovely, laughing-eyed Christian woman. Would he ever see her again? Why should he care? Angrily he dug his heels into the horse's flanks. Allah redeem him . . . he did care!

Within Saladin's tent the assemblage of officers and counselors had already convened. The tribunal had settled cross-legged upon thick cushions while Malik en Nasr paced the floor, his mantle flowing behind him. "There is no time left to us," he said softly, his black eyes heavy with despair. "There are barely enough provisions for the army, let alone these encumbrances which we have picked up along the way." He was referring to the masses of civilians who followed in the army's wake, as well as the bevy of Christian prisoners who were part of the exchange he was to have made with King Richard.

"After much thought," the mighty general stated sadly, "I can see no other way to free the army of responsibility to these people except to offer them at market."

Silence pervaded the octagonal tent, and turbaned heads were lowered in sympathy for this man who deeply regretted that he must sacrifice his own people for the sake of the army. "How many are to go?" Paxon asked curtly, breaking the silence.

"All of them!" Saladin turned to Paxon, his black eyes resolute. "Three hundred-odd of Christians, and, of course, those followers who have no means to support themselves. I pray Allah sees this not as a stain upon my soul, to put his faithful upon the auction block. I have deliberated and prayed, and it is the only answer I can find. It would be inhuman to set these civilians into the desert to die of hunger and thirst. No, the only answer is the auction. Once a price is paid for them, they are taken into bondage and their masters will see to their welfare. They can no longer remain a drain upon the army. The provinces of war come first."

Paxon looked into the concern-filled eyes of his general and felt pity. It was a hard decision to make, and one Malik en Nasr did not take lightly. The granaries were nearly empty, and Paxon was surprised that Saladin had kept the prisoners and tolerated the civilians as long as he had. A mighty general, a fierce warrior, and the heart of a mother for all people. "When will this be announced to the people?"

"This day!" The general's voice rang with a mournful timbre, and he invited the council to come forth with suggestions for the dissolution of the camp.

Hours later the decisions were made. The families of soldiers who were still living were to return to the city or place of their husband's origins. Those families of the dead could choose to return to their husbands' origins or to their own, or to test their fate upon the auction block. The camp followers, those women who

113

were without the protection of a husband, were to be taken to auction. They would have no choice. They were to be placed within the ranks of Christian prisoners on the drive to Damascus, where the auctioning would take place. The revenue from the sale would pay the tariffs on grain and the cost of supplies.

The news spread throughout the camp like a brush fire. Weeping women, their eyes sad and tear-reddened above their yashmaks, gathered their children close and mourned the separation from their husbands. A separation which could encompass eternity. Soldiers, their faces hard and set into grim lines of stoicism, took the time to help their women break camp and spend these last precious hours with their children. Indecision met with further indecision as plans regarding where the civilians would find a home were made and discarded. In the quarter of the camp where the single women, the concubines, lived, there was a great outburst of anger. They stood in the areas between the tents, hands on hips and voices raised as they cursed their fates. "We are not given a choice!" one woman with wide hips and a sallow complexion complained. "They send us into a life of hard labor only because we are not wedded. The unfairness of it!"

Another was heard to answer, "They know we would find our way into another general's camp. I myself would be most welcome at the camp of Saif ad Din. I have many admirers there."

"You!" a third exclaimed. "You were thrown from the camp of Saif ad Din! It was fortunate for you they could not prove you are a thief, else they would have cut off your hand!" Shrieking, the object of her insult flew at her in a flurry of bared teeth and raking nails.

Rosalan, who had been watching with Valentina from a distance, leaped into the fray to separate the women. "Stop this before you mark each other and a blind man would not have you!"

The women turned their anger on Rosalan. "You seem unconcerned that our livelihood is denied us!

114

One would think you had captured yourself a husband."

"No husband for me," Rosalan said lightly, excitement glinting in the depths of her velvety eyes. "I will be bought into a harem, and my master will be rich and handsome and kind."

"Bah! Who would have you, you carrier of disease?"

Rosalan's eyes darkened and her lips curled back in an ugly expression of hatred. "Watch your words, lover of dogs! Pray Allah would see all your teeth but one fall from your head, and may that one tooth pain you!"

"Ayee! She-dog! Curse of the—"

Rosalan turned her back, a smug smile on her lips, and walked toward Valentina, her hips swaying in an exaggerated manner which was meant to infuriate.

Valentina was laughing in spite of herself, and Rosalan joined her as they stepped into the shade of their tent. "Rosalan," Valentina asked hesitantly, "what will become of us?"

"It will be just as I told those cackling hens. I will be brought to auction and bought to enhance the harem of a kind and gentle man. I have no doubt. I am too pleasing to the eye for it to be otherwise. As for you, Valentina, the same fortune of fate can be yours. We will spread the word that you are Circassian. Those women are known for their gift of transporting men to the delights of passion."

"Rosalan, I have no wish to be taken into a harem. I want only to be reunited with my own people." Valentina's voice was strident with exasperation.

"Have faith, Valentina. Perhaps there is a way for you. We are to be among the ranks of Christian prisoners under guard. This is merely so we do not escape and find our way to Saif ad Din's army or that of another general. The drive to Damascus is many days, and you can keep your ear attuned for plans of escape. Perhaps you can include yourself in their plans and go with them. All will be well," Rosalan promised.

Today was the first day that Valentina had smiled since the two soldiers had burst into the tent and forced her to submit to them. Poor, poor pigeon, Rosalan thought, will she never learn to accept her fate? Would she never learn to put the past behind her and bless the new day? When would the tears dry on those smooth ivory cheeks? "Come," Rosalan said brightly. "Help me prepare the meal, and we will break camp."

Frustrated beyond tears, Valentina bent to stir the fire. Rosalan, although a proven and certainly dear friend, could be infuriating. All this talk about the fates and how no one can deny his destiny was ridiculous! At least Valentina hoped it was. With the direction *her* fates had been taking her, she would have to accept that she was bound for the auction block to be enslaved by a hard, cruel master and would never see another Christian face as long as she lived!

Rosalan had been wrong. The Christian soldiers captured by Saladin were too weakened from wounds and too close to starvation to plan an escape and overtake the Moslem guards. The long drive to Damascus ebbed the last of their strength, and many died along the way. Valentina herself would never have been able to walk the distance, but Rosalan had reminded several of the guards that Valentina was a brave girl and a killer of Christians, retelling the story of how she had been found near the dead body of a French foot soldier, the bloody dagger clutched in her hand. The reward had been a place atop a pack camel on the journey to Damascus.

The braying, nasty animal groaned in protest when it was commanded to kneel and accept its light burden of Rosalan and Valentina. Perched atop the cargo, Valentina thought the ground appeared to be miles beneath her, and her stomach threatened to retch each time the swaying beast took a step. Not even aboard ship, while crossing the great sea to the Holy Land, had the dipping motion of the vessel affected her as violently as this foul-smelling, four-legged beast of burden. When the caravan halted to make camp for the night, Valentina swore that never again would she climb upon the ship of the desert. But each day, after several hours of walking, her feet dragging through the sand and weighing down the hem of her garments, Valentina would look pleadingly at the drover, and he would help her onto the precariously swaying perch.

A long procession of blistering days beneath a persistent sun and chill nights that were too short to ease the aches of the trek to Damascus lay before Valentina and the thousand-odd dependents of Saladin. Women used to the climate of the desert carried their youngest child in a sling on their backs, and even with the added weight they were as sure-footed as the beasts of burden. Indeed, these women of the plains fared better than the Christian prisoners who were weak from lack of ample food and who had been stripped of their footgear. The only pain that was evident in the eyes of the women was caused by the separation from their men; a separation thrust upon them in the expediency of war. From the ancient city of Damascus they would go back either to their own people or to their husbands'. Still, there were among the caravan those poor desperate souls, who, having no family to return to, had only the auction block and the ultimate separation from their children looming in their futures.

Several times in any given night the crack of a whip could be heard, followed by the hysterical cries of a mother and the strident wail of a child. There was no guarantee that mother and child would be bought together, and rather than face separation, women would carry their young and attempt to steal away into the night. It was these victims of war who were most diligently watched by the guards, for they were the ones who would most likely attach themselves to the troops of another regiment.

Valentina and Rosalan would huddle together to protect themselves from the cold night air as they sought each other's warmth. Rosalan heartily cursed the order that no tents were to be erected in order to save the time it would take to set up and break camp

117

each evening and morning. Provisions were prepared by a company of men, and there were no individual cook fires. The meal of the day, usually at dusk, was served from great cauldrons to the endless line of travelers.

Valentina spread out the pallet that she and Rosalan shared, while Rosalan took their bowls and waited on the long line that snaked around the campsite. When Rosalan returned she handed Valentina one of the evening's rations.

"Ugh! This swill isn't fit for the swine!" she said disgustedly as she motioned to throw the grayish watery contents upon the ground.

"No!" Rosalan exclaimed, catching the bowl in midair. "If you don't want it for yourself, don't waste it. Give it to me."

"You amaze me," Valentina said, her face flushed with anger. "You throw yourself into that slop and toss it down with such relish."

Rosalan looked up from her bowl, her dark, luminous eyes wide, puzzlement scoring her smooth brow. This was quite a change from the Valentina who had undertaken the journey to Damascus with such silent resignation. There had been times when Rosalan was truly afraid for the morose and distant Valentina. This anger was the first the girl had exhibited since the start of the caravan's trek to Damascus. It pleased Rosalan. At last Valentina was showing some fight, some spirit. So often on the journey Valentina had limited her gaze to the distant horizon, neither seeing nor hearing anything around her. Even the pesty flies that plagued travelers on the plains had settled upon her face unnoticed and bitten with abandon into her smooth complexion. When Rosalan rode behind Valentina atop the lofty camel, she would cover the Christian girl's face and shoo away the pesty insects. Now, emerging from a complete state of lethargy, Valentina was at last showing some pluckiness.

Retrieving the bowl of mush, Rosalan began to scoop it out with three fingers and greedily sucked it into her mouth.

"You make me sick! How can you eat? Don't you care about what happens to you? Look how smugly you sit there sucking your fingers! God! You've thrown me in with barbarians! Nomads! Swine!" Valentina lifted her arms heavenward. "Rosalan, do you really think that a wealthy man will buy you and take you into his harem and place the riches of the world at your feet? How stupid can one girl be?"

Rosalan continued eating with all the gusto and relish she could muster for the repellent swill that was her supper. Covertly she looked up at Valentina, who was looming over her. Hands on hips, cheeks blazing with color, eyes wild and furious, Valentina continued her attack.

"Look at you, just look at you! Where's your self-respect? Where's that special, inner you? The core of your being! Bah! You'd sell yourself for a bowl of mush and a flea-infested blanket to wrap yourself in the cold night." In answer, Rosalan merely swept her three fingers through the bowl of swill and sucked greedily at the gruel.

"Stop making those disgusting noises! Can't you hear what I'm telling you?" Valentina shrieked. Dropping down to her knees and forcing herself to keep from hitting the Bedouin girl, Valentina took hold of Rosalan's arms and prevented her from bringing her fingers to her mouth. "Rosalan, listen to me, I beg you!"

As though noticing Valentina for the first time, Rosalan raised her eyes and affected an air of complacency. "You know my feelings about beggars. Give them anything and they are your lifelong responsibility. I am responsible only to myself."

Valentina shook her forcibly. "You must be the most exasperating creature God ever placed on this earth."

"Ssh! Lower your voice. You forget who you're supposed to be. If you must shout, be certain you leave your God out of it."

"When will you face facts?" Valentina demanded, her voice lowered but no less bitter. "You are marching toward your destiny, the destiny you say cannot be changed, only accepted. How can you accept a destiny that will see you enslaved for the remainder of your life? Has Allah shone his grace upon you thus far? Have you never looked about you, have you never seen what becomes of the women who live the life of a camp follower? Even in the short time I've been here I have seen women brutalized, their teeth missing, whiplashes on their bodies. And at the time of their monthly bleeding or after childbirth, when no man will touch them, what becomes of them then? I'll tell you. They go hungry! Their milk dries because they cannot afford to purchase even water from the vendors. Their children go hungry and fight the dogs for the trash thrown carelessly from the tents. You are still young and strong, hardly more than a child by European standards, but how many more years will you be young and comely? Open your eyes, Rosalan; see what lies before you. I shudder when I think of it, and I'm desperately frightened. If life as a camp follower is held to be superior to being a slave, just imagine what lies in store for us!" The tirade of her words left Valentina emotionally exhausted and spent. Tears shone in her eyes, which reflected the last rays of the sun in their pained depths.

Rosalan restrained herself from taking Valentina into her arms and calming her with soothing words. Instead, her voice was a clue to her barely contained fury. "Now it is your turn to listen to me, Valentina. I loathe this swill they feed us, yet I eat it because it is the wise thing to do. Death holds no attraction for me. And I keep the flies from biting my face because I have only my youth and beauty to trade upon. As for my soul, my secret core, as we have come to call that which is me, it is still mine! I don't trade upon it, I do all I can to keep it, to nourish it. This I cannot do if I am starving and I fall to my death. Speak not to me of whip marks! Do you see any on my body? No! Yet you came to me from the world of Christians striped and marked by *their* justice. You yourself have been brutalized by men. They forced their way into

120

our tent and raped you and worse. And what did you get for it? Nothing! Women will always be brutalized one way or another, but it is the smart woman who sees that she gains from it. If that gain be merely to keep body and soul together, so be it. It is my choice, the only way I know."

Rosalan set aside the bowl of gruel and moved closer to Valentina, her tone less hostile and forbidding. "Poor pigeon, you fear for the future. So do I. Yet I have hope."

Valentina still refused the bowl of gruel that night, and she spent most of the long hours until dawn shedding silent tears. Yet the next day, when the sun had climbed midway in the sky, she asked to be lifted upon the back of a camel, where she joined Rosalan in keeping her fair face covered from the ravages of the sun and the onslaught of the flies.

To Rosalan's satisfaction, Valentina rubbed sheep fat into the soles of her feet and took more interest in brushing her hair, freeing the raven locks from the stubborn granules of sand that seemed to imbed themselves in any part of her person she was careless enough to leave exposed.

Day after day the long, twisting, heavily guarded caravan covered the miles to Damascus, to their future. Because of the state of the prisoners and the need for frequent rests that were demanded by the children, it would be several weeks before they would reach the gates of that ancient city.

Following Rosalan's advice, Valentina accepted her rations of food, and the chill nights found her dutifully seeking sleep. Her hair once again became a night-dark cloud of gleaming tresses. Her hands and feet were once again soft and smooth, owing to the sheep fat, and along with the improvement in her appearance came a rebuilding of her spirit. A spirit that, Rosalan knew, was necessary for Valentina to survive.

One bright afternoon the caravan wound its way over a hill, and there before them lay the exotic city of Damascus.

The bevy of prisoners and women was tied at the wrists, hobbled at the ankles, and then marched in through the city gates. By this time the sun had set, and darkness pervaded the narrow streets and marketplaces. Valentina gripped Rosalan's hand and held it tightly, fearing separation from her friend. Rosalan's own hand was wet with sweat, which disclosed her own nervousness. "What will they do with us?" Valentina asked quietly.

Rosalan shrugged her shoulders. "Only Allah knows, Valentina."

The guard who was walking close beside them answered their remarks. "It will not be so bad," he said kindly. "Malik en Nasr has demanded the highest price for his own people. The higher the price the better you will be treated. For now, the women are to be separated from the men and will be taken to separate quarters, where you will have time to rest and bathe and prepare yourselves. There is no doubt in my mind that women as beautiful as yourselves will find a high place in a king's harem." He nodded encouragingly before he hurried to the front of the line.

"See, pigeon, what did I tell you?" Rosalan beamed a smile. "You yourself heard what he said. It will be to a scented harem that we will go. Bless your fates, pigeon. Allah is smiling on you."

In a walled enclosure Rosalan and Valentina, along with the other women of the caravan, were bathed and scented and dressed in gossamer soft fabrics and jeweled headpieces. Inexpensive bangles were clasped about their upper arms and soft kid slippers fitted on their feet. Rosalan helped Valentina dress in the strange garb and stepped back to admire her handiwork.

Valentina's costume was a royal shade of deep blue. The sheer skirt hung from a low-slung silver girdle, and the short jacket was of silver and blue threads. "Never have I seen such garments as these," Rosalan exclaimed, reaching for a brush to dress Valentina's hair.

Valentina felt naked. The silver girdle exposed her

flat belly, and the jacket was cut so short that it barely covered her breasts. Rosalan had wound strings of thin chains about her neck; they fell between the hollow of her breasts and were cool against her skin. The wide, circular skirt just reached her toes, and through the thin fabric her legs were clearly visible. "I won't go about in public dressed in this—this—"

Rosalan's patience was at a low ebb. She seized Valentina's shoulders and shook her. "You will, you must! It is better that you be bought by a wealthy caliph for his harem than be purchased for a seraglio. In the harem you will be called to your master, and he will give you the respect of a woman of his household. Do you want me to tell you what happens in a seraglio? Do you want to hear of the type of men you will be forced to service? For if you refuse you will be whipped unto death! Do you have any idea how long a woman can expect to live in the house of whores? I promise you, Valentina, it is not a long life! Men will bring you disease and whip you from the perverse devils in their nature—"

"Stop!" Valentina cried, pushing her hands against her ears to block out Rosalan's voice.

"Then use your wits!" Rosalan urged, her black eyes penetrating Valentina's. "In order to find yourself among your own people again, you must live to do it! Do not decry your . . ."

"Fates! That was what you were going to say. Do not deny my fates! Oh, I am so weary of hearing you say it!"

"Yes, I know you are, yet you do not really hear me. Do not deny your fates, true, but you must learn to become mistress of them! Will you always sit back and wait for someone to take care of you? Will you never learn to take care of yourself? Where is your spirit? Where is your fight? You deny your fates simply by not taking control of them. My fate would have been to die in the desert of starvation when my mother died. But I became mistress of my fates when I began to earn my own living. I did not deny my fates, but I did not let them rule me, either! Valentina, my friend, you are a very dull and stupid girl!" Disgusted, Rosalan walked away.

Valentina was stung to the quick by Rosalan's words. Was it true? Did she always wait for someone to take care of her? Did it seem so? Had she no spirit, no fight? Was she dull and stupid? Tears rolled down her cheeks, and she was about to give herself up to the heaving sobs that rose within her. No! She would not cry! All her life she had cried. She had cried for Berengaria's faithless nature, for the love of a king who could never love her, for everything and everyone. No more! She would do what had to be done! If it killed her . . .

The next few days were a test to Valentina's new resolution. Slave traders came to the compound and inspected the women, writing their names and numbers on tightly furled scrolls, and beside each name the price which they would command when placed on the block.

Valentina was terrified. The crude, impersonal manner with which the women were handled offended her. When she expressed these fears to Rosalan, the Bedouin girl gritted her teeth. "You make too much of it, Valentina. Think a moment. Would you buy a piece of ware without first examining your purchase?"

But Valentina had seen abhorrence in Rosalan's eyes, and her misery was easier to bear because she knew that Rosalan shared it. Yet she dreaded the moment when she would have to submit to those cold, knowing eyes and probing fingers.

The next morning, when the sun was still low on the horizon and spilled its promise of shimmering heat upon the land, a eunuch announced, in a peculiar high voice, that the forty women who shared the crowded compound with Valentina and Rosalan would come before the auctioneer for his inspection later in the day. Even as he announced it, Valentina could feel the dread which settled over the compound.

Rosalan immediately began to make preparations. Prodding Valentina to follow her example, Rosalan carefully brushed her hair and arranged it in a coif of several narrow braids, which she looped atop her head. The ration of water which had been distributed that morning was used to cleanse herself, and she made liberal use of the perfumes and cosmetics which had been provided for the women.

One of the other girls elbowed her companion and sneered at Rosalan. "Look at that one!" she jeered, raising her voice for all to hear. "She must think that the auctioneer will buy her for himself!" The others giggled and laughed at Rosalan who fumed at the other girl's gibes.

Ordinarily, Valentina would have expected Rosalan to fly at her attacker with nails and shrieks, but this morning she kept herself in control. "Pay them no attention," she told Valentina. "The stupid bitches think that the auctioneer is less than a man. He is a man, and like all men, he can be swayed by a comely face and shapely hips. But he also has a nose! If they used their heads, they would clean the smell off themselves and improve their chances to have a high price set upon them from the outset. Mark my words, the seraglios will claim more than half of them, and a pox be on them!" To emphasize her statement, she spit.

Just as the eunuch promised, the women were led from the compound to a low, walled building across the square, which they reached by a network of narrow, foul-smelling alleys that were inhabited by roving packs of dogs. The guards kicked and threatened, sending the starving animals yipping out of their hiding places.

When the procession reached the outer gates of the building, the double doors were flung open to receive the silent and expectant women. Valentina and Rosalan hovered near each other, taking comfort from each other's presence.

Upon entering, they were amazed at the contrast between the outside of the building and its interior. Rubble and offal glutted the alleyways and the street directly outside the perimeter of the low walls. What might have been a garden was a barren patch inhabited by stray dogs and their filth. But the interior revealed a different world. Here were wealth and opulence such as Valentina had never seen. Rosalan, who had never known such splendor even in her dreams, was wide-eyed and gaping, as were all the other women. Coming in as they did from the late afternoon sun, the darkness within made a full realization of the magnificence difficult. But their eyes gradually became accustomed to the light from the flickering oil pots that were scented with exotic perfumes and from the blazing torches set at precise distances along the tiled mosaic walls. The guards became hard pressed to hurry the bevy of women along.

One girl was heard to ask a guard why such splendor was masked behind the ugliness found outside.

"Do you think Abd Shaaba desires beggars to plague his household and thieves to ply their trade?" was the reply.

"Who is Abd Shaaba?" the girl asked.

"The most mighty and glorious of Allah's auctioners," was the angry answer. "He is the one you will have to please if you are to be purchased by anyone of esteem," he added impatiently.

Valentina, hearing the exchange, knew that Rosalan had again been correct in her judgment. Now she was glad that she had allowed Rosalan to press her into bathing and scenting herself and brushing her hair till it shone with blue-black lights. Abd Shaaba held her fate in his hands.

As they were led into another high, vaulted room, the women stammered and exclaimed over a huge ivory panel carved with intricate designs and ornamental relief work. Among other pieces of art flanking the walls, Valentina's eye was caught by an ivory horn in the shape of an elephant's tusk. Engraved on the horn were carved scenes of the goddess whom one of the women identified as Ishtar. Across the goddess's naked breasts were two feathers, and beside her sat numerous animals, griffins, and good-luck symbols.

Along the farthest wall were frescoes depicting several scenes of nymphs and satyrs engaged in numerous

126

positions of love. The double arches leading out to a portico were decorated with still more engravings of nudes, all of whom were women with large, well-shaped bosoms. Across the room was still another archway whose lintels were carved into masculine shapes with exaggerated sex organs. Rosalan looked down at her own breasts, which were barely concealed beneath her costume, and glanced worriedly at the female engravings. When she looked back across the room to where the satyrs were depicted, she hastily nudged Valentina. "Look, over there. To be certain, whoever carved them never met the men *I* have known!"

Everywhere Valentina looked there were innuendoes of lust. The group walked through to still a third room, where silk draperies were used to attract the eye to the niches in the wall containing statues engaged in a myriad of lascivious activities. The floor underfoot was thickly carpeted in jewel colors.

At the head of the room sat three men upon silk cushions. They were dressed resplendently in flaring khalats and brocaded tunics. The turbans of silk wrapped about their heads were studded with semiprecious jewels, and their beards were clipped to precise points, which gave them the look of the satyrs portrayed in the frescoes.

Valentina guessed that Abd Shaaba was the man in the center, for his cushions allowed him to sit higher than the other two men. Also, he was the one to whom the guards offered their salutes.

Without a word Abd Shaaba motioned the women to line the perimeters of the room. With another gesture the guards commanded the women to parade one at a time before the famous auctioneer. Valentina and Rosalan followed the line, and as they took their turns passing before him they saw him signal to one of the guards, just as he had when several of the other women had paraded before the dais.

In all, there were eight girls, including Rosalan and Valentina, who were detained, while the other women were led back to the adjoining room. For the first time Abd Shaaba spoke. His voice was like oiled glass, smooth and slick. "You will please disrobe."

Valentina glanced toward Rosalan, who was already engaged in removing her costume. "Everything, beads, bangles . . . everything, please," Abd Shaaba intoned. Valentina eyed the distance between herself and the doorway and then thought of how far it was to the exit. She would never make it; she was trapped. She had known for days that this moment was coming, and she had thought herself prepared. She was not. Her throat felt dry and parched and her heart was beating frantically within her breast. She was aware of the blood rushing to her face; she felt her cheeks burning.

"Hurry," a guard warned her. "Abd Shaaba has much else to do besides waiting for you."

"I can't . . ."

"Would you rather I strip you and save you the trouble?" was the guard's response.

Valentina shook her head and began to undo the bracelets which were linked about her wrists. Her fingers trembled and she clamped down hard on her teeth to keep them from rattling.

"Perhaps we should view the one whose modesty threatens to keep us here all the night through," Abd Shaaba said to his companions. "Long experience has taught me to be quick with ones such as her. Quickness is the keynote, else they tremble and shake, and some have even fainted in expectation of my attention." The other two men laughed and agreed. Valentina was to be first.

As she struggled with a length of golden chain, Abd Shaaba said, "Leave it. Come, stand before us. We would measure your worth."

Naked save for her hair ornaments and the length of fine chain, Valentina squared her shoulders and proceeded to walk to the center of the dais. Her face flushed pink and her eyes snapped a glittering green.

Abd Shaaba and his companions watched her with experienced eyes. They quickly noted her natural grace and the slow, sensuous sway of her slender hips. The fine chain which she had found impossible to remove had slipped around on one firm, coral-tipped breast, outlining its nubile perfection. Their eyes raked over her in speculative measure. There was no lust or sexuality in their glances, only the sharp knowledgeability of horse traders.

"Turn . . . please," Abd Shaaba commanded, and to her amazement Valentina found herself obeying him without hesitation. So cold and businesslike was he that she realized she could detach herself from the situation and do as she was told. "Again . . . please," he said, and Valentina turned once more to face the triad.

It was only when she saw Abd Shaaba rise from the cushions that her skin began to shrivel. Gritting her teeth, she forced herself to stand in place. Quickly and expertly, he ran his hands over her shrinking flesh. He began at her head, probing into her mouth and remarking to the others that there was no evidence of cankers or missing teeth. He lifted her eyelids and noted the brightness and clarity of her eyes. Moving down her neck and over her shoulders, his hands made contact with her breasts, testing their symmetry. Down her arms, plying her hands for flexibility, and over her feet and legs. "I noticed, when you turned about, the signs of a past beating. A lashing, actually. You have healed admirably, but I am quick to note such things. Fear not, it will not affect your salability." Abd Shaaba's hands coursed over the fine pink blemishes which still remained from Berengaria's whipping. "No, it will not impede your sale. You have much else in your favor."

The hands continued down over her haunches, the backs of her thighs and calves. Valentina stood as though carved from marble. The eyes of the other women burned into her as Abd Shaaba examined her for blemishes and imperfections. Just as she thought he was finished, he placed his hand along the inside of her thigh. She stiffened and pressed her legs together. "It is merely a formality," he soothed. "Only to see whether you are a virgin."

"I'm not," Valentina said simply, her voice low and throaty with emotion and humiliation.

"Nevertheless, for the record," he said. "I will be very gentle . . . come now . . . I assure you it is easier if I do it, rather than one of the guards."

Valentina shifted her glance to the guard who was closest to her and recognized his molten expression of desire. Squeezing her eyes shut, she allowed Abd Shaaba to perform his task. "So you are not," he stated simply, "but it is for the record; now it is written. Strange," he added as he peered deeply into her eyes, "from your maidenly behavior I would have guessed you were a virgin and had never tasted the delights of love. Still, I should have known that when a woman says she is not a virgin, then she is not. It is only when a woman claims to be in possession of her maidenhead that one should suspect she is lying."

This last comment drew laughter from the men on the dais as well as from the girls. Abd Shaaba's eyes were fathomless black pools that reflected the burning lamps. "A shame . . . we could have earned quite a price for you if you were virginal."

Turning back to his two business associates, he joked, "Although why men prefer virgins is beyond the intelligence Allah gave me. They are like untried steeds, disagreeable and undependable; incapable of giving a smooth ride."

Unable to contain herself, Valentina sputtered, "Perhaps you find this so because you have yet to learn that the quality of the mount depends on the skill of the rider."

The auctioneer was not a man without humor, and when the value of Valentina's words dawned upon him, he broke into peals of laughter.

"Beauty and humor . . . fatal charms for a woman to possess." He smiled. "Would that I were not burdened with this business for Saladin. Perhaps I could prove to you that I am an experienced rider."

As they were led back to their quarters, Rosalan's eyes glowed with pride. "I take back my words, Valentina. You are anything but a dull and stupid girl. I can understand now how that Christian fell beneath the point of your dagger." She threw an arm about Valentina, and the girls walked on, laughing. But each was painfully aware that the auction was to take place the next day and perhaps they would never see each other again.

Chapter Nine

The next day, an hour before dawn, the women were awakened and told to dress. Burly black eunuchs brought in trays of unleavened bread and urns of strong, hot teas sweetened with honey. The women grumbled at this poor fare but fell to the meager breakfast with relish.

An officer of Saladin's army stepped through the doors of the compound and ordered the women to assemble. "The mighty Malik en Nasr wishes the grace of Allah to go with you. You will be brought into the marketplace ten at a time. A great crowd has gathered to watch the proceedings and to make their bids. Allah go with you."

Outside in the bright sun Valentina found herself beside a tall, muscular Christian with wheat-colored hair. She did not recognize him immediately because it had been many weeks since he had shaved, and he wore a full beard, disguising his face. It was only when he spoke to her that she knew him to be an Englishman named Michael, part of the queen's guard.

"Lady Valentina!" he said, astonishment lighting his bright blue eyes. "Can it really be you! We all thought you dead!"

"Michael, I did not know you were Saladin's prisoner. How did you come to be here?"

Rosalan watched them with curiosity. Could this tall, pleasing man be Valentina's lover? Is that why she seemed so happy to see him?

"Rosalan," Valentina said excitedly, "this is Michael of Landslock. He is an English soldier. Michael was a member of the queen's guard, and we became friends on our long journey from Navarre."

Rosalan was no more informed than before. What was Landslock and where was Navarre?

"You haven't answered me, Michael. How came you to be here?"

"I could well ask the same of your ladyship," Michael answered.

"That is too long a story to tell." Valentina smiled. "Tell us of yourself."

"Lady Valentina, even I am befuddled by what happened to me. One moment I was a member of the queen's guard, and the next I am sent out on patrol. Our party met with the enemy and my steed was killed. I found myself wandering through the desert until I was captured by a warring party of Saracens. They took me captive, and from there I am here, about to be auctioned like a head of cattle." Michael's voice bespoke his bitterness. "Lady Valentina, I am a knight of the realm! My place is to be fighting beside my king, not here in this heathen bazaar!"

The line of captives moved forward into the marketplace. Valentina looked about at the milling throngs of people bartering their wares. At the far end of the market was a raised platform on which stood Abd Shaaba, holding a sheaf of papers and praising the worth of a comely girl being offered for sale.

Sudden dread clutched at Valentina, and she grasped Michael's arms to keep from falling into the dismal abyss which seemed to open before her. "Michael, I don't want to go!"

Michael laid a comforting arm about Valentina's shoulders, and the intimacy of the contact seemed to embarrass him. He was a knight of the realm, sworn to uphold the dignity of womanhood and chivalry. Even now, under these dire circumstances, Michael was careful not to give offense to a lady. However, Valentina had seen Michael avert his eyes from the sight of her legs, which were revealed by the wisp of gossamer skirt, and when he spoke to her, he was diligent in keeping his gaze limited to her face and neck.

A sigh escaped Valentina's lips. She wondered if Michael would be so gallant in his treatment of her if he knew that she had been ravaged by two Saracen warriors. "I have been a prisoner of the Saracens much longer than you, Michael. What news have you of our people in Acre?"

"Little if any, my lady. Except perhaps something you do not know of. It concerns Queen Berengaria. It is a closely guarded secret, but, as we both have little hope of ever seeing our own people again, there is no harm in telling you."

"What is it, Michael?" Valentina asked breathlessly.

"As you know, my good Lady Blanche saw fit to honor me with her company on more than one occasion." Michael's eyes became distant when he spoke of the fetching Lady Blanche. It was known among the queen's ladies that Michael of Landslock was soon to beg Blanche's hand in marriage from King Richard.

"Go on," Valentina prompted.

"Her Majesty, Queen Berengaria, met with . . . with . . ."

"Yes, Michael, go on!"

"On the eve of the massacre of Moslems, Queen Berengaria was . . . was . . . whipped!" he blurted.

"Whipped!" Valentina echoed. "By whom?"

Michael's eyes were troubled. "Lady Blanche helped Sena prepare a salve, but at the time she had no knowledge of who it was for or why. Sena, as you know, is quite old and taken to grumbling to herself. Lady Blanche overheard the old woman say that

133

the queen had been whipped. When she confronted
Sena with this, the old crone was shocked into silence,
but Lady Blanche persisted, saying that the welfare
of the queen was important to her ladies-in-waiting.
This was when Sena confided in Lady Blanche that it
was the Lionheart who had whipped her. My Lady
Blanche knew this could not be true, as I had told her
that I was to confer with the king on the building of
a new mangonel. When my lady questioned me, I
told her that the king never left his quarters. He had
remained with his officers for the entire night, drawing
up plans for the mangonel. Lady Blanche said this
could not be true, as she herself had seen the drover's
whip which the king had used to chastise the queen.
I, of course, did not insist that I was in the king's
company the entire night. It does not pay to pry into
women's intrigues."

Valentina gazed at Michael, slack-mouthed. Berengaria whipped! The drover's whip! Paxon! Poor 'Garia,
she muttered to herself, punished at the hand of her
adored Saracen. Valentina had a vivid memory of that
night and remembered Paxon's coming to her room.
She remembered the morning of the massacre and
Sena's telling her that the sultan was coming to take
her away. He had known what he would do and
wanted to save her from Berengaria's retributions.

Suddenly Valentina was pulled forward and jostled
along with Michael and Rosalan toward the auction
block.

Rosalan lifted her head and stepped up lightly beside the auctioneer. Shoulders thrown back, a comely
expression on her face, Rosalan looked lovelier than
Valentina had ever seen her. The rich gold color of the
Bedouin girl's costume accentuated the lustrous tones
of her skin. The ankle-length sheer skirt, which fell in
soft folds from her hips, alluringly revealed her firm
thighs and slim calves. Anklets of gold glinted mysteri-
ously from beneath her ribbon-bordered hem and jingled exotically with each step she took.

As Valentina watched the proceedings she realized
she was praying that Rosalan would not be purchased

by a bidder for a seraglio. The girl's temptress looks and full, pouting mouth hinted at her sultry nature; one which would be a valuable commodity in a house of prostitution.

The bidding for Rosalan was under way and proceeded at such a fury that Valentina found herself at a loss to follow it. Rosalan postured for the bidders, showing her fluid movements and suppleness. Valentina had heard Rosalan say that it was very important to be as appealing as possible in order to drive up the price. Seraglios declined to pay a high price for the girls they bought, since a woman did not usually live more than a few years. And the men who sought the pleasures of the brothels were not often very fastidious about their choice of female for the evening. The higher the price the better the chance of being sold into a rich master's harem.

Abd Shaaba halted the bidding and beckoned Rosalan to remove the short jacket that barely covered the top of her ribs. Valentina was surprised to see Rosalan balk. The girl had no scruples about being seen in the nude. Even on the long trek to Damascus, Rosalan had dutifully bathed herself within sight of passing guards and prisoners. When Valentina had shown her shock at the girl's lack of modesty, Rosalan had simply stated that she had nothing to hide and that sponging herself clean was much more important to her well-being than being modest. Now Rosalan's show of modesty in public puzzled Valentina.

"See how virtuous she is!" the auctioneer exclaimed, throwing Rosalan a look of approval. "This one is fit for the harem! Her beauty, her virtue! The breeding of a goddess! Imagine her among the women of your harems. Think of her and the fine sons she will bear. Sons of worthy blood!"

Immediately he commanded the bidding to begin again. This time he seemed pleased with the bargaining. With raucous shouts and silent nods, Rosalan's fate was sealed. "To the palace of Napur! Emir Ramiff has gained still another flower for his harem."

Rosalan's dark eyes danced with glee. A harem! Her

wish come true! And to the emir of Napur, an accomplishment beyond all dreams.

A wave of commotion arose beside Valentina and she felt herself stiffen. To her relief she learned that the auctioneer had called for five men, Christians, to be brought to the block. Valentina's relief fell away, however, when she discovered that Michael was among those to be sold.

Michael and the four other men, whom Valentina had never seen before, were herded upon the block. They stood there with heads bowed low, humiliated that they, soldiers for the Holy Cross, should come to be sold as chattel to the enemy.

Valentina turned her head away. At least she would not be witness to their degradation. The bidding began and ended with a look from Abd Shaaba and a grumbling amid the crowd. It was evident that none of the Christian prisoners would bring a good price. Word was out that Saladin wanted to be rid of his burden, and the prisoners of hostage could be gotten for a song. The conspiracy among the buyers resulted in a very poor cash benefit for Saladin. "For the costs of war to protect your land!" the auctioneer cried. "For the sake of the sacred jihad! Place your bids in good faith for the love of Allah!"

Still no response was given. The Christian prisoners would be bought to relieve Saladin of his responsibility, but it would be done at the lowest cost possible. From out of the crowd came a voice raising the bid by a few dinars. Disgust thickening the auctioneer's voice, he claimed that Michael and his four companions were sold to the highest bidder.

Valentina turned back to see the five men being led from the block and placed in a holding pen. There they would wait for their owner to claim them. Her heart sank to the pits of darkness, for she knew she would be called next.

Abd Shaaba's headgear fluttered in the wind. "It has been many years since I have had such a fair collection of maidens to present, as well as fierce warriors and white-skinned Christians." He turned to face Valentina, a lascivious smile peppered with greed spreading across his face. "See this one! Have you ever rested your eyes upon such skin, such limbs of grace, and hair the color of a raven's wing?"

Abd Shaaba's eyes fell upon a familiar face. "Mohab, keeper of the house for the warring lion Emir Ramiff. Think how pleased your master would be to receive such a one as this into his harem! Imagine how pleased he would be to have these soft and silken arms about his head, and these limbs cool and clean and most sweet for the caressing!" Valentina felt her face flush to hear herself described this way.

The auctioneer turned to his helpmate. "Undress her!" came the low command.

Against her struggles, Valentina was stripped to the waist. The auctioneer's slave held her arms tightly behind her back, causing her breasts to jut out proudly. "See for yourself!" Abd Shaaba continued. "These twin globes of alabaster, tipped with tiny roses! Think what delights await your master. What fair sons he could bear with such a one as this, to his delight and Allah's!"

The auctioneer turned to his servant again. "Strip her! I would that they see her limbs!"

The servant approached Valentina, and she felt as though she were being strangled. They would not do this to her! She would kill them first, and barring that, kill herself! Her hand moved with stealth as she reached for the auctioneer's poniard, a short dagger with a curving blade. She whipped it from its scabbard and whirled, slashing it threateningly at the servant.

"Seize her!" the auctioneer cried.

At once the guards were upon her, subduing her, grabbing the dagger from her grip. Michael, watching from the holding pen, struggled against his manacles to go to her aid, but the leather thongs were too strong and held his wrists firm. His eyes were pained for Valentina's humiliation, but he was helpless to do anything.

Valentina was finally under control, and the last vestiges of her garments were stripped from her. "Think of what sons such a one as this will bear!" Abd Shaaba continued, undaunted by Valentina's fray with the guards. The man whom he called Mohab signaled with his hand for the bidding to begin. What followed was masked in a haze for Valentina, who could not believe any of it was happening. She only knew that the man from Emir Ramiff's palace had offered such a sum as could be met by no other, and that at least Rosalan was also to go to the emir's harem.

Across the yard of the marketplace was a sandstone building which housed a favorite seraglio often frequented by the officers of Saladin's army. From under the richly embossed arch near the entrance emerged two men wearing the black and yellow uniform of Malik en Nasr, scowls upon their faces.

"We should have known better than to expect our usual service, Meshtub. It seems to me that half the city of Damascus has left their trade to watch the auction." Paxon handed a coin to the boy who had brought their steeds around to the front and mounted. His companion did likewise.

"I sometimes think my mother conceived me and birthed me atop a horse," Meshtub complained. "Why don't we stay and watch the auction? My back could do with a respite from this saddle. We have a three-day ride ahead of us, and there is no promise of diversion once we leave Damascus."

Paxon shot his friend a dark glare and gently kicked his heels into his steed's flanks. "There is no diversion. They're all gawking about and watching the auction. Come along, Meshtub, your complaining falls on deaf ears."

"As long as I'm voicing my complaints, I wish you would stop volunteering me for every mission you agree to undertake. I'm too young to die. What ails you, Pax? Ever since your last visit to the Engleysi queen, you've been like an itch that needs scratching!"

Ignoring Meshtub's last remark, Paxon looked across the marketplace to the lively proceedings of the auction. "Look upon those poor devils. They have only

Allah's mercy to cling to. They don't know what's in store for them."

Meshtub nodded agreeably. "Nadjar says there's a dark-haired Circassian to be sold who would make your eyes fall from your head with her beauty. Why not join the crowds and see?"

"No," Paxon said firmly. "If you're ready and your fat body can move, let us be on our way."

"Ride on, Paxon. I'll catch up with you. Look! There she is! Even from here I can see that Nadjar was correct as always."

Paxon looked with little interest toward the auction block, but his view was impeded by a string of passing camels loaded with wares bound for the market. "Stay if you like, Meshtub. I'll ride slowly and wait for you outside the gates."

Meshtub signaled with his hand that he had heard, but his eyes were riveted upon the scene taking place on the block.

Paxon rode on, picking his way through the city. Moments later Meshtub joined him, breathless with excitement. "Pax, do you hear what they're saying about her?"

"About whom?"

"About the Circassian!" Meshtub cried, exasperated by his friend's lack of interest.

"What are they saying, Meshtub? I know you'll devil me until I listen to you."

"She is beautiful! Her skin is white and unblemished, her breasts are like the budding of the jasmine flower, her limbs are long and slim and soft and clean . . ."

"Do you know this for yourself?" Paxon asked teasingly. "Or are you to take that thieving auctioneer's word for it? How often I have seen you fooled, my friend. Remember that carpet you purchased from a merchant in Jerusalem? I'll never forget how stupid you looked as you sat upon it and commanded it to fly!" Paxon threw back his head and surrendered himself to gales of laughter.

Meshtub's face clouded with remembered humilia-

139

tion. "How was I to know? I had heard tales of flying carpets . . ."

"We are all fools at one time or another, Meshtub. Forgive my insolence. But I will never forget how you looked when you at last admitted that you'd been played for a fool." Paxon again surrendered to laughter.

"I wasn't fooled this time!" Meshtub shouted. "I saw her for myself!"

"Who?"

"The Circassian! How many times must I tell you? Do you want to hear what she did, or do you want to hear it from someone else?"

"Very well, tell me before you burst."

Reining in close, Meshtub's eyes glowed as he told the tale. "She fought like a tiger! She seized the auctioneer's poniard and had murder in her eyes! It took three men to subdue her. Never have I seen a woman fight like that, ready to kill to protect her honor. I pity the poor soul who attempts to become her master!"

As Meshtub went on to embellish and retell his tale, Paxon's thoughts were inexplicably drawn back to Valentina. "Protect her honor," Meshtub had said. Somehow in his mind's eye Paxon could envision Valentina fighting not for her skin but for her honor.

Fool! he chastised himself. Men *have* honor. Women *honor!*

Chapter Ten

The journey to Ramiff's kingdom of Napur was long and arduous. The emir's caravan traveled at a leisurely pace, making camp late in the afternoon and resuming travel soon after dawn, before the heat of the sun blazed upon the plains.

Valentina traveled with Rosalan, guarded by eunuchs, those black sexless giants, trailing behind the main party. They rode in a little roofed pavilion that was perched atop a camel and shielded them from the sun. The water allotted them was plentiful, and twice, when camping near an oasis, they had been free to bathe and enjoy the cool respite from the day's journey.

They were treated royally, and when Valentina remarked on this to Rosalan, the young Bedouin girl gave her a puzzled look. "Of course we are treated royally. We now belong to the royal household. As possessions of the emir, we are treated as such. Valentina, don't you know anything?"

Valentina's ire was aroused. "This is not the first time I have been a member of a royal household," she retorted, and turned to complete her bathing.

Rosalan regretted her hasty remark, but her own fiery nature prevented her from admitting it. Valentina's retort reminded Rosalan that she was beneath her own station, and it rankled. "I pray to Allah that you are not as cruelly treated in the household of Ramiff as you were in the household of your queen," Rosalan lashed out.

Valentina's back visibly stiffened as she turned slowly to face Rosalan. Her features were darkened with rage. "At least I was not forced to lie with an Infidel. A whipping is far more to my liking than the thought of the slimy hands and foul breath of your Saracens."

"If your King Richard is any mark of a Christian man, I've no wonder that the thought of a red-blooded Saracen is foreign to you. I too have heard tales they tell of your Lionheart. He is not man enough to mount a woman! Small boys and music makers are more to his preference!"

The insolence in Rosalan's face incensed Valentina. Without a second thought she dashed the water from her basin into Rosalan's face. Swift as a cat, Rosalan was upon her, tooth and nail.

To ward off her attack, Valentina knocked Rosalan

to the ground and fell upon her, pinning her beneath her own weight. They tussled and writhed, each fighting with ferocity. For one instant their eyes locked and suddenly the tension broke. They helped each other to their feet, brushing the dust from themselves, laughing helplessly.

"Let me fetch you another basin of water, Valentina. Poor pigeon, I deserved that."

"No," Valentina protested, helping Rosalan brush the wet slices of dark hair off her face. "It was my fault. I don't know what's wrong with me."

"Nor me," Rosalan answered. "Perhaps it's been the worry and frustration of these past weeks. But now it's over, and we have been smiled upon by your God and Allah. We will have a home and food to eat and we need never worry again. Valentina, we will find a way for you to return to your people. Never fear. Look how far you have journeyed from Acre, where you were very nearly swept into the massacre."

"Yes, many miles separate me from my people," Valentina reflected, her blue-green eyes somber and lifeless even though she smiled.

"I am not speaking only of miles. I mean the change in you. When you first came to me you were a poor pigeon. Frightened and alone. Cowering at a sudden sound and timid in spirit. Now you have come into your own. The girl who first came to me would have accepted my tauntings and run off somewhere to cry. Not any longer. Now you are ready to fend for yourself. Did you ever think that you would kill a man to protect yourself? Did you ever think, even in your wildest dreams, that you would find the strength to go on with your life after being raped? Even on the auction block you showed your new spirit. Valentina, you are a different woman. The change in you has been complete. Now you face life knowing what must be done and doing it."

Valentina contemplated Rosalan's words and knew what she said was true. She *was* different; she knew her strength and would use it. She had withstood pain and degradation and was able to smile again. Looking

142

at Rosalan, she whispered, "Now that I have found my strength, the question is, what do I intend to do with it?"

"Why don't you decide what you want most in life? Then at least you will have a direction. Is what you want most to be returned to your own people?"

Valentina thought for a long moment. "No, somehow it's not quite as important as it once was. There's no one, nothing really, to return to. No one waits for me, and I'm not sure that this new Valentina I have become would belong any more in a world where women are treated so chivalrously." Valentina lifted mournful eyes. "Remember the Christian knight who was auctioned just before me? Michael?"

Rosalan nodded.

"I—I no longer felt at ease with my own kind. It was difficult pretending to be the same person I was, when I've seen so much and known so much." Her voice threatened to break and her eyes glistened with unshed tears. "No, returning to my people is not what I want most. But, God help me, I don't know what it is."

"You will know when the time comes, pigeon. Come now, let us both get fresh water and we can wash each other's hair." Rosalan pushed a ewer into Valentina's hands and picked one up for herself. "Now that you're nearly as smart as I am, and almost as stout-hearted, do you think you can be as swift of foot? I'll race you to the well!"

"Challenge met!" Valentina cried as she and Rosalan raced, laughing, across the campsite.

The track to Napur led upward toward the hills, across fields of cereals and verdant plains. Soon the track gave way to a more rugged country of hills and rocky reaches. At the entrance to the valley of Napur, groves rich with olives and figs appeared. High in the mountains, above the fertile plains, Napur stood like a glimmering jewel on an elongated ridge and commanded a panoramic view of the valley.

The people of Napur thronged through the city just

143

like the people of Acre and Damascus, going about their trades and bargaining. Only here, in Napur, the general condition of the peasants seemed far superior to those in other cities. The streets were cleaner, and there was an obvious lack of wild-dog packs roaming through the stalls.

The emir's palace stood in the center of Napur, upon a rise in the land that overlooked all perimeters of the city. Its white walls dazzled the eye and seemed to be carved from ivory. The windows were grilled in intricate patterns and the pinnacled roof was tiled. The high, surrounding walls enclosed a wide expanse of carefully tended gardens. A small, rectangular courtyard harboring citrus trees was furnished with stone benches and fearsome-looking dragons carved from the same dazzling white stone as the palace. A cool spring bubbled to the surface from between smooth, water-polished rocks and was the backdrop for huge flowering jasmine.

Valentina and Rosalan were led by Mohab through a secluded portion of the garden into the cool of the palace. Within were arcades flanked by marble pillars which soared to the frescoed ceiling and were broader around than a man could circle his arms. Rosalan looked about in awe, as did Valentina. "Close your mouth," Valentina whispered, "before a stray fly finds his home in it."

Rosalan snapped her mouth shut. "Allah strike me, I have never seen such beauty! You are familiar with palaces, but this is my first glimpse of what it means to be rich."

Valentina smiled, thinking how mistaken Rosalan was. The Bedouin girl assumed that because Valentina had been raised in King Sancho's palace, she was unimpressed with Ramiff's palace. There was a world of difference between the two. At home in Navarre, food was still served on slabs of stale bread called trenchers, and not upon the golden serviceware Valentina knew was the custom of the wealthy here in the east. Even the rich woven carpets were unknown

144

in Navarre, or even in the whole of Europe. Sancho had a fortress, Ramiff had a palace.

In Navarre the floors were still strewn with grasses and rushes cut from the fields, and changed twice a year when the odor became too much for even the least fastidious. Tapestries and carpets brought from the East were used as decorations on the drafty walls. Even the wondrous leaded paned windows, so familiar here in the Holy Land, were a marvel and a rarity in Europe. Napur and all its riches were a fable, a dream, inconceivable to anyone who had not traveled to the East and seen for themselves the boundless riches.

Valentina also knew that medical science and astrology and astronomy and mathematics were far advanced here in the land of the Saracens. As she looked about, Valentina caught herself thinking, "And the Europeans call them heathens! They are so far advanced they have left us centuries behind them."

Following behind the old man Mohab, Valentina and Rosalan were met by a huge black man. Mohab turned to them. "I leave you here. Beyond are the chambers of the harem, and as you know, entrance is forbidden by men. I go to report to the emir. I've no doubt you will be sent for later this evening. Allah go with you." Mohab bowed his salute.

The burly man who led them through the high wide doors into the harem was dressed in a turban of gold cloth and a short, sleeveless jacket of the same fabric that exposed his broad black chest. His legs were clad in bright red pantaloons that were nipped tightly at the ankle to expose his jewel-studded slippers with exaggerated points that curled back toward his ankle.

Valentina took several quick steps to come abreast of him. "Where are the other women from the caravan? Why are they not being brought into the palace?"

The black eunuch looked down at her and smiled, his large white teeth gleaming in his shiny face. "You are the only women who are to stay in Napur. The others travel on to other places to join the harems of several sheikhs. They are gifts from Emir Ramiff."

He turned away from her and discouraged further questions.

Valentina cast Rosalan a look which bespoke her gratitude that the fates had kept them together. Walking behind the eunuch, Valentina and Rosalan continued to look in awe at the luxurious appointments of Ramiff's palace. The floors were of colored marble fitted together and laid in an intricate design. The same motif was carried to the walls, where jeweled colors of red and blue accented with gold depicted ancient Saracen warriors mounted upon nimble-legged chargers.

The corridor took a sharp turn to the left, and even before the red-pantalooned eunuch opened the wide teakwood doors, Valentina and Rosalan could hear women's laughter coming from within.

Stepping through the doorway into the harem was like passing over the threshold into another world. The interior was a soft pastel blue and hung with silken draperies of white and yellow that billowed softly in the warm breeze filtering through the garden archways. The fragrance of perfume and exotic oils scented the air, and one of the women strummed idly on a stringed instrument. In the center of the room was an oval pool of clear, fresh water, and about its perimeters were rich cushions and low divans. Rugs carpeted the mosaic tiled floors, and their colors were repeated in the high, vaulted ceiling.

Suddenly Valentina and Rosalan found themselves surrounded by the women of Ramiff's harem, chattering gaily and asking them questions. Valentina continued her lie that she was Circassian. Here in the land of Islam Valentina knew that once a girl reached puberty, girlhood was put behind; but Valentina saw that most of the harem were younger than she or Rosalan, and all were beautiful. It seemed to Valentina that their backgrounds were as diversified as their skin colors; from the pale ocher of the Oriental to the rich black of the African. Valentina saw that the women numbered less than twenty, and this surprised her, for she had always heard that the harems of sultans held no less than one hundred lovely women.

As the girls buzzed around asking questions and making them welcome, Valentina lifted her eyes and saw a tall, willowy red-haired woman coming in from the garden. The woman seemed a good deal older than the others, but she was no less beautiful. Her eyes were blackened by kohl, accentuating their feline slant and her high cheekbones. As she walked she appeared to float, her silver-threaded caftan flowing about her.

Silence fell over the chattering women as they stepped aside to make way for the red-haired woman. "I am Dagny," she said imperiously, penetrating Rosalan and Valentina each with a cold, gray-eyed stare.

Inexplicably Valentina experienced an urgent desire to turn and run—away from this palace with its boundless luxuries, away from the chattering congress of women, but most of all, away from Dagny, whose gray eyes seemed able to peer past the surface to the secrets Valentina carried in her heart.

But run she could not. Instead, Valentina stood tall and faced Dagny. "I am Valentina," she said, her voice steady and unwavering. She saw that Dagny was near the age of thirty; fine lines fanned out from the corners of her eyes and at the sides of her painted mouth. The rice powder the woman used had accumulated in these shallow webbings and gave her a masklike, sinister expression.

"Valentina, is it? An unusual name. Did I hear you say you are a Circassian? I never heard of a Circassian by that name," Dagny mused, running the tip of her tongue across her rouged lips. Turning to the others, Dagny wrinkled her nose. "This one, this . . . Valentina, is much in need of a bath! She smells as if she slept with the camels! Now!" She clapped her hands and watched smugly as the girls of the harem hastened to do her bidding. It was obvious that Dagny ruled the harem with a jealous iron hand.

Two girls, Elan and Shidara, overtook the duty of seeing to Valentina's bath. Rosalan was led away and was attended to on the other side of the room. Although she didn't protest being separated from Valentina, Rosalan looked over her shoulder and cast her friend a warning glance which implied that Dagny could be dangerous, be careful! They took Valentina behind a three-sided screen, ornamented with embroidered panels depicting outrageously plumed birds, and stripped her of her garments. Dagny's voice came over the screen. "When you have divested Valentina of those rags, take them out to be burned! We will not have ourselves infested with lice!"

Valentina's face burned. She knew she carried the scent of the camel she had been riding, but her rigorous personal hygiene was *not* inviting to lice!

Elan hurried out through the garden doors with the small bundle of Valentina's clothes. "Bring the girl out here," Dagny commanded. Valentina wrapped a length of toweling about herself and stepped out from behind the screen. The expressions on the faces of the other girls were fearful as Dagny pushed Valentina to her knees. She ran her long, red-tipped fingers down the length of Valentina's dark hair. "Vermin are always a problem in these climates. It would be a shame if I should find evidence of lice in your lovely hair, Valentina," Dagny said smoothly. "Then I would be forced to have your head shaved."

Valentina's eyes drifted back to the girls and noticed that one girl's head was completely draped. From the fright and sadness in her eyes Valentina knew that Dagny had "found" lice in her hair. Refusing to suffer the same fate, Valentina threw off Dagny's hand and stood to face her. "Touch one hair on my head and it will be the last thing you ever do! I was purchased with my hair intact, and I intend to be presented to the emir still in possession of it!"

"So the Circassian has spirit!" Dagny said approvingly, touching a fingertip beneath Valentina's chin and trailing it down her smooth skin to the hollow between her breasts. Dagny's eyes glittered and her teeth bit into her lower lip. The familiarity of the gesture reminded Valentina of Berengaria, and her flesh crawled. Not again! Never again!

Valentina turned sharply on her heel to prepare for her bath, when Dagny's hand seized her shoulder and spun her about. "You will listen to me well, Valentina. I am mistress of Ramiff's harem and you are in my charge; my word is law and you will obey me!" Dagny's face whitened in fury. "Now wash the stink from your body." With a vicious shove Dagny pushed Valentina into the pool's scented water.

Breaking the water's surface, gasping for air, Valentina retaliated by grasping Dagny's leg and pulling her into the pool. Like two spitting cats, they went at each other with a show of claws, tearing at one another's hair, fingers stretching toward eyes, lips curled back over snarling teeth. Dagny, being taller, had the advantage, but Valentina was quick and agile. The water churned with their struggles and the girls shrieked in support of the newcomer.

Valentina's waist-length hair was a handicap, and Dagny grasped a handful, dragging Valentina to the bottom of the pool. Water rushed into her nostrils and down her throat; she held her breath till she thought her lungs would burst. Dagny became overconfident and allowed Valentina to slip out of her grasp just far enough to become vulnerable. Valentina seized the opportunity and clutched the redhead about the knees, upsetting her balance and pulling her under. Dagny went down with a choking yowl and gurgling bubbles.

Valentina's fingers found Dagny's coronet of braids and hauled her to the surface. Dagny sputtered, the fight gone out of her. The black kohl around her eyes ran down her cheeks, and the scarlet rouge on her lips had smeared, lending to her mouth a hideous grotesqueness. "Now *you* hear me and hear me well, Dagny," Valentina said hoarsely in a tight-lipped rage. "I will never obey you unless it pleases me to do so. You will never be my mistress and I shall never be your servant!" Valentina shook the terrified Dagny until the redhead's teeth rattled. "I have known a woman such as you and I will never fall victim again! If you should ever touch my person, even by chance, you will regret it to the end of your days!" She pushed Dagny to the edge of the pool. "Take her out. I wish to complete my bath!"

Valentina completed her bathing in peace. Dagny had retreated to an anteroom to repair the damages, while Elan and Shidara attended Valentina. Her long hair was washed and rinsed until it squeaked. Then they took her into the garden where the sun could dry it, and brushed the thick, heavy locks into a becoming style. The top and sides were pulled back from her face into a sleek topknot, while the back was allowed to hang free in a shining cascade down her back. To complete her toilette, she was anointed with rare perfume. Shidara brought forth an array of garments and finally selected a jacket of green silk edged with gold braid and a low-slung circular skirt of six layers of silk gauze, each layer trimmed with the same gold braid. Soft green sandals of leather were fitted on her feet, and Elan hung strands of fine gold chains around her neck and bangles of gilt on her arms. At last Valentina met with their giggling approval: she was ready to meet Emir Ramiff.

Rosalan peeked timidly from behind a yellow silken drape. Coyly she stepped toward Valentina, her gold skirt rustling seductively. "How do you like me! Am I beautiful? Is this palace not beautiful?" Arching her arms gracefully over her head, Rosalan pirouetted across the floor.

Valentina laughed, her voice rich and deep. "I like you, you are beautiful."

Rosalan stopped in midstep. "And the paláce?"

Valentina glanced around, looking toward the screen behind which Dagny made the repairs to her appearance. "Beautiful but decadent."

"Be wary of that she-devil, Valentina. I thought she would have you killed. She still may see to it."

"Be still," Valentina soothed. "She will do no such thing. Aside from her haughty attitude, Dagny knows her place and would not jeopardize it by offending the emir with my death."

Rosalan peered deeply into Valentina's eyes. "There are worse things than death, Valentina, mark my words. Dagny bears watching!"

They were interrupted by the same black eunuch who had led them through the palace to the harem. His eyes held humor and a peculiar tinge of respect as he spoke to Valentina. "I am to take you to the emir. He wishes to meet the slave girl who fought like a tiger upon the auction block."

Valentina's eyes narrowed. So soon? What would the emir be like? What would he demand of her? Rosalan cast her a meaningful look. Be brave, her expression said, but be pleasing! Do not fight him, he is your master. It is to him we must look for our security and our fate!

Finding herself incapable of reassuring Rosalan, Valentina turned quickly on her softly slippered feet and followed the eunuch to meet her master, hoping beyond all hope that he would be kind.

Chapter Eleven

Valentina was led down a marble corridor and into a vast room which opened onto a balcony overlooking the city. Rich carpets adorned the floors and hung from the high stone walls. A gold throne-like chair rested at the far end of the room with mounds of colorful pillows scattered around its base. Valentina was led to the center, where she was told to kneel before the emir. She did as instructed, her head high. The old man on the throne looked her over appreciatively and motioned her to stand. "Your beauty pleases me," he said in a voice as dry and cracked as old leather. "Your name?"

"Valentina, master," she said huskily.

"Your name is as beautiful as you are," the emir said gallantly. "You will be a welcome addition to my harem. I'm pleased with my purchase."

"Kadi," Valentina said hesitantly, referring to Ramiff by the honored title of "teacher." "May I speak?" The old emir frowned at her words but nodded.

Valentina licked dry lips and lowered her head to her knees. "Please, please don't send me back to the harem. I would do anything, anything you want, if only you don't send me there. I would scour these marble floors till they glisten, I would work in the stables. I can read and write. I'll read to you, I will learn to care for you, to anticipate your every need even before you yourself realize your wish. Have pity on me, I beg of you."

Emir Ramiff was puzzled. What manner of woman was this? "Speak to me with truth, child. Let there be no lies between us. You will be happy and content and live well." The old emir clasped his hands together and watched the girl. Valentina lifted her eyes, and the honesty Ramiff found there startled him.

Kneeling before him, Valentina raised her head proudly and held her shoulders straight. The green on her jacket was reflected in her eyes, and Ramiff's glance fell on her graceful neck and the warm ivory tone of the flesh between her breasts. "Tell me!" he commanded.

"Kadi, your humble servant has no liking for the society of women. Even in the short while I was there I noticed . . . relationships between your women . . ."

"Ah!" Ramiff interrupted, his aged face crumpling into lines of amusement. "They merely entertain themselves; make nothing of it."

"I must make something of it," Valentina insisted quietly. "I have been at the mercy of a woman who made advances to me, whose fingers reached out to touch me, whose lustful glances made my flesh crawl.

I would rather die," she said, her voice a soft purr of resolution.

Ramiff experienced a sharp stab of apprehension. Would one so lovely actually consider taking her own life? He leaned forward and peered into her unwavering aquamarine eyes and saw there the answer. Something about this girl struck a chord in Ramiff's heart. How sad it would be if her obvious intelligence were wasted, and how delightful it would be to always have her loveliness within his failing sight.

"You say you can read and write?"

"Yes, Kadi. And I speak many languages. I was taught alongside Queen Beren—" Too late, she realized her mistake.

"They said you were Circassian!" the old emir said sharply.

"I lied. I had no wish to die," Valentina said simply. "My dark hair made the lie believable. I was a noblewoman in Queen Berengaria's entourage. We grew up together."

"So you are an Engleysi. A noblewoman! How came you to be here?"

Valentina related her story, ending with, "Christian or Moslem, one does what one must to survive."

"All of what you have said to me has the ring of truth," the emir said thoughtfully. "Is this so?"

"I have spoken the truth."

"Then I shall tell you a truth. I am an old man, as you can see. I am king of this province and control all matters of state. My eyesight is failing me by the day. It will not be long before I can see nothing. My heart pounds in my chest so that I can barely catch my breath. One day soon I shall go to join Allah. I have spoken of this to no one save you. You shall be by my side. You will do as I instruct you. You must give me your loyalty and your allegiance. There must be no lies between us. If you agree to these terms, then we shall begin immediately. One other thing," he said, raising a gnarled old hand. "There will be times when visitors of state will arrive here for negotiations. If they desire a little pleasure you will oblige them, is

153

that understood?" Valentina nodded humbly, her eyes thankful. The old emir clapped his hands and a eunuch appeared. "Have Mohab sent in here to me."

Valentina stood, her eyes wary and full of misgiving. What was he going to do with her? What did he have in mind?

"You're little more than a child," the emir said, his voice full of what sounded to Valentina like surprise.

Valentina flinched at his words. If what he said were only true. How wonderful to be a child with no worries or fears. Those long-ago days when she played with Berengaria on equal terms were the happiest of her life. Her eyes were sober and lifeless when she answered the emir. "I am not a child, and I have not been a child for a long, long time. When one is a child, life is uncomplicated and happy. My life is, at this moment, complicated, and I am not happy. I know that you hold my fate in your hands, and there is nothing I can do about it."

"If given the chance, would you do something?" the emir asked craftily.

Valentina pondered the question a moment before replying. "But of course I would do something. I have a great desire to live, to survive, and I would fight for my life if I had to. Wouldn't you, if the situation were reversed?" she asked quietly.

Ramiff didn't answer for a moment. "Sit down, young woman; let me look at you. I detest to have a female tower over me. You need have no fear of me. I am not an ogre. Your eyes look upon an old man with crippled bones and eyesight that is failing. I have told you that before. Tell me, what could I do to you?"

"Perhaps you would do nothing by your own hand, but there are others who obey your commands," Valentina said, perching as if poised for flight on the stack of scarlet cushions Ramiff had arranged for her.

Ramiff frowned. "I have never killed a woman. None that I am aware of, at any rate. Is this what you fear? That I would take your life?" His faded old eyes watched her carefully as she suddenly relaxed against the colorful cushions. He could almost feel the loosening of her muscles and was puzzled.

"I believe you," Valentina said softly.

"Why?" the emir asked bluntly, chagrined at her quick response.

"Because what you say is true. You are an old man. I see the way your lips tremble and the way your hands shake. Your eyesight is failing and you must squint to see me. When one grows old, one has a tendency to mellow and be forgiving. I am truly sorry for your infirmities and wish there were something I could do to help you. I'm young and strong and my eyesight is keen."

"I am too old for a woman," the emir answered testily. "For now, all I have are my memories and my thoughts of Allah. Mohab sees to my welfare and takes care of me. He has been with me since we were children."

"Alas, he grows as old as you, Emir," Valentina said softly. "Since he entered this room, I have watched him as he waits on you. His hand is no longer steady. His eyesight is little better than yours. His legs are painfully crooked and he finds it difficult to walk. He doesn't want you to know this, and with your failing sight you fail to notice. It is a wonder he is able to function at all. It was a long, tiring journey from Damascus even for the young. Yet he made the journey, and without rest he is here to serve you."

"So I am inconsiderate of my servants, is that what you are telling me?" Ramiff scowled.

"Ask Mohab for yourself. He returns with your tea."

"Mohab, is what this woman says true?" the old man demanded petulantly.

"She lies! All women lie," Mohab answered defensively, instantly fearful that the days of his usefulness to Ramiff were ended.

"Forgive me, old friend," Ramiff said compassionately. "I did not notice. Forgive me my demands and my wrath. I am an old fool to think that I could grow old and you would remain nimble and youthful enough to see to my needs." He laid a gnarled old hand on Mohab's arm, and tears glistened in his eyes.

"A twinge now and then, it means nothing," Mohab said quietly.

"A twinge, eh? If your twinges are like mine, may Allah take you quickly, my friend." He fixed a glistening eye on Valentina and demanded to know what else her keen eyes saw.

Feeling more secure in the knowledge that Ramiff was a loving and compassionate man, she answered softly, "Many things. Your great palace is in disrepair. As a matter of fact, it is filthy. Your servants are lax and insolent. I see Mohab's working many hours to manage things has been insufficient."

The emir bowed his head. "May Allah forgive me, but I must ask you, a woman, for assistance. My heart hears truth in your words, and my own people have played me for a foolish old man. They see I cannot even keep my house in repair. Tell me, what should be done?"

"It is not for me to say," Valentina answered. "I am grateful to be alive. Beyond this I have no thoughts."

"Come here, child," Ramiff called kindly. Valentina slipped from her seat of cushions and knelt before him. Tears gathered in her eyes when he laid his hand on her head. It had been so long since she had felt a gentle touch that the threatened tears welled and overflowed. "You have no cause for worry. Mohab will take you to a room far from the harem. You will be safe and no harm will come to you. You have my word. Go now; my bones ache and my eyes cry for sleep. We'll talk later when I wake. Mohab, take this lovely woman to the apartments across from mine."

Mohab stirred himself painfully and got to his feet. He motioned Valentina to follow. The old emir cackled delightedly. "I saw that, I saw how painful it was for you to get to your feet. And you say the woman lies! May Allah snatch you baldheaded when you go to meet him, you old fox."

Mohab looked at Valentina and grinned, showing short, stained teeth. "I thought he would never notice."

156

"You misjudge the emir, Mohab. He knew long before I mentioned it. He had no desire to upset you by allowing you to know that he recognized your pain."

Mohab shrugged. What manner of woman was this? She seemed to read one's mind. Women, he thought sourly, were the ruination of all men. He grinned again. If one had to be ruined, at least it would be pleasant to be ruined by one as beautiful as Valentina.

"Mohab, I could mix some herbs for you in a tea that would make your pain a little easier to bear. My father was a physician, and I learned many things from him as I grew up."

Mohab's eyes lit. "Would you do this for the emir also? His twinges are worse than mine."

"But of course. I would be honored to help."

Mohab trotted back to the emir's quarters after he situated Valentina in a lavish apartment overlooking the gardens. He shook the emir's shoulder and spoke gently. "She is safe in the apartment across from yours. Listen to me, Ramiff. She says she knows much about herbs because her father was a physician and she learned at his knee. She says she can make our twinges less painful."

"Allah be praised," the emir said happily. "I would give up my kingdom to be free of this damnable pain. Sit, my friend, and we will talk. I will talk," he amended. "You will listen."

Mohab nodded and lowered himself gratefully to the scarlet cushions and waited patiently till the emir put his thoughts in order.

"I heard many things in the woman's voice. I heard fear and I heard hope and compassion. My eyes saw a beautiful woman who has been abused and misused. I saw a slender back that is straight and a will that is unbending. She has eyes that are truthful and loyal."

"You saw all of those things, and yet you profess to have overlooked my painful, crooked legs," Mohab snorted indignantly.

"One sees what one wants to see, no more, no less," Ramiff said gruffly. "I apologized, did I not? I don't think she should be placed in the harem. I would like to have her read to me. I find her pleasant, and her voice soothes me, not like your grumbling tones. And," he added peevishly, "I would wager she wouldn't cheat if we were to throw dice. You cheat, Mohab."

"It is you who cheat, Ramiff," Mohab said defensively. "Already I have won Napur from you eleven times!"

"And eleven times I won it back!"

"Yes, but by cheating. But I allowed you to cheat because it makes you happy," Mohab said magnanimously.

"And that is still another thing," Ramiff said harshly. "Where is that game from the Far East? I want to play something different."

"It should arrive any day now," Mohab soothed.

"And when it does, will you know how to play? I know how tricky you are. You say there are two sets of rules, one for me and one for you. You think me a fool!"

"No, Ramiff, it is you who make the rules to suit yourself," Mohab laughed, knowing the emir enjoyed baiting him. Of late Ramiff had little pleasure in his life. If badgering gave him pleasure, it was fine with Mohab.

"Well?" Ramiff demanded.

Mohab sighed. He knew the expected response by heart. "I cheat and you are the honest player. Eleven times I cheated you to win Napur, and eleven times you regained it honestly. I always make my own rules, and I make them so I can cheat."

"May Allah have mercy on you," Ramiff said piously. "You see, confession is good for the soul. In a little while you will feel so good that you will want to play a game of dice."

"You are correct as usual," Mohab laughed.

"Now that that little matter is taken care of, let us get back to the woman. As I said, she pleases me. What do you think of taking her in here and allowing her to help you? She says she can read and write. She could be our nursemaid," the emir said happily.

"She could wait on both of us and make our last days happy. With certain conditions, of course," he added hastily. "When I wake from my afternoon rest, I will test her."

"How will you do that?"

The emir gave an elaborate sigh. "It is a simple matter. We'll have her read the reports you have drawn up. I want to see if she'll tell me if you made any errors. Then we'll play dice with her."

"What if she doesn't know how to play?"

"Then, Mohab, I will teach her. If she cheats, we'll send her to the harem. If she's honest, we will keep her here to help us and let her assume some of your duties."

"How can you teach her to play honestly when you don't know how yourself?" Mohab asked testily.

"I will think of something," Ramiff grumbled. The two old men glanced at each other and laughed. "You see, Mohab, Allah is pleased with my decision. I can tell by the way we feel better already."

Mohab rolled his eyes and looked heavenward. He was too tired to argue, and his knee joints were paining him more by the hour.

Seating himself comfortably on a low, soft divan while the emir rested in his high bed, Mohab massaged his painful knees and felt tears prick his eyelids. For a moment the pain lessened, and he prayed to Allah to take the emir first. He knew in his heart that the aging old man would die on the spot if he went to join Allah before him. Perhaps the woman was the answer. Ramiff seemed to have an uncanny sense about such things. Mohab offered a small prayer to Allah that she wouldn't cheat in the game of dice.

When Ramiff awoke, Mohab went to fetch Valentina. She watched his slow, painful progress down the corridor and suggested that they go to the kitchens so that she could brew some herbal tea for both him and the emir.

Mohab was only too glad to agree, and escorted Valentina with a flourish, chattering all the way about the old emir and his painful joints.

In the ample-sized kitchen, Mohab watched in delight as Valentina dug her long, slender fingers in first one crock and then another, filling a small pot with various herbs. She added water and waited patiently for the mixture to come to a boil. Carefully she poured the scalding liquid and replaced the lid of the pot.

"Tell the cooks to keep this tightly covered. The longer the brew stands, the more beneficial it will be."

Mohab followed her orders and led her from the kitchen, the teapot clasped securely in his old hands.

Back in the emir's apartments, Valentina poured the tea into delicate cups and handed one to Ramiff and one to Mohab, who took it graciously, entirely convinced that he would be able to romp and run through the great palace as soon as he had consumed it.

"In a little while you will begin to feel the benefits of the brew," Valentina assured them. "You must drink it several times a day, and especially before retiring for the night."

"While we sip this fragrant tea, perhaps you would be kind enough to read to us," the emir said. "Mohab, fetch some of the reports from my desk."

Valentina rose to her feet. "Tell me which reports you wish and I will get them. You should stay off your legs as much as possible," she said to Mohab.

The gentleman nodded spiritedly and gave her instructions to find the ledgers. He decided he liked being waited upon, and the woman had his vote of confidence as of this moment.

The heavy ledger in her hand, Valentina returned and sat down cross-legged on the crimson cushions. She opened the dusty book and began to read the various entries. From time to time she frowned, and the emir watched her as she made notations in the columns of figures.

The tea worked its calming magic, and both men relaxed and listened to her low, husky voice as she read off dates and figures. Emir Ramiff interrupted her once to ask a question. "Your tone tells me something is amiss. Are the figures inaccurate?"

160

Valentina chose her words carefully before she replied. "It is difficult to read some of the entries."

"There is no need to spare my feelings," Mohab said quietly. "At times my fingers do not work as quickly as my head, and at other times my head works faster than my fingers."

"It is a small matter and can be rectified," Valentina said, making a notation. "Did you do all this yourself, Mohab?"

"Ramiff trusted no one save myself," Mohab answered proudly.

"It is too much to expect of one person to do all this and not make an error."

"You old fox, she is defending you," Ramiff said sharply. "Thank the woman properly."

Mohab nodded his thanks.

"You must be more careful in the future," Valentina said, "for if you are not, the next time the sultans come for grain they will think they have more coming to them than they do. So far," she said thoughtfully, "the shortages are all in the sultans' behalf, especially Saladin's." Her head bent over the ledger, she failed to see the roguish wink that Ramiff bestowed on Mohab.

"I have had enough of these dull reports. Would you care to join us in a game of dice?"

Valentina readily agreed, a smile on her face.

"Do you know how to play?" Mohab asked.

"No, but I'm willing to learn."

The emir was in his glory as he began to explain a rather intricate set of rules. Valentina frowned. "But that sounds so complicated and tedious. Would it not be simpler just to set the goal at one hundred points and shake the dice till each player reaches the highest number in a determined number of rolls?"

"I knew it!" shouted the emir, shaking his fist in the air. "Two sets of rules, one for you and one for me. Now I suppose you're going to tell me that there is another set of rules for women!"

"I would not tell you any such thing." Mohab scowled. "We will all play just the way she said. What will be the prize?"

"I have the perfect prize," said Ramiff, looking at Mohab with a crafty light in his eyes. "The bells."

Ramiff explained this to Valentina. "Mohab ordered a box of silver bells with the intention of tying them upon my slippers so he could hear where I walked. Now I know, Mohab, that your hearing is leaving you and you can't hear my footfalls. Bells on my feet! When I go to Allah, you can festoon my body with bells to alert him to my coming, but not before then."

Valentina suppressed a smile as the two old men badgered each other; she marveled at the way Napur had been governed.

"I only wanted the bells because you have become a sneaky old man," Mohab complained. "You think you can roam the corridors at night and find your way back without injury."

"Bah! What you're saying is, you wanted me to roam the palace with bells on my slippers so my entire household would think I'm a lunatic!"

Valentina interceded. "The box of bells belongs to whoever reaches one hundred points first." She watched as the two men began to play with a vengeance, each trying to outcheat the other. Since it was Mohab who was keeping score, she offered no complaints.

Two hours and three cups of tea later, the emir was leading the game with a rousing eighty-seven points, with Mohab close behind with eighty-five. Valentina had only thirty-seven and was being soundly trounced. When the emir announced a short time later that he was the winner, Valentina smiled at the knowledge that he had won the bells. It was a deceitful victory, and she knew it.

Mohab waited for the emir to nod his head at her small victory, and he correctly interpreted Ramiff's meaning and smiled happily. Now he too could wait for Allah and have a major portion of his responsibility to Ramiff lifted from his shoulders.

Back in her own quarters, Valentina pondered the looks that had passed between the two old men. They were up to something. Whatever it was, she knew instinctively that they meant her no harm. In the short time she had been in their company she found them likable and charming and was pleased to know she could serve them well and do some small things to ease their aging pains.

The days raced into weeks as Valentina went to the emir's lavish apartments every morning and read to him. She waited patiently for the day when he would tell her he wanted to talk to her, but for now she bided her time, making the two old men as happy as she could. They seemed to wait for her each morning, and their lined and tired faces would light with smiles as she entered the room with their tea. She knew that when Ramiff was ready to tell her what he planned to do with her, he would do so, and not a moment before. For now, it was sufficient that she was well fed with a roof over her head and that there were no threatening soldiers about to force themselves upon her.

In the afternoon they would play a game of dice, and when the old men napped she altered and corrected the ledgers. Another day or two and all the ledgers would be in order, and then she would have nothing to occupy her time.

She had just closed the next-to-the-last ledger when Mohab literally ran into her room, flourishing a large box. "It's the game from the Orient. It just arrived this very moment. Ramiff!" he called boisterously. "It has come! It's here! Come, we will begin the new game!"

Ramiff seated himself in a deep throne-like chair and waited impatiently as Mohab removed a multi-colored board depicting squares and rectangles and hundreds of embossed tiles. "Well, do you know how to play? Let me see it! Is this what you're making all this fuss about? It's too small!" he exclaimed in disappointment.

Mohab was crestfallen. Ramiff was correct. It was too small. With their eyesight being what it was, they could never make the proper moves.

Valentina eyed the colorful pieces and said to the

emir, "May I offer a suggestion? There are many artisans here in your palace. Why couldn't one of them make a large table board and engrave larger tiles? That way the table could stay right here in your room and not have to be moved. The tiles could be carved from jet or ivory, just like these, but on a larger scale."

"Now why couldn't you think of that, you old fool?" Ramiff snarled at Mohab. "Does it take a woman to show you are losing your brains as well as your youth?"

"May I remind you, o mighty emir," Mohab began soberly, and Valentina winced. She knew that whenever Mohab became overly respectful to Ramiff, a stinging gibe usually followed.

"Remind me of what?" Ramiff grumbled. "That it took a woman to solve your problem?"

"Remind you, Ramiff, that as you yourself did not think of the solution, I, your humble servant, am not the only old fool who is losing his brains as well as his youth."

Ramiff's eyes nearly popped from his head. "You insolent—" Suddenly he broke out into gales of laughter. "Do you know what I was about to say, Mohab?" Again he laughed, great roaring guffaws. "I was about to say 'insolent young pup'!"

Valentina laughed, and so did Mohab. They both joined Ramiff and laughed till their eyes watered.

"Do you know something else, Mohab?" Ramiff said tenderly, a softness in his voice that had not been there before. "I think it was the smartest thing you ever did, to purchase this woman at auction. She has brought new life and laughter to both of us, and I will never let her go."

Valentina's eyes watered again, but this time it was tears of gratitude that sparkled on her cheeks.

With the passage of time Valentina learned the ways of the palace. She was both loved and feared by all those in attendance on the aging emir. She guarded him jealously and saw to his every whim. She would wake him in the early hours of the morning with a bright smile and a bunch of wild grapes spar-kling with dew. As always, she would converse in her low, throaty voice, which he found so pleasing. Three months after her arrival at the palace, she was pre-paring the emir's bed for the night when he cried out for her to light the candles.

"Kadi," she said softly. "They are all lit. What is it? Can you see nothing?"

"A shadow here and there," the old man said halt-ingly. "I thought I would be prepared when it hap-pened. I don't like the dark," he said petulantly.

"Let me help you," Valentina said quietly. "You need have no fear of the dark. I'm here, and I shall stay near you at all times. Don't fear the darkness—at times it can be a friend." She led him to the high bed. "I will be your eyes," she said humbly. "I shall never leave your side, you have my promise." Ramiff patted her hand and fell back against the mound of pillows. "Kadi, I have a favor I wish to ask of you. Will you grant it?"

"Why do you ask?" the old emir said testily. "You know I do as you say. You ask as a formality. What is it?" He pretended annoyance.

"Rosalan, the slave who was purchased in Da-mascus with me for the harem. May I have her here to help me? I shall need someone."

"Another woman," the old man said tartly. "Soon I'll be surrounded by women. What will Allah say when I meet him?"

Valentina laughed softly. "That you are a good and wise man. What else could he say?"

"Where will you spend the night?"

"Here in this room, on the floor. I told you I would never leave your side."

"Valentina," the old voice croaked. "Can you carry on? Will you be able to manage all these affairs of state as I have instructed you?"

"But of course. Mohab has taught me well. He says that I do a better job than he ever did," Valentina laughed.

"And Mohab is right. Tell him to send the woman

Rosalan to you. I grant it. Does this mean that I shall be confined to this miserable bed for my last days?"

"It means no such thing," Valentina said firmly. "You shall move around all you wish, and I will be at your side. When there are visitors, I shall arrange for you to sit in the shadows, and no one will notice. Rosalan will be invaluable to us."

"We shall do as we agreed. There is always one who wishes to take over the reins." Ramiff referred to his son Homed, who was now an acting general under Saif ad Din and had been sent by Ramiff, under protest, to his duties in the war. The old man held Homed in contempt and knew him to be a power-seeking reprobate who would deplete the treasury of Napur and betray his people. Ramiff settled back against his pillows and thanked Allah that this girl who had become so dear to him would not have Homed's jealousies and treacheries to contend with as long as Ramiff was alive. As a favor to the old emir, Saif ad Din had assigned Homed a post far to the north. If Ramiff should die, Valentina's freedom had been arranged and she would be returned to her own people. The old man felt guilty keeping Valentina at his side when it was in his power to grant her freedom. But the girl had never asked this of him, and he was loath to face the end of his days without her tender ministrations.

"I think what we shall do is have me remain here in my private quarters. This way, when I am confined to my bed, no one will know, and they will become used to my withdrawal. Do you agree?"

"As you wish, Kadi."

"My days are numbered, Valentina. I have grown weaker. I didn't want you to know."

"I knew," Valentina said simply. "You lean a little heavier on my arm, you eat less, you walk less. You can't hide it from me."

"I thought so," the emir grumbled. "I can't keep anything from you. Talk to me so that I may sleep."

"What would you like to talk about?" Valentina asked.

"You. And none of your tricks! Every time I ask you to talk, you manage to turn everything around, and I do the talking and you do the listening. I want to know about you. You talk to me this evening," he said sternly.

"Kadi," Valentina said softly, "there is nothing to tell. I have led a simple life and have nothing to reveal. You, on the other hand," she said impishly, "have led a wild and colorful life."

"Tell me!" Ramiff said firmly. Valentina sighed. "Tell me how you managed to get yourself whipped. How is it that you didn't talk your way out of that as you did with me for the harem?"

Valentina laughed. "The queen had me flogged because she thought one of her lovers bedded me."

"Have you ever had a lover, Valentina?" Ramiff anticipated her answer to be in the negative, and Valentina did not dispute it. She knew the old man had come to care for her, and she had no wish to disturb him with knowlege of a long-passed injury.

"Why? A beautiful woman like you. I don't understand."

Valentina laughed throatily. "Before one can lie with a man, one has to be asked. I haven't been asked."

The old emir roared. "You speak the truth, child. Did you not explain to your queen that what she said was untrue?"

"I tried, but she chose not to believe me. The man in question was her lover—a Moslem."

"Treason!" Ramiff shouted hoarsely.

"Yes, treason. She didn't care, and the man . . . he thought of his pleasure, I'm sure. How many men can boast they bedded the queen of England?"

"Who was this daring man?" the emir questioned.

"Paxon, sultan of Jakard, first general to Saladin."

"Ah, your voice turns to honey when you speak of the man. What does he mean to you?"

"Nothing," Valentina said defensively. "What could he mean to me? He's a Moslem and I am a Christian.

167

I helped him in his . . . affair with the queen, and that's all there was to it."

"I have the feeling that there is something you aren't telling me. I don't say you lie, but you evade me."

"So you will pick at me till I tell you, is that it?" Valentina asked fondly. "Very well. The sultan kissed me. I think the queen observed it and mistakenly thought I was also bedding him. That's why she had me beaten."

"And what sort of feelings did you have when the sultan kissed you?" the emir persisted.

"Kadi, that is a personal matter. I have no wish to discuss it."

"And why not? You know everything there is to know about me! I entrust my empire to you, and you won't tell me how you feel about a kiss. I want to know. Remember, we have truth between us."

"I knew from the moment I looked into his eyes that he was a man who would demand the ultimate from a woman. Her body and her soul. Now, tell me about the time you rode into the desert with only a handful of men and single-handedly wiped out the caravan of bandits and stole all their gold after you killed the horses and set the caravan to a smoking fire. I love that story!"

"There's nothing left to tell; you just told it to yourself. You even take that pleasure from me," he said grumpily.

"Then, how about the story of when you and Saladin stole the nine women from Emir Noraf's harem and locked them in yours? Tell me how you bedded all of them, and don't leave anything out, not even about the one who got away from you."

"Leave me!" Ramiff shouted. Valentina laughed and walked to the wide windows that overlooked the palace courtyard, gazing down at the lush gardens enveloped in the warm night. She would make all the arrangements tomorrow for her new role as personal attendant to the old emir. He was right, he had not many days left. Would she be able to do as she had promised him? Could she save Napur from his son, the power-hungry Homed?

Valentina looked longingly down upon Ramiff's city, the city he had helped to create and to free from the long bondage under the hands of his uncle, Marduk.

Ramiff had been a young boy when his father, then the emir of Napur, died, leaving him in the care of his own brother, Marduk. Marduk was the mirror opposite of the dead emir. He was crafty and conniving and lusted for wealth and power. That he had been the second son, and by that accident of birth had lost the title to the throne of Napur, had always stirred a deep hatred in his heart. When Mohammed Jufin, Ramiff's father, was presented with a son, all hope of gaining the throne died for Marduk.

Throughout his boyhood Ramiff clung to the memory of his father and prayed for Allah to hasten the day when he himself would reach the age to manage the kingdom of Napur alone, without his uncle Marduk as acting regent.

Each day news reached his ears of Marduk's further injustice and injuries to his people. The taxes placed upon crops and property were exorbitant, far exceeding what the land was worth and certainly more than a hard-working peasant could afford to pay. Lawlessness became synonymous with the name of Napur. For healthy bribes villains and thieves could continue their business under the eye of the law. Houses of prostitution lined the streets. Gambling and murder were the order of the day, while respectable citizens were the victims.

Ramiff, with his boyhood friend Mohab, waited for the day when law would be reinstated in Napur. When at last that day drew near, Marduk plotted Ramiff's murder. It was Mohab who saved the young emir's life by keeping a wary eye on Marduk's movements and by handing out some healthy bribes of his own.

Strangely, during Ramiff's struggle to regain his throne, Marduk was discovered dead. Poisoned by his own hand, it was said. But there was no state funeral for Marduk; instead, his body was interred somewhere

169

on the plains, with little to mark the grave save a covering of stones.

Throughout the next few years Ramiff was busy restoring order and justice to his land. Now, when his death was imminent, he had still another enemy of the land to torment him. His own son, Homed. Ramiff would sigh when he thought of him. "So like my uncle," he would whisper, "greedy, insatiable, power-hungry. My beautiful Napur, to think it should come under the rule of a tyrant within one lifetime."

Touching his bent head, Valentina pledged a silent vow that she would do all in her power to help Ramiff save Napur from Homed. Tears glistened in her aquamarine eyes and spilled onto her smooth ivory cheeks. Yes, old man, she thought, sweet old man, your time to join Allah is near. And God help me when Allah takes you, for I have come to love you as a father.

A sob catching in her throat, Valentina fled the room, leaving Ramiff to his dreams of youth and a time when he had only his future before him.

Chapter Twelve

Emir Ramiff became resolved to his blindness. By day Valentina sat beside the old man and read or talked quietly of things that were and things that would be. By night, in the dim candlelit portion of Ramiff's room that she had assigned herself, she would read the official papers of the kingdom, making a note here or there, and stamp them with the emir's official seal. At times her eyes would grow weary, and Rosalan would snuff out the candle and gently lead her to her divan in the dimmer recesses of the emir's apartments. But Valentina always remained close enough so that if Ramiff cried out in the night she could be with him in seconds, murmuring soothing words of comfort or bathing his head with herb water.

One warm, sun-filled day Valentina and Rosalan had propped the emir upon a mound of satin pillows that were placed on the balcony overlooking the city. His discomfort was emphasized by his annoyance at his complete dependence on Valentina. "Why do you persist in this fruitless effort of saving my life?" he asked her. "I believe you would breathe life into my body if you could. You make me sit in the sun and eat these foods that are only fit for babes in arms. Why don't you allow me to take to my bed and wait for Allah?" he grumbled.

"Allah isn't ready for you yet, Kadi. I have no wish to see you die. And while there's life in my body, I will do everything possible to keep you beside me."

"Surrounded by women!" the old emir complained as his gnarled hand reached out to pat Valentina's. "What will Allah say when I arrive?"

"Kadi, have I not served you well? Have you a serious complaint about either Rosalan's treatment of you or mine?"

"Of course not," the emir said quietly. "You have treated me better than my own people, and for that I am grateful. Valentina," he whispered, "you must never, never allow anyone to know you are a Christian. When I am gone they will kill you, and Rosalan also. I cannot go to Allah with that on my mind."

"You need have no fear, Kadi. I will follow your instructions to the last letter. You must rest now, for I wish to talk with you. A messenger has sent a gift from Saladin. In a week Malik en Nasr will be here for a conference with you. Rosalan has gone to fetch the gift. Saladin says, in his missive, that he has matters of grave importance to discuss with you. We both know why he is coming and what he wishes."

"Saladin is like a son to me," Ramiff said sadly. "I wish I could look upon his face again, but it is not to be. My instructions stand. You will arrange the conference outside this room and leave this door ajar. I will listen, and, if necessary, you will send Saladin to the door and I will converse with him."

"Kadi," Valentina said, touching Ramiff's arm lightly, "all this becomes too involved. Hiding your infirmity from the servants is difficult enough. But from what I know of Saladin, he is not easily fooled."

"It must be done!" Ramiff shouted, his agitation causing his voice to quake. "Should that treacherous son of mine learn how close to death I am, he would return here to push me over the threshold! Homed is too much like his great-uncle Marduk." Ramiff curled his lips in fury. "He shares his greed and cares nothing for the people of Napur."

"Kadi, dear one," Valentina whispered. "It pains me to say this, and my heart is devoted to your purpose, but you yourself know that one day Allah will call your name. Then Homed will return and the result will be inevitable. Your last days should be spent in peace, preparation, and prayer. Do not deny yourself these things."

Ramiff's wizened face curved into a wry smile. "You are not the keeper of all my secrets, Valentina. I have a plan, and if I am successful, Napur will be safe from Homed. Now, what else have you discovered concerning Saladin's arrival?"

"He brings many soldiers and very little gold," Valentina said quietly.

"The gold matters little. My question is, Valentina, can you discuss the position of the Moslems who now hold Jerusalem? Will you be able to speak impartially, knowing that the Lionheart has pledged to regain the city and recapture his Holy Cross? By Allah, this shall not happen! Allah ascended into heaven from the Rock of Jerusalem, and no Christian will deny us Moslems our sacred shrine! Speak words of truth to me, Valentina. Can you conduct this council meeting and not give a hint to your birth? What I ask is something I do not take lightly. You must give me your word."

"I shall do as you expect of me. No one will know

that I am a Christian, and my birthright will not interfere with my conducting the council meeting."

This was not the first time Valentina realized the truth behind her words. Since coming to Napur and living under the guiding hand of Ramiff, she had learned much about the Moslem religion. It was this knowledge which had made her realize that a man's worship for his God was universal. Jerusalem was as much a part of the Islamic religion as it was for the Christians. Ramiff's feeling that the Moslems should not be shut out from their sacred shrines was just as strong as that which she had witnessed among the Christians and had experienced herself. The only answer for both worlds was peace. Peace, and a tolerance of different beliefs.

"What do you think Saladin is sending you?" she asked in a girlish whisper.

"Who knows? Something I don't need or want," the emir said testily. "Saladin is a remarkable man in many ways but remiss in others. I would like a basket of peaches, ripe, succulent peaches. I would like to eat them and feel the warm, sweet juice trickle down my chin. Perhaps he's bringing peaches." The old man closed his eyes in the warm sun.

"Perhaps," Valentina said softly. "I will arrange for the peaches." She looked down fondly at the emir and felt tears of inadequacy sting her eyes. He was right; if she could breathe life into his body, she would. How much longer could she keep him alive? Days, weeks, months?

A sound pricked at her ears as Rosalan came out on the balcony, a wicker basket in her arms. "The emir's gift from Saladin," she said.

"What is it? Did you open it?" Valentina questioned excitedly. Rosalan smiled but shook her head.

"What's this? What did you say?" the emir asked petulantly.

"Your gift from Saladin," Valentina said. "Shall I open it for you?"

"You're going to open it, anyway, so why must you continually ask my permission?" he replied tartly.

"What has the wily fox sent me? Hurry and tell me it is peaches!"

Valentina laughed. "Oh," she said softly. "How beautiful!"

"Well, is it peaches?" the emir asked querulously.

"Better than peaches, Kadi. It is a panther cub. A female, and pure white!"

"Your eyes must be playing tricks on you. There is no such thing as a white panther," Ramiff said testily. "I wanted peaches, and what does he send me? A bogus panther."

"I speak the truth, Kadi. She is pure white, an albino, and the most beautiful animal I have ever seen," Valentina crooned softly as she scratched the animal's soft white ears.

"Then she is yours. I give her to you," Ramiff said imperiously. "But," he warned snidely, "She can't be real. Saladin must have dipped her in something, for there is no such thing as a white panther. He always tries to trick me. He knows I love peaches," he continued to complain.

"You would truly give me this magnificent animal?" Valentina was fearful that the emir would change his mind.

"I said she was yours. Don't be surprised when the cat turns black like all the others. This is one of Saladin's tricks."

"Thank you, Kadi. I shall treasure her," she said humbly as she laid her head against the emir's dry cheek.

"I wanted peaches," he said, drifting off to sleep.

"Rosalan," Valentina said, "go below to the kitchens, talk with the cooks, and find out where you can get peaches. Ripe, pink peaches. Send someone to the bazaars, and don't return without them."

"Where will anyone get peaches at this time of year?" Rosalan questioned.

"I have no idea," Valentina said as she stroked the white cub.

"If anyone can obtain them, it is Ahmar. He knows

everything," Rosalan said with confidence. Quickly she turned to leave.

"Rosalan, stay a moment. I wish to speak with you." Valentina hastened over to Rosalan standing in the doorway and asked in a low voice that would not disturb the emir, "Who is this Ahmar of whom you speak so often?"

Rosalan's face flushed and she smiled shyly. "Ahmar is the guard of the harem, the captain of the guards who watch over the women."

Valentina perceived a coquettishness about her friend and waited for her to continue. Rosalan's attitude concerning this man was puzzling. She had always considered men a means of livelihood, never as objects of affection. This softness in Rosalan's voice and the shine in her black eyes were new to Valentina.

Suddenly Rosalan began to talk about this man Ahmar with an animation that made her already pretty face even lovelier. "Oh, Valentina, he is so wise, so strong! Yet there is a gentleness about him. And when he looks at me I feel all giddy inside. Oh, Valentina, he's so wonderful!"

Valentina's first emotion was happiness for Rosalan. Then a thought occurred to her. "A guard in the harem, you say?" Rosalan nodded. "But, Rosalan . . . I never thought that . . . that . . ."

"That a man in the harem is still a man. Is that what you are having difficulty saying?"

Valentina's expression told her this was so.

"There is much you do not know about life, Valentina." Rosalan giggled. She pulled Valentina through the doorway, out of earshot of the emir. "Valentina, whether a man is a true eunuch or not depends upon how old he was when they . . . castrated him. Ahmar was nearly in his twenties, and believe me, his manhood is not lost to him, only his ability to impregnate a woman."

"But he was made a guard of the harem. Surely no one knows that Ahmar is still . . . potent?"

"There are a few women who know his secret, but they will keep it to themselves. It would be their heads

175

if they admitted they had lain with anyone other than the emir, or anyone whom the emir had gifted with their pleasures. Never fear, Ahmar is safe. Even so, he is much too smart to lie with those cows in the harem. He only sought his pleasures outside the palace."

It took a moment for Valentina to digest these words. "Rosalan, you haven't told this man that I am a Christian, or what I have promised to Ramiff, have you?"

"No, Valentina, that is our secret, and I would never share it without your permission. Besides, I remember my mother warning me not to tell a man *everything* about yourself. It always pays to have an air of mystery." Rosalan left Valentina, a new lightness in her step. As Valentina looked after her, she prayed that Rosalan would heed her mother's advice. If Ahmar lied about his masculinity, he could well be lying about other matters as well. Valentina's father had given her advice, too. Beware the fly in the ointment, he had warned her. For Rosalan's sake, Valentina prayed that the fly was not Ahmar.

"Valentina, Ahmar has returned from the marketplace, and there were no peaches to be had," Rosalan said fretfully. "What will you do?"

"There must be peaches somewhere. I'll go to the bazaar." There was a note of panic in her voice. "I must find peaches for the emir! I promised that he would have them. I can't go back on my word without trying to find them."

Rosalan shrugged. If Valentina could make peaches materialize out of thin air, then so be it. All manner of strange things had been happening of late. A few peaches would not surprise her. "Would you like me to accompany you to the bazaar, or would you prefer it if Ahmar went with you?" she asked in a tone that clearly said that it made no difference who went with Valentina, they would not find any peaches anywhere.

"I'm convinced that Ahmar did not look in the right

places. Gold can buy anything. I promised Ramiff, and I'll not return unless I have at least tried. You may come with me, if you like. We'll show Ahmar that women cannot be deterred from their objective."

Rosalan shrugged again. She could see by the determined look on Valentina's face that she meant exactly what she said. She would find peaches if it was the last thing she did, and woe be to Ahmar when the elusive fruits materialized. "Do you wish to leave now, Valentina?"

"Immediately. The sooner we leave the quicker we return. Fetch a basket. No, get two. One for you and one for me. We'll get as many as we can carry so Ramiff can eat to his heart's delight."

Rosalan hurried off to fetch the baskets, an amused look in her eyes. Valentina actually believes that she will stroll through the bazaar and there will be baskets and baskets of peaches for her to choose from! Honestly!

Valentina and Rosalan weaved their way through the throngs in the bazaar as beggars clutched at their abas, begging for a coin. Valentina shrugged them off while perusing first one stall, then another, and still another in her search for peaches. The aroma of ripe cheese and flowers mingled with the odor of livestock and humanity.

"Why wouldn't you believe me when I told you there were no peaches to be found?" Rosalan asked petulantly.

"We have not yet covered the entire bazaar," Valentina said as she looked up at the glaring sun. When she lowered her eyes and blinked to adjust them, she heard the cry of a vendor.

"Peaches! Peaches! Ripe and succulent peaches! Fit for a king! Firm and delicious! Peaches! Peaches!" The merchant held out a plump, pink peach as he stood before Valentina. "Ah, lovely lady, see how firm and sweet they are. It's a beauty and equaled only by your own."

"You see," Valentina whispered to Rosalan. "Didn't

177

I tell you there would be peaches? One just had to look for them!"

Rosalan looked at the merchant in his white garb, his headdress billowing about him in the hot, errant wind off the desert. His expression showed his amusement, and in that one moment Rosalan realized he was no ordinary merchant. She watched as the man's sun-bronzed hand offered the peach to Valentina.

"We'll take all you have," Valentina said happily. "How much is your price?"

Rosalan groaned. Would Valentina never learn? She pulled on Valentina's sleeve and whispered, "Haggle. Remember how I taught you to haggle? Make no mention of price," she said sharply.

"For you, lovely lady, they are a gift. A beautiful fruit for a beautiful woman," the merchant said softly, his voice deep and intimate.

Valentina's eyes widened as she watched a luscious peach topple from the heaping basket and roll away. Her eyes fell to the soft, bark-colored boots that peeped out from beneath the man's flowing caftan. She had seen those boots before today! She raised her eyes and stared into laughing dark eyes. She became mesmerized, her breath catching in her throat as it had that day in Messina.

For that one brief moment time stood still as she continued to return his gaze. The hot sun was now a warm caress; the shrill cries of the vendors became soft words of nothingness. The vibrant colors whispered to her, and the hot, dry wind cloaked her in a softness she had never before experienced. Her heart thumped madly in her breast as she reached out to take the peach from his hand. Their fingers touched, and a current so strong, so forceful, made Valentina close her eyes in a remembered thrill of ecstasy.

Suddenly a babble of voices rang through the bazaar as a horde of tattered children raced past the over-crowded stalls. Rosalan pushed Valentina to safety, but not before she pulled the basket of peaches out of harm's way. When Valentina regained her composure, she was startled to discover that the dark-eyed vendor was gone.

"Now look what you've done!" Rosalan snapped, Valentina looked down at her hand and saw that the peach she had been holding was now a pulpy mass of trickling juice.

Her eyes were wild as she stood on a stool and raked the milling throngs. He was gone! The sun was again a hot, brutal mantle of heat, the shrill cries of the merchants fell tumultuously on her ears, and the persistent wind was torturous to her fair skin.

The baskets of peaches in their arms, Valentina and Rosalan fought their way through the jostling crowds. "It would be wise if neither of us questioned the other as to where these fruits came from," Rosalan said in a nervous voice.

Valentina smiled. "Let us just say it is a taste of eternity." She shivered as she recalled the vendor's piercing gaze and incredible touch. Was he the man she longed for?

Valentina worked diligently the entire week to ready the palace for Saladin. Food was brought from the massive storehouses and prepared in advance. Flatware and goblets were polished till they gleamed. Every assortment of fruit and cheese available was brought for Valentina's approval.

When she at last had a few moments to herself, she drew Rosalan aside. "Saladin's caravan is due a little before sundown. I must admit to a few qualms. Everything is in readiness, and the women in the harem are as excited as young virgins. I have just come from the banquet hall, and all is prepared. At midday tomorrow the conference will take place. The emir is in a state of frenzy, which is detrimental to his health. Twice during the night I had to go to him because he complained he couldn't breathe. I pray that somehow, by some miracle, I can keep him alive for the length of Saladin's stay. When the dignitaries arrive, they will be shown to their quarters and a guard posted. I will join them at the banquet. They must not be allowed to roam the palace."

Valentina prepared for Saladin's arrival by dressing in a costume of soft yellow trimmed with jets. She affixed the face veil, the yashmak, to her head and peered into the polished metal to see her reflection. She approved of the yashmak covering the lower half of her face. It gave her an air of mystery, which coincided with her emotions. If the truth be known, Ramiff had become very dear to her, and she prayed that she could protect his secret of failing health. The old man lived in dread of his son's succeeding to the throne, and Valentina vowed she would protect Ramiff from Homed whatever the cost.

"Is all in readiness?" the emir questioned in a feeble voice.

"Yes, Kadi. I can see from the balcony that the guests have arrived. It is an impressive sight. The caravan is long and the black horses magnificent. Saladin dismounts now. His generals are behind him." Her voice faltered as she narrowed her eyes into the setting sun.

"What is it? What is wrong? I can tell by your voice that something is amiss."

"The sultan of Jakard rides beside Saladin. I was not prepared for this, Kadi," she said in a quavering voice.

"Then you must prepare yourself now. Did you think Saladin would travel without his first general? Why does this bother you? The truth, Valentina."

Valentina tore her eyes from the sight below and knelt beside Ramiff. "For one thing, he knows I am a Christian."

"And the other?" Ramiff asked.

"The other, Kadi, is the sultan himself. I knew from the moment I looked into his eyes that this was a man who would demand everything of a woman. He would take the essence of a woman and consume it until she was part of him, until he owned her and could mark her as one of his possessions." Valentina's throaty voice was heavy with emotion.

Ramiff grasped for her hand and held it tightly. "And this you do not want, is that it? You fear Paxon of Jakard because you are not ready to belong to any man." It was a statement, rather than a question.

Valentina answered quietly, her voice a purring whisper, "No, Kadi, I fear the sultan because I can so easily *want* to belong to him, to accede to his demands, to be consumed by the fires of his passion . . . and so I fear him because I am not ready to give my soul to another."

"More because he wants to own your soul, or more because he knows you're a Christian?"

"Both," Valentina answered softly. "Both, Kadi."

"I will lie for you. I will say you are a Circassian. Allah will forgive me if he will add it to the list of my wrongdoings. There is none who will dispute my word."

"You would do that for me?" Valentina asked tremulously.

"You know I would. Do you think I believed your story that Malik en Nasr sent me peaches? Saladin doesn't know a peach from a fig! We Moslems are fatalists, Valentina. What will be will be. Allah proclaims it! You will do as we intended, and young Paxon will just be another guest. If you should find yourself drowning in his eyes and succumbing to his charms, remember what you told me, that you are not ready to give yourself to a man. I have faith in you, young Valentina."

"Oh, Kadi," Valentina cried, tears streaming down her cheeks, "I will make you proud of me, truly I will." She touched the dry skin of his cheek. "Your faith shall not be misplaced."

"I wish to rest now; send Rosalan to me. If you wish, you may bring Saladin to these rooms before you retire, and I will speak to him in the darkness. I can do no less than make him welcome, as he is like a son to me. Go now; see to the preparations. If there are any peaches . . ."

"Rosalan has them for you, Kadi, a whole basketful."

The emir felt her presence leave the room. Rosalan joined him at his bed and spoke quietly to him. "Valentina is disturbed, I feel it," she said simply. "What if the sultans do not accept her? What if she cannot control them?" Rosalan was worried.

"Have you so little faith in Valentina? I thought you women had boundless faith in everything," the emir said petulantly.

"She is a woman. It's as simple as that. The sultan of Jakard is no fool. He whipped the queen of England. What do you think he will do to Valentina if he finds her here, which he will?"

The emir was unperturbed at Rosalan's words. "He will know that Valentina sits at the banquet table at my request. Neither Saladin nor Paxon would dare to question my authority. I shall speak to Saladin myself in the evening, in the darkness of this room. If Paxon is as enamored of Valentina as she is of him, then he will say nothing. We can be a close-mouthed lot when we choose, eh, Rosalan?"

The girl smiled and touched the old man's hand comfortingly. Yet her eyes betrayed her fears.

Valentina positioned herself at the end of the corridor which led to the banquet hall. She watched as the visiting sultans were ushered into the cavernous room, where they were seated on floor cushions near a long, low table. Squaring her shoulders, her heart hammering in her chest, she opened the heavy doors and strode into the room. She walked slowly to the head of the table, her carriage stately. She smiled slightly at the stunned looks on the men's faces but carefully avoided seeking Paxon's eyes.

Paxon stopped in midstride. His constant companion, the slinky black panther, pressed closely against his leg. Paxon could not take his eyes off the young woman. His eyes bored into her, trying to see behind the concealing yashmak. It couldn't be! Yet he knew it was, and his heart thundered in his chest. What blessing of Allah! Valentina, here in old Ramiff's palace! But how did she come to be here? The last he knew of her, she was lying upon a bed of pain, suffering from the lashing doled out by the Engleysi queen, Berengaria. He willed her eyes to turn to him, to recognize him. Stupid, of course she recognized him! Valentina, Valentina, his heart sang, here, beside me!

Valentina was aware of Paxon's scorching glances. She could barely keep her sensibilities. Her blood warmed with his nearness, and she yearned to lift her eyes to meet his gaze. But terror prevented her from doing so. A bevy of mixed emotions raced through her veins. Delight at once again being in his presence, and horror that he, one of Saladin's generals and a Moslem, might consider his responsibility to reveal her for what she was. A Christian!

"Emir Ramiff asks me to bid you welcome to his home. He regrets that he is unable to attend this banquet and asks your forgiveness." Her tone was low and throaty, almost a seductive whisper. "I am Valentina," she said simply as she lowered her head in respect, leaving the men to speculate on her exact relationship with Ramiff. As Valentina seated herself she heard the low buzzing of masculine voices. One of the sultans made a move as if to leave. "Do not be so foolish as to leave this banquet table, mighty General, for if you do, the emir shall hear of it," Valentina purred.

Throughout the meal at which only the men dined, it being the custom that women eat last, Valentina kept up a conversation with the sultans in her low sensual voice. The visitors listened and answered in grunts and sighs. Only Paxon's face remained unreadable, his dark eyes fathomless. What was he thinking? How much longer was this meal going to last? Her insides were churning at such a speed that she thought she would faint. Why doesn't he say something, do something? She brought her thoughts back to the present when Saladin addressed her. "How did the emir like my gift?" he inquired.

Valentina smiled, her eyes bright aquamarine jewels above the yashmak. "He wanted to know why you sent him a white panther when all he wanted was peaches. The cat is in my care, and I assure you she is being well cared for." Valentina smiled again as her eyes went to the black panther at Paxon's feet. "The emir asks that you accompany me to his quarters after the banquet so that he can chastise you and welcome you before you retire."

Saladin looked at Paxon and asked in a low voice, "Have you ever seen such a beautiful woman? Where did that fox Ramiff get her, and what is she doing sitting in his place at the head of the banquet table? It's unheard of!"

"Your tongue works at a furious pace, Saladin," Valentina interjected. "Ask me what it is you wish to know, and I will tell you. Speculation is for fools and children. Too often one decides upon the wrong answer."

"You have a bold tongue for a woman," Saladin said quietly, his bejeweled hands pulling at his close-cropped beard.

"How so?" Valentina asked huskily. "One could safely say that rank does have its privileges, does it not? Is that not the way it is in your armies? When in this palace, you will defer to me in all matters. If the emir wishes to speak with you, then I will take you to see him; if not, then you will conduct all matters through me." She rose from the table. "From this moment until your visit is over, you will speak with me and me alone. You will please show me the respect the emir demands of you. I shall listen intently and grant what you ask, if I am in a charitable mood." Her eyes bored into Paxon as she spoke, willing him to make some sign. His dark eyes remained inscrutable as he watched her leave the room, Saladin, the king of Islam, following in her perfumed wake.

"What in the name of Allah—?" The room took on a life of its own after the departure of Valentina and Saladin. Paxon listened, a smile tugging at the corners of his mouth. So what if she was a Christian, what could she do? A woman. A pretty face. Ramiff was a brilliant man. In no way could she pose a threat to Paxon or the other sultans. Since that day in Acre,

184

Paxon had allowed his mind to be troubled by her less and less, but he had never been completely able to forget her. Her eyes, sapphire-blue in happiness; her mouth. Even through the yashmak he could discern the sensitive mobility of those warm, moist lips. Even now he could remember their softness, taste their sweetness. Paxon was drawn back into the conversation, but his mind was on Valentina and the way her breasts rose high and proud beneath the thin silk of her garments.

Saladin followed the slim-hipped Valentina down the marble corridor, a faint stirring within him. The slight swaying of her narrow hips sent his heart to hammering in his chest. The high, taut breasts straining against the filmy material of her tunic made his senses reel. Perhaps . . .

Valentina thrust open the door of the emir's rooms and stood back to allow Saladin's entrance. She noticed the long look he gave her and the way his eyes traveled to her breasts, just as Paxon's had done. What was Paxon doing? What was he thinking? Was he, at this moment, revealing her identity to the others?

"Kadi, Malik en Nasr is here to see you," she said, leading the way to the oversized bed in which the emir lay.

"So the great warrior has arrived," the emir laughed heartily. To Valentina's practiced ear, she realized that this conversation was going to cost the emir in more ways than one. "How was the banquet? Is your belly full and are your eyes drunk with the sight of this lovely woman? Don't answer," he joked. "I know you too well. My eyesight may not be what it once was, but I can read your emotions as well as I used to when you were younger."

Saladin bowed in deference to the emir, his eyes speculative as he gazed at the old man propped up in bed. "What do you mean that your eyes are not what they used to be? You had the eyes of a hawk."

"Ah, yes, at one time, but now my eyes have this

devilish film over them, a sign of approaching old age," the emir laughed. "But I can still appreciate a beautiful woman."

"True, one need not be young to appreciate a woman's charms," Saladin agreed. "Tell me, Ramiff, what is this all about? Who is this woman who sits at the head of your table and presides over matters of state? My sultans question this—this—"

The emir interrupted him. "You question me, after all these years? You have no right, Saladin. Allah makes his decisions; I, Ramiff, make mine. If you do not like the way Napur is being controlled, then take your generals and your petitions away. I wish to hear no more about it." His tone was firm. "I allowed you to speak your mind because you are like a son to me, and because of this I listened. Let us speak of other things. The panther, where in Allah did you come across a white panther?"

Saladin laughed. "I thought my gift would delight you. The panther was bred for you. There were two of them; unfortunately the first cub died. You have the only one in the world. There will be no other. I'm happy my gift pleased you."

"I would rather have had peaches," the emir grumbled.

"So your tastes have not changed. I remember the days when you would gorge yourself with baskets of the succulent fruit."

"And while I was doing that, you were gorging yourself on ripe cherries."

"My one weakness," Saladin conceded. "It has been years since I have had cherries. At times I would almost give up my life for their sweetness."

"Ah, you see, and you send me a white panther." Both men laughed.

"The hour grows late, Saladin. Speak to me of what it is that concerns you."

"My spies tell me the Lionheart pushes on toward Jerusalem. This, of course, was inevitable, but he plans to do it much sooner than we expected. Philip has returned to his throne in France, and rumor has it that he and King Richard parted in anger. Richard must not take Jerusalem! We make preparations to see that this does not happen. The men of Islam are ready to fight to the death."

"Yes, to the death. Jerusalem is ours! Allah proclaims it! What of the slaughter of our people? How did this happen?"

Saladin's voice was bitter. "I do not know. I was on my way to the conference to discuss the exchange of prisoners when it happened. I threatened to retaliate, but I could not kill so senselessly. Men, women, and children . . . I should then have been as ruthless as the Lionheart. It was a slaughter! I cannot forgive or forget that atrocity."

"Very good, my son," Emir Ramiff said sternly. "And tell me of this first general of yours, Paxon of Jakard."

"Paxon," Saladin said thoughtfully, "is like that wild stallion he rides. He is young, lusty, wild; a magnificent general. He never fails!"

"And what of *Sheikh al Jebal,* that Old Man of the Mountain? Tell me what he has been up to in that Eagle's Nest."

"As you know, his power stretches from Persia to the Holy Land. He has citadels all over the mountains. He becomes more powerful each day the sun sets. His assassins are so well trained that they move freely among Moslem and Christian alike. *Sheikh al Jebal* is as elusive as a spirit. His *fedawi* roam the mountains and the plains at will and unafraid."

"Do you believe these tales?" Ramiff asked sharply.

"Yes. *Sheikh al Jebal* is powerful."

Valentina had been sitting in the shadows listening with fascination to Saladin's description of Paxon and the mysterious *Sheikh al Jebal.* Now she moved forward to interrupt the conversation between Ramiff and the Moslem king. She knew instinctively that it was time to intervene. The emir's voice was tiring, and she had no wish for Saladin to notice this.

"The hour grows late, Kadi," she said firmly. "To-

187

morrow is another day, and the conferences are to begin early."

"Forgive me, Ramiff. I apologize for the late hour, but we always manage to find much to speak of." Malik en Nasr rose and bowed low, his eyes on Valentina in the dim light of the room.

"Saladin," the emir said softly, "my harem is open to you. Make a choice to warm you this night, and Allah be with you."

"I have no need of the harem," Saladin said quietly as his eyes bored into Valentina. "When a man sees perfection, he will settle for nothing less. Another day," he said, bowing his white turbaned head toward Valentina. She smiled into his eyes, aptly reading his message, and was flattered. This Saladin, although in his forties, was a most attractive man. There was a lean look about him, no doubt from his years of soldiering. His face was deeply tanned to a shade of worn leather, and his graying beard lent authority to his chin. Most fascinating of all were his eyes, black and soulful beneath heavy brows. In their depths Valentina sensed a pathos and wisdom. Those ageless pools did strange things to her sensibilities and made her flesh tingle.

"But," the emir said harshly, "you take nothing that is mine unless it is offered or asked for, is that understood?" The old man's blind gaze shifted in Valentina's direction.

"It is understood, Ramiff," Saladin said quietly. "Rest in the arms of Allah, Ramiff."

Valentina led Saladin to his quarters and bowed low as she opened the door to his chambers.

"Do my eyes deceive me, or is this man a guard on my door?" Saladin asked sharply, nodding at the man leaning against the wall.

"Your eyes do not deceive you, Malik en Nasr. A guard will patrol this entire corridor."

"Am I to understand that we, the guests of my good friend Ramiff, are to keep to our quarters?" The general's black gaze rippled through her, and Valentina felt her knees tremble in the face of this formidable man.

"If this is what the mighty general cares to believe, so be it," she answered softly.

"Would you have me ignore the obvious?" he demanded.

"Malik en Nasr is a most discerning man," Valentina countered guilelessly.

"By whose orders?" Saladin demanded.

"By my orders," Valentina said in her low, throaty voice. "Do you question them or my right to issue them?"

"Praise be to Allah, no! Ramiff was more than explicit. But know this. If I had the desire to leave this room, your guard would be unable to stop me."

"Perhaps you would wish to try and make good your boast," Valentina purred. "I will see you in the morning," she said, her eyes meeting his in a clash of wills. She bowed low, offering the traditional Moslem salute of touching forehead, lips, and breasts, and stepped backward in a show of respect. Then, turning, she walked down the corridor, head held high, aware of his eyes following her every step.

Chapter Thirteen

Valentina cast a last, critical eye around the conference room. Silver bowls of desert flowers graced each end of the long, gleaming table. Stacks of parchment and quills were centered within reach of any of the visiting officers. She adjusted the colorful silken hangings a fraction so that the room would be dim, yet not dark. Bright sunlight was subdued by deep rose draperies. Valentina looked down at her feet to see the white panther nuzzling her ankle. She smiled as she scooped her up in her arms and gently stroked the silken head. "You have a wish to attend this conference, is that what you're trying to tell me? Very well, you shall attend." The panther cub purred deeply as she settled herself comfortably in Valentina's arms.

Cradling the animal fondly, Valentina entered the emir's rooms. "Kadi, all is in readiness. Do you have any last-minute instructions for me?" she asked nervously. The emir's voice was tired and weak as he struggled to get up from the high bed. "No!" Valentina said sharply. "You must rest! Your meeting with Saladin has taken a toll on your strength. I will leave the door ajar so you can hear every exchange of words. If there is something that is beyond me or that I feel I can't deal with, then I will come to you. You must promise me, Kadi, that you will remain quiet and rest. It's not time for Allah to take you. Please," she pleaded, "your promise."

"Badger, badger," Ramiff complained in a weakened voice. "I am nothing but a bedridden old man, no use to anyone. Leave the cat for me to stroke. The feel of her will remind me I am still of this world. I am not yet ready for Allah."

"Kadi," Valentina teased lightly, "what manner of talk is this?" One moment you say you want to go to Allah, and the next you wish to hold on to something so he cannot reach out for you."

"Badger, badger! Am I not the emir, and can I not complain? What good am I if I cannot change my mind seven times a day? Besides, I have decided that I am afraid of Allah," he said in a childish voice.

Valentina laughed. "I think it is Allah who is afraid to take you with him. I don't think he is ready for one such as you. He is probably thinking that he has no need for an emir who sucks on peaches all day." While her tone was light and teasing, her blue-green eyes were sad.

"What name have you given this atrocious cat? Has she turned black yet? Saladin thinks I am a fool. There are no white panthers. You must trick him as he did me and find out what the wily fox dipped her in. I want to know," he said petulantly.

Valentina trembled as she thought, Oh, Kadi, have you forgotten Saladin's words that he spoke only such a short time ago? He explained the cat's origin. Tears burned in her eyes at this evidence of the old man's feebleness.

"I shall find out," Valentina said quietly. "I will trick him, as you suggest. I think you're right. There is a black speck on her ear," Valentina lied.

"I knew it!" the old man chortled. "He thinks because I am old and my eyesight is gone that I would be fooled. Go now, and remember what I told you. Leave the door ajar so I can hear. Pray to Allah that I do not fall asleep," he said, his eyes closing, the cat purring beside him in contentment.

The council had assembled, each member wearing black and yellow robes, the colors of Saladin's holy jihad. Saladin took his place on the floor cushion to the right of the head of the table. Paxon took his place beside Saladin. The men's eyes turned expectantly to the head place, awaiting Ramiff's appearance.

Valentina was unsure of herself and allowed the men to speculate on Ramiff's appearance for several moments. She noticed Paxon turn to watch her. She wished with all her heart that he had not accompanied Saladin to Napur. Ever since she had first set eyes on him, he had complicated her life. And he did so even now, when she could feel his gaze as though it were a physical touch sending flames coursing up her spine and warming her skin to a faint flush. Would he reveal that he knew her to be a Christian, an enemy of these men who sat in counsel? She returned his gaze, her eyes falling upon his virile, handsome features and lithe, muscular physique. In spite of herself, she remembered the feel of his mouth clinging to hers and his arms crushing her in a breathless embrace. Valentina found herself locked in a deep, meaningful gaze with the handsome Saracen until she was aware of a glint of mockery in his night-dark eyes.

She lifted her hand for silence, opened a ledger-type folder, and held her quill in readiness. "Tell me what you wish and what you will pay, in gold," she said firmly. "I will then tell you if the emir agrees to the exchange. Before we begin, there are several errors which must be rectified. Malik en Nasr"—she glanced at him—"your payments are greatly in arrears. Your promise of payment for the last quarter has not been received. Before we can continue, your arrears must be paid."

"That is impossible," Saladin said coolly. "Payment in gold was shipped to the emir on the agreed date. I have the seal of the emir proclaiming it."

"There is no seal in the ledger," Valentina told him. "Perhaps you would care to examine it."

Saladin was leaning over her shoulder, a scowl on his face. "Here," he said, withdrawing a slip of parchment from inside his loose-flowing caftan. "The emir's seal. See with your own eyes!"

"What you say is true," Valentina said, her blue-green eyes furious. "It would seem there is one in this palace who lines his pockets with the emir's gold. Very well, the matter is ended. Tell me what you wish."

"Grain and provisions. My armies are in short supply and my people need more than ever before. The last shipment to my armies fell into the hands of a Christian raiding party."

"And the price?" Valentina asked in her throaty whisper, her eyes narrowed.

Malik en Nasr mentioned a figure. Valentina laughed mockingly.

"Do you take me for a fool? I could go to the bazaars and sell the provisions for five times what you offer." Her eyes narrowed even more. "Because I am a woman and sit here in the kadi's place does not make me a fool. I will not haggle. Triple your offer to consider the supplies yours. There will be no haggling."

"I demand an audience with Ramiff!" Saladin said angrily.

"Denied," Valentina said coolly.

Paxon listened to the verbal exchange between Valentina and his commander. A slight smile tugged at the corners of his strong jaw. By Allah, she had denied Saladin a conference with the old man! Would Saladin bow to her power, or would he defend his request? The black panther growled deep in his throat as Paxon stroked the glistening raven head.

"I demand—" Saladin said, rising from his position at the conference table.

Valentina said, with a dangerous purr in her voice, "When you sit at this table, you have no rights other than your bargaining power. All other rights belong to me. You will remain seated or you will be escorted from the conference."

"By what right—?" Saladin choked off his words.

The small white panther, tired of lying on the emir's chest, jumped from the high bed and scampered into the conference room and leaped on Valentina's lap. Valentina smiled fondly at the frisky cub, then looked deeply into Saladin's eyes. "By my own right," she said. "If you have no wish to continue with the conference, then you may leave. I have no patience for your impatience. Give me your answer." She continued to fondle the cub. The black panther raised his massive head and snarled. Paxon laid a hand on the beast's head and he immediately quieted. Saladin, his eyes furious, seated himself and stared at Valentina.

"Let us continue," she said, looking at Paxon. The dark eyes bored into her as she stared at him, mesmerizing her with their dark depths. She watched the sun-bronzed hands stroke the cat's silky head and imagined what they would feel like on her body. Her cheeks flushed a rosy hue as she tore her gaze from his. What was he thinking? What was he feeling?

"I agree to your terms," Saladin said coldly.

"Malik en Nasr has made a wise decision. May I offer a suggestion? Perhaps it would be to your advantage to purchase an extra supply of grain in the event that King Richard's men waylay the supply caravan. Divide the goods between two caravans, each taking separate routes. I merely suggest this. The decision is yours."

"What would you have me pay the tariff with? My purse is empty. You refuse to 'haggle,' as you put it. I'm in no position to buy more than I can afford!"

"Emir Ramiff would be most pleased to make you a gift of the grain."

"Ramiff cheats himself," Saladin said suspiciously.

Valentina's eyes ripened to a deep blue. "Emir Ramiff never shorts himself. The grain is yours for the exchange of three horses."

"Agreed!" Saladin exclaimed triumphantly. His devilish look told her that he thought her a fool and Ramiff an even greater fool. Women, he derided, had no head for business.

"Your forbearance, mighty General," Valentina said smoothly. "You haven't heard which three horses I have in mind. Emir Ramiff admires the three white stallions in which you profess your pride. Is the mighty general still agreeable?"

Saladin's expression darkened and his steady gaze held fury. "Agreed," he said harshly, his lips tightening into a thin line.

Paxon shifted his position on the thick floor cushion and felt admiration for Valentina. His ebony eyes darkened momentarily as he watched her slender hands stroke the sleeping head of the white panther, her touch light and sensuous. His thoughts were interrupted by Valentina's raising her eyes and gazing into his. Again he felt as though he were drowning in a pool of shimmering blue-green water. The muscles in his thighs tingled, and the cat at his feet stirred restlessly. If only he had taken her away with him on the night she had tasted Berengaria's whip! She would now be his!

"We are gathered here for other reasons than to supply our armies," Saladin said to his generals, re-assuming the dignity of his rank. He turned to a swarthy man in his middle years who was holding several scrolls of parchment. "Everyone here is familiar with our noted chronicler, Baha ad Din. As we are all gathered here, I felt it would be opportune for us to hear what Baha ad Din has written about the jihad. His sources of information are impeccable, and we can trust that all he writes is truth."

At Saladin's nod, Baha ad Din rose to face the assembly, his scrolls in hand. "Much of what I report is common knowledge; yet, because of the distance which separates our armies, Malik en Nasr has requested this report to rout out rumor and realize fact. May I begin?"

The notable assembly nodded, and Baha ad Din read from his scrolls: "Richard, king of England, captured Acre. This report takes us from the inhuman massacre of our people. The Lionheart made his first move by marching his armies down the coast, with his fleet of ships following behind to the city of Jaffa, the port of Jerusalem, whose distance is said to be sixty-five miles away from the mother city, as the crow flies. The date was summer, August twenty-five, eleven hundred and ninety-one. He led his troops during the season of heat, when the streams and wells are dry. We, the Moslems, kept abreast of his actions by the use of spies and mounted patrols. Along the way to Jaffa, Malik Ric ordered the destruction of three towns which were in his path to Jaffa, and when he arrived in that much-needed seaport, he destroyed the fortifications and continued to march south. Moslem patrols, with the aid of Allah, marched beside him, out of sight within the hills."

The turbaned heads around the conference table nodded. All were aware of this. Baha ad Din continued.

"It is reported, and justly, that the Christian army did not march unmolested. The men of Allah harassed King Richard's rear guard with bowmen, but we failed to engage the Christians in an encompassing battle. The Lionheart struck a strange formation of troops. He had his army march in three columns. The one closest to the hills—and to our patrols—consisted entirely of infantrymen in close ranks. Those in the exposed outer files carried bows and crossbows and wore tunics of mail. They handled their weapons with fury and their armor shielded them from our arrows. Their compatriots within the files carried spears and swords and stood ready to fend off an attacking charge."

The eyes beneath the turbans narrowed, and the men leaned imperceptibly closer, clinging to Baha ad Din's words.

"In the second column, shielded by the screen of infantry, were mounted knights and horsemen protected from our avenging arrows, which would have taken an expensive toll of their horses.

"In the third column, nearest the sea and separated from our attack, moved the supply carts and the wounded. From the ranks of this third column came relief men for the infantry.

"Our great and wise leader, Malik en Nasr, and his honorable brother, Al Adil, rode out to inspect a wide plain which lay before the route of the Christians and found it a likely site for battle. For two days Moslem horsemen had been unsuccessful in coaxing the Christian cavalry to break ranks. The Crusaders refused to be brought into battle. The Christians moved forth like a great armored centipede across the plain. Combat was inevitable.

"The battle raged for hours. Banners were trod beneath the feet of dying horses; fallen men lay dying in the gore upon the plain. Still, the losses were evenly matched on both sides. Some of our Turks hid themselves in wooded copses, and others climbed trees to gain an advantage. The enemy found itself more and more entangled within our grasp, and we became expectant of victory. Then their cavalry amassed and charged us. The battle raged fiercer than before. The Christians labored to repel, while the men of Islam sought to destroy.

"All the way to Arsouf the Christians pushed onward, repelling the forward attacks of our honorable general, Taki ad Din. The might of Malik Ric was seen and witnessed that day by the men of Islam, and his name will range in Moslem legend through the centuries."

Valentina listened and silently applauded this news of her king. Richard had proved himself a worthy adversary to these Moslem generals, and she knew that his valor and leadership had confounded them.

Baha ad Din continued to read from his chronicle. "Malik en Nasr conferred with his generals and altered his campaign. Seeking to bide for time, rather than take part in endless skirmishes, the Moslem forces were divided. The defense of Ascalon, the southern key to Jerusalem and the caravan route to Egypt, was temporarily abandoned. Instead, Malik en Nasr wisely decided against crippling his armies by shutting themselves within the walls to defend it. Another loss such as we experienced at Acre would be avoided.

"From the dawning of the day our king busied himself with the tearing down of Ascalon. All the grain stored in the city was allotted to the workmen. Every house within those walls was burned, and the towers were filled with wood and also burned.

"Throughout Ascalon was a sound of grieving, for the city was pleasant and its walls were strong and its houses were beautiful. Sick to his heart, Malik en Nasr did what was necessary."

Valentina saw the grief wash over these powerful men's faces. Ascalon was known as the Bride of Syria, and its beauty was vastly admired. Never in her wildest dreams had she imagined she would sympathize with a Moslem loss while the other half of her heart rejoiced for the Christian victory.

"Baha ad Din took his seat, and Saladin spoke. "Malik Ric has sent an envoy requesting a meeting with the leaders of the Islamic army. Al Adil, my brother and counselor, will accompany me. Arrangements must be made. It is unseemly for a leader of men to see to these arrangements. It was my intention that Ramiff of Napur do this." He turned to face Valentina, his meaning clear.

"The emir agrees," she said smoothly, although her heart was racing. To be in contact with her own people again! "I will see to it myself, Malik en Nasr, and I pray all arrangements meet with your satisfaction.

Emir Ramiff has arranged a festive evening as a farewell for your generals who must return to their duties on the morrow. He asks that you will attend." Her announcement met with approval, and she fixed a bright blue gaze on Saladin as she asked softly, "Will you assign your own men to oversee the transfer of grain and supplies to your caravans? If you will excuse me now, I go to the emir."

She bowed low, a graceful movement, and touched her heart, lips, and head in salute. She looked at Paxon, her face calm and serene. As always, he wore an aloof expression, his eyes dark and unreadable. Would Saladin assign him to oversee the transfer of grain? Her eyes fell to the black panther at his feet, a beautiful beast, and one that seemed to be in perfect harmony with his master. The cat stirred, one curving paw stroking the cool marble tiles, his ears straight, his purr a deep rumble. It would seem that the Saracen was feeling contented. Suddenly the cat snarled and sprang to his feet. Paxon's dark eyes narrowed as he met her stare with a questioning look. Questions he would soon demand to be answered!

Chapter Fourteen

Valentina, resplendent in her gauzy emerald silk, her hair swirled atop her head in a coronet entwined with strings of pearls, glanced around the huge banquet hall. Mounds of colorful cushions were placed in a wide circle in the middle of which braziers laden with simmering lamb and succulent squash rested on brilliant tiles. Huge wooden bowls of fresh figs and fruit graced the squat iron braziers. Flickering candlelight cast mysterious shadows over the frescoed walls.

Her thoughts again turned to Paxon. Would he let his eyes linger on her as he had at the conference? How would her body react to his muscular manliness? She gave a delicate shudder and called the panther cub to her with a soft word. At her tone the cub frisked about, nosing into the bowls of fruit and leaping over the silken cushions. She came to rest at Valentina's feet and purred sensuously against her ankles. Valentina bent down and fondled the cat with gentle hands. "I believe you're getting too big and awkward to frisk about like this. It's time you were chained when guests are present. Soon you'll be as big as the black panther who sits at the sultan's feet. Will you guard me as well as the huge black cat does his master?" In answer, the albino purred even louder. "Come, this is no place for you to romp and play. Soon the sultans will arrive and the evening's festivities will begin." The cub trotted behind her obligingly as she led her to Ramiff's apartment and the place where she was to sleep.

Valentina looked in on the sleeping emir and felt saddened. He slept more and more of the day away. Soon he would close his eyes for the last time, and then she would be alone. Would she be able to carry on? Her thoughts drifted from the sleeping emir back to the visiting sultan and his black panther. So far he had said no word, but his eyes said many things, and that was what made her tremble. How would she feel when he did speak? Would his voice send ripple after ripple up her spine, as it had that day on the dusty road? Did he remember the feel of her in his arms? What, God, what did he feel? How long would she be able to look into his dark eyes and not succumb to him? Whom would he choose from the harem this night? Would he choose? Or would he simply sit and stare at her?

She shook her head to clear her thoughts, gave a last, lingering look at the old emir, patted the panther cub, and walked from the room. Taking a deep breath, she entered the banquet hall and almost gasped aloud at the resplendent attire of the visiting sultans. Each one seemed to outdo the other. Her eyes settled on

Paxon. Tonight his headgear was all white, his bronze face complementing the stark whiteness. His caftan was also white, with bold slashes of crimson and black. Soft kid boots, the color of his panther, graced his muscular legs. Her heart fluttered madly as she tore her eyes from his magnificent form and seated herself amid the cushions. She clapped her hands lightly, and the musicians began to play the soft, haunting melodies of the East. Servants scurried forth to serve the food and drink, while jesters and jugglers displayed their skills, demanding their audience's attention.

Throughout the long, leisurely meal Valentina was silent, presiding over the banquet with a watchful eye to the needs of Ramiff's guests. The men soon relaxed in her quiet presence and regaled each other with ribald stories and tales of derring-do. An uneasy feeling began to settle over her as she watched the musicians approach the center of the room. For some strange reason her heart was beating wildly and she was finding it difficult to breathe. Her eyes raked the room and came back to rest on the musicians as they weaved in and out among the dancing girls.

Suddenly the musicians moved to form a circle, and a man dressed in colorful attire entered it, a flute to his lips. The melody was that of a night bird, true, pure, and simple. The haunting tones sent a chill up Valentina's back. Her eyes narrowed as she stared into the circle of musicians. It couldn't be! It was! She moved on her seat and perched as if to run into the circle. The flutist eyed her for a moment, correctly interpreting her intention. The slight negative shake of his head went unnoticed by everyone save herself.

The desire to run was so great she could barely contain herself. The circle broke and the flutist wandered among the sultans, carefully avoiding Paxon and the sleeping cat who lay at his side. Gracefully he made his way to Valentina and stood behind her. Her shoulders tensed at his nearness, her eyes wary and haunted at the same time. She wanted to reach out and clasp him to her, to never let him go. Again time stood still as the haunting melody came to an end. She turned slightly to nod her approval at the flutist, and shock raced through her body at the dark-eyed stare that met her gaze.

"I can't wait for eternity," she whispered softly.

The flutist bowed low and returned her whisper. "If it is meant to be, it will be." Tears gathered in her eyes as she watched him back away from her and exit the room. Suddenly her eyes filled with horror as she remembered how the evening was to end.

She had to put the Saracen from her mind. The rest of the evening loomed before her, and she needed her wits about her. It was provident that no one could see into her heart and mind.

More dancing girls entered through the wispy draperies at the end of the huge hall. Soft flute music wafted around the circle of cushions as the girls, tiny tinkling bells on their feet, danced and twirled for the sultans. Gold tassels covered the tips of their breasts, and lacy cobwebs of fine-spun silk graced their slender legs. Gold and silver bangles adorned their arms and wrists. The music was soft and seductive as the flute players followed the swaying women. The banquet was coming to an end. The sultans were nodding approvingly and pointing to this one and that one, their choice for the evening.

Valentina watched Paxon out of the corner of her eye, waiting for him to make his choice. He didn't raise his hand, nor did he seem particularly interested in the graceful dancing girls. The panther got to his feet, looked around, and began to purr, Paxon's hand on the silky head. Paxon gazed at Valentina, his eyes hooded and, she thought, dangerous. Every muscle in his body appeared taut, ready to spring. The cat stirred restlessly and opened one slanted yellow eye. His tail twitched and made a slapping sound on the marble floor. The other slanted eye opened, and both eyes went around the room in a slow, catlike gaze. One huge paw snaked out from his curled body as Valentina tore her eyes from the scene and forced her mind to concentrate on the dancing girls. Their dance over, they bowed low as they waited for first one sultan and then another to make his choice for the evening. At last all the sultans, save Saladin and Paxon, had made a choice.

Valentina looked around in alarm. Fear leaped into her eyes as the obvious direction of their intentions settled on her. All eyes were on her as Saladin looked first at Valentina and then at Paxon. Paxon nodded slightly, deferring to his superior. The black cat snarled and was on his feet, his eyes glaring wildly at the circle of men. Paxon smiled, white teeth gleaming in the flickering light. A gentle touch of his hand, and the animal again rested at his feet. Paxon had bowed to Saladin, but he didn't like it. The cat bared his teeth and growled deep in his throat.

Paxon smiled, his eyes boring into Valentina, forcing her, compelling her, to look at him. The cat purred as Valentina's eyes widened, her heart hammering in her chest, her tongue swelling in her throat. She licked dry lips, her gaze locked in his as she fought with herself to conquer this strange emotion that threatened to choke the life from her body. The black cat continued to purr softly, his rest contented. Which was worse, the soft purr or the dangerous snarl? She had to do something, anything, to get her mind back to the evening's entertainment. She clapped her hands and the harem girls returned and this time they danced to a more festive tune from the flute player. The music was low, sensual, and throbbing. The tempo of the music increased as the girls danced more daringly, spinning closer and closer to the sultans. Wicked grins of delight settled on the men's faces as they playfully reached out to snatch at the jangling bangles.

How long before they couldn't wait any longer? How long before she had to go with Saladin and feel Paxon's eyes on her back? Men servants continued to serve the rich, spicy food. Paxon ate nothing, Valentina noted. From time to time he would slip a piece of meat to the watchful cat at his feet.

Valentina smiled until she thought her face would crack with the effort, all the while her thoughts racing to the close of the evening. The sultans were now in a playful mood. Who was to signal the end of the night's festivities? Surely not she! The emir had said nothing about how the evening was to end.

Seeing her indecision, Saladin rose from his mound of cushions and clapped his hands. The sultans arose as one, Paxon included, and stood watching Saladin. He nodded slowly, and the men followed the women of their choice. Paxon narrowed his dark eyes and reached for the chain around the cat's thick neck. His exit from the room was slow and deliberate, the cat snarling and straining at his leash. Paxon said something soothing and the big cat licked his master's hand. Valentina fought the urge to run after him, to call him back. Instead, she smiled at Saladin and waited for him to lead the way to his quarters.

Lengths of silken cloth billowed and rustled in the fresh breezes off the desert. Inside the opulently appointed room, Valentina set about arranging the silken pillows and lit the small pot that held a sweet-smelling incense. When the room was in readiness, she turned to Saladin in rapt attention.

"You're a beautiful woman, Valentina," Saladin said quietly. "Quite the most beautiful woman I have ever seen. Tell me," he said, his voice low and conversational, "how you like your duties here in the palace."

"Thank you for the compliment." Valentina smiled. "I find my duties . . . myriad. I have much to learn. You might say that I am feeling my way. I made a mistake today with your account. I will not make the same mistake in the future."

"When I first saw you, I knew that I had seen you before, but I could not place you immediately. I remember now where it was that I had seen you. You were in my camp and were sold at the auction. I regret it, but there was no other choice. When a human has to be sold, it tears at my heart. There are many times that I feel I was not meant for war. I command my armies well, make no mistake, but when I was a young man I had the wish to be a teacher. I thirst for knowledge of other lands, other peoples. I think I would have made a fine teacher; the desire to mold young minds has always been a passion with me. Unfortunately it was not meant to be. My people needed me, and I had to come to their aid. In the days when I served under Ramiff, he constantly goaded me about my books and quills. He told me when I was an old man I could learn. For now, experience would be my greatest teacher. Sometimes I think he is right, and at other times I think him wrong. How much longer do you think he will live?" he asked suddenly.

Valentina flinched at the abrupt turn in the conversation.

"In the words of Ramiff, when Allah is ready for him. He is well taken care of and should live a long and fruitful life."

"You lie," Saladin said quietly. "It makes no matter. Ramiff has his reasons and I will not dispute them. If he thinks you are capable of controlling his kingdom, then I shall not question it again. I speak only for myself; the other sultans may not be so gracious. Be warned, young Valentina," he said softly as he grasped her arm and pulled her to him. He made no move to kiss her or embrace her, content with having her near, his strong hand stroking the softness of her arm. Again he spoke suddenly, catching Valentina off guard. "Have you lain with a man?"

"No," Valentina said hesitantly. "I have been taken by a man forcefully, but I know nothing of love-making."

"Then I will be your teacher. There is lust and there is love. You must learn the meaning of both so that, in the future, you will not barter your body for some foolish reason. You are much too beautiful and intelligent a woman to make so serious a mistake. Love is a magnificent thing. Only once in my life did I love a woman so much, I would have given her my soul. Allah saw fit to take her from my arms when she gave birth to my son. Months later my son died. It was just as well, for then I could get on with my life with no tormenting memories. Lust, young Valentina, is something one feels for another much the way animals do. It is physical and means nothing. A man can walk away and never look back. When he looks back and smiles, that is love. You must learn the difference between the two. You feel something for young Paxon and he for you. If nurtured like the young seedlings, perhaps it will grow to something. Be not too quick about making decisions. Not by deed or look would he let me know he desired you this evening, but he couldn't fool me. We have a saying in our armies that rank carries its privileges, and I chose to exert my rank this evening because I desired you for myself. I shall be gone tomorrow to my armies. Paxon and his men will remain to see to the supplies. Now, enough of this prattle; let me hear you speak."

Valentina felt confused. "There is little to speak of. I am an inexperienced woman in the ways of the world. I will bow to your knowledge and your teachings. The emir has told me you are a gentle and wise man. He has told me many stories of your youth. I especially like the one where you and the emir stole nine women from a sultan's harem."

Saladin laughed. "That was a daring feat indeed. We were lucky to escape with our skin intact. Ramiff was a lusty man in those days. His need for women was constant and all-consuming. Now all he has are his memories and failing eyesight. One day I will be in that position myself. Until such time I will take my pleasure where I find it." He drew her to him, crushing her lips. Tendrils of fire raced up her spine as Saladin's hands expertly explored her body. The bruising passion of the man delighted her as the sparks of desire snaked into dancing flames.

Pulling her to her feet, Saladin gazed at her with narrowed eyes. Valentina stared at him, her mind and body receptive to whatever it was he would do, willing him with her eyes. He backed off a step and looked at her again with wide eyes and a smile on his face. He motioned her to step closer. She obeyed and smiled at him, her body quivering, her mind racing. Slowly he reached out to open her tunic. His rough, calloused hands, bronzed by the sun, removed her scanty blouse, exposing her breasts. His sun-darkened fingers clasped her breasts and caressed them with gentle, soft strokes. When he saw her lips part and her tongue dart out to moisten them, he removed the gold girdle, his eyes on her swelling, quivering breasts. The golden girdle dropped to the carpeted floor as his hands maneuvered the gauzy emerald skirt down over her hips. The soft, slithering sound of the silken fabric against her was loud in the silent room.

Completely naked, Valentina stood still, her breathing ragged, her eyes glazed with sensuality. Moments later the caftan he wore slithered to the floor and he drew her to him.

His mouth sought for and found hers, locking her in his hard embrace. Wave after wave of desire coursed through her as she answered his kisses, her tongue darting into the warm recesses of his mouth. His hard hands caressed and stroked her back, bringing her still closer to her desires. Her breasts were taut and hard beneath his hands as he gently lowered her to the mound of silken cushions. She circled his broad back, straining to bring him closer. Soft moans of ecstasy escaped her parted lips as he proved himself to be a gentle and artful lover, arousing her to the heights of passion, teaching her about her own body and allowing her to experience to the fullest the broad spectrum of her desires. He devoured her with his eyes and covered her with his lean warrior's body. Teasing touches of his tongue against her fiery skin ignited her sensuality. His fingertips grazed the softness of her inner thighs, and, helplessly, she felt her body arch to aid him in his explorations.

Her fingers curled in his close-cropped hair, Valentina felt the tautness of his muscled back and the hardness of his thighs as they entwined with hers. A deep wave of yearning spread through her belly, drawing up her knees, bringing her closer . . . closer to him. Her eyes a deep smoky blue in the dimness of the room, she gazed into his smoldering eyes. Her tongue darted out to moisten her full, parted lips. With her breath coming in short, light pants, he brought her to the ecstatic culmination of womanhood.

Spent, her eyes closed, Valentina lay against the satin cushions, her hand resting on Saladin's massive chest. Saladin, his eyes contented, his body completely relaxed, smiled at the woman beside him. He laughed fondly as he let his fingers trail over her breasts. "You're a beautiful woman, more so now that I've tasted your charms."

Valentina laughed throatily. "And you're a beautiful man," she returned coyly.

"Listen to me, Valentina. This is love for now, two people caught up in a moment of time, two people who want nothing from each other save the moment. The ultimate is when you love another with your heart and soul. Then that which you give will have a meaning, a meaning even I can't explain to you. When this happens you will know it. That love is like no other and is rarely experienced more than once in a lifetime. I shall wish with all my heart that you find such a love."

"Will I know what to do when I find it?" Valentina asked huskily.

Saladin laughed. "My dear Valentina, you will know, just as I knew and the emir knew, and all the others before us. You will know!"

Dawn arrived in all its purple mystery as Saladin dressed, his eyes warmly caressing Valentina as she languished beneath the silken covers. He felt desire rise in him again as he gazed down at her beautiful face. Her eyes were smoky-blue again as she watched him from beneath her dark, winged brows. Her black hair, spread against the pillow, framed her face, and her skin was a warm ivory against it.

Saladin reached out and tenderly rubbed those long ebony strands between his fingers, remembering how they had twined about him like a curtain that separated him from worldly matters and freed him to soar to ethereal heights with this smooth-skinned goddess who welcomed him to taste her delights.

"Your eyes speak to me of many things, Valentina, and they implore me to return to you. Another time, another place," he said quietly, touching her lips with his and feeling them part beneath his, drawing him, prolonging the tender contact. "Such beauty, so feminine," he whispered huskily. "Your mouth was created for kissing, your body for adoration. You wonder if you pleased me. Never wonder, Valentina. Last evening I told you I would be your teacher, and at the onset I was, and you were a magnificent pupil, so eager and willing to learn about yourself. Soon after our roles changed, and you became the teacher with your cool, smooth limbs and firm, ripe breasts. You have given me a beautiful memory to take with me on my journey. Until we meet again, young Valentina." He kissed her again and felt the spark ignite.

Valentina, tears brimming in her eyes and tumbling down her cheeks, rose to her knees. The coverlet slipped as she extended her hand, exposing satiny twin globes which rose proudly on her slender torso.

"You beckon me like the hot sirocco wind which blows off the desert, and I am loath to leave you," he said, his voice a husky whisper which made her spine tingle as she remembered how he had murmured soft phrases in praise of her during the night. "We shall meet again in the desert with the sands of time whirling about us. Good-bye, Valentina."

"Never good-bye. I look forward to our time in the desert," she said, smiling into his eyes. Then he was gone.

She sprang from the bed to the balcony, draping the coverlet over her. She watched with a closed throat as the caravan made ready to move. The rich vibrant colors of the camel drivers' robes and the heavily laden camels were a majestic sight. Then she saw the cat! Where the cat was, Paxon was! She shielded her eyes from the sun and searched him out. He was standing next to Saladin, his legs slightly parted, his hands on his slim hips, the panther at rigid attention. Saladin, sensing her presence on the balcony, raised his head, and Valentina waved. Saladin nodded as the panther strained on his leash. Paxon also raised his head. Even from this distance Valentina could hear the snarls and see the bared teeth of the huge cat. She shuddered as she walked back into the room and prepared herself for the coming day.

She would see that Mohab went to the granaries with Paxon, and she would read to the emir. Her plans were soon dashed when Mohab entered the chamber. "Valentina, my old friend has lapsed into a deep sleep, and I am unable to wake him." Mohab was visibly shaken. He shook his head sadly and tears brimmed in his rheumy eyes. "We knew it would be soon. We can't make him live because we wish it. It won't be long now, perhaps only hours."

Valentina was stunned. "Has he any pain?"

Mohab shook his head. "I gave him a little opium shortly before dawn because he demanded it. Then he fell into his deep sleep, and there was nothing I could do."

"We must be near him, he must not be alone."

"But the sultans, the granaries," Mohab protested worriedly. "Word must not be allowed to filter out that Ramiff is near his end."

"Yes, there is always the business of the living, isn't there, Mohab?"

"I would stay with my old friend and see him safely into the arms of Allah. I could never keep my mind on accounts and bins and contracts."

"You will remain with Ramiff." Valentina's mind raced for someone to see to the delivery of the grain. "Mohab, send Rosalan to me, and then I will join you in the emir's room. Quickly, Mohab. I will wait for her here."

"Rosalan! She has difficulty counting the spots on the dice. No, mistress, she would never do. And the sultans, they would be offended to have a mere woman—" Mohab snapped his toothless mouth shut. Looking at Valentina and recognizing her strength, he vowed he would never use the phrase "a mere woman" again.

"Rosalan's counting may be faulty, but not her

judgment of character. Quickly, Mohab, do as I tell you. Ramiff is my first concern."

While waiting for Rosalan, Valentina donned the same costume that Saladin had so seductively removed the night before. She imagined that his aroma still lingered in the room, and when she looked at the low divan on which they had spent the night in each other's arms, a sensation of longing filled her. But when she tried to see his face, the image would not come to her. The man of her desires was faceless. Last night had only been a taste of what true love and real passion could be. Not even Paxon's face fit the image of her dream man: the man who would love her beyond all else and recognize that she was a person unto herself and love her for it.

Valentina chastised herself for daydreaming when Ramiff, a man who had only shown her the kindness of a father, lay dying on his bed. She knew that with Ramiff's death her responsibilities to the kingdom of Napur would be endless. At all costs it must appear that the old emir lived, so that word would not reach the infamous heir to the throne, Homed.

Rosalan entered the chamber and moved toward Valentina, her arms open, ready to give comfort. "Poor pigeon," she murmured, and Valentina found herself enclosed in the girl's warm embrace. "Poor pigeon, so much responsibility. So great a weight for such pretty shoulders. I have just come from the emir. He still sleeps and seems to be at peace. His passing will be quick and painless. Ramiff has made his peace with Allah, and only paradise awaits him on the other side of this life."

Valentina's cheeks were wet with tears. "May Allah smile upon him," she whispered.

"Allah will smile," Rosalan assured her, "and in the paradise to which he goes, he will be young and strong again and will hunt the wild goat. It is not Ramiff for whom I fear, pigeon, it is for you. I know of the promise you vowed to the old man and of the danger in which you place yourself. From what I have heard of this son, Homed, he is a man to be feared.

210

In the harem Dagny counts the days until Ramiff goes to Allah and Homed is called back to take the throne."

"Dagny? But why should she care who sits upon the throne? Her position here in the palace is safe."

"Valentina, once I told you that you don't know everything. Dagny dallies with women, true, but that's all it is. A dalliance, a passing of time, a seeking of pleasure. Since there are no men made available to her, she seeks release from her passions through women. But, Valentina, it is well known in the harem that Homed and Dagny have been lovers. Also, she claims to come from royal blood. I am certain her sights are set on sitting beside Homed as his wife when he takes the throne."

Valentina's mouth turned downward in a sneer. "Impossible. Surely Homed has followed the Islamic custom of marrying at a young age. Surely he has other wives."

"Other wives, yes, but none who have claim to royalty. I told you, Dagny claims and evidently can prove that she is of worthy blood to share the throne with Homed. It was only last week that she received a missive from him. And it is not the first that she has received. Apparently Homed shares her feelings. And he is most grateful to her for keeping him informed of his father's health. After she received this missive, she was most curious about your relationship with the emir. It would be safe to say that Homed is already aware of your presence here in Napur and your closeness to his father."

"I see," Valentina said softly. "Homed's most reliable informant is Dagny. Then she must be banished, gotten rid of, anything, but she must leave Napur."

"No. She must stay here so we can watch her. If you send her away, Homed will arm himself with another informer. One who could be more dangerous, since we would not know who he or she is."

"Of course, you're right. I should have thought of it myself. It is as I told Mohab. There is no better judge of character in all the Holy Land. What would I do without you?" Valentina cried, hugging Rosalan.

Embarrassed by this praise, Rosalan quipped, "You would have perished the first day in Saladin's camp." Disengaging herself from Valentina's embrace, she said, "Now tell me what you will, for it was not to shower me with praise or affection that you had me sent here to you."

"Yes." Valentina cleared her throat of husky emotion. "I want you to tell me more of this Ahmar who makes your eyes dance and your cheeks flush. What kind of man is he? To whom does he owe his allegiance? Think well, Rosalan. Whether I remain your poor pigeon or a cooked goose depends on your answer."

"There is little I can tell you other than that I know him to be a man of kindness and good character. Wily, cautious, yes, but he needed these traits to survive. And who among us can blame him for keeping the truth about his manhood to himself? To admit it would have meant death."

"Yet he admitted it to you." Valentina looked at Rosalan questioningly.

"Agreed, but to no other. He loves me, Valentina; that is why he told me his secret."

"And do you love him?"

Rosalan's cheeks flushed under Valentina's scrutiny. "Yes—I mean no! I can't love him. The one thing that Ahmar cannot give me is the one thing I know I must have. A child. For this reason I cannot love him."

Valentina decided it would be most unfair to press Rosalan any further. That she could come to love this man, give her heart to him, and trust to cherish that part of herself which she called her secret core were reasons enough for Valentina to trust him. She had to trust him; there was no one else!

"Rosalan, can Ahmar read and write? Do you know?"

The look the Bedouin girl gave her was rife with puzzlement. "Yes, I do know. He is the one who keeps the harem's household accounts. He is apt with figures also."

"Wonderful! Now tell me again, can he be trusted? To what extent can I place my faith in him? I must know now, this moment. The sultans are waiting at the granaries for the delivery of grains and foodstuffs. I want Ahmar to take charge. And there will be other matters which will need a man's hand, and Mohab is too old to see to them. Do you think Ahmar is our man?" Valentina's voice was urgent.

"Ahmar is our man," Rosalan said simply. "I would trust him with my life."

"It may just come to that, Rosalan," Valentina said solemnly.

Chapter Fifteen

Valentina returned to her room to change out of her gay costume of the night before into something which reflected her sorrowful mood. She had just finished arranging the dark green veil that matched her long, loose-flowing gown when Rosalan entered, saying that she had brought Ahmar. "Leave us, then, Rosalan. Go to the emir and stay with Mohab. The old man needs someone just now. Neither of them should be alone."

Valentina looked frankly at Ahmar to see what effect her words would have on him. She watched carefully for a reaction that would tell her he already knew of the emir's condition. A shifting of the eyes, a shuffling of the feet, some sign as to whether or not to trust him. Ahmar stood at attention, his tall, well-built frame filling the doorway. He wore the bright, gay dress of those who were part of Ramiff's harem. Somehow the bright yellow silks and the beaded tunics were not so effeminate on him as they were on the other eunuchs. There was a sensuality about this man, and Valentina wondered that the others had not seen it. Still, she thought, what reason would they have to look for it? They could see no farther than his label of a eunuch.

"You are Ahmar. Do you know who I am?" she questioned with a ring of authority in her voice.

"You are known by many names," he answered, "yet I believe the name you prefer is Valentina."

Shocked that Ahmar could be so candid, Valentina looked for a hint of insolence in his handsome countenance, but there was none. His features, though rugged and swarthy, nevertheless bore a trace of refinement. If this were Europe, it would be said that he had the look of a gentleman or a knight of the crown. He was clean-shaven save for a length of side whiskers, and his jaw was square and well-defined. While he did not have a burly physique, he had a sinewy look of strength about him. His hands were broad, with a dark fuzz of hair on his knuckles. But it was his eyes that struck her. Light gray, the color of the sky just before dawn, before the sun casts its rosy glow over the world.

"Where do you come from, Ahmar? You do not appear to be of Turkish blood. Your eyes, for one thing . . ."

"I am of Turkish blood. My mother was a Turk and my father was a Frank. A Christian." Ahmar stated this simply, without the hostility common to other Moslems of mixed blood. Seeing that Ahmar did not continue his explanation, Valentina did not pursue the subject.

"Rosalan speaks very highly of you, Ahmar, and it was she who suggested to me that you could be of some help." When Valentina mentioned Rosalan, Ahmar's face betrayed his feelings for the young Bedouin girl.

"I am honored that Rosalan has some small regard for me. I would not care to disappoint her. Anything I can do to serve you would be my delight."

"I understand you have a good knowledge of figures and the written word. I have need of your knowledge out at the granaries. The sultans have come to see to their delivery of foodstuffs. Do you think you could manage this for me if I gave you their contracts and ledger books?"

"I would do all I could to serve you and Emir Ramiff." Ahmar's expression changed to one of pride, and Valentina imagined that he would be glad to prove that his talents exceeded the demands of the harem.

"How much do you know about me, Ahmar? What have you been told?"

The man lowered his eyes, avoiding her gaze.

"You may speak frankly," Valentina urged. Still he did not meet her eyes.

Finally he said, "I only choose to believe that which Rosalan has told me. Nothing more. I know you have enemies here in the palace, and I would not make myself a party to their viciousness. Let it suffice to say that I am your servant, yours and my leader's, the emir. I owe no allegiance to any other, and I would not pledge myself to you if I did not know you to be sympathetic to Emir Ramiff's needs."

Valentina smiled. She could appreciate why Rosalan, honest and painfully frank herself, would choose this man. "Come with me, then, Ahmar. I will fetch the ledgers for you and show you what must be done."

Ahmar bent to salute her with the traditional touches to the heart, mouth, and forehead. In his eyes she saw there a friend.

Valentina sat for hours, her hand resting upon the clawlike hand of the old man. From time to time she would bend her head and put her ear to his chest to listen for his feeble heartbeat. As dusk settled over the palace, the beloved emir joined Allah, his death peaceful and quiet. The white panther cub emitted a low howl and bared her small pointed teeth. Valentina looked at the animal and narrowed her eyes. "So you are growing up. We shall miss him!" she said softly, tears coursing down her cheeks.

Mohab knelt beside his lifelong friend, a low keening sound surging from his throat. They sat there for a long time, Rosalan, Mohab, and Valentina, each sharing the other's grief at the passing of a good and noble ruler.

When the moon slid behind the clouds, they buried the emir, scattered the ground, and tossed small rocks and pebbles upon his grave beneath a Judas tree. Sobbing, Valentina rushed back to the emir's quarters and flung herself on the bed where the old man had joined his Allah. The cub jumped on the bed and nuzzled her cheek, purring loudly for her attention. Gently she stroked the cat's head and then scooped her up and sobbed all the louder.

This solitary funeral was wrong! Ramiff had been a good and kind leader to the people of Napur. He should have had his people's tears of grief and a funeral ceremony befitting his stature. But this was what he had wanted, what he had trained her for, what she had promised. Ramiff had warned her that she would tread on dangerous ground. It would not be easy to conceal the death of Napur's leader.

"A truce is inevitable between Christian and Moslem," he had said, his white-filmed eyes pleading. "Save Napur, save my kingdom from Homed, that feral-hearted son whom Allah saw fit to curse me with! When the truce is signed, go to Malik en Nasr. He will help you. He will be free of the ties of war, and he will see to your safety and protect Napur from Homed's insanity."

How could she have refused this gentle man? He had nowhere else to turn. Even Saladin himself could not deny Homed the right of his inheritance. Only she, Ramiff had implored, could do that for him. When a truce was signed, Saladin would appoint a regent, as was his right, to watch over Homed and see that Napur did not suffer from poor leadership. "It would not be for long, Valentina. A treaty will be signed within a year, two at the most! Homed has been banished from Napur until my death. You will not have any interference from him, and the people in

216

my palace dread his return as fervently as I do. They will not ask questions."

And so Valentina found herself pledged to conceal the old man's death until a truce was made.

For three days Valentina remained in seclusion, alternating between tears of sorrow and tears of anger that Allah should take the one person in this new world whom she had come to love. On the fourth day she dressed carefully in white khalats and a deep blue tunic. She covered her head with a blue headcloth and a white turban. In the center of the turban folds she placed an ornate pin set with a blue sapphire which Ramiff had given her, saying he imagined it matched her eyes perfectly.

When Valentina reached the courtyard, Ahmar was waiting for her astride a fine roan horse. In his hand he held the reins for the white Arabian stallion she had bartered away from Saladin.

"How did you anticipate my taking a ride, Ahmar?"

"Rosalan, mistress," was his simple reply. "She thought you would have need for a guard. Mistress, the emir's stable is not equipped with a lady's saddle. If you would like, I can ready a cart . . ." From the expression in Valentina's eyes Ahmar knew he had blundered.

"And just what do you know of ladies' saddles?" she asked sternly. "Do you doubt that I would ride astride? The truth, Ahmar. Why do you think I would have need of, much less know of, a lady's saddle?"

"Would the mistress let it suffice to say that one of Christian blood can sense another?"

"Who told you?" Valentina demanded, realizing to her dismay that she had just admitted that which she had been ready to deny. "Rosalan?"

"No, mistress. Rosalan said nothing. Behead me, yet I swear I speak the truth. Forgive me, but yesterday I spied you sitting alone in the secluded gardens, near the solitary Judas tree. You were very quiet for a long time, and I hesitated to interrupt you. When you were ready to leave, I saw you touch your hand to your forehead, then to your breast and to each shoulder. My mother once told me that this was how my mother prayed to his God. She said it was the sign of the cross."

Fear tinged Valentina's eyes, turning them a murky green.

"Fear not, mistress. I was alone when I observed you. No one else saw you."

"So now you know that I am a Christian and that I have never ridden astride. What are you going to do about it?" she challenged, watching for hidden signs of his intentions.

"About the fact of your being a Christian, I intend to protect your secret. As for your never having ridden astride, I intend to teach you."

Valentina smiled in spite of her trepidations. She was coming to like Ahmar very much, more each time she encountered him. "How do Moslem women ride, Ahmar?"

"They don't. They are always perched upon a camel or are driven in carts. Mostly they walk behind their men."

"Then I shall be the first, Ahmar. Let my enemies do with it what they will. I will ride!"

Ahmar leaped down from his roan and assisted her in mounting the stallion. It felt strange to Valentina. "Now I can see why men are better riders than women." She scowled. "Sitting astride gives the rider a keener sense of security and more control."

"So you have discovered our secret," Ahmar said lightly as he mounted the roan. "Keep the secret to yourself, mistress. We men have no desire to be outdone by women."

"Outdone it will be! Come, Ahmar," she challenged, "I will race you to the granary."

Valentina spurred her horse and raced ahead of Ahmar. Unbeknownst to her, Ahmar's horse lost a shoe, and he stopped to tether his mount to a tree. He loped back to the stables for a new mount, knowing Valentina would be safe on the short ride through the meadows and fields. Nothing could happen to her. So intent was he on his errand that he failed to see a distant rider race after Valentina.

Valentina laughed delightedly as the wind whipped at her face, her hair billowing behind her. She knew she would beat Ahmar by very good lengths. Suddenly her horse stumbled and threw her off balance. A long arm reached out to steady her and to slow the mount beneath her. She drew in her breath as she stared at the Saracen from Messina. Her lips trembled and tears gathered in her eyes. They were alone. His gentle touch on her arm felt like a scorching brand. "Please," she whispered huskily, "you must tell me who you are and . . ."

Dark ebony eyes laughed into hers. "Let us say I am a man who is captivated by your beauty. Allow me to be your humble servant," he said, bowing to her from his position on his horse.

Valentina moistened her lips. It was difficult to speak with her breath coming in ragged gasps. "I have no need for a servant," she finally managed.

The rider laughed, a low, husky laugh that sent shivers of delight down Valentina's back. "In truth, I have no desire to be your servant. I merely thought the suggestion might please you."

"Why?" she cried in a tormented voice. "Why are you doing this to me? You're laughing at me."

The laughing eyes sobered. "No, I would never laugh at you. My heart is breaking for your tears."

"Who are you? Why do you keep seeking me out?" Valentina cried in an anguished voice.

"One day I will have an answer for you," the rider said simply.

"Please, you must not do this to me. I cannot think, I cannot function after I see you. My mind and my heart are in a turmoil. Please tell me why," she pleaded.

"This is not the time for answers. Look to the west, your man approaches."

"Will I see you again?"

The rider chose not to answer this question but replied instead, "One day all things wise and beautiful and wonderful will be yours. You have my promise."

"You speak of eternity. Those things are not meant for me in this life," Valentina cried in a tormented voice.

"You have my promise," the rider called over his shoulder as he raced off, his horse sending spurts of sand high into the air.

Ahmar brought his mount to a skidding stop and looked sharply at his mistress. He did not fail to see the tears in her eyes. "Who was that?" he demanded harshly. "What did he do to you? Tell me! I will ride after him and—"

"No, Ahmar, he is a friend. Come, we must go to the granary. Forget that you saw the rider. Another time we will discuss him."

The sound of hooves in the distance captured Valentina's and Ahmar's attention. "That will be the Sultan of Jakard," Ahmar said. "I would know that magnificent black Arabian of his anywhere."

Valentina steeled herself for the confrontation with Paxon. Within moments they met him in front of the wide granary doors. His black stallion was snorting and pawing the ground, and the panther, who kept pace with his master, was snarling and spitting as Paxon dismounted. His long-legged stride brought him within inches of her.

"Sultan," Valentina said huskily as she bowed and offered him the Islamic salute. "I am sorry for the delay, but your shipment is ready. I understand this is the last of it."

"Yes, we ride out at sundown," Paxon said coolly as he gazed at her in the dimness of the cavernous granary.

Valentina was aware of his intense scrutiny and felt discomfitted. She had to do something, say something. "I shall pray for your safe journey," she said quietly.

"Will you pray to your God or to Allah?" Paxon asked mockingly as his fingers played with the heavy chain attached to his panther.

"To my God, for I am a Christian, as you well know," Valentina replied, an edge to her throaty voice.

Paxon continued to mock her. "A Christian in charge of a Moslem kingdom. If you are ever discovered, you will be crucified. Are you aware of that?"

"Fully aware," she answered quietly. "For now you are the only one who knows. I have wondered at your silence."

"I thought you would." Paxon smiled, his white teeth gleaming in the dimness. Valentina's heart raced. She heard rather than saw Ahmar close the lid of a granary bin and walk out into the bright sunshine. Paxon remained motionless, compelling her with his eyes not to move. The cat at his feet purred loudly and nuzzled his master's boots.

The Saracen tilted his head to the side, reading her emotions. "I recall a time when you rested in my arms as though Allah himself deemed you should be there. I recall tears and a whipping you received because of me. For that reason I have remained silent. I would have come back for you, but the massacre prevented it. I wanted you to know this," he said, his voice dangerously soft in the stillness of the granary. "One day you will be mine and mine alone. I shall see you in the desert in two weeks' time. For now you can think of me and that approaching time. You will be mine," he said confidently, a smile tugging at the corners of his mouth. Jerking the panther's leash, Paxon walked jauntily out of the granary.

Six days before the conference between the Lionheart and Saladin was to begin, Valentina linked a slim chain around the white panther and set out in the garden for a walk. She had to calm her mind. Shadjar ad Darr was the name she had given the cat. The name meant "Pearl Spray" and seemed fitting for the sleek white animal who was the essence of feline femininity. Shadjar's disposition varied. One moment she would purr and the next she would snarl in outrage as her mistress paced the confines of her elegant quarters. At this moment she walked sedately at Valentina's side, purring contentedly. Valentina sat down on a marble bench under a Judas tree and stroked the cat at her feet. "My body and my mind are making demands of me that I can't cope with," she said quietly to the cat. "Do I listen to my heart, or do I listen to my body?" Her mood changed and she laughed, the panther stirring at her feet. Valentina, queen's procurer. Her laugh was high-pitched and shrill, and Shadjar snarled and spit as she began to paw the soft earth beneath the tree.

Leaving the glistening city of Napur, Valentina rode at the front of the long, winding caravan heading for the place of meeting between Richard the Lionhearted and the Moslem king, Saladin. She was dressed simply, all in white from her khalats to her headgear. She rode upon the white stallion beside Ahmar, who had proved invaluable to her in the preparations for hosting the meeting between the warring factors.

Rosalan stayed behind in Napur with Mohab, seeing to it that the emir's death remained a secret. Earlier in the week Valentina had confided in Ahmar, telling him of Ramiff's passion and the pledge she had made to keep the news from Homed until a truce was signed. It had seemed so logical when she had made that pledge, but now, with the pressures mounting between Moslem and Christian, and with Dagny's spies within the palace, she wondered what she could have been thinking of at the time. Guiltily she confessed to herself that she had done it to keep herself out of Dagny's clutches. How long could she maintain this guise? Even with loyal counterparts like Rosalan and Ahmar and Mohab, how long would it be before she made another mistake, like making the sign of the cross when she finished her prayers? Until a truce is signed! her mind screamed, and terror plunged its icy finger into her heart. A truce. How much could she, a woman, do to secure one?

A wild howl behind her caused her to smile. Shadjar ad Darr rode into the caravan and was protesting the confines of the cage. "All of us, Shadjar," Valentina whispered, "are entrapped in one way or another."

With her Valentina brought a huge pavilion and

gifts to both leaders, camels and saddled horses and an entourage of cooks with their supply of meats and pastries and fresh fruits. The dromedaries were burdened with the trappings containing the tents for the large procession from Napur. A brilliant cortege of horsemen followed along the winding path to the meeting place.

Valentina rode in silence, her thoughts upon the three men whom she was to see. Richard, flaming sun god of the north, king of England, keeper of her allegiance to her faith. Saladin, fearless warrior, a man of letters and an expert in strategy and, not the least of all, a tender teacher. Paxon, a dark firebrand, sultan of Jakard, bestower of black looks, arouser of passions, keeper of secrets. To them she rode, three men who had a place in her life, in her heart. And the mysterious man who came to her in many guises and promised her many things, where was he placed, in her heart?

Valentina and her entourage were to join Saladin's camp at one end of the fertile plain which separated him from Richard's camp. As she was seeing to the preparations of her tent, an officer from Malik en Nasr's camp approached her. "A thousand pardons. I seek a woman named Valentina."

"I am Valentina of Napur," she answered. "Why do you seek me?"

"Not I, but Malik en Nasr; he calls for you. The general fell into the throes of fever two days past and, in his delirium, asks for you."

"Take me to him immediately," Valentina cried, a myriad of emotions clutching her heart. "How sick is Malik en Nasr?"

"Most gravely," the officer answered.

Her steps quickened to keep pace with the cloaked officer. Would his illness affect the outcome of the negotiations? How could a truce be made if Saladin was on his death bed? How much longer could she live this life of deceit? Saladin. How much of her heart wished him to live for the truce, and what part of her heart prayed for his recovery for the woman?

The interior of Saladin's tent was dark; he lay on a divan, his face still and lifeless. She looked to the men in attendance, her question asked by her eyes.

"Malik en Nasr calls for a woman named Valentina. Are you the one he seeks?" an attendant asked.

"Yes," she breathed, stepping closer to the divan and noticing the dark hollows beneath Saladin's eyes and his ragged breathing. "I am Valentina, for whom he calls. What manner of illness is this?"

"We are the physicians to Malik en Nasr. He suffers from a desert fever known as *hubta*. It has struck him down before this, and these bouts have weakened him. We ask Allah for his mercy."

Valentina had heard of *hubta* and knew it was a fairly common desert ailment characterized by raging fever and severe pains in the head and along the spine. Saladin stirred; his eyes spoke his pain, his voice no more than a whisper. "Valentina . . . Valentina . . ."

"I am here, my master," she cried, falling to her knees beside the divan. His hand reached for hers and she took it, feeling the dry heat which emanated from it. "I will stay with you until you are well."

"No . . ." He shook his head fitfully. "There is . . . much for you to do."

"And I will do it. Save your strength. I will see that all is done."

"My brother . . . Al Adil . . . he will take my place. Seek him out . . ." Saladin's head fell back to the pillow, and there was not even the sound of his ragged breathing to reassure her.

"Do something!" she cried to the physicians. "You must not let him die—you must do something!"

"Malik en Nasr refused treatment until you arrived. At times the cure is as deadly as the disease."

Through the tent flap came two *mamlūks,* slaves trained to arms. The word *mamlūk* meant, literally, "the possessed," and most were of Turkish origin and were both loyal and formidable warriors. The *mamlūks* began heating iron brands in the glowing coals of the brazier, and when the tips were glowing red, Saladin's physicians turned back the covers, exposing his

bare chest. Even before the brands, searing and hiss-
ing, touched his flesh, Valentina knew what they were
going to do. She recalled having felt his healed scars
from previous brandings and that he had told her they
were the result of his treatment for the *hubta* fever.

Saladin groaned in pain as the first brand burned
into his flesh, and then he was quiet, allowing the physicians to go about their cure. "Now we will pray to
Allah," one man murmured as he applied a soothing
salve to the wounds he had inflicted.

Miraculously the cure seemed to work. Within an
hour Saladin began to perspire profusely, and the physicians proclaimed him cured. His recovery would take
many days, they warned, and there was no need to sit
beside his divan. They would care for him.

When at last Valentina stepped out of Saladin's
black and yellow tent, darkness had fallen and the velvety sky was filled with shining stars. Weary and anxious for Saladin's return to health, she stumbled in the
direction of her own pavilion through the masses of soldiers who were waiting vigilantly for news of their general. She nodded her head and smiled. A great cheer
went up among the men. Many threw themselves upon
their knees and thanked Allah for bestowing this blessing on their leader.

Paxon had been waiting for her, and he took her
arm. "I will return you to your tent. You have had an
exhausting day; you will need your rest. Tomorrow negotiations begin, and your duties will be many."

Valentina walked beside Paxon, grateful for his
presence. When they arrived at her camp, she saw that
her tent had been erected and that a dim light from
the brazier glowed within. An old woman, a slave from
the kitchens in Napur, slept outside, waiting to serve
Valentina her dinner. Everything seemed to be in perfect order, and she turned to Paxon questioningly.

"Your man Ahmar and I saw that a proper camp
was made," he told her. "One thing you must learn,
Valentina, is that slaves and servants do only what you
tell them, nothing more. No doubt they would have

awaited your return for the order to erect the tents and prepare the meals."

Her eyes shone with gratitude. "I thank you," she said softly.

He felt himself becoming lost in her loveliness. It would be so simple to embrace her, to feel the fragile framework of her crushed against him, to press his mouth to hers, to feel its warmth and sensitive moistness, to partake of the sweetness he knew he would find there. He must have her!

As if reading his thoughts, Valentina retreated a step. She didn't trust herself not to throw herself into his arms and make herself his.

Mistaking her intentions, Paxon interpreted her backward movement as a rejection. "I will leave you to yourself. No need to repeat your thanks for my waiting to walk you to your tent. I knew I would not have to wait long. Even a Christian woman would not demand a night of love from a dying man!" His words were a slap, a physical affront.

"Do you hurry to leave because of your fear that I would instead demand a night of love from *you?* Walk on, sultan of Jakard. If it is love I seek, I would not look in your direction!"

Never had a woman spoken to Paxon this way! His hand came up as if to strike her, but she showed no fear. "So, I do not frighten you! You are as obstinate as a braying she-camel. My embraces you would reject, and yet would accept my blows. There is only one way to tame an obstinate beast, and that is to be more obstinate than she!" Without warning, his arm reached out and pulled her close. His mouth crashed down upon hers, and the stars seemed to leave the sky and fill her head. His mouth lingered upon hers, and when he drew away he pressed his mouth close to her ear. "And once having trained the obstinate beast, it is best to remind her who is the master," he whispered softly.

Valentina's hand flew up and slapped him soundly across his cheek. "I take you at your word, Sultan. *I am the master,* and you are the obstinate beast!"

Paxon retaliated in kind, bringing up his hand and

slapping her across the face. Her head snapped back at the stinging blow. Her pride was stung, and she hissed at him in low-voiced curses while he merely laughed at her. Seeing that her words had no effect, she ran off into the darkness, his laughter loud and obscene in the velvety night. On and on she ran, with no mind to where she was going. When she fell, she lay there with her head in the crook of her arm, sobbing uncontrollably.

Strong, gentle, familiar hands gathered her close, and whispered words found their way to her ear. These arms were the only safety she needed. Only these arms that held her close and the soft, safe whispers were all she needed for now and forever. There was no need to look into the dark eyes; she knew what she would read in their depths. She burrowed her head in his chest and sobbed until his gentle words soothed her. Strong yet tender hands stroked her matted hair from her forehead. She moaned softly as she felt him kiss her cheek, her throat, her mouth.

Valentina settled herself comfortably in his arms, a strange peace enveloping her. His touch was calming, hypnotic, and eventually she began to doze. Soft murmurs escaped her from time to time, and Menghis smiled as he cradled her dark head to his chest. When she was fully and deeply asleep, Menghis brought up his hand, and within minutes men surrounded him. "Take her back to her tent and be careful not to wake her," he said.

Valentina felt her sleep being disturbed, but she knew that she was safe. Unbeknownst to her, she slept in the arms of the devoted ones, Menghis's *fedawi*.

Chapter Sixteen

Because she was a woman, Valentina was not allowed inside the tent where the negotiations were taking place. She was compelled to rely upon news of the proceedings from the servants who tended the men during the meeting.

Time was heavy upon her hands, and after her third visit to Saladin's tent that morning, she sought out Ahmar, who was making himself useful by instructing the bevy of servants from Napur on the preparation of the meals.

"Ahmar, I have an errand for you. Take two men and ride back to Napur. Go to Mohab, and he will give you a basket to bring here to me."

"Napur? Yes, mistress. Has this something to do with the pigeons you sent to Edessa just after you agreed to host this meeting here?"

"Yes," Valentina said coyly. "I once heard Saladin say he would give his life for ripe cherries, and the best grow in the orchards of Edessa. I commissioned an envoy to carry dozens of homing pigeons there. When the birds are released, each will return to Napur carrying several tree-ripened cherries."

Ahmar smiled. "Your inventiveness would amaze even Allah."

"How long will it take you to reach Napur?"

"I will return with the cherries by eventide."

"Allah go with you, then," Valentina whispered as Ahmar sprinted off to saddle his mount.

Word from the negotiations was not good. Both parties agreed that the war had gone on too long and that the losses of men and horses were uncountable. Richard had taken the initiative and stated, "Jerusalem must be yielded up, and the Moslems must retire beyond the Jordan River." Al Adil, brother to Saladin and his counselor, refused with pride.

Back and forth the bantering went, neither side gaining a point, and a truce seemed unreachable. The time arrived for evening prayers among the Moslems, and the negotiations ended. Richard and his men were invited to partake of the banquet being prepared, and he accepted.

Valentina dressed for the evening's festivities. A large hip bath was brought into her tent and filled with heated water, a luxury here in the desert. A serving girl laid out a gown of white silk embroidered with colors of the peacock. Golden cloth slippers and a girdle were arranged near the gown, as was an assortment of jewelry.

Valentina's hair was brushed back from her face into a free-falling cascade down her back. The hair above her ears was braided with blue ribbons and looped back to show her dainty ears and the golden hoops in her lobes. The cool silk of her gown was soothing against her body. It was cut in a wide scoop over her breasts and fit snugly along her midriff and hips, ending in a swirling circle just above her toes. The sleeves were long and full-cut, edged with embroidery about the hem. As she viewed herself in the polished metal hung above the divan, she frowned. The gown was too revealing; her breasts were seductively outlined and threatened to spill from the bodice. The garment would have been a scandal in Navarre, she thought. But, of course, this was not France!

The great pavilion had been erected that day. The crimson silk which formed its walls and ceiling caught the rays of the setting sun and dazzled the eye. Thick Turkish rugs had been strewn about the floor and topped with floor cushions the colors of the rainbow. Servants walked to and fro, carrying trays laden with food and fresh fruits. Shadjar ad Darr followed Valentina about the camp as she saw to the last-minute preparations. Everything taken care of, she took the panther back to her own tent and chained her.

"Shadjar, you sense my hidden feelings, don't you?" Valentina asked softly as she petted the glossy white head. "I have never felt this way before. I am drawn to the sultan and I am drawn to the man in the doe-skin garb. No, that is not true, Shadjar. The man called Menghis has crept into my very soul. My flesh might succumb to another, but never my heart. For me there can be no other. He stalks my dreams and invades my every waking hour. My destiny and my mind are his. He is a man to whom I can give myself totally. I know that somehow, in some way, my life belongs to him. Perhaps it will happen in the desert, where the sands of time stand still. It will be one moment in time, when that one moment will be an eternity for me, and for him. I see in his eyes what is mirrored in mine." Valentina gave the cat one last comforting pat and stepped out into the cool desert night.

The yashmak, covering the lower half of her face, fluttered in the light breeze. She spied Ahmar and his companions leading three pack horses into the camp-site. Her slippered feet sank into the soft sands of the desert as she ran to meet him. "Ahmar," she said breathlessly, "did the birds carry back the cherries from Edessa?" Her eyes flew to the pack horses, trying to see between the slats of the hampers containing the pigeons.

"Aye, mistress, the plan worked admirably. Every bird returned with four cherries each, and I think it is safe to say that every single fruit was picked within the last twenty-four hours."

"How did they manage it?" Valentina asked, tapping one of the hampers as if she didn't really believe it contained cooing birds.

"Mohab instructed that little pouches, those which normally contain herbs and medicines, be attached to the pigeons' legs. When the birds were brought to Edessa, cherries were fitted into each pouch. The birds were then released and flew directly to Napur.

230

When I went to retrieve them, Mohab was waiting outside the dovecote, his eyes skyward, looking for the last of them to return."

Ahmar reached into one of the hampers and withdrew a gray pigeon. The tiny pouches were still attached to the bird's legs. Valentina held out her hands, and Ahmar dropped four ripe cherries into her palm. "They're still warm from the sun," Valentina marveled.

"Aye, and taste them! By all that's holy, I don't think anything sweeter has touched my lips!"

"Save Rosalan's lips, eh, Ahmar?" Valentina teased. Ahmar's handsome face flushed a deep red. "Forgive me; at times my pleasures seem perverse," she apologized with a laugh. "Go and have someone give you something to eat. I will have servants carry the hampers to Saladin's tent."

Outside Malik en Nasr's great tent bearing his standard, Valentina stopped to relieve one of the pigeons of its burden. She heard her name being announced by the man standing guard over the general, then heard Saladin bidding her to enter.

The interior of the tent was dim, lit only by the low fire in the brazier.

"I have come to wish you a return to health, mighty Saladin, and to bring you a small gift."

"Your presence is gift enough. Come sit here beside me and tell me what has kept you from my side all this day." Saladin's voice had regained its authority but was still weak from his bout with the desert fever. It seemed to Valentina that the odor of burning flesh still hung heavily in the atmosphere. She marveled that he should seem so well on the road to recovery. Another mystery in this strange land, she thought: a desert cure for a desert ailment.

"There was much that needed to be done, the food, the pavilion, endless little details . . ."

"And a commendable job you have made of it! Yes, I have my little spies, and they have informed me how diligently you have applied your talents." His hand reached for hers across the covers, and the contact with him was reassuring. There was strength in his grasp and his eyes were bright and alert, although dark shadows were smudged beneath them, the evidence of his ordeal with the fever. "You say you have a gift . . ."

"Yes," she said, remembering the four little fruits clasped in her hand and hidden beneath the folds of her gown.

"First, remove your yashmak. I wish to see your face. Can it be as lovely as I dreamed while I lay here?"

Valentina lifted her hand and pulled the sheer silk away from her face.

"That is better," he sighed, "and you are more beautiful than I remembered. Now, the gift, what is it?" He smiled. "Hummingbird tongues? The horn of the great unicorn? A hair from the head of Mohammed?"

"Better than all of those together," Valentina laughed, a sweet, throaty sound. "You will never guess in a thousand years!"

"But you haven't given me a chance! Where is it, there in the hand you hide beneath your skirt? Ah, then, it is small . . . what could it be?"

Valentina held her hand out, the four cherries glistening in her palm.

"Cherries!" he exulted, reaching for them.

"No!" she tormented. "Not until you say they are more fitting a king than hummingbird tongues and unicorn horns. Admit it before I take back my gift and leave you to dream of their sweetness all through the long night!"

"It is admitted. Now bring them here, else you force me to rise from this bed and chase you through the camp! Would you see me humbled for a few cherries before the eyes of my men?"

Valentina knelt beside his bed like an obedient servant. She presented her gift with upraised hands while she bowed her head low. "Never to see Saladin humbled," she laughed. "Would that they had no stone; then they would be fitting a king."

"A cherry without a stone is like a woman without a heart!" He bit into a luscious ripe fruit, his eyes widening. "Where did you come about these, Valentina? I would swear by the Prophet's beard that they fell from the trees in Edessa. How did you come by them? I would swear they are still warm from the sun!"

"Would you believe me if I told you they came here to you by the wings of birds?"

"Beautiful lady, I would believe you command the hearts of men but never the birds of the sky."

"Believe it, master, for this is how I came by the cherries. Shall I prove it?" Valentina clapped her hands, and six pigeons were released into the tent and came to rest atop his bed. Deftly she captured one and removed the tiny pouches from its legs, presenting him with four more cherries.

"By the eyes of Allah!" he exclaimed. "How did you know . . . ?"

"I once heard you say to Emir Ramiff that there were times you would give your life for the fruit ripe from the tree. I had no wish for you to give your life for something I could so easily provide."

"The woman is a wonder!" he exclaimed, looking off into a dark corner of the tent.

Valentina had supposed they were alone except for the guard, and she turned abruptly, astonished to see the sultan of Jakard standing quietly at attention, his eyes boring into Valentina's face.

Time seemed to hang suspended as they glared at each other. Valentina was the first to lower her eyes. It seemed to her that she could still see the imprint of her hand upon his dark cheek, and the harsh sound of the slap she had dealt him echoed in her ears. Valentina's eyes became panic-filled as it occurred to her that he might seek retaliation for that affront by revealing her identity to Saladin. Was that the reason he was here now? Had she interrupted his plan? Was this why his night-dark eyes gazed unwaveringly into hers?

Saladin was watching them both, his eyes drifting

speculatively from one to the other. The long, still moment was broken by the entrance of a servant bringing in a large basket of cherries retrieved from the birds in the hampers. A moment later a loud fluttering and flapping of wings was heard as the pigeons were released for their flight back to Napur.

Saladin broke the silence. "Valentina, your gift is the most magnificent gesture ever bestowed upon me. I have received jewels and rarities, all given to a king, but this . . . this was for me, the man." The words were spoken humbly, his voice on the verge of breaking. He was deeply touched by her gesture and was too honest a man to hide his emotions. "Paxon, come here," he called gruffly, reaching out a hand to him. Paxon moved forward and placed his hand in that of his king.

Valentina threw Saladin an imploring look, reading his thoughts, hoping she was mistaken.

"Your hand, Valentina."

"Kadi, no, please, I beg you, don't do this." Her tone was deep and husky.

"Your hand, Valentina."

She threw herself on her knees, pressing close against his chest. "Kadi, I beg you, if you have any feeling for me!"

Saladin patted her back soothingly. "It is because of the feeling I have for you that I do this. Your blood is hot and strong, too strong for a man my age. I give you over to Paxon's keeping," he whispered. "Go now, and leave me to my cherries." The Islamic king took her hand and placed it upon Paxon's palm.

The contact with Paxon's flesh sent tingles of expectancy coursing through her veins. She remained on her knees, refusing to look up into Paxon's eyes, for if she did . . .

"Leave me now," Saladin commanded in a voice more harsh than he had intended.

Paxon helped Valentina to her feet. She grasped his sun-darkened hand and stood there feeling small and powerless before his muscular strength. She felt his eyes compel her to look at him, and in spite of herself

234

she obeyed. All will and determination seemed to evaporate with his touch.

He led her to the tent flap and she hesitated, glancing back at the divan on which Saladin lay. The general felt her gaze and turned his head to face her. "Why do you hesitate?" he asked. "I gave you over to the sultan of Jakard!"

Valentina's voice was a low, throaty sound that seemed to fill the stillness within the tent. "I go, Kadi, as you order me to do, but I will not make it easy for him!"

Paxon walked beside her, glancing at her in the darkness. The shimmer of starshine reflected off her face. She had not bothered to restore the filmy yashmak, and her face was bare to the night breezes. As he walked beside her, he was aware of her withdrawal, her resignation, this woman-child who could evoke the deepest sympathy with her tears and a gut-churning passion with her allure. Paxon had been as shocked as Valentina when Saladin placed her hand in his. He had felt the icy fingers, the bloodless fragility of them, the lifelessness, the cold of death. Yet there had been a hunger in her eyes, a hunger he meant to fill until she cried for mercy and slept tranquilly and sated in his arms.

"Where are you taking me?" she asked, her voice low and tremulous.

"To the other side of the oasis, not far now." When no reaction registered on her face, he added, "Are you so eager that I should take you here, now?"

"You planned this!" she accused, turning to him, her face a soft glow of ivory in the starlight.

"No, but I could not have planned it better." He reached out a hand and held her arm tightly, afraid she might run away as she had the night before.

"Release me!" she commanded, her low voice heavy with threat.

"You are mine! Given to me by Saladin, the king."

"Not yours, never yours!" she spit, wrenching her arm away.

235

"We shall see," came his reply, more dangerous and threatening than the trumpets of war. Seizing her arm again, he marched her forward at a quickened pace toward the edge of the oasis, away from prying eyes and the scent of camels.

Beneath the light of the stars, beside a tall date palm which whispered in the wind, Paxon stopped and removed his cloak, spreading it upon the grass which grew beneath their feet.

A slim beam of moonlight pierced the heavy foliage of the date palms and shone down upon Valentina, illuminating her features in silvery radiance. Paxon's face was in the shadows and inscrutable, but his gaze was a tangible thing; she felt it touch her and was aware of his closeness and the flames of anger running through his veins.

"It should not be this way between us, Valentina. Come to me of your own will." His voice was a warm throb that became one with her heartbeat.

"As I told Saladin, I will not make it easy for you," she said resolutely, and he felt a coldness all the way to the pit of his stomach.

"You were willing enough with the general," he reminded her cruelly.

"And I am here with you now because Saladin commands it."

He stepped closer to her. "And you always obey your king. To which king do you owe your allegiance, Lady Valentina of Navarre?" He could see her breasts heaving beneath the thin silk of her gown, and he thought how easily that fragile fabric would rent beneath his hands. "If you have no desire to walk back to camp with your gown in tatters and your flesh exposed for the whole of Saladin's army to see, I suggest you remove your gown."

She knew he spoke the truth. Here, alone with him, isolated from the rest of the world, he could take her as he wished, and she would have no recourse because Malik en Nasr had given his approval.

Holding him in an unwavering gaze, she silently began to remove her gown. When she at last stood before him divested of her clothing, she made no move to cover herself. He filled his sight with the look of her, drank in her lissome curves, and knew he wanted her as he had never wanted another woman.

She mocked him with her eyes and beckoned him with a slow, sensual smile, her full, ripe mouth parting over her white teeth. Paxon held her with his eyes as he tore the garments from his back and came to her.

His arms slipped around her and his skin was cool and smooth against her own. He pulled her close, so close, flattening her breasts against his chest. He bent toward her slowly.

She turned her head away, back and forth, resisting the moment when his lips found hers. He buried his hands in her hair, his fingers twining in the heavy ebony masses, holding her head immobile.

He found her mouth.

It was ice, the same bloodless cold that was her hand when Saladin placed it in his.

Still, there was that need for her, the hunger for her.

His lips clinging to hers, he pressed her down onto the cloak he had spread for them. Valentina tore her mouth away, gasping for breath. "There is a difference between lovemaking and ravishment," she gasped, the sound of her voice urging his passions.

"Only a slight difference," he breathed, forcing her down until she felt his cloak against her shoulder blades. He kissed her mouth, cherishing it with his own, imprisoning her body beneath his hard, lean strength.

Her struggles were futile, all her strength expended from the force of her desperation. His mouth became more demanding, savage in its urgency. His hands caressed her breasts and his mouth left hers to explore the softness of her throat, trailing the touch of his fingers with the warmer touch of his mouth.

She ceased her struggles, realizing that she was no match for his strength. She lay still, motionless, passive beneath him. He kissed her ear and breathed soft Saracen love words as his fingers traveled down the length of her, teasing, arousing, till her breath came in short pants and her body turned beneath his touch, opening itself to him like the petals of a flower.

His searching fingers adored her, his hungry mouth worshipped her and traced patterns on her skin. His head moved lower, grazing the tautness of her belly down to the softness between her thighs.

He felt her flesh grow warm to his touch; the ice had been thin, and beneath it beat the pulse of a woman. He parted her thighs with his knee and felt her move beneath him, arching her back to receive him. Her mouth was exotic and sweet and flamed beneath his. She accepted him, his maleness, his hardness, as he drove into her, and his pulses beat in his veins and crescendoed into endlessly long thunderings.

She felt him move upon her, demanding her response, and she offered it, moving beneath him, reveling in her own femininity, trailing her fingers down the length of his muscled torso. She urged him on, hearing the tattoo of her heartbeat in rhythm with his. And between the beats of her heart she heard another sound, the sound of his voice as he promised to make her his. And the sound of her own voice promising it would not be easy. Words, only words. This was real, the feel of him, his need for her, his becoming part of her, her becoming one with him.

Rosalan's voice, ". . . the core of you . . . the essence that is you . . . no one can take it . . . it is only yours to give . . ."

Her own voice, ". . . I will not make it easy . . . easy . . . easy . . ."

Her arms fell to her side, her body lay passive. It was only when he had taken his pleasure of her and withdrawn that he showed his anger. He leaned close to her, and she could feel his hot breath on her cheek. He scowled, his dark eyes filled with fury. Yet she did not draw back but returned his gaze with an indifference which reflected her lack of response.

"I am not a fool, Valentina, so be wary of playing me for one! I felt your mouth cling to mine and your breasts rise proudly beneath my touch. Did not those

238

long and lovely limbs curve over my back and imprison me within you? Is it me you resist or yourself? Don't answer," he said gruffly as he rolled away from her. "Perhaps your coldness was the reason Saladin found you lacking, and even now, at this moment, he is doubtless laughing that he foisted you on me!"

Valentina's nails itched to rake the flesh on his cheek. What he said was true. She had responded to him. She had wanted him more than any other man, more than anything. But neither her response alone nor the pleasure of her body would ever be enough for a man like Paxon. He demanded of her things she was not ready to give. He excited her, yet he frightened her. There was a hardness about him, and unyielding intractability. He was a warrior first, the sultan of Jakard second, and a human being last.

"You smite me, Valentina, and this is something I do not take lightly from a woman."

"You would take all else from a woman, why not a rejection?"

"Never your rejection!" he threatened, pinning her back against the cloak. "If I cannot have you, no one else will! I promise you that! I have only to place my hands about your throat and kill another Christian to add to my record."

"Why don't you, then? Have you suddenly developed scruples against the killing of women?"

"You are less than a woman. You forget I've witnessed the ice which runs through your veins. No, not yet. I have decided you will live a while longer. Your eyes are asking me a question, Valentina. You wonder why I have not yet revealed your true identity to Saladin."

"You misunderstand, mighty sultan. I was wondering how long it would take you to use that threat against me," Valentina snarled, her eyes blazing.

Gripping her shoulders more fiercely, Paxon gritted his teeth and growled, "I have allowed myself to be placed in an untenable position. By not revealing your deception immediately I became aware of it, I have placed myself in the position of becoming your accessory. A most unhealthy position for a man such as myself who makes ready to become part of the leadership of this land. Secondly, I bestowed my forbearance upon you because I cannot imagine what harm you could employ against the Islamic nation. I know Ramiff to be a staunch and loyal man. He will keep you in line. And last of all, but not the least," he growled more fiercely, his hands still holding her prisoner, "I am not yet prepared to see you face your death. There is still the matter of who will win the war we wage between one another. Heed me well, Valentina, I will win. I always win! One day soon you will be mine and the battle will have been won!"

Paxon suddenly released her and left her lying upon the cloak while he gathered his garments. Stunned, she waited for him to return. The night had turned chilly, cold even, and her flesh rose in protesting little bumps.

She felt bruised, beaten, more so than the night in Saladin's camp when she had been raped by the two soldiers. She had come so close, too close, to trusting him, to surrendering herself to him. There was no love between them. All she represented to him was a new vista to conquer. A battle not yet won. He wanted her because she represented a challenge. There was no tenderness, save that which he would display to aid him in his quest. There was no faith, no trust . . . nothing. Sexuality, lust, yearning . . . all things of the body . . . but what of the heart? Where was the camaraderie? The sharing of spirit? The cherishing that could withstand the events of a lifetime?

Fully dressed, Paxon came back with her clothing. Dropping down on one knee, he fitted her slippers on her feet as though she were a small child. She had to quell her hand from reaching out to soothe his injured pride. She pressed her lips into a tight thin line to keep herself from explaining her passivity.

He tossed the white silk gown at her. "Dress, else I'll be forced to drag you back to camp naked as the day you were born." His tone was mocking and edged with contempt, and Valentina felt all explanations die in her throat.

He watched her as she dressed, and she did not attempt to hide herself from his gaze. In spite of himself, Paxon felt his desire for her renewed. "I thought I had melted your reserve, and at the last moment you proved me wrong. I promise you this. There will be another time, many times, when I will make love to you, and bit by bit I will chip away that icy indifference. Heed me well, Valentina, you will be mine!"

To argue would be a waste of breath and would only prolong the time till she could be alone with her thoughts. Valentina silently moved across the oasis in the direction of her camp, walking mutely beside the Saracen. Apprehension swelled in her heart at the thought that one day soon Paxon would make his threat come true.

Chapter Seventeen

Throughout the next day Valentina stayed close to her camp, tending to the endless duties required of her as proxy hostess for Emir Ramiff. She filled her mind with routine chores, refusing to think of the night before beneath the stars at the edge of the oasis.

The afternoon found her exhausted, and she retreated to her tent to refresh herself. Stretching down on the low, narrow divan on which she slept, she found it impossible to direct her thoughts away from the Saracen. In the solitude of her tent, the memory of him became sharp and vivid. Had it only been the night before when she had lain under his tender touches, when his warm mouth had pressed against hers and evoked emotions from the desert shadows of her heart?

"Mistress," came a call. "May I enter?" It was Ahmar.

"Yes, enter," she answered, grateful for a distraction from her thoughts of Paxon.

Ahmar entered and lowered himself beside the divan. "The negotiations are at an end. A truce was impossible."

Valentina sat up. "An end? Ahmar, are you certain?"

"Nothing could be more certain. Richard has ordered his men to break camp. The Lionheart came here for one reason alone, to show the world that he was willing to negotiate. It was the only thing he could do to recover his honor after the massacre. You will never believe what came out of this meeting."

Valentina looked questioningly at Ahmar, waiting for him to speak.

"The Lionheart seems to think that a marriage between Christian and Moslem would be the end of the war. He offers his sister, Queen Joanna, to Saladin's brother, Al Adil. This done, both Christians and Moslems are to surrender their holdings in the Holy Land to the new couple, and Jerusalem is to be held in peace by both sides. He asks that the true cross be given back to the Christians."

"It will never be," Valentina said softly. "Queen Joanna is a fervent Christian and abhors the Moslems. She will never agree, and Richard will have no recourse but to accept her decision. She is the widow of the late king of Sicily and, until she gave over the throne to her husband's cousin Tancred, was a queen in her own land. As such, she has her rights and will never agree to marry Al Adil, cultured and affable though he may be."

"The Lionheart is well aware of this, just as we are. He was grasping for the moon."

"What does the Lionheart plan to do now? It is clear he cannot in all truth expect this marriage to come to pass."

"There is talk that he goes back to rebuild Jaffa. He still holds the city, and in its present condition, it is

242

open to attack. The winds of war blow bitter as the winter squalls from over the great sea."

October passed, and November, and Valentina continued with her duties in Napur, each day listening for information on the continuing war. Richard had left a contingent of men to rebuild Jaffa, while he himself led raiding parties and engaged in skirmishes throughout the plains, hunting down hostile patrols. Inch by inch, the Crusaders had penetrated the plains, quartering themselves in empty towns and dismantled towers. Through their efforts they had gained the edge of the foothills, and before them the road to Jerusalem, twelve miles away, rose between gullies and barren hills. But time was their enemy and the seasons changed. Rain came behind the cold north wind and chilled the bones. Most of the men were ready to march upon Jerusalem, but their leaders delayed them, realizing the difficulties which lay ahead. A plan was needed, and Richard could not think of one.

Rain and hail beat upon the Crusaders, overturning their tents. Horses died from lack of shelter, and the rain and dampness rotted the meat and molded the biscuits. Shirts of mail were seized with rust, and men dropped in their tracks from hunger and disease.

Impatient with their lot, the French insisted on pushing ahead to Jerusalem but were ordered back by Richard, who, because of his lack of resolve, brought down the rancor of the French. The army was in no condition to undertake the siege of the Holy City, Richard decided, and ordered that everyone must go back to Jaffa.

Discouraged, the French parted company with Richard and went away with the Duke of Burgundy. Richard and his nephew, Henry of Champagne, went on to Ibelin. Each day was worse than the one past, and finally they reached Jaffa, which they found being slowly rebuilt.

Through his network of spies Saladin knew that the Christians had returned to the shores of the sea. He then told his Saracens to return to their own countries until the early spring. They all went willingly, for it had almost been four years since any of them had seen their homelands.

When Valentina heard the news that Saladin was breaking ranks among his men, she became frightened that Ramiff's son, Homed, would return to Napur and find that his father was dead. But Ahmar and Mohab reassured her that this would not come to pass. Homed was exiled from Napur, and Ramiff's death was still a well-kept secret.

The new year heralded 1192, making it nine months since Valentina had arrived in the Holy Land. Nine short months that had seen the end of one life and the beginning of another. From her life as a tormented lady-in-waiting in Berengaria's retinue to that of regent of Napur, though no less tormented.

It was not easy to learn of the Christians' defeats. Ahmar assiduously kept her abreast of the war, gathering information and relating it to her. Ahmar assumed she was so interested because the war affected prices and because the information was important to her in her newfound capacity.

Ahmar's latest news concerned the English king. Richard was still at Jaffa, spending his time seeing to the rebuilding of the city. Not only did he have an ensuing struggle against the Moslems, but there was disorganization in his ranks. The French were weary of delay and nominated Conrad of Montserrat to bring the factions together and lead them as king of Jerusalem to which Richard gave his consent.

All was being made ready for the coronation of Conrad when news reached the Crusaders that the newly appointed king had been assassinated. The unfortunate man had been riding home from a banquet in his honor when he was struck down by cutthroats. The act of another murder was attributed to *Sheikh al Jebal,* the Old Man of the Mountain.

The death of Conrad did much to heal the rift between the French and the English. Young Henry of Champagne was elected to take the crown awarded to

Conrad. Being a nephew to both Richard and Philip Augustus made him the likely choice. But the coronation of Henry did not alleviate the sufferings of the Crusaders. Supplies were still short and the death toll was high. Richard himself fell ill and had himself carried about Jaffa in a litter as he directed his men with the rebuilding.

Ahmar returned to Ramiff's palace with news. "Mistress, I have just come from the city, and what I must tell you is not pretty. Malik Ric's men are dying like flies. They say Richard is as sick as his men. They've taken to killing their horses for meat. The animals were disease-ridden, and the men are so sick they lie in camp and wait for death. The camp is vermine-infested and the flies are as thick as the clouds overhead."

Valentina was more distressed than she would admit to Ahmar. Richard's men dying. Her people dying! Lying in the fields and the rock-strewn roads, dying of hunger and starvation-related diseases while she had command of vast storehouses of food supplies.

Shadjar, the white panther, had grown at an alarming rate, although she still possessed the playfulness of a young cub and was sometimes awkward in her explorations. This time the young cat had overturned numerous bottles and jars of ointments and cosmetics on Valentina's dressing table. Even the chore of cleaning up the disaster that the cat had created could not distract Valentina from the guilt she experienced.

The Christian army was dying. Surely King Richard would now move more quickly along the path to a truce, rather than lose thousands of men to the scourge of starvation.

Perhaps she could secretly send out a supply. Not even Rosalan would have to know. The thought of all those men, most of them her countrymen . . . Fool, she raged at herself. What could you do? A woman . . . Still she tormented herself. Perhaps she could lead the caravan herself. . . . Stupid . . . you are needed here . . . you have a pledge to honor.

And where would she find the manpower to move

the caravan? No, she would not betray the trust Ramiff had placed in her.

Starving . . .

Even if she could find the manpower to move the caravan, *Sheikh al Jebal,* the Old Man of the Mountain, would probably steal them away from her. Wasn't he part of the reason why both Richard's and Saladin's men were struggling to feed their warriors? *Sheikh al Jebal* availed himself of every caravan he could overtake, and then he resold the stolen food to the highest bidder for twice the price. The Old Man of the Mountain was a nonpartisan in this war. The only victory he sought was that of becoming even more powerful through wealth.

No, she couldn't possibly arrange to send foodstuffs to Richard's men. Still, Saladin and his men were thriving. They had returned to their homelands and were recuperating from the hardships of war in their own homes among their families and loved ones. The Christians had no one here. Even the comfort of loved ones was denied them by the separation of thousands of miles.

Perhaps . . .

And if she should meet a contingent of Saladin's men? What then? How could she explain herself? And in the spring when the war was resumed, how would she explain the missing food from the warehouses? Food that had already been paid for by the Islamic forces! No! It was impossible. Yet . . .

She thought of what she knew of the Old Man of the Mountain. Very little, save that he lived on Alamut, his Eagle's Nest atop a mountain less than a day's journey from Napur. It was known to be an impregnable fortress. No one had ever heard of an outsider climbing his mountain and returning alive.

She must be going daft, she mocked herself. Imagine thinking of going to *Sheikh al Jebal* for help to aid the Christians! Still, she knew of many deeds which had been wreaked against the Moslems. Men of his own faith and his countrymen! It was evident that *Sheikh al Jebal* had created for himself a third world in which he was neither Moslem nor a man of Islam. He was powerful unto himself and cast his allegiance to no country, no faith. What possible reason could *Sheikh al Jebal* have for helping her secure food for the Christians? Wealth, came the ready answer. Else why would he trouble himself with waylaying caravans and reselling food at twice the price? Wealth was the primary concern of the old leader of assassins.

There was no doubt in her mind that Richard could pay for the foodstuffs in amounts sufficient to compensate *Sheikh al Jebal*. Gold was plentiful, but not grain or meat. Besides, she would never deplete the treasuries of Napur to pay *Sheikh al Jebal*. She still held sacred her pledge to Ramiff, and she would not take from the people of Napur.

All through the day and through most of the night Valentina wrangled with her indecision. Whatever her decision would be, she would have to bear it alone. This was something she could not ask Rosalan or Ahmar to help her with. The decision would be hers, and she would face the consequences.

Throughout the restless night Shadjar ad Darr moved about, stalking the room. Her mistress was torn, the cat could sense it as she let her paws scratch at the carpeting beside Valentina's bed.

The early morning hours were cold, yet as the sun rose in the sky it warmed the air. Valentina rode the white Arabian, Shadjar keeping pace alongside. Occasionally the panther stalked a bird or a rabbit but always returned to Valentina's side, catching up with the Arabian stallion in swift, graceful bounds.

Throughout her ride to the base of the mountain on which perched Alamut, Valentina could hardly believe that she was making this journey to meet with a legend. A living legend of evil. *Sheikh al Jebal*. Over and over, she asked herself why she was making this perilous journey. Why had she left a note for Ahmar and Rosalan, saying that she was going into the desert to make a retreat and meditate? They were her friends. Yet here she was, riding to Alamut . . . betraying them. And old Mohab, grief-stricken since the death of Ramiff. Looking to her for words of comfort and the opportunity to be useful. Each day Mohab would carry meals into Ramiff's empty quarters to keep suspicions from being aroused. Each day Rosalan would carry out bedding and clothing and bring them down to be washed, even though no one had used them. And Ahmar, that wonder of a man, who devoted his life to the keeping of Ramiff's secret.

By what right did she put her life in danger and thereby threaten the best friends she had ever known? Why was she doing this?

The answer was there for her to see, and yet she turned away from it. Admit it to yourself. Because you are a Christian. Know yourself, Saladin had told her.

Admit it. You want this fierce decision taken out of your hands. You want to be able to sleep at night. Leave the decision to *Sheikh al Jebal*. When he laughs at your request, the matter will be resolved. You will be vindicated. You will have taken action and your heart will rest easy. You expect to be denied. Laughed at, even, and yet you still climb to the Eagle's Nest!

Valentina opened her bright purple cloak and let it drop to the saddle behind her. Her khalats were a deep earthy brown, but her tunic was a vibrant shade of rose. She had purposely worn bright colors to attract the eyes of the *fedawi*, who, she knew, monitored her every movement. She rode boldly ahead, her cloak fluttering behind her, refusing to give them cause to consider her a spy.

Upward she rode, Shadjar beside her, up to Alamut, the Eagle's Nest of the Old Man of the Mountain. She was surprised when no move was made to stop her. The sun was high in the sky when she paused to rest. Her eyes raked the deep foliage and the undergrowth. Why hadn't she been stopped? How far up the steep terrain would she be allowed to climb before she was stopped by the *fedawi,* followers of *Sheikh al Jebal?* If there was someone who stalked her ascent, the cat would have shown some sign.

Nothing. Her nerves on edge, Valentina resumed her climb, the stallion slipping and sliding on the hard rocks.

The sun was falling in the sky, red and brilliant golden rays streaming a path as Valentina accomplished the mountaintop. Here, instead of the barren wasteland she expected to find at the mountain's crest, was a wide grassy knoll splashed with sunshine. The perimeters were dense with trees, and before her were the vast high walls of Alamut.

There was not a sign of life anywhere. Valentina, astride the stallion with Shadjar at her side, rode the length of the grassy knoll toward the citadel, whose white walls appeared russet in the last rays of daylight. She knew fear as she approached the gates, and squared her shoulders in resolution. Above the gates read a legend:

AIDED BY GOD,
THE MASTER OF THE WORLD
BREAKS THE CHAINS OF THE LAW.
SALUTE TO HIS NAME!

She stood there a long moment contemplating the meaning of the inscription. From behind the immense gates of the stronghold she heard a sound, and suddenly the gates swung wide, admitting her. Cautiously she advanced, calling softly to Shadjar to follow. If human hands had swung wide the gates, she saw none, but the feeling of eyes upon her was almost tangible. All was quiet, all was still, and hardly daring to breathe, Valentina advanced. She glanced toward Shadjar, and the cat seemed calm, her ears erect and her tail held aloft. This had a soothing effect on Valentina, who could trust the cat to sense danger.

Before her path stood another gate, this one leading to the inside of a high-walled tower. Magically, as her stallion came within yards of the gate, they swung open, silent on their hinges. She dismounted, leaving the stallion, knowing somehow that when she was ready to return down the mountain, he would be there for her.

She entered a dim room lit only by the inconsistent flare of torches paraded around the high walls. The air was fragrant with sweet incense, which seemed to tickle Shadjar's nose. Slowly Valentina walked forward, the panther keeping stride. Hesitantly she approached the far side of the room, and as her eyes became accustomed to the dimness, she perceived a man sitting upon a gilded thronelike chair that stood before a drape of glistening beads. Pots of incense smoked near his feet. The flickering torchlight cast the wizened man into ghostly shadows. His face was skull-like; the skin stretching over his cheekbones was paper-thin, with blue veins standing out starkly. Thin, straggly gray hair hung to his scrawny shoulders. His body appeared wasted to the point of emaciation. Clawlike hands were folded in his lap, his stick-thin legs crossed in front of him. The smoldering incense wafted around him in small puffs, spiraling upward. His eyes remained closed, his mouth compressed into a tight line.

Valentina shuddered. How could this wizened, feeble old man help her? He must know she stood before him, yet he gave no sign. She hadn't come this far to turn around and go back without at least trying. Hesitantly she spoke, her voice soft and pleading. "I need your help, o *Sheikh al Jebal*. I am Valentina from Napur. I wish your men to aid me to transport grain and food supplies to the Christian armies," she said simply. "Perhaps we can reach an agreement to share the payment the Lionheart will make for the foodstuffs." She was saying it all wrong! Why was she trembling with fear? Not fear for her life for having the affront to come to Alamut, but fear that she would be refused. The knowledge was staggering! She realized she would beg *Sheikh al Jebal*, crawl to him, anything! She could no longer deny that the welfare of Richard's men was more than a whim. It was paramount! Vital! They were her people and they were starving, and she had the food within her grasp!

Her voice shook with emotion. "If you find that you cannot give me your men, then will you give my transports safe conduct?"

The wizened old man gave no sign he heard her words, continuing to sit in his cross-legged position, the sweet-smelling incense wafting about him.

Valentina lowered herself to her knees and reached out a slender hand. "Please help me," she begged in her low, throaty whisper. "Please, I will do whatever is necessary for your help."

The beaded curtains behind the throne parted, and a tall man stood gazing down at Valentina's dark head. He laughed, his head thrown back in merriment. "You beg prettily, Valentina, consort to Ramiff."

Valentina, stunned beyond measure, stood immobile. Her blue-green eyes were full of wonderment. Everything left her mind, the wizened old man and the reasons for her coming to the top of the mountain. Only the happiness of seeing the man with the laughing dark eyes was important. She had found him. This was the man from the tourney in Messina. This was the man from the bazaar and the man with the flute. This was the man she had told she could not wait for eternity. Her heart pounded madly as tears glistened in her eyes. "Who are you?" she whispered. "Please, you must tell me."

Time stood still while she waited for his answer. His face, his laughing dark eyes, his tall, lean, hard body, were forever branded in her heart. She had no need to hear him say his name. This was Menghis.

Chapter Eighteen

Menghis laughed, showing perfect, gleaming white teeth. His face was square and chiseled, his laughing mouth sensual as he gazed at her. His head was bare of headgear, and tendrils of inky hair fell low over his forehead. His hand stroked the full mustache he wore on his upper lip. *"Sheikh al Jebal* does not hear you. He is in deep meditation, waiting for his death."

Valentina forced herself to come back to the moment. Her legs trembled, and she could not control the pounding of her heart. "If he cannot hear me, then whom shall I ask?"

"You may ask me. I heard your request and I find it strange. You control a Moslem kingdom, and yet you plead for the Christian cause! Tell me why I should help you?"

"Because I beg you. The Christians need food and supplies. Without them they will perish."

The laughing dark eyes were sober and solemn. "And if I refuse, what will you do?"

Her voice, when she replied, was low, husky, and full of emotion. "You would let armies die when you could help. I don't understand. Where is your honor?"

Menghis laughed as he cupped her face in his hand. His touch sent a scorching streak of fire through her, and she felt herself grow weak at his nearness. "Come, we will stroll through the gardens, it is a beautiful evening. We will discuss my honor further in the cool, clear night, where this incense does not rob the senses."

A violent shudder ripped through Valentina as he

took her hand in his and led her from the room and into the garden. Dusk had fallen and stars were just becoming visible. In the grayness before dark he led her down the narrow garden path and out another gate into the open. While they walked they were silent, each feeling the presence of the other and the effect that this nearness had on their emotions.

Valentina felt as though she had been away and had returned home to be met with love and tenderness. Words were not necessary.

Menghis measured his steps with Valentina's. He prided himself on having made the better choice that day in Messina at the tourney celebrating the Lionheart's marriage. Valentina was vibrant and daring, as well as beautiful. He studied her profile from beneath lowered lids and appreciated her finely chiseled nose and determined chin, which was in perfect balance with her brow. Her hair was loose and tumbled down her back in lovely disarray. He had to force himself to refrain from reaching out to run his hands through its wealth of darkness. But it was to her mouth that his eyes always returned. Full and ripe, yet firm and well shaped. A mouth which would cling in a kiss, a mouth made for kissing. He knew that the touch of that mouth upon his would be soft and cool, and he knew he could drown in that sweetness.

Menghis led Valentina to a narrow stream near a small waterfall and sat beside her on the embankment. "You questioned my honor. I have none," he laughed.

"Will you help me?" Valentina asked softly as she stared into his dark eyes.

"Why should I help you? I know what you said, because you asked and men will die if I refuse you. Men should not go to war if they are not prepared to die. Unlike most Moslems, I am not a fatalist. Each man is the victim of his own destiny and should expect no help to avoid that destiny. What do you have to offer should I agree to help you?"

"I have nothing. It is Malik Ric who will pay in

gold. Twice what the delivery is worth. Half for your help and the other half to reimburse Napur."

Menghis laughed again, his white teeth startling in the descending dusk. "I find your request more than strange. A moment ago you questioned my honor. I should like to question your honor. You are a Christian masquerading as a Circassian. You are the consort to Ramiff of Napur. Forgive me, the late emir." At Valentina's gasp Menghis smiled. "I knew the moment the emir joined Allah. I know more of you than you know yourself. You claim to be a neutral, is that not what you profess? You control the emir's kingdom and will steal his grain and food supplies to aid the Christians. And you question *my* honor?" Menghis wore an amused expression as he waited for her reply.

Valentina flinched at his words. "It was a question of survival," she said slowly. "I had no other choice. I had no wish to die. What you say about me is true. Yet I cannot let men die when I have it in my power to aid them."

"You speak in riddles, beautiful Valentina. You can do nothing unless I help you. And when the Christians are well fed and strong again, they will slaughter the very people who aided you and allowed you to survive. Tell me," he said mockingly, "where is your honor?"

"I have prayed for a truce," Valentina protested. "Yet none seems imminent. While I pray, men starve."

"Yes, I know of the starving men. I know of hardships in the name of war on both sides." The handsome lines of his face fell into a scowl. "Will men never learn that nothing is gained by war? In the name of their gods they destroy each other, they inflict misery upon one another, and they say they hear the call of their faith. It sickens me."

"You say 'in the name of their gods,'" Valentina whispered. "Who is your God, Menghis?"

"Not who, What. The forces and laws of the universe are my god. Hence, all things are God, and each of us has the touch of the immortal. To go against the goodness in the nature of man is to blaspheme against my idea of 'God.' The doctrine is simple. God is all things and all things are God. War is against this doctrine. Peace is the natural order of things, hence peace is God."

Simply and touchingly, he professed his beliefs to her. His voice was mellow, and there was a timbre of longing behind his words. She believed him. Regardless of the fact that she had found him here on Alamut, a den of assassins and thieves, she believed him.

A conflict roared through her. If Menghis could take the responsibility of whether or not *Sheikh al Jebal* would help her, was he not also responsible for the misdeeds credited to the Old Man of the Mountain?

"I ask you again, Valentina," he said softly, no hint of mockery in his tone this time. "Where is your honor?"

"Believe what you will, Menghis, but if the situation were reversed, I would aid the Moslems. Will you help me?"

"I will give you my answer in the morning."

Valentina looked deeply into Menghis's eyes and smiled. "Does this mean you will make me wait for eternity?"

There was no need for Menghis to reply. Gently he cupped her face in his two strong hands and gazed into her eyes for a long time. All her worries, all her fears, fled with his gentle touch and deep gaze. She belonged to him, now, for tomorrow, forever. They would walk into eternity together. Menghis was her destiny.

"Time here in the Alamut has no meaning. I wish you to be my guest for the evening. Perhaps," he said, smiling wickedly, "I will keep you here for my own."

"Please don't say things like that to me unless you mean them," Valentina said huskily.

"And what would you say if I told you I was serious in my desire for you to stay here?"

Fear clutched at Valentina's heart. She would have to refuse him. "I would tell you I cannot stay

. . . now. I would tell you that there might be a time when I . . ."

"Yes, I know," Menghis whispered huskily.

"Tell me," Valentina asked quietly, "when *Sheikh al Jebal* joins his God, who will sit in his chair?"

"Very astute of you, my dear Valentina. It is I who will sit in that chair and grow to look as he does."

"No! No! You can't sit in that chair. If you do, that means . . . No!" she screamed desperately.

"It is my destiny," Menghis said, a strange tone in his voice.

"You told me that men are victims of their own destinies, yet knowing what yours will be, you do not avoid it?"

"It does seem a paradox, does it not?"

"Explain it to me so that I can understand," Valentina pleaded tearfully. "That was what you meant that day in the desert, isn't it? When you said if not here, then in eternity." Her voice was tormented.

"I am deeply sorry for seeking you out. I had no right. I wanted to indulge myself, can you understand that? From the moment I saw you in Messina I knew I had to see you again. And the day in the bazaar and again in the desert, I could not help myself. I told myself that when I sat on the throne, I would have the memories of those times. But to answer your question. When I speak of destinies and fates, I speak of other men. I am unlike other men. I can be likened to your kings in Europe who know their destinies even if they wish something different for themselves. I am successor to the throne of Alamut. I do not sit alone here on the mountain. I am a figurehead, someone to whom the *fedawi,* the devoted ones, can look to. A part of the myth of *Sheikh al Jebal* is that he is immortal. By the look of that old man in there preparing for his death, you know it is not so. You know that the Old Man of the Mountain is credited with many assassinations. This is not so. There are men in this world who would push the guilt away from themselves and have their enemies killed in my name. This goes unrefuted because it helps to perpetuate the fear of *Sheikh al Jebal* in men's hearts."

"You say you are not alone here in Alamut. Who sits beside you?"

"If you are attempting to learn if there is a special woman in my life, I tell you there is not. I am not alone here because there are many men behind the throne of *Sheikh al Jebal*. Men who make decisions . . . Allah be praised that I am not responsible for what they choose to do in the name of *Sheikh al Jebal*."

"And Alamut? What is this secret of Alamut, the secret which calls for loyalty in the hearts of your *fedawi*? It is said that they are so successful because they care nothing for this life but look forward to death."

"Yes, another myth, although there are certain here among us who are such as you say. The *fedawi*, the devoted ones. The secret binds their hearts and makes them court death, the secret of Alamut."

Valentina listened, enraptured by his words. She was about to learn a secret that had puzzled scholars throughout the centuries, and she would learn it from the lips of *Sheikh al Jebal* himself.

"Here on the crest of this mountain lies the world of Alamut—Eagle's Nest—and from here an eye on the world keeps its vigil. Within the walls of Alamut is a garden, a garden of Eden. Here among the exotic trees and the marble fountains that toss flavorful wine into the air is every delight of the senses. Carpeted pavilions of silk welcome one in from the sun; tiled kiosks and sultry music add their charm. For here is a world which all men seek.

"And only the *fedawi* can enter this paradise. They are told when they are brought to Alamut that they will be shown what their death and eternity will be like. If they are agreeable, then a drug is administered to them, only once. When they wake, they then make the decision if they are to stay or not. It must be each man's decision. Valentina, can you think of any man who would not give up the suffering of this world for the delights of heaven? I see by your expression that you thought Alamut was a den of drug-induced men. It is not true. We have no wish to rob men of their minds. If we did this, how could the *fedawi* function and carry out orders? There are many stories and legends of the *fedawi,* but I wanted you to hear the truth." His voice was heavy and somber, and there was sorrow in his eyes.

"Thank you for telling me," Valentina said softly. "I shall keep your secret."

"I know you will, otherwise I would not have told you. If you were to utter one word of what I said, a *fedawi*'s dagger would find its way to your heart. Rarely is my judgment wrong. No, I am not concerned. You have proved to be trustworthy in keeping Ramiff's secret, even at the expense of rejoining your fellow Christians. You are an unusual woman, Valentina; honor is not a word women often understand."

"Perhaps it is because so rarely are women dealt with honorably," she defended.

Menghis laughed. "Aptly put, Valentina, aptly put. Now that you know my destiny, tell me of yours."

"I do not dwell on destinies," Valentina said. "I live each day as it comes."

"Then we are much the same, are we not? You have no life beyond today, and one day soon I shall have no life beyond tomorrow."

Valentina felt saddened at his words. Such a waste of life, and what of her own? Once she aided the Christians, she would have to make decisions concerning her future.

"Look!" Menghis said, pointing to the small growth of trees near the embankment. He moved from his relaxed position and held out his hand. A fawn on still wobbly legs teetered over to him and gently nosed his outstretched hand. Valentina was surprised to see kernels of corn in the dark palm of his hand. "Make no sound," Menghis warned. "Soon this baby's mother will be here for her evening feeding."

Valentina watched as first one doe and then another appeared. Daintily they ate the corn in Menghis's hand and backed off, staring at him with dark, beautiful eyes. Menghis crooned soft words ·of reassurance to them, a smile on his face. When the deer scampered off, Valentina laughed. "And you talk to the animals. I find it beautiful that they should trust a human," she said.

"Strange? They ask for nothing. Their trust is implicit. Would you kill one of my animals?" he asked coolly.

"To survive, yes. I will do what I must to survive."

"At times, when it is convenient, you speak the truth; at other times you skirt the edges. Why is that?"

"Because I must survive. I must," Valentina said savagely. "How is it that you know so much of me? Do you have spies in the palace?"

Menghis laughed as he stretched long, lean legs in front of him. "I have men everywhere. I knew of your intention to climb the mountain when you left Napur. I knew of your progress up the mountain from the moment you started your climb. I know of every word that was spoken in the conference room at the desert meeting. I know that you lay in the arms of the sultan of Jakard, and before that in the arms of Saladin. Tell me," he laughed mirthfully, "when will you bed the Lionheart? Speak the truth, young Valentina."

"You're hateful!" Valentina cried, jumping to her feet. "You have no right to say this!"

"Truth is truth, is it not? Why are you afraid to have it spoken aloud? Enough of this. Come, I will take you to the women's quarters, where you may refresh yourself. Afterward you will join me for the evening meal."

A young sloe-eyed girl of no more than ten met Menghis and Valentina inside the walled garden. Menghis released Valentina to the child's care with a promise to sup with her within the hour.

The child led her through the doors to the women's quarters. Valentina had expected to find several or more chattering women but instead discovered that she had the palatial quarters to herself.

More magnificent than the apartments of the harem

in Ramiff's palace, the room into which the child led Valentina was like stepping back in time to what legend has said the palaces of ancient Rome were like. Arcades were fashioned along two sides of the room, and beneath each tiled and marble arch stood braziers which were burning brightly to give both light and warmth. Long, low divans upholstered in marvelously rich fabrics ringed the room. The floor beneath Valentina's feet was carpeted in the most lush jewel-like colors of the rainbow, having a translucence which made them appear thicker and more welcoming to the foot. Tapestries, which Valentina recognized as coming from French looms, were hung about the high, vaulted walls, and pedestals supporting figurines and statues of goddesses gave the long, wide chamber a furnished feeling yet did not detract from the simple sweep of architecture.

Far off to one end of the room was a pool fed by an outside stream, and floating atop the blue-tinted water were rose petals and fragrant pomanders studded with spices. Upon closer examination, Valentina discovered that a pit had been fashioned outside the perimeters of the pool, and within this pit were polished rocks heated by burning, fragrant oil. Valentina dipped her hand into the clear water and tested its temperature. Pleasantly warm, soothingly so. The continual runoff from the pool emptied itself into a trough which fell beneath the floor and ran to the outside. Never in her life had she ever imagined such luxury. Who had devised the mechanics of it? That person was a genius!

Delighted with her surroundings, Valentina turned to smile at the child, who said, "I am Aloe Bud, beautiful lady, and the master wills it that I see to your needs."

"I am Valentina," she answered, smiling, "and you are also beautiful." And the child was. Small yet sturdy, with skin the color of pale tea that made a striking contrast with her thick black hair, which was brushed severely back from a wide, intelligent brow. The plumpness of childhood rounded Aloe Bud's chin, and her eyes were widely set beneath finely arched brows. An entrancing child, with the entrancing manners of the East.

Aloe Bud giggled. "Am I really beautiful?" she asked with the direct manner of a child.

"Most definitely, Aloe Bud. Has no one ever told you so?"

"Yes, Valentina, but I love to hear it!" she said shyly, lowering her gaze.

Valentina laughed. "Then I will tell you so whenever we have a chance to speak."

A great yowling and scratching sounded at the door. Aloe Bud nearly jumped out of her skin and ran to Valentina, clinging to her in fear. "No! No!" she cried, her voice bridging hysteria.

Valentina dropped to her knees, drawing the child into her arms, comforting her. "Aloe Bud, hush, little one!" But the yowling continued and the scratching at the door became more violent as Aloe Bud's cries increased. "Little one, it is Shadjar ad Darr, my good friend. Come, I will show you!" The child clung tightly, unbelieving. Valentina managed to extricate herself from the child's grasp and go to the door. Aloe Bud ran behind a divan and crouched low, her round little face a study in horror.

Valentina pulled open the door and there was the white panther. She sprinted in, her yellow-green eyes looking at Valentina guardedly.

"See, Aloe Bud, it is as I said. This is my friend Shadjar ad Darr. She was given to me by the emir of Napur. I have raised her from a cub."

Timidly Aloe Bud raised her head and peered at the panther. Her eyes grew round with wonder. "A white panther?" she said. "A magical white panther!"

Valentina laughed. "Well, yes, I suppose there is a magic about Shadjar. Come over and meet her. You will be the first little girl she has ever met."

Aloe Bud cautiously approached Shadjar, who promptly rolled over on her back for Aloe Bud to scratch her soft white belly.

"See, she likes you. The two of you can be friends," Valentina said.

Aloe Bud laughed, a high, little-girl's laugh, and wrapped her arms about Shadjar's neck. "My own friend, my very own friend!" The child looked at Valentina. "Will Shadjar protect me from the things that move in the night? Will you let her stay with me?"

"What things that move in the night, Aloe Bud?" Valentina asked softly.

"Things, people without faces, spirits." Her face lost its smile and clouded over in fear. "I am too young to sleep here with the pretty ladies, and the nights are so long and lonely. I hear things that frighten me."

"This is why you were so frightened when Shadjar scratched at the door?"

Aloe Bud nodded. "I thought it was *him* coming to get me!"

"Him?"

"Him!" Aloe Bud insisted. "The man who caught me in the garden! He talked to me, so nicely at first, but then he picked me up in his arms, and he was so strong! I cried for him to put me down, but he only laughed and said that I would be his good little girl! Oh, Valentina, I was so frightened. He squeezed me so tight I could not get my breath, and then his hands . . ." Aloe Bud could not continue; she had begun to cry. Wracking sobs shook her young shoulders as she buried her head in Shadjar's white coat.

Valentina smoothed the child's dark, shining hair to comfort her. "Did you tell anyone what this man did, how he frightened you?"

Aloe Bud raised her head, tears streaming down her cheeks as she said, "Who is there to tell? Sometimes I am so lonely that I hide under the trees in the garden and cry and cry."

A wild heat of rage consumed Valentina as she cradled the child in her arms. How well she knew the fear Aloe Bud described. Pictures flashed through her mind, and she saw herself small and helpless as the hulking French soldier pressed her back against the wall outside the prisoners' compound in Acre. The two

262

Moslems in Saladin's camp had also ravaged her. "Cry, little one, cry it all out, cry until the tears come no more." For an inexplicable reason, Valentina cried, too.

Bathed and dressed in a caftan of soft yellow silk, Valentina left Shadjar with Aloe Bud and went out to meet Menghis. Darkness had fallen and the sky was star-studded. He stood in the shadow of a tree, and she felt his eyes devour her as she walked toward him. He led her silently across the garden and held open a door, and Valentina stepped into a small room in which a low table had been placed with floor cushions of silk and brocade strewn beside it. The table was set for two, and the gilded flatware shimmered softly in the candlelight. When they were seated, Menghis clapped his hands and a manservant brought in trays of food. There were delicacies of cheeses and small breads surrounded by fresh fruits. The wine was sweet and mellow and the haunch of lamb done to a turn.

Menghis ate heartily, while Valentina picked at her food. He noticed her lack of appetite and commented upon it. "Is not the food to your liking?"

"The food is much to my liking. It is the company I keep which robs me of my appetite," she answered in a voice which rang with hostility.

"How have I offended you, Valentina? Tell me, and I will amend it," he said magnanimously.

"There are things which can never be amended," she shot back, angry at his confidence that he could make all things right. "I have no liking for the company of one who is an enslaver of children!"

He watched her eyes turn to chips of green glass, cold, hard, and deadly. "And who is this enslaver of children whom you so detest?"

"Would you have me believe that *Sheikh al Jebal* has no knowledge of the things which take place in his Eagle's Nest? Do you take me for a fool? I speak of Aloe Bud!"

"Who?"

263

"Aloe Bud! The little child who saw to my bath! You don't even know her name?"

"Ah, yes, the little child. Save your reproaches, Valentina. Would you have me believe that you know the name of each slave and servant who dwells in Ramiff's palace in Napur?"

Valentina was stung. He had spoken the truth. "Nevertheless, a child! An innocent child left to her own devices and put to the perverted desires of those soulless men you bring here to become members of your *fedawi*. Devoted ones! Hah! Devoted to molesting children is more the truth!"

Menghis's dark eyes flashed with fury as his upper lip curled back, his manicured mustache a ribbon of black against his white teeth. "Enough!" he shouted, slamming his fist on the table. "Enough! I will have none of your woman's nagging. You will sit there calmly and tell me of this child Aloe Bud. I have no knowledge of a child being mistreated here in Alamut. Why did not the child tell someone?"

Valentina felt her heart pound furiously in her breast. His anger had quelled her accusations and struck fear into her. His rage was enormous, deadly, and she knew he had the power to choke off her last breath with the huge hand that he had curled into a fist and pounded on the table.

"Now," he said in a calm voice. "You will tell me what has happened."

Finding her voice, Valentina told him how Shadjar had scratched at the door, putting terror into the child's heart. "And who is there to tell? Your women? They take no notice of the child. Yourself? How could such a little one come to the great *Sheikh al Jebal* and tell him this? She wept when she told me that at times she is so lonely that she hides beneath the trees in the garden and cries. Menghis, you who are so kind to the animals are blind to a little one here in Alamut who needs kindness and affection more than the wild beasts of the forest."

He lowered his eyes in self-reproach. "I myself will see to Aloe Bud's welfare." He raised his eyes, looking deeply, searchingly, into hers. "Do you believe me?"

"I believe you," Valentina whispered, somehow knowing she would always believe in this man.

"When next we meet I will tell you of the arrangements I have made for the child, and I will hope that you will be pleased." He said this without a trace of mockery, and Valentina's heart eased for Aloe Bud. She knew Menghis would do all in his power to see that the child was cared for, just as he saw to the welfare of his animals.

Menghis and Valentina finished their meal in silence, neither very interested in the food placed before them. They lingered long over the wine, their eyes meeting above the golden goblets. The very atmosphere seemed charged simply because they were with each other.

Menghis pared a winter peach and offered her a slice of it. She extended her hand and felt the little shock when his warm fingers placed the cool, wet slice of fruit in her palm. The fruit was sweet and juicy, and her tongue licked at the sweet wetness on her lips.

Menghis, his eyes half closed and hooded beneath his heavy dark brows, thought of what he knew of this remarkable woman across from him. Her beauty was evident and a delight for his eyes, but it was her spirit which called to him and excited his senses. He had never known a woman like her. A woman who could sit in the presence of kings and warriors and be their equal. A woman who could speak her demands in that curiously husky voice and cause men's ears to listen. From what he knew of her past, she was a girl of noble birth under the protection of King Sancho of Navarre, certainly not quite the background to prepare her for assuming the duties of the wealthy state of Napur. He had traveled Europe and knew that women were held in the highest esteem, but their intelligence was left to embroidery and household tasks. How had Valentina gained the confidence and capability to be regent of a Moslem state?

Menghis was aware of almost every detail of Valentina's life since she had come to the Holy Land as part of Berengaria's entourage. What he did not know did not matter. It was enough for him that the girl who had come to Acre with the Christians had become a woman among the Moslems. A woman whose very presence excited him, whose eyes could draw the truth from him, and whose voice was a balm for his loneliness.

The long silence between them was not discomforting to Valentina. She was alone with her thoughts, yet not alone. She could feel his gaze wander to her and was aware of the deep stirrings of excitement within her. Her eyes told her he was handsome and her head told her he was not an evil man. But her body, the stirring within her, told her more. She knew the evening would end with her in his arms, and she was not disquieted. What had happened to that innocent young girl who had come to Acre? she wondered. Where had she learned that the pleasures of the flesh were not a thing to be denied? Had she remained in Navarre, she would have stayed chaste until her marriage and even then the pleasures of the marriage bed would be denied. To keep her husband's respect, she would have had to hide her emotions and accept his lovemaking as a wifely duty. It occurred to her that she might not have succeeded in this. She knew herself to be a sensual woman. Saladin, in his wisdom, had taught her that. With Paxon she had experienced an earthshaking response and yet had willfully denied herself the ultimate consummation for fear of losing herself to him.

Yet she was not a wanton, she told herself, in spite of actions which would have branded her as such in Navarre. Perhaps it was because she now dwelled in the world of men. Yet when Menghis looked at her and touched her, she was reminded that she was not a man. She was a woman with the emotions of a woman! And in the face of his masculinity she was aware of her own frailties.

The danger of finding herself with child left her

undaunted. The child of any of these men would be a remarkable child, indeed. The blood of royalty would flow through its veins, and its heart would be brave and bold, its eyes flashing and its character intrepid. But a child of Menghis's would inherit that intangible core of spirit which could make all dreams possible. A child to shape the world!

The silence between Valentina and Menghis ensued, each alone with their thoughts yet ever aware of the other's presence. The wine was sweet and left Valentina lightheaded. The silence between them seemed more eloquent than words, and when he at last reached out his hand to her, she took it readily. Out into the chill night they walked, hand in hand. She filled her lungs with the bracing air and felt a slight, pleasant buzz in her head. She looked up at him as they walked, conscious of his height, his maleness. His hand was warm in hers, and her shoulder brushed his arm and tingled with the contact. They walked across the gardens, out onto the grassy knoll. Beneath the cover of the trees, hidden from the stars, they stopped. He took her in his arms and the universe clashed.

His mouth became a part of hers, and her heart beat in wild, broken rhythms without pattern. They strained toward each other, caught up in the designs of yearning. Together they mounted the obstacles of the flesh and toiled to join breath and blood, flesh and spirit.

They tore at each other, each seeking that which the other could give. There in the shadows of the trees, away from the prying light of the heavens, they devoured each other with searching lips and hungry fingers.

When at last sensibility returned, they touched mouths with lips swollen by passion and tasting of salt. The salt of blood, the salt of tears. They lay together in the chill night air, feeling only the warmth where their nakedness touched, and when they sought each other again, it was with tenderness. Their mouths were gentle and their fingers caressed. And when her passion quickened, Menghis calmed her with his touch and crooned to her words known only to lovers.

He was as gentle with her as he had been with the deer of the forest. His movements were reassuring, his touch on her naked breast light and soothing. He gentled her passions the way he would gentle a wild mare, with a sure touch and a crooning voice, allowing her to place her trust in him. He tamed her wildness yet loved her wild; he quieted her moans with his mouth yet evoked cries of passion with his touch. When passion was renewed again, it was pure.

Dawn was fast approaching when at last they awoke in each other's arms and, without abashment, held each other close for the pure joy of touching. After a while, when the sun had an opportunity to rise above the horizon, he led Valentina to a quiet cove, where they surprised several deer drinking from the clear spring. Words were unnecessary as Menghis divested himself of his garments and helped Valentina with hers.

The water was icy and bracing. Their breath hazed about their heads in pluming clouds in the chill morning air. Splashing and frolicking like two children, Valentina and Menghis reveled in their closeness. The water was waist-high, and Valentina's breasts were firm and their rosy crests erect and hard from the coldness of the water. She saw Menghis's eyes drift to them time and again, his pleasure evident by his sultry look.

Once he bent to grasp her knees and pull her down, the water closing over her head. Whooping for revenge, Valentina splashed and tormented him by threatening to run from the pool and steal his garments. "Then see how your *fedawi* will worship their *Sheikh al Jebal* when they see him sneaking back into his own palace shivering with cold, his clothes stolen away by a woman."

Laughing, Menghis captured her and threatened to dip her beneath the surface again. Screaming for mercy, Valentina clung fiercely to him, her arms locked about his neck, her face pressed close to his.

Suddenly time stopped, the birds were silent, and nothing and no one existed in the whole world, save the two of them. Two lovers rapturous with each other and reveling in that private world which only those who love can enter.

Gently he embraced her, cradling her head in one of his hands while the other supported her haunches. Backward, backward he dipped her. Into her line of vision swept the treetops and the sky, which was growing brighter with every passing moment. Slowly, deliberately, he bent his head, beads of water shining on his dark hair. Closer and closer his mouth came to hers. Tighter and tighter became his hold on her, as if he were clinging to her, desperately cleaving to this moment of time, cherishing it, remembering it, burning it into his memory, searing it into his soul.

And Valentina gave to him. Without reservation, without doubt. She gave herself to this man who was a paradox. And she knew, without a doubt, that he would cherish the part of herself that was her secret core. Her soul, her mind, her heart, her body. She became his in that one gentle, searching kiss, and she knew she could never belong to another.

Later, after they had breakfasted together, after a meal shared without a word between them, yet with an understanding that far surpassed words, Valentina dressed again in the clothes in which she had arrived.

She stood on the edge of the grassy knoll, her eyes sultry, smoky-blue in the early morning light. Menghis leaned against a giant tree, his own gaze smoldering as he watched her.

"Why?" she asked softly. There had been no words needed between them. What she meant was understood.

"You ask me why I have decided to help you. Not for the reasons you think. I wish to see how you control your destiny. In order to do that, I must help you. You may well come to rue the day you climbed this mountain. When you can accept your destiny, you will be at peace with yourself. If I can aid you to reach this plateau in your life, then so be it." He picked up a small hamper which rested near his feet. A soft gray dove clung to his fingers, a slim golden tether hanging from its stick-thin legs. Menghis perched the bird on her shoulder and fastened the tether to her tunic.

"When you have the need to climb this mountain again, loose the dove and I will be waiting."

Chapter Nineteen

The early twilight fell over the courtyard, weaving lacy patterns over and beneath the Judas tree. Valentina watched from her position on the balcony as Mohab dropped to his knees, his head bowed. Poor old man. She must do something about him. If he were allowed to continue on these pilgrimages to the garden, he would reveal the secret of Ramiff's death. She had noticed of late that at times his vague conversation made no sense at all, but he frightened her with his imagined omens and constant references to Ramiff's son, Homed.

Valentina shivered slightly in the evening air. Mohab was lingering longer than usual. Was he willing his body and mind to follow Ramiff into the soft earth beneath the Judas tree? As she watched him the lavender shadows deepened and lengthened, cloaking the small private garden in soft, caressing blackness. When she saw Mohab struggle to his feet, she withdrew from the balcony and settled herself on a chaise to wait for him. He did not disappoint her and soon entered the room, a wild, terrible look on his face.

Valentina was frightened and waited for him to speak. Something was wrong. Dear God, please don't let him be ill, she prayed silently. "Tell me," she said gently, "what is it that troubles you, Mohab?"

Mohab shifted his weight from one foot to the other and wrung his hands in agitation. "Evil. There is evil all around us. I have prayed for my old friend and that what I fear is not true. Yet Allah confirmed my suspicions this night while I prayed beneath the Judas tree."

Valentina frowned. "I don't understand what you're saying, Mohab. What evil? What suspicions? You must tell me, and perhaps we can do something about what is worrying you. Please, we are friends, are we not?"

Mohab lowered himself painfully onto a mound of sky-blue cushions and looked at the young woman with sad, tortured eyes. "It is Ramiff's son. He is coming here. I prayed to Allah for days to give me some sign that my suspicions were true, and this night I saw the sign that he meant me to see."

"Mohab, Ramiff banished Homed. What makes you think he will come back to Napur?"

"I don't think he will come here. I know he will come! I saw it in the stars weeks ago, and I had my fortune told by the sand painter. Why do you think I spend so much time beneath the Judas tree? I have been waiting for my prayers to be answered, and they were. Somehow Homed has learned that his father is dead, and he is coming to claim Napur. My dear old friend Ramiff knew his own son's evil, and he was banished for the sake of Napur—it has even been rumored that he once killed a woman who was with child, so evil is he."

"Mohab, what you say is foolishness. There is no one, save ourselves, who knows of Ramiff's death. I swear to you on my life that Rosalan and Ahmar have not given away the secret. There is no way that Homed could know."

"He knows," Mohab said fretfully. "I saw it written in the stars, and tonight Allah answered my prayers. When I was coming through the palace, I saw the woman Dagny with a missive in her hands. I watched her as she read from the parchment. When she was reading it she wore a wicked look and whispered Homed's name before sticking the missive between her udderlike breasts. When she realized I was watching her, she spit at me and said I should enjoy my life now because soon all things would be changed. Those were her exact words, Valentina."

A chill washed over Valentina as she tried to comfort the old man. "Mohab, fetch Ahmar to me. Also Rosalan. We'll discuss the matter. Perhaps they know something about what is going on in the harem. Do it quickly so that your mind can be eased."

Mohab slowly left the room, his old eyes tortured with his thoughts. He knew he was right. Homed would return and make trouble for the entire kingdom. Ramiff would never forgive him if Homed was allowed to come back. From his perch on Allah's shoulder Ramiff must be grumbling and complaining that Mohab was doing nothing to stop what was about to happen. Sooner or later the emir would leave his safe refuge and begin to walk through the heavens. When he did, the bells on his slippers would signal to Mohab that he knew his old friend was doing his best. Ramiff had to know that somehow, in some way, Mohab would protect Napur from Homed.

If he had to, he would kill the treacherous son. He would do it joyfully! Ramiff would make it right with Allah so that there would be no black mark against his name when he too entered the heavens.

Rosalan and Ahmar looked at each other, puzzled by Mohab's firm request that they follow him to Valentina's apartments. When they arrived, Valentina motioned Mohab to tell his story to them.

Ahmar nodded his head in agreement after Mohab finished speaking. "Yes, mistress, I saw her with my own eyes. It was a missive brought to her by a nomad. She paid him highly for his delivery. And it is as Mohab says. She wore the satisfied look of a cat."

"When the night comes I will kill her for you," Rosalan offered. "She won't torture you any longer," she soothed, placing her arms about Mohab.

"You will do no such thing!" Valentina said sternly. "For now we will be on guard and watch her. Ahmar, you will keep a constant watch on her. See that she doesn't manage to slip away."

"And be sure that's all you do while you're in the harem," Rosalan sniped. "It isn't true what they say, that Dagny likes women. She likes women but she loves men. She'll have you in her bed before you can get your shoes off."

Ahmar looked smug as Rosalan narrowed her flashing eyes, her fists clenched at her sides.

Mohab continued to fret as he listened to the exchange between Ahmar and Rosalan. "I have not heard the bells as yet. Ramiff is displeased with me," he said petulantly.

"Mohab, what bells?" Valentina asked. "I did as you asked. When we buried Ramiff, we placed the bells on his slippers."

"But I haven't heard them! Ramiff told me that when he was tired of perching on Allah's shoulder, he would climb down and take charge of his new life. He can see everything. He knows what is happening here, and yet he does nothing!"

Rosalan rolled her eyes heavenward and pointed a long finger at her head.

"Mohab, I want to be certain I understand what you're saying. Did Ramiff tell you that if you heard the bells, everything would be well and you could do whatever it is you think should be done?" Valentina shook her head. Her own words didn't make any sense to her.

Mohab sat down and looked at the three faces staring at him. He sighed and spoke patiently, as if he were addressing backward children. "Before Ramiff joined Allah, we made this agreement. He would wear bells on his slippers. He had it in his mind to perch on Allah's shoulder and offer to help manage the heavens," Mohab said, pointing toward the sky. "Ramiff said that when the agreement was sealed, and he promised not to cheat, he would climb down from his perch and the bells on his slippers would let me know that all was well. He said that he would be able to look down here on earth and he would send me messages and I would know what to do. If I hear the bells, I know I'm doing what is right. Now do you understand?"

Rosalan rolled her eyes and grimaced.

Valentina laid a gentle hand on Mohab's shoulder. "Yes, I understand. You must rest now, and no more journeys to the Judas tree this night. We'll talk more in the morning. You need have no fear of Homed. Now that we know of your suspicions, we'll guard against them. Rest well, Mohab," she said, kissing him lightly on the cheek.

"Since Ramiff died, he has grown more peculiar by the day," Valentina said quietly after Mohab had shuffled from the room. "His time is near also. Soon he'll join his old friend, and only then will he be happy. And if it's bells he wants to hear, then it's bells he will hear. Ahmar, before you go to the harem I want you to tie a bell to the very top of the Judas tree, where it will be hidden by the branches. If he wants to hear a bell, then he will hear a bell!"

Ahmar winked at Valentina as she handed him a tiny silver bell.

"Be sure that you secure it well so it does not fall to the ground. I don't even want to think of what Mohab might do if he thought a bell fell out of the sky." The three friends laughed then, and some of the threatening tension was relieved.

Days passed, with Mohab more and more withdrawn. He no longer would rise to Valentina's teasing, and wanted only to spend all his waking hours beneath the Judas tree.

Valentina waited patiently for him to make some mention that he heard the bell tinkling, but he said nothing. She was becoming alarmed, as were Rosalan and Ahmar. One afternoon she joined him beneath the tree and stood listening to the silvery tinkle of the little bell. Watching Mohab covertly, she was shocked when he gave no sign that he heard the merry little tinkle. "Mohab, do you hear what I hear?" she asked softly.

"I hear nothing," Mohab said sullenly.

"Listen, can't you hear the sound?"

Mohab listened, then shook his head stubbornly and rose to his feet, leaving her standing beneath the tree with a foolish expression on her face.

The following morning, shortly after sunup, Valentina was shaken awake by a wild-eyed Rosalan. "He's here!" she whispered, her face a mask of fright. "Homed's demanding to see his father and says he'll kill anyone who stands in his way. Mohab is on his way now to the great hall. You must hurry, Valentina. Homed is going to kill old Mohab, and then he'll never hear the bells!"

"Go for Ahmar. Tell him to come at once," Valentina said briskly, fully awake. "Tell Mohab to fetch Homed to me, but have him wait till Ahmar gets here. Quickly, Rosalan."

Within moments she was dressed and had her hair in place. An opaque yashmak concealed the lower portion of her face. The veil would give her a certain degree of security, for with it she felt her emotions could not be easily read. She had just seated herself behind an impressive-sized table piled high with ledgers and loose papers when Ahmar charged into the room. "Where is he?" he demanded.

"In the entrance hall. I told Rosalan to have Mohab bring him here. He should be arriving shortly. He mustn't be allowed past this room, Ahmar."

Ahmar had no sooner taken his position at the foot of the table when a belligerent and perspiring Mohab and two of the palace guards half dragged, half carried a vicious-tongued Homed into the room. Mohab gave him a shove and the man sprawled across the room, landing at Valentina's feet. His face was suffused with hatred and he spewed threats and obscenities.

Homed began to struggle to his feet, and Mohab made a lunge for him, knocking him down again. "Leave him," Valentina commanded.

Mohab stepped away, disgust pinching his features, loathing curling his lips.

275

"Why have you come here and what is it you want?" Valentina asked coldly.

"I came to claim what is rightfully mine," the travel-soiled young man replied.

Valentina looked at him and felt her stomach heave. The camels of the desert smelled better than he did. He wore a filthy facsimile of the uniform of a member of the Islamic Guard. Narrowing her eyes, she stared at his thin, pockmarked face. His small beady eyes were those of a desert rat or a weasel, and his long nose jutted out from his face. A long, unkempt beard, which was too sparse to be attractive, disguised a weak, receding chin. His neck was long and scrawny and bulged with purple veins.

"There is nothing here that belongs to you. When you were banished from this kingdom, you were told never to return until Ramiff rested with Allah."

"Who are you, and what right do you have to sit at my father's table?" he demanded in a nasal twang.

"By the right of your father, Emir Ramiff. I've taken over Mohab's duties. I owe you no explanations. I answer to no one save your father."

"My father is dead!" Homed shouted. "Everyone in this palace knows he's dead, and you're trying to deny me my rightful inheritance!"

"Your father is alive. There are no tricks being played, except possibly by you."

"If my father is alive, then I will see him," Homed demanded. Valentina saw Ahmar stiffen, ready to attack if Homed tried to burst out of the room in search of Ramiff.

"Your father knows you are here and has given orders that he will not see you. He also says your only thought in returning to Napur is to line your pockets. There is nothing for you here, Homed."

"I have traveled many miles to come to Napur. I demand to see my father. Saladin has broken ranks for the winter and I have been relieved of duty. I have nowhere else to go. And I will not leave until I've seen my father."

"You speak as though the breach in your relationship occurred only recently. I happen to know from Ramiff that he banished you years ago. But I will be charitable and allow you to stay two full days. You may bathe and fill your stomach. If you have the need of a horse or camel, one will be provided. Beyond this there is nothing for you here. The guards will show you to your rooms and watch that you do not travel this palace in the night. Your father wishes you a safe journey and bids you another farewell." Valentina rose from her chair to indicate that the meeting had ended.

"You lie!" Homed hissed. "I don't believe a word you said. I think you killed my father with the help of these people." He pointed a finger at Mohab, Ahmar, and Rosalan. "My father would never allow a woman to have as much authority as you seem to possess. Women are stupid and have but one use."

Valentina bristled but remained silent.

"I'll want a woman from the harem for my use," Homed said sneeringly. "I do not return to my post until spring. Before I leave I will know the truth. Send me that woman Dagny; she was my favorite when this was my home and not yours."

"Rosalan, see that Dagny fills his needs."

Homed shrugged off Ahmar's grip and walked from the room with royal bearing. Before leaving, he peered at Valentina, malicious contempt visible on his swarthy face.

Again Valentina felt the sting of conscience. True, Homed was despicable and dishonest, and Ramiff had hated his only son enough to retard his taking the throne. Yet that was all it was, all it could ever be; a delay. Even if Ramiff knew he could not keep Homed from ever claiming Napur, he could only beg for the time when Saladin would institute a truce and would then be able to oversee the managing of Napur and make Homed answerable. What right did she have to interfere with the natural order of events despite a pledge made to a dying old man?

"You cannot force him from the palace," Mohab complained. "You can threaten till your face turns blue, and it will do no good. Without a face-to-face confrontation with his father, he'll never leave. What will we do now?" Mohab wailed.

"The first thing I'm going to do is prevent you from making any more visits to the Judas tree. You must give me your word that you will not visit Ramiff's grave till I tell you it's safe."

Mohab knew she meant what she said. For a moment Valentina thought he would balk at not being able to spend his days near the emir, but in the end he agreed grudgingly and left the room muttering his hatred of Homed to any and all who would listen.

Valentina collapsed onto the chaise and wiped her perspiring brow. Dagny. How in the name of God had she forgotten about Dagny? Who was watching her if both Ahmar and Rosalan were here? She would have no peace till she knew that the sly, perfidious bitch was safe behind the closed doors of the harem.

Digging into the jewel casket on the ornate carved chest next to the table, she came up with a large heavy key and left the room.

Inside the women's quarters, Valentina called the women to attention. "Where is Dagny?" she asked, her voice dangerous and low. There was no reply. "If one of you does not see fit to use her tongue in the next few seconds, the lot of you will find yourselves at the mercies of Saladin's army. The decision is yours."

One of the women, the one whom Valentina had noticed when she had first arrived at the palace because of her shorn head, minced her way to Valentina's side and whispered, "She has gone to see a friend who has just arrived in the palace." The girl's guarded looks told Valentina that word of Homed's arrival had already spread.

Hastily Valentina turned on her heel and left the harem. Mohab was right. Trouble was just beginning. Her fears had come to fruition, and she would need all her wiles and wits to combat Homed.

Homed stepped from his bath, his thin, stringy body so scented and perfumed that the atmosphere was suffocating. Ahmar withdrew from the room in order to breathe fresh air. There was no way for Homed to leave his quarters except by the one door. Ahmar smiled to himself. Homed could take as many baths as he wished and use bottle after bottle of scented oils, and he would still look as though he had been dipped in lard. Ahmar thought of his own powerful physique and then grinned at what he had just seen stepping from the bath. Wild chickens had more meat on their bones than Homed. Arms akimbo, Ahmar assumed his stance and waited outside the door.

What seemed like hours later, he was startled by wild sounds from below the balcony. He frowned, undecided if he should investigate. The commotion grew more furious and rowdy by the moment. He backed up slowly to the wide balcony and opened the grilled doors to see what was taking place below.

A deep roar of laughter escaped him. Rosalan was straddling the supine Dagny, one hand pressed against her throat and the other clasping her hennaed hair. The screaming Dagny was shouting for help and cursing Rosalan with every breath she took.

"What are you doing to the she-dog?" Ahmar shouted to be heard above the screams.

"Dagny is to be allowed to go to Homed, and I wanted to be certain that her condition befitted him! When I finish with her here, I'll drag her to the stables, and then she'll be suited for the likes of him," Rosalan panted as she suddenly drove her fist into Dagny's stomach.

"Bitch!" Dagny screamed hoarsely. "I'll kill you for this!"

Rosalan laughed. "Not if I kill you first."

Two of the guards from the other end of the corridor walked over to the balcony to see what all the commotion was about. Ahmar explained and sent them both to guard Homed's door. He then leaned over the railing and felt pride flood through him as he watched Rosalan give the squirming Dagny a loud crack on her jaw. "I can't say that I disapprove of

279

what you're doing, but there has been a slight change."
Ahmar laughed.

Rosalan raised her eyes and waited for an explanation.

"The plucked chicken looks and smells like . . ."
Words failed him. "What I'm saying is, he's had a bath!"

"Then the bitch will have a bath, too," Rosalan laughed delightedly. "I'm curious to see what she looks like beneath all her powder." She gave Dagny's head another vicious jerk and dragged her to her feet. "You can tell the rooster you guard that his woman will join him shortly."

Chapter Twenty

Valentina raced for the holy mountain and Menghis. Only on the Alamut could she find peace and be free of the pressures that surrounded her in the palace.

In her wild scramble up the mountain, her only thought was that Menghis would calm her tortured being. He was right, the Alamut was beautiful and would soothe her.

When Valentina reached the citadel, she was surprised to see Aloe Bud. "Darling child, what are you doing here? I thought Menghis took you to safety below the mountain."

"He did, Valentina, but I ran away," Aloe Bud said happily. "I could not live below, so Menghis has allowed me to return. He has placed me under his protection and has allowed me to feed his deer. Isn't he wise and wonderful? He knew I would die of loneliness if I stayed below. The Alamut is my home."

Valentina looked around. "Where is Menghis, Aloe Bud?"

"He sent me to greet you and to fetch you to him. He wanted me to tell you that I am happy and for you not to be sad that I am back on the Alamut. Come, I'll bring you to him," she said, placing her hand in Valentina's, a happy smile on her round face.

"If you are happy, little one, then I am happy also."

Valentina walked beside Aloe Bud into a large circular room lavishly decorated with silks and brocades. Mounds of brilliant cushions and pillows were placed next to ornate gold chairs. *Fedawi* were being indoctrinated into the loyal order. Valentina frowned. "You should not be here, Aloe Bud."

"I know; that is what Menghis said. I'm to leave as soon as I bring you to him. Later I will serve you tea and cakes. I have learned many things since I came back to the Alamut," she said impishly. Valentina nodded as the child scampered off.

Her eyes went to Menghis, and she felt herself grow weak at the sight of his beloved face. "Come," he said softly. "We'll sit in the far corner of the room."

Valentina shuddered and wanted to flee but could not move. "Menghis, I don't think I want to stay here and watch the men succumb to the drugs that will be given to them."

"You will not have to see that which you have no desire to. The men received the drug hours ago. From time to time you may hear one or more of them speak, but that is all. There is nothing for you to fear. Come, we will talk. I see there is much we must discuss. Listen to me carefully. The men have come here of their own choosing. Who is to say heaven and eternity are not what they imagine? Who is to say this time is not meant to be? If the gods whom you and those below the mountain pray to did not want this to happen, then some manner of divine, earthly intervention would take place. It is the way of the Alamut, and I cannot change it. In the beginning I too asked questions out of fear. That fear is no longer with me."

Valentina was less agitated now that she rested next to Menghis on the silken cushions. Seeing nothing to disturb her, she moved closer to him and pressed his hand to her cheek. "Tell me more of the drug. I wish to know."

"This particular drug is called Angel's Trumpet. The name symbolizes heaven. It was brought to the Alamut from Turkey many, many years ago. Now it grows on the mountain. It is very potent. If used unwisely, it can cause death. Too much or too little can do harm. For years the drug was tested before it was given as it is now. Only *Sheikh al Jebal* knows the right proportions. Even I do not know what they are."

"Do they know they are . . . what I mean is . . . do they think?"

"They know they are on the Alamut. They know that before they can be considered *fedawi,* they must see their heaven and their own special glimpse of eternity. If you wish, you may speak to any or all of them, and they will answer you in a rational manner. The drug is wearing off now."

"Tell me of your experience with the drug," Valentina said inquisitively.

"It was a magnificent experience and I have no regrets. Each man wishes to see heaven and eternity. I have no desire to repeat the experience. It is like seeing and tasting perfection. If it is to be repeated, then it means nothing. We have no desire to use drugs to cripple and eat the mind. We are not fools, Valentina. It is the way of the Alamut, and as I said, I cannot change it, nor do I have a desire to do so."

"It frightens me," Valentina whispered, her eyes dark pools of concern.

"Listen to me, Valentina. As a Christian, you believe in many things. You believe in God and in heaven as a place to go after death. If there is a heaven, would it not be beautiful? Would you see angels and heavenly beings? Would smells have colors, would you be able to see sounds? Heaven is supposed to be the epitome of all things. Is not this what you and other Christians were taught to believe?"

"Yes. But heaven is only for those who are good and who die a natural death."

"Are you telling me your God would forsake those who have made a mistake, and if they died a violent death He would reject them?"

"I'm confused." Valentina looked at him, perplexed.

"The men are not dying; they are imagining what death will be like and seeing their place in eternity. Each man is seeing and feeling his own eternity. Since neither you nor I know if there is a heaven or what heaven is like, who are we to judge? I don't say it is right or wrong; it is the way of the Alamut. Speaking for myself, as I said, I have no regrets. I see that you are still frightened. We will speak of it no more."

"No, I'm no longer frightened. When I'm with you nothing frightens me. It's just that when one is under a drug, one does not have control of his mind and body."

"Valentina, everyone fears death. It is the one thing the mind cannot conceive. There is no one to tell us what life after death is, if indeed there is such a thing. The drug, given in the right proportions, lets the *fedawi* see this. I no longer fear death since I saw what my death and eternity would be like, and my fears were put to rest."

"Tell me, Menghis, what was your hereafter like? Please tell me, I would like to know."

Menghis's eyes were sad as he cupped her face gently in his strong hands. "That is the one thing I cannot share with you. Each person's hereafter is his own." He could not bear to tell her that she was not in his vision of eternity. "Come, we will go to my quarters so that Aloe Bud can show you what she has learned. She has been beside herself since she learned you were coming up the mountain. She thinks of herself as my protector. Every time I turn around she is making me some tempting dish to nibble on."

Valentina looked around the room at the men and no longer felt uneasy. If they were experiencing their eternity, who was she to dispute it? As Menghis said, it was the way of the Alamut.

While Menghis and Valentina walked back to Menghis's quarters, Aloe Bud, who had been hiding behind a curtain, scurried to the kitchen area. This was her chance to show Valentina that her coming back to the Alamut was not a bad thing. She would make the tea and serve the cakes, and then both Valentina and Menghis would see that she was helpful and she would never be sent away again.

She looked around the tidy kitchen and at the glowing brazier. A kettle was simmering, so all she had to dc was add the tea leaves and let them sit for a few moments. She glanced at the crocks that held the herbs and teas and was undecided. She should have asked the cook which ones were the best to use. She had been so excited when Menghis sought her out and told her Valentina was climbing the mountain that she had forgotten, and when she did remember, the cook was gone. She sighed and then brightened. She would smell the leaves, like the cook did, and whichever smelled the best she would use. She especially liked the shiny green leaves of the mint. That was what she would do, she decided; she would mix the mint leaves with another leaf and make a different tea, one that Menghis and Valentina had never tasted.

Aloe Bud tiptoed around the huge kitchen, happily sniffing one crock and then another. The mint leaves in one hand, she stood back and looked at the various sizes of the crocks, surmising that the largest crock held the best blend of leaves and was the one that was used most often. She sniffed again and decided she liked the sweet, tangy scent of the fresh leaves, which smelled like they had just been picked. How much should she use? She sighed again. If she was going to make only two cups of tea, then she wouldn't need much. She would use one leaf of each. She nodded happily as she dropped the two leaves into the simmering kettle and sat back, waiting for the tea to steep. She placed a freshly picked flower on the white cloth of the tray and added the small rice cakes. Carefully she poured the tea into two fragile cups and surveyed her handiwork. Satisfied, she picked up the tray and walked carefully, balancing the tray, to Menghis's quarters. She set the tray onto a low table and smiled at Menghis and Valentina.

"What a good child you are," Valentina praised Aloe Bud's thoughtfulness.

"I hope you like the tea." Aloe Bud smiled as she hugged Valentina good night.

"I will drink every drop, and while I am sipping it I will say to myself, 'Aloe Bud made this tea for me, how lucky I am!' Sleep well, little one."

"Fickle women," Menghis laughed after she had gone. "Before you came she was kissing me good night."

Valentina laughed at his pretense of annoyance. She sipped at the tea and remarked that the mint flavor was delicious. When she finished the tea she relaxed deeply back in the cushions, but she became thirsty, thirstier than she had ever been in her whole life. Then suddenly her body became hot, and she felt as if she were burning in fire. She glanced at Menghis and saw him rubbing at his neck, a puzzled look on his face. Her heart began to beat furiously, and the room around her changed colors in swirling, rapid succession. It reminded Valentina of the day she met Menghis at the bazaar, all the fantastic, brilliant colors whispering to her now as they did then.

Then Menghis became a tall, graceful tree, stretching out his branches to entwine her in his sweet embrace. Fascinated, Valentina watched as if outside herself as her own body became the earth and the sky, to nurture this tree that quested for her very soul. Then her body became, not the elements, but her own star-exploding galaxy as Menghis crept into her soul and made the sparks rain back to the heavens.

Together they tumbled down endless corridors into prehistory at the dawn of their love. They traveled back slowly, hand in hand. Valentina looked at her panther, her beloved Shadjar, and saw her ears standing erect, a pulsating dome between them, strung with colorful lanterns blinking and winking high musical notes of love.

She saw from afar creamy-smooth white words . . . words of timeless devotion flowing from Menghis's mouth. Valentina watched in amazement as the words rolled across the floor, pausing to tickle Shadjar before scurrying out the door.

Valentina stared deeply into Menghis's eyes as he entered her womanly shrine, his eyes a river, his eyelashes sapphire wands, and she wanted to drown in the flowing motion of the rivertide, touched softly by magic wands that lit her way.

Her body exploded into thousands of shimmering, shattering jewels as the tide swept her under, and she rose to the surface in a field of wild strawberries. She lay back, contented, and listened to them grow around her. Her life flashed before her, and the sound of her laughter came strangely to kiss her ears. Suddenly, no longer aware of the tall, rugged tree that had been Menghis now shedding its leaves beside her, Valentina felt another presence.

A beautiful blue shape knelt beside Valentina and licked at her face. The mellow notes of a flute darted from behind the blue shape and consumed her in its sensuous notes. Her lover had taken yet another guise.

Time passed quickly, too quickly, as Valentina reached new heights of consciousness she had never before dreamed possible. She met and spoke to God, liked Him, and humbly asked Him to look out for Ramiff and Mohab. She asked for forgiveness for what she was doing, and He said He forgave Judas and that He would pardon her also.

She fell back into the wild strawberries and felt their pain as she crushed them beneath her back. Gentle wafts of scarlet wind circled the room from the open window. She marveled at the deep, vivid purple sound of the cat's tail as it thumped on the tile floor.

Suddenly Valentina became aware of a white glow all around her. The tree that was Menghis, free of its leaves, beckoned her. She reached out, clutching at the tough, sinewy branch that was his arm, and felt him draw her body into his. The single crystal tear in his eye was a waterfall of shimmering diamonds, making them take leaf.

They were reborn in each other's arms.

They slept.

Menghis woke, his heart pounding, his mind racing. Gently he touched Valentina to be sure she was all right, and then he relaxed. His eyes went to the tea cups and he shuddered. The child must have mixed up the . . . was it Aloe Bud? Of course it was Aloe Bud. Valentina was right; the child should have stayed below the mountain. An innocent mistake, and they could have both died.

He cradled Valentina's head to his chest and waited for her to awaken. His heart ached for her and what she would say when she opened her eyes.

Hours passed.

Valentina woke when the sun was high. Her hand immediately reached out for Menghis's, and she held it close to her breast. She spoke quietly. "The child made a mistake. It was a beautiful, terrifying experience. Now I know why you said once was enough. I do not blame you, Menghis. You must not look so tormented, my love. Your eyes are full of anguish for me. I was inside your soul, Menghis. Your breath was my breath. I felt us reborn as one," she said softly, her eyes brimming with love.

"You could have died. How can I live with that thought?"

"The child made a mistake. We must learn by our mistakes. You will say the right thing to the child, and she will never make that mistake again. She only meant to please us; no harm was intended. I can forgive her, and so must you."

For an answer Menghis crushed her to him, the tears in his eyes blinding him for the moment.

"I wish I could stay here forever, but I must go back down the mountain. I needed to see you and feel your arms around me. Now that I have been with you, I can go back to the palace and do what I must do." Gently she kissed his eyes, his cheek, his mouth.

"You will be in my thoughts every moment, every second of the day." She smiled at him. "Come, walk me to the edge of the mountain, as you walked with me before to the beginning and the end of time."

Chapter Twenty-one

Winter was upon the Holy Land. February was the month of the rains, and the heavy droplets beat dismally against the windows. Valentina's spirits were as dreary as the day.

As she paced the confines of her apartment, Shadjar's yellow eyes kept track of her progress back and forth across the carpeted floor. Valentina's thoughts were high on Alamut, her heart with Menghis. So often in these weeks since she had lain in his arms Valentina dreamed of him and imagined herself still locked in his loving embrace. No longer was she tormented by dreams of a faceless lover to whom she could give her heart and soul. The lover had a face now, he was Menghis.

The first caravan carrying supplies to Richard's army had left the granaries of Napur within three days of her return from Alamut. Quickly and silently, Menghis's *fedawi* had seen to the loading of the pack animals and wagons and had left Napur before the sun crept over the horizon. Within a week there was delivered to her a purse containing half the gold from the sale to Richard. This was immediately deposited in Napur's treasury. If her conscience pricked her that she was availing herself of the foodstuffs which had been purchased by Saladin's generals, she did not dwell upon it. Valentina only knew that she was doing what must be done. It would have weighed much heavier upon her mind if she had access to supplies and allowed her compatriots to die of starvation.

Shadjar lifted her head and looked to Valentina's door beyond the alcove, hung with bright yellow draperies. A moment later a light tap sounded on the heavy carved door.

"Enter," Valentina called, composing herself quickly. The transportation of the supplies was her secret alone, and she had no wish to burden her friends with her misery.

Rosalan entered on light, slippered feet. Valentina looked at her friend and marveled at the change in her that living in Ramiff's palace had brought about. No longer forced to live the hard life of a wanderer following behind a constantly moving army, Rosalan's beauty had flourished. Her creamy ocher skin glowed with health, and her dancing dark eyes were bright and clear and still betrayed her dauntless nature. The girl took great care with her dress and grooming, the effects of which were evident in her shining black tresses and fastidious costuming. In the few short months they had lived in Napur, Rosalan's once-calloused feet were as soft and carefully tended as her pretty hands. As Rosalan stepped into Valentina's apartment, the bangles and bracelets she was so fond of wearing jingled enticingly.

"Where's Ahmar?" Valentina teased affectionately. "He usually trails behind you like a lost puppy." Something in Rosalan's eyes dimmed, and Valentina knew she had said the wrong thing. "Is anything wrong, Rosalan?"

Rosalan cast her eyes downward and was silent.

"Have you and Ahmar quarreled?" Valentina persisted. This was so unlike Rosalan, who was known to always speak her mind.

"No, we have not quarreled. It is just that I have become weary of his company and I told him so. I sent him away."

"Away!"

"Not away from the palace," Rosalan hastened to explain, "just away from me. I have other things on my mind, and I cannot bear his constant company. There are times when a woman needs to be alone," Rosalan defended.

Valentina remained silent, not knowing what to say. That Rosalan was troubled was clear, and all she could do was wait for her friend to share it.

Dropping down to her knees, Rosalan patted Shadjar's head and the cat rolled onto her back, begging for her belly to be scratched. Rosalan complied, speaking softly to Shadjar and laughing at the cat's antics. Valentina snapped up a brush from her dressing table and began to whip the bristles through her hair. When Rosalan needed someone to talk to, she would be ready to listen. Otherwise, she knew it was useless to pry. Rosalan could be the most cryptic of all the people she had ever known.

Tiring of Shadjar, Rosalan rose and stepped over to Valentina's dressing table, picking through odd bits of jewelry and perfumes. Almost at once she dropped a length of beads and went to stand by the window, looking morosely out at the rain, her face as gray and lackluster as the day. Finally she began to pace back and forth, just as Valentina had been doing when Rosalan arrived.

As Valentina brushed her hair, she watched Rosalan covertly. What could be troubling the girl so greatly that it was tearing her to distraction? Suddenly Valentina became frightened. Had Homed done something to Rosalan? Had he discovered that Ramiff was dead? The supply shipment to the Crusaders—had someone implicated her in it? Her thoughts racing, terror clutching her in its grip, Valentina jumped up from her seat near the dressing table and rushed to Rosalan.

Grasping her by the arms and turning her about sharply to face her, Valentina demanded, "What is it? What's wrong? Tell me, I can't bear the waiting! Has Homed . . ."

Rosalan covered her face with her hands, her shoulders shuddering with uncontrollable sobs. "No, no, not Homed," she protested. "It is me."

Slowly she brought herself under control, and the

sobbing abated. Her eyes, meeting Valentina's, revealed undisguised pain. Valentina hardly knew what to say. Rosalan had always been the stronger of the two. She had always shared Valentina's troubles and had been the one to comfort her. In the end, it was Rosalan who had offered the soundest logic. Following Rosalan's teachings, Valentina gathered the girl close and allowed her to cry before pressing her further for any answers.

Together they sat on the low divan which was Valentina's bed, one comforting the other's tears. At last Rosalan raised her head and reached into the neckline of her caftan to withdraw a rumpled handkerchief which she had stuffed between her breasts. From the condition of the small white square of cloth it was evident that Rosalan had done a good deal of crying before coming to Valentina's apartment. Her heart breaking for her friend, Valentina asked, "Can you tell me about it? I will understand if you don't want to, but I hate to see you suffer so, Rosalan. Let me help you."

"No, there's nothing you can do. There is nothing anyone can do, there is no help for it. But I must tell you, for it will not be long before you discover it for yourself."

"Discover what?" Valentina prodded, still fearful and expecting the worst. There were so many secrets she carried in her heart. Which of them had been discovered?

"Discover that I am with child," Rosalan blurted, her voice on the point of breaking.

"A child—Rosalan—how wonderful! It is what you've always wanted!" Rosalan began weeping again. "Stop your weeping. Are you afraid you will be banished from the palace? Silly girl."

"No . . . but I am so unhappy. I have always longed for a child of my own, and now I carry one beneath my breast. I should be happier than ever in my life. Here I live in a palace, able to provide for my child . . . still I'm miserable."

"But why?"

"Because of Ahmar," Rosalan confessed, misery filling her great dark eyes. "The child is not Ahmar's."

"This I have already surmised," Valentina said softly. "You yourself told me that although he is still a man in every sense of the word and capable of making love to a woman, he cannot father a child. Oh, I see. . . . Ahmar is angry with you."

"No! That is just the point," Rosalan interposed before Valentina could continue with that line of thought. "Ahmar is not angry! He's delighted! He knows that I have longed for a child. No, Ahmar is not unhappy."

Valentina was confused. "What is the problem, then? If Ahmar is happy about the child for your sake, and he still loves you . . ."

"Oh, Valentina! Don't you know anything? Can't you see that Ahmar is only saying he is happy? I've lived too long in the desert. I know how men think. If it is not their child, they have no regard for it."

"Rosalan, this is not so. I know of many men who love and accept children whom they have not fathered. Many of these men even give the child their own name to bear and bestow a rightful inheritance upon them. Ahmar loves you. He will love your child."

"Perhaps this is the way of men where you come from, but not here."

"Ahmar has said he is happy you are with child. Has he told you he still loves you?"

"Yes," Rosalan whispered. "But I know it is only words. When he sees me grow big of belly, he will feel differently. He will not want a crying babe who needs his mother. No, Valentina, all men are alike."

"That is not true, Rosalan. All men are not alike," she said softly, thinking of Menghis and how different he was from Paxon. "You do Ahmar a great disservice to say he is like all other men. If this were so, why have you never fallen in love before?"

"You don't understand. I do love Ahmar, but I know in the end he will hurt me, and that I could not bear. So I have put him away from me. We no longer share the same bed."

"And he left? Without trying to make you see that he loves you?"

"He left because I threatened to kill myself if he did not go. All his explanations are useless. I know what he feels in his heart." Rosalan began to sob again and Valentina held her close.

There were no words to ease her misery, and Valentina's heart was heavy. At last Rosalan blew her nose and dried her eyes before readjusting her yashmak. Still the great dark eyes above the veil were filled with sorrow.

"Rosalan, if you have made your decision concerning Ahmar, then you must think of your child. All this weeping can't be good for either you or the babe."

"I know it isn't good for the babe, yet I can't help myself. When I think of Ahmar and how good he was to me, so gentle . . . so loving . . . But my thinking of him must stop. I have someone else I must think about and care for. My babe."

As Rosalan mentioned the child she carried beneath her breast, her eyes lit for the first time since entering Valentina's apartment. "It will be a boy, I know it. Strong and virile, and I will teach him all I know and see that he learns from only the best teachers. He will make something of himself one day, my son will. Listen to me! What if the child is a girl? Poor child. Life is not easy for us women, is it, Valentina? But I will love her all the more and teach her to survive in the world of men." Rosalan's arms closed about Valentina's neck. "We will both teach her, eh, good friend?"

"Yes," Valentina laughed, wondering how long it had been since she had held a tender babe in her arms. As she thought of it she felt a small yearning for a babe of her own. Menghis's child. Clearing her thoughts, she asked, "Can you tell me whose child you carry? I thought that since Ahmar had captured your attention you had eyes for no other."

"I can tell you, and when I do you will understand why I have such hopes for this child's future. If it is a son, he will be a most remarkable child. His father

is the sultan of Jakard," Rosalan stated simply, un-
aware of the shocked expression on Valentina's face.
"Remember when Saladin and his generals came to
purchase foodstuffs? It was the night before Emir
Ramiff died, and you had spent the night with Saladin."

Valentina nodded, showing she remembered the
night, but her movements were mechanical and stiff.
Paxon!

"The sultan and I met in the halls of the palace.
Very simply, he invited me to spend the night with
him, and I accepted. I knew what an affront it would
have been to the emir to refuse, even though I had
already come to know Ahmar."

"Paxon," Valentina whispered.

"Yes, that is his name," Rosalan continued, un-
heeding of Valentina's distant manner. "Had I tried,
I could not have chosen a more handsome or intelligent man for my child's father. Already the babe's
destiny is taking shape. Imagine if I were still living
among the ranks of Saladin's army. So many men,
night after night. And so often I prayed that I would
find myself with child, but it never happened, and I
thought it was Allah's will that I was barren. Instead,
one night with a powerful man like the sultan of
Jakard, and my life is changed. I am to be a mother!"

Valentina's brain was whirling in spirals. Paxon, father to Rosalan's child! It was almost beyond her
grasp.

"Valentina," Rosalan's voice intruded upon her
thoughts, "have you heard anything I've said?"

"Of course," Valentina answered brightly. "There
is a child on the way. A very special child. And not
because his father is a sultan, but because his mother
is a remarkable woman."

"Then you are happy for me?"

"Happy, and I rejoice for you. I only wish you
would give the matter of Ahmar more thought. A
child could do with a father in this world, and Ahmar
would set a fine example for any child."

"I have thought about it, and it can never be.

Each day the child would remind him that he can never father a child of his own. How can I believe him? I could never take the chance that my child would feel unloved." The sadness had crept back into Rosalan's eyes. It was apparent to all but the blind that she loved Ahmar deeply.

Rosalan adjusted her yashmak, tucking it into her hair. "I must leave you now. I still must gather the laundry from the emir's room. We can't afford to be lax, since Homed and that she-dog Dagny keep such a watchful eye on the goings and comings from the emir's apartments. I wish we could get Homed out of the palace! Even Mohab, poor man, is growing nervous about the food he brings into Ramiff's chamber. Each day he sits there alone and eats the food meant for his friend. Each day is a painful reminder that Ramiff has no further use for the nourishment of this world."

"Go to him, then, Rosalan. Tell him I will come to Ramiff's chamber after our evening meal and we will play the game he had sent from the Orient. Mohab likes that game the best. I fear for his health since Homed has returned. The strain is too much for him to keep up this guise."

"He'll be happy to hear your message. I also try to spend more time with him, and now that Ahmar and I are no longer together, I will have even more time for him."

"That would be kind of you, Rosalan. But don't overtire yourself. In fact, from now on, Ahmar will see to gathering the laundry from the emir's chambers. I don't want you to strain yourself. This child means too much to you for you to take any chances."

"Do not worry about me. I'm young and healthy, and so will the babe be," Rosalan laughed, her delight over the child obvious. "I'll see you at meal time." Her skirts rustling, her feet soundless on the thick carpet, she left Valentina to her thoughts.

Rosalan, bearing Paxon's child! Valentina was not jealous, but she wondered if she would have been if she had never come to know Menghis. Yes, she told herself. I would have been insane with jealousy.

Still, she wished that Rosalan's child had been fathered by another. Anyone but Paxon. The very thought of him threw her into a panic. He knew too much about her. At any time he could reveal her true identity and place her very life in danger. If it was ever discovered that Ramiff was dead and that she had been instrumental in keeping Homed from his rightful place upon the throne, she would be stoned to death. Worse; if Paxon ever discovered that she had been sending to Richard, supplies that had already been purchased by the army of Islam, she would be crucified! Paxon would see to it! She knew this as well as she knew her own name. No one, least of all a woman, could ever betray Paxon and interfere with the success of the jihad and live.

Now each time she looked at Rosalan she would be reminded of Paxon and the danger he represented. Not for a moment would she find respite from the thought of what he would do to her if he should return to Napur and find the storage bins empty of their larder.

Icy fingers of fear touched the base of Valentina's spine, and she felt as though she had just brushed death.

Rosalan was sitting near the window when Ahmar saw her. The afternoon light made a halo around her head, and her expression was complacent and lovely. In her hands she held pieces of soft cloth which she was carefully stitching into garments for her child. Ahmar was certain he had never known anyone lovelier. As she bent her head to her task his eyes fell on the soft nape of her neck, and he longed to place his lips there and breathe in the feminine fragrance of her. Rosalan's concentration on the new and arduous task of fine stitching was so great that she did not notice Ahmar's presence.

In the process of stitching, Rosalan's tongue darted between her lips, giving her the appearance of a small child intent on play. For all her experience, Ahmar thought, she is still like an innocent child. His heart swelled with love for her. If only he could convince her that he loved her and would love the child as well.

Suddenly Rosalan pricked her finger with the needle. She dropped her work and lifted her finger to examine it as a bright red droplet of blood appeared. Grimacing, Rosalan put the injured finger in her mouth. Her lips pouted, her brows drawn down into a scowl. Ahmar almost laughed aloud. Even the smallest of her gestures brought him joy. Unable to resist the impulse, he was beside her in two long strides.

Her surprise at seeing him registered in her eyes. Ahmar spoke before she could send him away. "Look what you've done to yourself," he sympathized. "Here, you're doing that all wrong. Let me see it."

Without protest, Rosalan offered him her injured finger. Ahmar knelt at her side, taking her hand in his, and tenderly placed pressure on the tiny wound. "You should be more careful, little one. Someday you will do yourself a terrible injury."

Rosalan smiled. It was good to have Ahmar near her again. She had missed him terribly these past days when they had avoided each other. Tenderly he ministered to her finger, wrapping it in a small scrap of cloth from her sewing.

"Wait until the bleeding stops, else you'll stain the little one's clothes before he has a chance to do it himself." Ahmar's voice was light and teasing, yet his eyes were unfathomable reaches of gray.

"Thank you," Rosalan whispered, trying to keep her voice level. "I will be careful." She expected him to leave, but he continued to stand there looking down at her. At last she raised her eyes and saw on his face the pain she was causing him. Her own heart constricted with emotion.

Suddenly Ahmar's arms were about her, pressing her close, just holding her. When he raised his face again, she discerned a glistening in his eyes that matched hers.

Wordlessly he lowered his head again and pressed it against her belly, where the child was beginning its life. "Rosalan, I love your child," he whispered, his voice tight and controlled.

Tenderly Rosalan touched his dark head and held him closer to her. Her heart beat with joy, for she knew beyond a doubt that she believed this man. He loved her and he loved her child. He would find no joy in this world without the two of them.

He raised his head, marveling that at last she seemed to believe him. Rosalan pressed her mouth against his; their tears mingled.

Against her ear Ahmar murmured, "I imagined you were only using the babe as an excuse to put me aside. I thought you considered me half a man because I could not give you a child."

"Hush, Ahmar," Rosalan soothed. "Without your love I am only half a woman." She silenced him with her lips.

Joy had returned to the world, and they found themselves laughing and crying and trying to speak their hearts.

"Enough of this talk," Ahmar commanded, lifting her into his arms.

"Foolish man! Where are you taking me?" Rosalan demanded, wrapping her arms tightly around his neck and nuzzling against his cheek.

"To my chamber, where we can be alone and where I can hold you in my arms and we can make love and pretend that this is the first day of our child's life."

In answer Rosalan covered his mouth with her own and found there the sweetness of life and the reason for living.

Mohab kept a close watch on Homed and the woman called Dagny. He spied upon them when they walked the corridors, and he was outside their door when they ate and made love. Never once did he remove himself from their presence. He slept little and ate nothing. His wizened features took on a gaunt look and he spoke not a word, not even to Valentina. Only his eyes were alive, and full of hatred.

Once, while he stood outside the door, he heard both voices raised in anger, and he smiled to himself. Dagny was telling Homed that he was a fool to allow Valentina to continue with her duties as regent. She insisted that Napur was his because the emir was dead. When Homed demanded proof, she could offer nothing save her suspicions.

"Demand to speak to your father, and do not take no for an answer," she prodded. "Together we'll rule this kingdom. You promised me."

"I need proof, and what is it you think I can do, guarded as I am night and day? I'm not welcome here and my father refuses to see me. What do you want me to do? Force myself upon him? And if he is alive he'll banish me again. Then where will I pass the winter?"

"Do something! Leave the palace, bring back hired cutthroats. The promise of gold will secure their loyalty to you, and when they hear you will be the next emir, they will do whatever you ask."

"Words are easy," Homed protested. "But how do you expect me to leave? That burly Ahmar will kill me and slit my throat if I look at him out of the corner of my eye."

"There are ways for Ahmar to be taken care of, and I'll see to it. He will be occupied when the time comes."

"It would appear that you have a great deal of confidence in your charms," Homed sneered.

"Much confidence," Dagny answered shortly.

"And how do you expect to outwit that old man Mohab, who is our constant shadow?"

"There are ways to take care of him also. You are a man, and you should be the one to do all the thinking. Why must I do everything?"

"Because it was you who sent me the missive, and it was you who decided that my father was dead, and

299

it was you who convinced me that the time was right for me to take the throne. You said you had many abilities."

"One day soon, when the time is right, we'll kill the old man. You're young and fleet of foot. You will simply make your way through the grounds and away from here."

Mohab listened, his face puckered into a frown. They were speaking just a shade too loudly. It was almost as if they wanted him to hear what they were saying.

While Mohab listened outside Homed's door, Valentina was expressing her alarm over what she called Mohab's condition to Rosalan. "He no longer hears me when I speak to him. His eyes look through me as if I were not here. I fear that his mind is leaving him and I feel so helpless. I did a foolish thing when I told Homed he could stay in the palace for two days. I must have looked very foolish. Now we must keep him here, a prisoner. Even I, inexperienced as I am, know that if he were to leave, he would return with a band of cutthroats."

"He should be done away with," Rosalan said quietly. "And Dagny, too. Everything was peaceful and Mohab was happy until Homed returned and they began their plotting."

"Rosalan, you know I can't kill the emir's son, regardless of how I feel about him. I simply couldn't do it."

"You wouldn't have to do it, Valentina. There are those who would do it for you willingly."

Valentina sighed. "No, Rosalan, it is the same thing. His death would be on my shoulders, and I can't allow that to happen. Right now my main concern is for Mohab. There must be something I can do for him. Something I can say that will ease the burden he carries."

Rosalan persisted with her logic. "But, Valentina, they are plotting our deaths. Right now, this minute! And you have fears of doing them in? I don't understand you. They are like two fleas on a dog. Who will miss them? No one," she answered herself. "They serve no purpose and should be done away with."

"I don't want to hear any more on the subject," Valentina said firmly. "For now they are well guarded and there is nothing they can do. Leave me, Rosalan. I must think of what I am to do for Mohab."

"How long do you think we can keep them prisoners?" Rosalan persisted.

"I don't know! I don't know anything at this point! But prisoners they will remain, be it for a day or a year! As far as anyone is concerned, Homed returned to Napur and left again. I don't even want anyone to know that he's still here in the palace. Do you think Ahmar can manage that?"

"It has already been done. Ahmar has great foresight, Valentina. And as for keeping them under guard, it will be done and none the wiser. And those two will never see the light of day as long as the sultans are in Napur for their supplies. Never fear, Valentina, Ahmar will see to it."

Regardless of Rosalan's assurances, Valentina's brows were drawn into a frown.

"I still say it would solve all our problems to kill them now!" At Valentina's stern look, Rosalan turned on her heel, muttering to herself that she must go and inform Ahmar.

Chapter Twenty-two

In the long and lonely hours before dawn, Valentina tossed and turned upon her silken-covered divan and found sleep impossible. Thoughts of Menghis filled her head, and her body cried out for his embrace. Each day the yearning for him mounted, and each night found her dry-eyed yet heartsick for the sight of him. She threw back the covers with such suddenness that the sleeping Shadjar leaped to her feet, startled and snarling.

"Hush, you foolish cat. Go back to sleep," Valentina ordered, feeling a bit foolish talking to the panther. "Look what you've done. You've got Menghis's dove slapping his wings and spilling his seeds all over the carpet." Shadjar winked her bright yellow eyes at Valentina and tilted her head to one side as if she understood.

Valentina gazed at her reflection in the looking glass. The desire to see the tall, dark-haired man was so strong that she began to tremble. She slammed the looking glass against the heavy ebony chest and spun around to Shadjar. "How would you like an outing?" she asked the attentive white cat. "And you, too, my key to the kingdom of love," she cooed to the dove Menghis had given her. "Will you fly ahead and tell him of my need to be with him?"

After changing into her riding costume of warm khalats and long-sleeved tunic, topped with a cloak to protect her from the cold, Valentina slipped Shadjar's chain about her neck and loosed the dove from his perch, attaching his golden tethers to her shoulder.

Her heart pounding within her breast, she ran down one corridor and then another, till she was outside the doors of the palace. She knew as surely as she must draw her next breath that she had to be with Menghis and gaze deeply into his laughing dark eyes. All thoughts, all feelings save this all-encompassing yearning, this ache for him, fled.

In the gloom of the stable, which was heavy with the scent of horseflesh and hay, Valentina saddled the white Arabian, whispering soft words of comfort to calm the startled animal. Out into the cold night air she led her assemblage of horse, panther, and dove. Once beyond the fence of the stable yard, she mounted the animal and whipped it to a fast gallop, the dove hugging close to her neck for warmth and Shadjar keeping pace.

When she began to outdistance Shadjar, Valentina reined in and waited for the cat to catch up. Looking up at the sky, the stars silver beacons in the velvety darkness, Valentina's yearning became a strong, steady throb. Love. It was love. She had given this feeling, this yearning, a name, and she was easy with it. Love. She loved Menghis.

Crystal tears welled, crested, and overflowed down her cheeks. Love! her heart joyously announced. Prodding the Arabian, Valentina and her strange entourage moved toward the place where her heart would know its ease. Toward Menghis.

Through the dawn, onward beneath the noonday sun, and shadowed by the red glare of sunset, Valentina rode to her love. Midway up the mountain Valentina released the dove and watched it circle overhead. It found its bearings and then soared high in the sky toward the pinnacle of the mountain. To Menghis.

Driving the animal beneath her, Valentina fixed her gaze upward. Her hair had come free and loose and streamed out behind her as she urged the horse faster, always faster. To Menghis. To Menghis.

Achieving the top, the citadel in sight, Valentina slipped from atop her mount, the strain on her muscles from so long a ride going unnoticed. She stopped once on the footpath to get her bearings and to take a deep breath. She could sense the eyes of the *fedawi* all about her. Instead of making her feel menaced, the unseen eyes made her feel safe in the descending darkness.

The round golden circle of a moon crept from behind a dark cloud, making way for a galaxy of twinkling stars which lit up the ebony sky. It was to be a night made for love beneath the stars, love with Menghis.

Emotion welled in her throat as she stepped over the rise and raced across the clearing. "Menghis," she called softly. "Where are you?"

She was in his arms, his kisses searing a path from her mouth to her neck as he crushed his lean, hard body to hers. Their lips sought each other's as they lost themselves in a love so desperate that the only release possible would be an explosion of passion and desire.

Menghis tenderly picked her up and cradled her to him. She burrowed in his embrace, kissing him wantonly. He laid her down gently on the soft, thick carpet of leaves and crushed her lips beneath his. Her head reeled with the intoxicating scent of him mingled with that of the woods into which he had carried her.

Wordlessly he worshipped her. Valentina's arms clasped tightly about his neck as she answered his kisses. Her breasts swelled against their confines. Her breath came in a scorching spasm as a low animal groan began deep within her and escaped her lips.

His head fell to the pinnacle of her desires as his lips teased and nibbled, driving her to the brink of frenzied wantonness.

The throbbing of his manhood was searing the tender flesh of her inner thigh, and she arched her back and imprisoned him with her hand; leading him toward her, closer, closer, until a flood tide of exultation consumed them both and made them one.

Menghis slept, his dark head cradled against her breast. Valentina lay quietly, her body at peace at last as she watched the stars in the heavens signal one another in the jet vastness of the sky. Soon they would disappear with the first warning rays of the sun. But they would return. They would always return. Just as she would return. For now, for always, forevermore.

Shipment after shipment was sent out over the following weeks. Word reached Valentina that Saladin's officers would soon arrive to fill their caravans. Her inspection of the near-to-empty granaries and the dwindling foodstuffs filled her with alarm. What was she to do? The harvest wouldn't be reaped for months. Visions of her naked body being tied to a cross assailed her, and she trembled violently. Crucifixion was the penalty for treason and treachery. How was she to explain the shortages to Saladin and his generals? Would Menghis aid her again? Each of the three times she had gone to Alamut, she found it harder to return to Napur. When she rested on the grassy knoll or in the arms of Menghis in his apartments, she was content, at peace. Now it would appear that her pigeons had come home to roost.

Should she ask Menghis to help her? She negated the thought almost immediately as she recalled his words: "I wish to see how you handle your destiny."

No, she could not ask Menghis. She would climb the mountain and see him and give her weary mind a rest. When the Moslems returned, she would take whatever punishment was in store for her. It had been her decision to aid the Christians, and she would live with that decision. Even if she died for it!

Without hesitation she strode from the palace, the dove on her shoulder and the panther at her side. Now that she was familiar with the terrain, she found the hard climb easier each time she made the long trip up the mountain.

Would she come back down this time? Her heart pounded at the thought. What would it be like to spend the rest of her days in the Eagle's Nest?

Even as she thought it, she rejected the idea. She now knew enough from Menghis to know that his role as the future *Sheikh al Jebal* had almost been preordained. He had been selected when still a child, almost before he could walk. When he approached manhood, he had been sent to stay on Alamut, his only companions the *fedawi* and the servants and the women of the harem.

But when he knew that the time for him to take the throne of Alamut was fast approaching, Menghis had insisted on seeing a bit of the world before assuming the title of *Sheikh al Jebal*. It was from this journey that he was returning when he decided to join the tourney honoring King Richard's marriage to Berengaria.

"Pax and I are very old friends. He is my half brother. Our father was the former sultan of Jakard."

Valentina could not imagine two brothers more dissimilar. Paxon was a warrior, loving the conflict of battle, while Menghis was at heart a peacemaker. What was it he had said? All things are God. Yes, that was Menghis, and that was why she loved him. He possessed a deep and profound respect for life. Unlike Paxon, who could crush a life as easily as crushing an insect.

Loving Menghis as she did, she was still not prepared to leave all scruples behind and take up a life atop Alamut. She abhorred the citadel and all it stood for. It represented murder and a society of ruthless men who would stop at nothing to achieve their ends. And the lives wasted in the process! Those poor unfortunates who believed they had visited heaven and who risked their lives, indeed even sought death, in order to return. A vision of the little girl Aloe Bud rose in her mind's eye. What kind of place was the Alamut in which to raise children? She had only to recall how Menghis had had to send Aloe Bud away from the only home she had ever known in order to protect her from meeting one of the men who had been drugged into believing that the Alamut was heaven, where all desires were granted.

No, much as she loved Menghis, she knew she could never spend the rest of her life in Alamut. Although Menghis had often asked her to stay, he had never uttered a word about leaving the mountaintop to make a life with her in the outside world.

But she would not think of that now. All that mattered was seeing Menghis again. Sighing deeply, Valentina released the dove and watched it soar upward and then settle into a slow, easy flight. She began the climb, thoughts of seeing Menghis pushing everything else from her mind.

At the tip of the knoll, her breathing ragged, she raced to the open doorway of the citadel and threw herself into Menghis's arms. Sobs tore from her throat. Menghis spoke to her quietly, as he did to the wild animals, and soon her sobs subsided. "Just hold me," she cried brokenly. "Just hold me."

A smile played around the corners of Menghis's mouth as he cradled her head against his chest. She did such strange things to him, this long-legged Christian girl. How had he allowed her to get into his blood this way? It could never mean anything for either of them. Yet here she was, filled with torment and unhappiness.

He knew why she was here. The Moslems were returning for their quarterly supply of provisions, and she had none to give. What would she do? Would she ask again, or would she accept what her destiny ordained? He felt his heart pounding in his chest at what he thought her decision would be. "Come, we shall watch the animals. I have a new fawn to show you, a long-legged, graceful creature like yourself."

Valentina's turmoil quieted, as did her trembling body, with Menghis's touch. Knowing full well that this might be the last time she would see him, she stayed on the mountain for five days and nights.

The warm sun filled their days as they bathed in the cold sparkling springs, and the stars blessed their nights as they lay with their arms twined about each other. On the last night before she was to leave for Napur, she rested beside Menghis, her body content, her mind at peace.

Menghis stroked her dark hair and was saddened. She had not asked for his assistance; she had demanded nothing save his closeness.

This beautiful woman whom he loved knew she would be facing death when the empty bins in the granary were discovered. Yet she took the responsibility for her actions and had come to him only to share their love. Not to beg his aid.

A silent tear slipped down his face as his arm tightened protectively about her. She was his heart, his life. Valentina was his love.

In the early hours before dawn, Valentina awoke and found herself pressed tightly against Menghis's lean, hard body. His breath was warm against her cheek and his arms held her close.

Silently she rose and dressed, careful not to wake him. Before leaving, she stood over him a long time, burning his features into her memory. She leaned toward him and gently pressed her lips against his. He stirred in his sleep, and for an instant his lips clung to hers. Hastily Valentina turned away and opened the door leading out onto the knoll.

Menghis lay still, listening to the sound of the door closing. Anguish tore at his heart. Why hadn't he asked her to stay? he tormented himself. Why hadn't he begged her?

Sighing, he realized all too well why he had done neither. He loved her and wanted her beside him always, yet he understood that she had made a pledge to Ramiff; a pledge she would keep regardless of the cost. And her decision to aid her King Richard had been hers alone. If there should be consequences to meet stemming from her decision, then she meant to meet them.

Menghis turned on his side, his emotions racing through him, bringing pain but also the remembered ecstasy of their love. The scent of her perfume was still in the room, and the place beside him was still warm from her body. He had felt her rise from the divan and knew she was dressing in preparation for her departure. When she had leaned over him and pressed her lips to his, it had been all he could do not to gather her into his arms and answer her love.

Now he was glad that he hadn't allowed her to know that he had been awake. She had burdens enough to carry without the additional burden of a sorrowful parting.

On Valentina's descent from Alamut she eyed the long caravan as it snaked its way across the plain far off in the distance. She looked to the sun and calculated the time. If she hurried, she would have a few hours to spare when she reached the bottom of the mountain. When the caravan and the sultans arrived, how long would it be before she met her death? Days? Hours?

Would her death be gory and bloody? Who would tie her to the cross? Would Menghis know when she met her death? Menghis loved her, Menghis wanted her to stay on the mountain with him—Menghis loved her!

Later, back in the palace, her body clean and perfumed, she waited for the sultans to arrive. She would arrange for the evening's entertainment but would not attend. Let them think what they wished; she no longer cared. She would stay in her apartment and mourn. She would cry till her eyes were burned from her head. She would cry for Menghis, not for herself, for Menghis and what might have been. Always for what might have been.

Rosalan tapped lightly on Valentina's door and was bidden to enter. The Bedouin girl's eyes held many questions concerning Valentina's absence from the palace, yet she did not inquire.

"Rosalan, I'm glad you came. I wanted to see you." Valentina's voice was tightly controlled. How she longed to share with Rosalan the love she had found for Menghis, but it would not be fair to burden Rosalan with the secrets she held in her heart. There was too much to explain, and she couldn't reveal the secret that Menghis would one day be *Sheikh al Jebal*.

"Rosalan, word has come to me that the sultans will arrive shortly for their quarterly supplies. Would you see to the preparations? Also, Homed and Dagny must be kept under very close guard. They must not leave their quarters for even an instant. If they ever told Saladin their suspicions, it would not go well for us."

Rosalan nodded, her black eyes serious, her mouth drawn downward. "Rest assured it will be taken care of. We all have too much at stake to have Homed babbling his suspicions to anyone."

"Night and day, Rosalan. Tell Ahmar. No one is to be allowed to see Homed or Dagny. No one is even to know that he is still in the palace!"

"Ahmar has had them under constant guard, and

they're not allowed to leave their quarters. But I'll see to it that the vigilance is not relaxed. Our secret will remain ours."

But would Valentina's secrets remain hers?

Chapter Twenty-three

Saladin sat beside Paxon as the evening's entertainment began, his mind rejecting Paxon's words. "I say you are mistaken," he said harshly. "There are no traitors in our midst."

Paxon demanded angrily, "Are you going to tell me that it is a coincidence that Richard's men are suddenly hale and hearty and their storehouses are full? I sent a scout, and he reports to me that the emir's wagons unloaded provisions on five separate occasions. Where did the provisions come from and how did they get to Richard? I demand answers!"

"The morning will be soon enough for your answers. If what you have learned is true, then the granaries will be empty. If your sources are wrong, then the matter is ended and we'll know that the Christian people have raised up their arms to help Malik Ric. As to the wagons belonging to Ramiff, that could be easily explained. With *Sheikh al Jebal* looting as he does, he leaves the wagons where he attacks them. He's interested in their contents. Has he not in the past sent his cutthroats out to capture our own supply caravans? Then, in a few days' time, they are offered back to us for sale at twice the price."

Something in Paxon's brain clicked. It concerned the linking of Ramiff's wagons with *Sheikh al Jebal*. Ramiff's wagons with Valentina . . . Menghis . . . *Sheikh al Jebal*. Valentina and *Sheikh al Jebal!*

Paxon lowered his eyes guardedly. Not even Saladin knew that Paxon's half brother was soon to be the next *Sheikh al Jebal*. Still the image of Valentina and Menghis boiled through his brain. Instinct told him he was right in his deductions. Again his turmoiled mind saw them as they had been on the day of the tournament in Messina. Menghis laughing . . . Valentina squealing more in delight than in protest. Paxon also recalled his brother's inclinations for peace and Valentina's loyalty to her own people. It all fit!

"What will we do if the granaries are empty?" Paxon demanded, garnering a hostile look from Saladin, whose enjoyment of the meal was disturbed by Paxon's suspicions. "How will we feed our men? The harvest is not for many months!"

"It does no good to speculate now, the hour is late. Morning will be soon enough." Saladin deliberately turned his back on the young sultan of Jakard, letting his intentions be known that he meant to relax and enjoy the night's events.

Paxon, stung by Saladin's slight, rose from his cross-legged position. "Morning is not good enough. I want to know now!" He left the banquet hall, the black cat snarling and spitting by his side.

He barged his way into Valentina's apartment and grasped her arms. "The keys to the granary. Give them to me!"

"By what right do you demand this?" Valentina retorted.

"I need no rights. I demand them, and you will relinquish them to me. I won't tell you a second time. The keys," he said, holding out his hand.

"Do you wish to buy or to observe?" Valentina asked huskily.

"I will purchase when I see the bins in the same condition as the last time I was here. Your king has been aided by someone, and I think that someone is you. My mind tells me you would never take so foolish a risk, but my instincts tell me you would do everything in your power to aid the Christians."

"Have you voiced your suspicions to Saladin?" Her eyes pierced him, challenged him.

"If you mean have I revealed your true identity, no. Not yet!"

Dread filled Valentina as she withdrew the keys from her coffer and followed Paxon from the room. The sooner she settled the matter, the sooner she would die. They rode in silence. Valentina reined in her horse and slid from the animal, her heart in her throat. What would he do? Would he kill her immediately, or would he make her death an example to all the others? Licking dry lips, she unlocked the huge doors and waited for Paxon to push them inward. Carefully he lit the lantern and walked into the darkness of the cavernous storehouse. Valentina followed him, dreading the moment when she would be forced to peer into an empty bin, the first of many. God, help me, she begged silently.

The lantern was held high as Paxon opened the first bin: filled to overflowing. The second and third were the same. Valentina drew in her breath as Paxon made his way down the long line of bins. They were all filled to the brim. The dried fruits and sugar sacks were piled neatly, one atop the other. Valentina felt faint as she tried to fathom the mystery.

Paxon held the lantern near her face and looked at her angrily. "I don't know how you did it, but I know you are the one who has aided the Lionheart. One day I will find out, and at that time you will have many answers to give me. These bins are filled higher than they should be. There has been no harvest. Yet the sacks of dried fruits and sugar are higher than before. Where did they come from?" he demanded threateningly.

Valentina shrugged. Menghis! Menghis had done this for her! She had to go to him. She had to go now! Her heart raced as she realized what Menghis had done for her. He had given her back her life even when she chose not to stay on Alamut. She would go back and stay with him. Forever, if he wished!

"Why? Why did you do it?" Paxon persisted.

"Do what?" Valentina purred. She had to get back up the mountain. She had to leave now, *now,* as fast as she could.

"Why are you looking at me so strangely? You made me a fool and I won't forget it," he said. "I know you are the one who sent the supplies to Richard. Valentina, you are forcing me to a dangerous decision!"

Make all the decisions you want, her mind screamed. I won't be here to hear them. She tossed the keys to Paxon and left him standing in the granary with a dumbfounded expression on his face. She mounted the Arabian stallion that had once been Saladin's pride and raced in the direction of Alamut. To Menghis.

As Valentina made her way up the steep grade of the mountain she heard the soft cooing of a dove from time to time and knew that the *fedawi* were reporting her progress to Menghis. Once she heard a strange sound, a calling sound, echoing through the air. She shivered, knowing instinctively that Paxon was somewhere behind her in the indigo darkness and that the *fedawi* were calling their warning.

She reached the top and made her way across to where Menghis was feeding his deer in the moonlight. "When do you sleep?" she whispered softly.

Menghis smiled as he continued to feed the deer. "When a guest arrives at the Eagle's Nest, the host must be awake to greet him. Regardless of the hour. You made miraculous time, my love. It wasn't that long ago since you stood in the granary with Paxon and wondered over the brimming bins."

Valentina would never understand how Menghis was informed so quickly about her actions. Then she heard the coo of a dove and understood. "My time was quicker tonight because Shadjar is not with me. She slows my pace."

"Do you know that we will have another guest shortly?"

"Yes, I know. It is Paxon. I thought I evaded him, but evidently he was more clever than I thought. I'm sorry, Menghis."

313

"There's no reason for you to apologize. Sooner or later the sultan would have found his way here. Now is as good a time as any. Pax was never one to allow things to simmer, not when he could bring them to a boil. He's a bull and acts like one."

"He was enraged when he saw the filled bins. The bins are the reason I have come. To thank you. But Paxon is ready for murder. I've never seen such rage!"

Suddenly Menghis laid his hand on Valentina's arm. "Be very quiet now," he whispered. "I want you to see something. You must not make a sound, for if you do the performance will be over."

A graceful, long-legged doe walked daintily into the moonlit garden and stood quietly waiting for her fawn and stag to arrive. Another doe arrived, and then another and another. Soon the garden was filled with the huge-eyed animals. The does and stags maneuvered themselves to the far side of the garden, giving their offspring the center of the garden. Valentina watched in delight as the young animals frolicked and scampered about the tight circle made by their parents. The night birds swooped down and joined their play. Their song was pure and sweet-carrying in the night air. Valentina drew in her breath as she saw one of the more precocious youngsters try to escape the tight circle of observant parents.

"Now watch, Valentina," Menghis whispered. "Each stag will come and lead his offspring away. It's a miracle how they know which is their own."

Suddenly there was a commotion and the deer scattered wildly. A voice bellowed, "Menghis, you bastard! Come out here where I can see you, and none of your damn tricks!"

Menghis sighed. "Didn't I tell you he was a bull?"

"Don't mumble. Come out here where I can see you," Paxon roared.

"No one can ever accuse you of being nimble-footed, Pax. You managed to shake half my mountain loose during your climb."

"If I don't kill you tonight, the day won't be far off," Paxon continued to roar. "Why? Give me one good

314

reason why you have helped that damn Christian woman, and don't lie to me."

"Lie? Me? When have I ever lied to you, Pax? In order to lie, I would have to know that I did what you are accusing me of. Explain yourself. What is it I am supposed to have done, and when did I do it?"

"Valentina has been sending stores to the Crusaders and you have helped her do it! Then you filled the grain bins and food sacks in Ramiff's warehouse. Don't deny it!" Paxon had murder in his eyes as his hands clenched tightly at his sides.

"There's no need for me to lie about something I didn't do. I haven't left Alamut in months. Look somewhere else for your culprit, warrior."

"I meant what I said, Menghis. If I ever find out that it was you, I'll kill you!"

"Just like that, you would kill your own brother? Would you weep over my body, Brother, or would you chortle with glee? And while you're killing me, what do you think I would be doing, Brother?" Menghis asked quietly.

"Dying!" Paxon answered curtly.

Valentina tried to absorb what she was hearing. Gentle Menghis, arrogant Paxon. Fire and water.

"Pax, I'm asking you as your brother to end this matter now. I want no ill feelings between us. End it, Brother. If you have more to say, say it and let's be done with it. You accuse and I deny."

"It's not over, and it will never be over until you stop helping this harlot! Do you know what she's doing? Or has she lied to you, too?" Not waiting for an answer, he continued. "She's aiding the Christians! And," he added harshly, "by doing so she is killing our own people. How can you be a party to this?"

"I have no people, only the *fedawi,* or did you forget? Your people are your people, her people are her people. From this moment on, Pax, be very careful you do not make war on the Alamut."

"So it is to be brother against brother, after all," Paxon snarled.

"Only if you make it so, Pax. Go back down the

mountain to your people and do what you must. Leave me here in the Eagle's Nest with what is mine. This time you will arrive at the foot of my mountain safely. If there is a next time . . ."

"The next time you will try to kill me. You will take notice I said 'try to.' Hear me well, Brother. If we meet in combat it is you who will die. You have my word on it!"

Even from where she stood Valentina could read the deep sadness in Menghis's eyes.

"A safe journey to you, Brother," Menghis said, extending his hand to grasp Paxon's. Paxon made no move to accept his offer.

Still holding his hand extended, Menghis stared deeply into Paxon's jet eyes. "Regardless of what you say, regardless of what you do, you will never be able to kill the love I feel for you as a brother," Menghis said softly.

"Then I will kill you as a stranger if you ever get in my way again," Paxon said, ignoring the outstretched hand and turning his back to descend the mountain.

Turning around, he addressed Valentina. "And as for you, mistress of Napur, don't sleep too soundly at night. I have not forgotten what you have done to aid Malik Ric. I will never forget, rely upon it!"

"I did what I had to do, Paxon. Men were starving and I had warehouses full of provisions. They are my people, and even though I pray for peace, they are still my people." Valentina's voice was throaty with emotion. Too much had happened, and all so quickly. Her mind reeled with the knowledge that the only two men she had ever cared for—brothers, too!— were at dangerous odds with each other.

Paxon's harshness eased. Although he knew he was a fool, he did understand. Strangely enough, this betrayal, this turning back to help her people, was something Paxon the warrior could easily understand. He knew he would have done the same if he had been in her position. He took a step toward her, his eyes penetrating the darkness to read her expression. "Valentina . . . come away with me. Now. There is nothing for you here on Alamut. No one will ever have to know what you did. I will never betray you. Come with me now. Life awaits us down off this damnable mountain."

Valentina stepped closer to Menghis and clutched his arm for courage. If she went with Paxon now, she would be free of the danger she had placed herself in, yet this was something she could never do.

"As I told you, Paxon, go back down the mountain and leave me with what is mine." Menghis's voice was quiet, yet there was a ring of hard metal beneath it.

Paxon's eyes widened and hatred spewed forth. "So you think she is yours! She is MINE! From the first day I set eyes upon her she was MINE! And I will have her!" Paxon snarled these last few words through clenched teeth and Valentina's heart constricted. More than overbearing and possessive, the man was vengeful and dangerous.

Stepping close to Valentina, so close she could feel his hot breath upon her cheeks, Paxon exhorted, "Come with me now and all will be forgotten."

Menghis's arm tightened beneath Valentina's hand. Pressing closer, Valentina whispered, "I stay with Menghis."

Paxon made an involuntary move and Menghis stiffened, ready to protect Valentina. At the last instant Paxon changed his mind and turned from them. Rage made his back ramrod straight and his head high. He left them to make his descent down the mountain. He would not forget this lost battle.

The following morning the sun shone brightly upon Alamut, oblivious to the dark struggles which took place in the breasts of the two lovers. Valentina looked about, drinking in the sight of the wide grassy knoll and all its memories, certain that she would never return to see it again. Menghis stood beside her, his eyes tortured. If the day were to match their emotions, there would be a storm the likes of which the world had never seen.

"Valentina, stay here with me. Don't leave,"

Menghis said suddenly, his voice husky with emotion. "Stay with me, and I'll love you for all eternity. We will leave here; the Alamut will be behind us. Together we'll find a place for us in this world. Stay. I can give no assurances for the future save that I will always love you."

A vise of iron closed around Valentina's heart, making her incapable of speech. He read the decision in her eyes and smiled sadly. She had committed herself to a cause and had given her pledge. Tenderly she held him close; he felt her heart pounding.

"Stay with me. There is nothing in this world but our love. With the strength of your love I will put the throne of *Sheikh al Jebal* behind me. For your love I will turn my back on an obligation I committed myself to long ago, before we found each other."

Still she gave him no answer. Her decision was in her eyes as she turned and started down the mountain.

This emptiness, this unbearable emptiness, Menghis thought; this is what it will be when I sit on the throne as *Sheikh al Jebal*. My life is over. There is no life for me without Valentina.

Fearing to look back, Valentina led the white Arabian down the mountain. Her heart felt as though it had been ripped from her chest, and a great welling of tears rose in her throat and threatened to drown her in sorrow.

The black Arabian snorted and pawed the ground, his massive head thrown back, his mane swishing violently. The black cat snarled and bared his teeth as Paxon brought the Arabian under control. The animal soothed, Paxon slid from the horse and tethered it to the nearest tree. He freed the black panther and started his climb up the mountain. His destination: the Alamut and Menghis.

A jagged streak of lightning ripped across the sky, followed by a roaring thunderbolt. Before long the approaching storm would be as savage as he felt. Another streak of lightning ripped down and struck a tree directly in Paxon's path. Man and cat leaped to safety just as the giant tree fell. Paxon's ebony eyes narrowed and his square jaw hardened. He knew it was an act of nature, and still he wanted to lash out at whatever lay before him. The wind whipped itself into a frenzy and bent the huge trees of the mountain till the branches touched the ground. Deep, hoarse rolls of thunder shook the heavens as streak after streak of lightning lit up the mountain, bathing the immense trees and rocky terrain in an eerie, spectral light. The sudden onslaught of rain startled Paxon when it poured from the heavens. The cat swung his head to look at his master and then continued with his sure-footed climb up the mountain. Paxon lowered his head as he followed the cat, his shoulders hunched, into the driving rain and whiplash winds. He fell once and narrowly missed striking his head on a huge boulder.

When he set foot on the grassy knoll, a sudden gust of wind drove him backward. Strong arms grasped him and led him to the palace in the Alamut. Paxon looked around the bright candlelit room, shook the rain from his head, and crossed his arms over his broad chest to warm his chilled, drenched body.

"This mountain is becoming well traveled of late," Menghis laughed as he entered the room. "Perhaps I should conduct guided tours—for a price, that is. Welcome, Pax. To what do I owe the honor of this visit?"

"Your humor escapes me," Paxon said savagely. "I didn't climb this damnable mountain in the middle of a brutal storm to listen to you and your humor. I came here for a reason, and as soon as you give me some dry clothing, I'll get on with the matter."

"The first door on your right in the corridor. The clothes have been readied for hours. Even the storm couldn't blot out your climb up my mountain. I understand a tree almost felled you. The gods must be watching out for you, Brother."

"It wouldn't surprise me if those creatures who serve under you didn't have something to do with it," Paxon snarled as he ripped the sodden caftan from his body and strode from the room.

"You'll never change, Pax. You always did have a suspicious nature," Menghis called after his brother's retreating back.

When Paxon returned to the room, Menghis offered him a goblet of wine and smiled crookedly. "Welcome to my home, Brother. I didn't get the chance to welcome you when you arrived. Are you always so surly when a storm rages? Shall we drink to your health or mine?" he inquired affably.

"Whatever . . . amuses you," Paxon said curtly as he downed his wine in one gulp and extended the goblet for a refill.

Menghis's eyes grew serious. "Why did you come here again? What is it you want?"

"Do my ears deceive me?" Paxon said mockingly. "I find it hard to believe there is something you don't know." His voice hardened as he gazed at his brother. "You know why I'm here as well as I do. This is no time for your games and charades. I came here to ask you, not to demand, but to ask you to stop your *fedawi* from raiding our wagons of grain."

Menghis laughed, his strong white teeth gleaming in the candlelight.

"And who is it that says my *fedawi* are responsible for raiding your wagons?"

"The word 'fool' is not branded on my forehead, Menghis. Your *fedawi* raid the wagons and then sell them back to Saladin for twice what they are worth. Our treasury is low, our people hungry. I want you to stop it," Paxon said coldly.

"And if I refuse?"

"Man of peace," Paxon snarled. "You don't know the meaning of the word. You're a master of deceit and trickery. You're aiding the Christians, but you refuse to help your own people. In my eyes you are guilty of the one thing we were both taught by our father to fear—treason!"

"You're a fool, Pax. When I came to the Alamut I renounced all things. I have no people, save the

320

fedawi. I owe your people nothing and I owe the Christians nothing. In case you don't understand me, let me make it clear."

"Don't bother," Paxon said harshly. "I told you once before that you aren't God, Menghis. I meant it then and I mean it now. It's the woman, isn't it? You'll help her, but when I ask you for the same help in the name of our people, you refuse."

Menghis laughed. "And, Brother, the word 'fool' is not branded on my forehead, either. Do you think for one moment that *I* think you came here for the reason you stated? Foolish man. You came because of the woman. You want her, admit it. You've always wanted what was mine, ever since we were boys. You used to say what was yours was yours. What was mine was ours." His voice took on a clear, hard ring. "The woman is mine. Not yours, not ours, but mine. Understand that, Paxon, and don't ever again make that mistake."

The black panther stirred from his position near the flaming brazier and looked at both men. A deep, low growl erupted from him, and then he was still.

"We aren't boys any longer," Paxon said curtly. "That was another life and a long time ago. This is now. The warrior has come to the man of peace to ask for help, and the man of peace refuses that which the warrior asks. And if the warrior were to say the woman does not enter into the discussion, what would the man of peace say?" Paxon asked sarcastically.

"The man of peace would be forced to say the warrior lies," Menghis said coolly.

Paxon's eyes were as bitter as his tone. "I knew it was a mistake to come here, but I prayed that we could resolve our problem."

"Your problem, Pax, not mine. What made you think I would help you? Because we are brothers? You know the meaning of *Sheikh al Jebal* and the Alamut as well as I do. If you had told me the real reason for coming here, I would have helped you. Saladin has all the foodstuffs he needs, and his treasury is full. It was the woman. Don't make matters worse and lie to me further. There should be truth between brothers. Go back down to your world and leave me to mine. And, Pax, don't climb this mountain again, for if you do you will never go back down to your world."

Paxon laughed cruelly. "And what happens to your woman when you sit on that damnable chair with that incense floating about you? What happens then, Menghis? She's flesh and blood. She has passions and desires, as you and I do. Once you sit on that throne, you'll be nothing more than a memory. Do you think for one moment that she will go into a nunnery? Now who is the fool? I see by your eyes that the man of peace carries hatred in his heart," Paxon mocked. "For now she is yours. Later she will be mine! Remember that when you sit on your chair of gold and your mind becomes eaten away with opium!"

"You would be wise if you left this mountain now!" Menghis said quietly.

But Paxon wasn't finished. "Regardless of what you think, regardless of what you say you know, I came here because of Saladin and the wagons. I came to ask for your help. If the time ever comes when I have to lay down my life for you, I will. We're brothers. I haven't forgotten, nor will I forget in the future. You have our father's blood in your veins, the same as I do. If you choose to turn your back on me and our people, then there is nothing I can do. I won't beg you, Menghis. And I make no promises to you, save one. When you sit there on that throne, that is when I will take Valentina. You will live with that thought every day for the rest of your life. I will win, Menghis, just as I did when we were boys. Remember that I always won what you wanted most." Paxon's tone was arrogant.

"I remember," Menghis said softly. "I also remember that I always got it back."

"But this time you won't be able to get it back," Paxon mocked.

"There are more ways than . . ."

"One to skin a cat. Is that what you were going to

say?" Paxon continued to mock. "Rest easy, Brother. From time to time as the years pass I will bring Valentina here so she can see you grow old in your Eagle's Nest."

"You would do that, wouldn't you?" Menghis said harshly.

"Of course I would do it. I just said so, didn't I? I don't wear two faces as you do."

"I should have killed you that day in Messina."

"Yes," Paxon taunted him. "That is what you should have done."

"Good-bye, Pax. Remember what I said. No more trips up the mountain. Give my regards to Saladin. And, Pax," he said as an afterthought, "the next time you find yourself in Baghdad, check the cave near the water. You may be pleasantly surprised to see just how rich Saladin is. It would take my *fedawi* weeks to carry his wealth to another cave for safekeeping. A full, rich life to you, Pax."

Paxon narrowed his eyes as Menghis walked from the room. Was he lying? No, Menghis never lied. He called the cat to him and left the Eagle's Nest, his mind and his heart confused. The bitterness stayed in his eyes as he walked into the raging storm to start his descent down the mountain. Down the mountain to his world.

Chapter Twenty-four

Valentina was sullen. It had been raining for over a week and everything was sodden and damp. Her skin felt clammy and cool, almost as if the blood had left her veins. She walked to the balcony and stood looking down at the dripping Judas tree. "I promised you, Ramiff," she whispered, "that your son Homed would be prevented from knowing of your death until the war was over. He is constantly under watch, and so far our secret is still safe."

Saladin and his generals had left the vicinity of Napur, and she had not seen or heard from Paxon since he found the filled bins and followed her to the Alamut. Free from threat, Valentina should have been put at ease. Instead, she felt torn in so many directions that she was no longer certain of the validity of her actions. Was it right to keep the people of Napur from knowing of their beloved emir's death? Was she wrong in preventing Homed from taking his rightful place among his people? Perhaps Ramiff had been exaggerating Homed's greed and diabolical ways. By what right should she take all this responsibility upon her own shoulders and make decisions which affected other people's lives?

"Oh, Ramiff," she whispered to the place beneath the Judas tree, "if only you were here to talk with me. Soon your old friend Mohab will join you, and I will have lost another dear one."

She wiped at the tears with the backs of her hands as she watched the rain beat against the Judas tree. Suddenly, without warning, the rain ceased and a sudden wind whipped up and lashed against the twisted tree until it almost touched the ground.

Valentina blinked. Was there someone down there in this weather? She narrowed her eyes against the driving wind and saw Homed and Dagny. In the sudden gusts Dagny had been forced to grasp one of the low-hanging branches to hold herself upright. When the gusts died away as suddenly as they had come up, Valentina heard Dagny's voice.

"I'm telling you, your father is buried right here, beneath this tree. Why else would the old man Mohab come here to pray? I brought you out here in this accursed storm because they would never think anyone would venture outdoors. Well, Homed, what do you say now? If you look closely, you can see that the earth is raised and has been disturbed."

An unnatural brightness bathed the garden, which reminded Valentina of the Saint Elmo's fire that she had once seen aboard ship. Valentina knew she should leave her post at the window and go down to the garden, but she was unable to move as she waited for Homed's reply.

Suddenly she noticed Mohab stalking through the garden, carrying something in his hand which glistened in the eerie light. Soundlessly he came upon Homed and Dagny.

Dagny whirled and saw Mohab just as he brought up his arm to strike out with a long, curved scimitar, aiming straight for the center of Homed's back. Dagny screamed, a high, piercing scream that made the fine hairs on the back of Valentina's neck stand on end.

Homed backed off, dancing out of Mohab's reach just as Rosalan entered the garden. Her movements were heavy and awkward with the child she carried. "Mohab, where are you?" Rosalan called, oblivious to the drama taking place just a few feet from where she stood.

"Oh, dear God, no! Please, no!" Valentina wailed, sensing the danger Rosalan was walking into. The unnatural brightness in the sky began to dim, and the light breeze began to whip into gusts. Even from where she stood on the balcony Valentina could hear the musical sound of the silver bell in the Judas tree.

As the last vestige of light waned, the tiny bell slipped from the branch and fell near Mohab's feet. The old man's step faltered and he straightened his stooped shoulders. He lashed out at Homed, slicing deep into his chest, spilling his life's blood.

Dagny jumped on Mohab's back, beating her fists into his bony ribs. Rosalan rounded the corner near the path and rushed to the old man's defense, gripping Dagny by her bright red hair. Just as she got a hank of it in her hand, Dagny was shaken loose from Mohab's back and reeled backward, forcing Rosalan to the ground.

It was impossible to see, and Valentina screamed

for Ahmar, who had just entered the garden in search of Rosalan. With one savage yank he grabbed Dagny by the arm and flung her against the tree.

Valentina heard Dagny's head crack and her neck snap, and then there was silence in the garden. The wind lessened and a light drizzle began to fall from the heavens while a low gray mist wove its way through the foliage.

Mohab bent and picked up the tiny bell. Slowly he walked from the garden, the bell pressed against his withered, leathery cheek. Ahmar gathered a sobbing Rosalan into his arms and carried her into the palace.

Valentina raced down the corridors and found Mohab. She clasped the old man to her, and her eyes fell on his clenched hand and the silver bell. She led him into the emir's apartment and gently helped him into Ramiff's favorite chaise. Mohab sank into the softness and closed his eyes; his features were a portrait of complete exhaustion.

Once the old man opened his eyes and smiled weakly at Valentina. "Just a few moments more and Ramiff will come for me. See," he said, pointing a finger upward, "he comes. Slowly, but he comes, and he wears only one bell on his slipper. Even now he cannot bear for me to have anything of his. Quickly, Valentina, fasten this bell to my slipper. Once it is attached, he can do nothing about it. We will be equal. It is just, is it not, Valentina?"

A sob tore her throat, but she answered him calmly. "Very just, my good friend." Then his ancient eyes closed and Valentina fastened the bell to his slipper, the tears streaming down her face. Her head jerked upright when she heard Mohab begin to mutter.

"It took you long enough to come for me, Ramiff. You look well, old friend. No tricks. I too have a bell, and we are equal. Allah will see to it that you don't cheat me any longer and practice your deceitful ways," he grumbled weakly. "I am ready, Ramiff."

The sobs which were held in check erupted, and Valentina dropped her head to the old man's knees.

326

There came to her the tinkling sound of a bell. Then there was a profusion of ringing bells, and Valentina knew in her heart that the two old men were dancing their way to the heavens. The friends were together again—this time for eternity.

After a long while, she dried her tears and rose to her feet. She had to find Ahmar and Rosalan and tell them about Mohab. The old man must be buried near the Judas tree, close to his lifelong companion. Her eyes fell to the old man's feet. Slowly she raised her eyes and then looked down to the floor again. The bell she had just fastened to Mohab's slipper was gone!

Dropping again to her knees, she scoured the floor from one end to the other. The bell was gone. Her face broke into a smile as she looked upward. "It was the least you could do for an old friend," she whispered softly, new tears gathering in her eyes.

Finding Ahmar and Rosalan, she quickly told them of Mohab's death. "Poor old man," Rosalan wept, and Ahmar comforted her.

"Homed is dead, and so is Dagny. She broke her neck against the tree," Ahmar said regretfully. It was evident he hadn't meant for Dagny to die. "Will you stay with Rosalan while I see to the carnage in the garden? It would be better if they were not discovered there. Questions are sometimes difficult to answer."

When Ahmar returned, they discussed Mohab's burial in low tones. Ahmar frowned and spoke haltingly. "Mistress, Rosalan and I heard something strange."

Valentina waited, knowing what Ahmar was about to say.

"We heard bells before, hundreds and hundreds of bells. They were light and chiming. They rang and pealed and were all around us."

"I know about the bells, Ahmar. It was Ramiff, coming to help his old friend to Allah. It was the emir's way of making amends to Mohab for leaving him behind. It is simple, is it not, Ahmar?"

He looked at Valentina, not certain if she was jesting. Finding no ready answer in her tear-glistening eyes, he smiled. "Of course. What other explanation could there be?"

"What other explanation, indeed," Valentina said softly.

Rosalan, heavy with child, stood beside Ahmar and Valentina alongside Mohab's grave. Tears coursed unashamedly down their cheeks as they looked upon the grave which Ahmar had just covered. No words were needed in eulogy, for each had come to love the old man who was so faithful to Ramiff and to each of them. Mohab had been laid to rest not far from the Judas tree that shielded the emir's grave from the scorching sun and drenching rains.

Rosalan dropped an early rose upon the grave and began to chant a prayer for the dead, intoning the words in a tear-choked voice. With a low murmur, Ahmar joined her, his face a mask of grief for the loss of a good friend. Alone, Valentina waited for their prayer to end. In her hand she clutched the old men's favorite gaming dice.

So much had happened in this strange land of the East. Her life had changed so drastically since she had set foot in the ancient city of Acre, where she had been part of Berengaria's entourage. In this land she had found unquestioning friendships and deadly intrigue. She had no need to wonder whether, if she had it to do all over again, she would make the same choices. The answer would always be an intractable "yes." For in this land where men made war, she had found love. She had found Menghis.

At the mere thought of him her heart swelled. Soon, soon she would be with her love! Homed was dead and Napur was safe! Soon the death of Ramiff could be revealed, and her pledge to the old emir would be fulfilled. No one would question the death of Dagny, because in this land the death of a harem slave was insignificant. Their only worry had been to hide the fact of Homed's death. This Ahmar had taken charge of with great aplomb. Homed's body was carried out in the night, and Ahmar buried him somewhere on the plains. Before the death of Ramiff was made public, the rumor would be circulated that Homed had met with desert cutthroats.

Richard's men had been helped through the winter, and now that spring was nearly upon them, he would be better able to provide for his troops through his own wits. Valentina's responsibility to the Crusaders was also at an end. Soon, soon, her heart sang, soon she would be free to fly to Menghis's arms.

Rosalan and Ahmar finished their prayer. Silently their hands reached out for each other, and Valentina felt a deep loneliness. Her need for Menghis was greater than ever when she saw the loving glances which passed between the two lovers.

Suddenly Valentina remembered the gaming dice which she held in her hand. Wordlessly she bent over Mohab's grave and dug a shallow hole into which she dropped the dice. "So they can resume their games," she whispered, fresh tears coursing down her pale ivory cheeks. Rosalan turned to Ahmar and buried her face against his chest. He held her tenderly, soothing her grief.

As Valentina watched them her need for Menghis's arms became more than a need. It was an obsession. Now the time had come. At last she was free! Free to fly to Menghis and live within the circle of his arms and the warmth of his love.

It wasn't until she left the stable yard, Shadjar at her side, that she thought of Rosalan and Ahmar. She reassured herself that they would know how to carry on without her. She would send word to them later, after she and Menghis were together.

Onward she rode, careful not to press the stallion and making certain that Shadjar kept pace. Onward to her glorious love!

As Valentina raced across the grassy knoll she found herself crying, sobbing, happiness flooding her heart and quickening her steps. The moonlight was waning over the citadel, and the climb in the darkness had been more difficult than she had anticipated. But she was here now, here close to her love.

Tears flowed freely, and Valentina was lifted beyond herself with exultation. Her life was beginning, truly beginning. "Menghis! Menghis!" she called, expecting him to appear and rush toward her, catching her in his arms and smothering her with his kisses. "Menghis . . ."

To the citadel, whose doors were opened by silent *fedawi.* Through the corridors lit by torches, throwing the whole interior into eerie shadows. As if by magic, doors were opened for her as she raced through them headlong, calling his name.

"Menghis!"

Into the inner regions of the citadel she sped, alone, seeking, searching. Her heart became filled with an unknown terror as she hurried down winding corridors, along dimly lighted passageways, calling to her love.

Reaching the end of a long passageway, Valentina was suddenly met by two *fedawi.* Silently they walked beside her, leading her to an open door which was guarded by several men standing at attention. Peering into the darkness beyond, Valentina's heart was filled with dread. The room was high and vaulted, and she knew she had been there before, once long ago, when she had first dared to climb the mountain to Alamut.

The sweet fragrance of incense wafted upon the air, and Valentina recognized it as the heady aroma which had filled the air when she had come upon the wizened old man who sat cross-legged upon his golden throne. "No, no. Dear God, don't let it be!" she cried aloud as she entered the room.

Through a curtain of beads she recognized the golden throne upon which the dying *Sheikh al Jebal* had sat. The old man who Menghis had said was awaiting death, the man whom he would replace as the society's new *Sheikh al Jebal.* Sobbing hysterically, she rushed through the beaded opening behind the throne.

She gasped, stunned at the sight which met her eyes.

Menghis! Dear God, not Menghis! Falling to her knees, tears cascading down her cheeks, she reached out her hands, imploring him to look upon her.

"Menghis!" she sobbed. "My love. Come with me down the mountain. We'll go away together. Please," she begged, her voice husky and heavy with emotion. "I'll go anywhere with you, do anything. But come with me. We can be together for all time, for all eternity, as you said. I'm begging you, Menghis. Come with me. I love you! Don't turn me away!"

He sat as still as death, seeming neither to see nor to hear. "Open your eyes and look at me! You hear me! I know you hear me!" she screamed. "I'm free now. Free! Nothing awaits me. All obligations have been met. I didn't want to turn my back on you when you asked me to stay. You understood that; I know you did." Heaving sobs wracked her body, the fragrance of the incense was making her ill.

"Menghis, my love," she implored. "What will become of me without you? What will I do without you? How can I live without you? Can you take my life so easily? Do I mean nothing to you? Please, Menghis, please. Love me, come with me . . ." She fell forward, her head resting near his feet, and she stayed there for what seemed an eternity, waiting for him to respond, willing him to answer. Something soft brushed her face, and looking up, she saw Shadjar staring at her with curious yellow eyes.

Drying her eyes with the backs of her hands, Valentina stood and looked down at Menghis. Her heart breaking, she reached out and touched him, begging him to acknowledge her. Still he remained silent, his breathing quiet in the darkened room.

"I know you can hear me, Menghis. I'm going to leave. You asked me once what I had to offer you, and I told you I owned nothing. I gave you my heart and my love. Just as I know you understood why I had to go back to Napur and see my obligations through, I will try to understand why you are doing this. But you must not be alone. I will leave you

331

Shadjar ad Dafr. She is the only thing that is mine to give, my darling."

Valentina spoke softly to Shadjar, commanding her to stay before she left the darkened room, leaving behind her love, her life, her future.

Menghis heard rather than saw Valentina leave. If he had opened his eyes, he would have followed her as she asked; down the mountain, never to return. But just as she had had the strength to meet her responsibilities, so must he have the strength to meet his. Could he do any less than she had done?

Slowly, silently, he reached out a hand and laid it upon the white panther.

Time was endless for Valentina now that she no longer could climb the mountain and have Menghis to talk to and love. She went about her daily routine in a trancelike state. Everywhere there were whisperings and fear. Questions were asked concerning the old emir's health to which there were no answers. The palace buzzed with talk that Ramiff was dead, but there was no proof. None dared to investigate to find the proof.

Petitions were sent to the emir and were returned with his official seal. The black eunuchs looked at each other with questioning eyes. The women of the harem smirked behind their face veils, but the palace held fast to its secret.

Bored with the everyday routine of the palace, Valentina grew fretful and hostile. Her hostility turned to recklessness as she continued to aid the Christians with her supplies of grain and foodstuffs. Soon her daring spread to far corners. It became known that Richard had a benefactor among the Moslems. As always, when the bins were depleted they were miraculously refilled.

Valentina began to notice strange faces in the palace. The faces watched her and marked her every move. She knew they were the *fedawi* sent to her by Menghis. The more reckless she became, the closer they hovered near her.

When she could tolerate her lonely life no longer, she would ride like the wind across the plains, return exhausted, and fall asleep, only to have her dreams invaded by a tall, dark-haired man with smoldering eyes. And she would awake crying. Menghis was helping her, and she was just as certain that somewhere Paxon was lying in wait to trap her.

Chapter Twenty-five

Spring again returned to the Holy Land. It was the fifth year to see the yellow and black banners of Malik en Nasr cross the Jordan. The brown grasses of the plains were replaced by greener, fresher grasses upon which the sheep grazed. Streams ran clear again, free from the silt and mud that had been churned by the winter rains. Cedar and poplar trees stood their lonely vigil along the rims of hillocks and mountain ranges. The heather was sweet and the bees buzzed lazily. Yet the lonely figures of men garbed in mail still turned their thoughts to war. A war which had its beginnings beyond memory and which would have its end beyond a lifetime.

It was heard among the men of the Crusaders that a miracle had occurred in the Holy Sepulchre at Eastertide. Saladin had made his pilgrimage there to sit before the darkened tomb where the dark lamps hung. Miraculously, the dark lamps lit up before the eyes of the Moslems. The Christians were certain that the lighting of the lamps had been a sign and a portent. Victory would be theirs!

Richard rode his men along the plains late that spring. He stormed the fort of Darum, and every Moslem within its walls was slaughtered. Onward they rode to the gardens of Gaza, where it was rumored that the Lionheart would desert the Holy War to return to England. Word had come to him that his brother, John Lackland, had formed an alliance with Philip Augustus to take England from Richard's hands. Philip would never forgive Richard for slighting his authority with the French army and, it was rumored, for the greatest injury of all, that of turning his affections away from Philip for the company of a mere lute player.

Amid the cheer of at last seeing the Holy Sepulchre, the men made ready, packing a month's provisions, though poor those provisions were. Out of the cities they marched, gathering at last in the hamlets and towns of the area known as Beth Nable.

Valentina thrust open the doors of the granaries and stood back to allow Paxon to enter. A smile played around the corners of her mouth as she settled herself atop the white Arabian. Let the Saracen close the doors.

When Paxon slid the bolt on the heavy doors, his dark eyes were narrowed and angry. "There is only one way you could manage this," he said coolly.

"Only one way to manage what?" Valentina smiled as she leaned over to hear the tall man's words. "Why do you persist in coming to Napur to torture yourself? You know the bins will be full."

"And I know who fills them! You sell yourself to *Sheikh al Jebal* in return for supplies and his aid in getting them to the Christians. Everywhere I look in the palace I see his *fedawi*. They guard you as though you were *Sheikh al Jebal* yourself. Whatever you want they will do for you. How clever you are, Valentina. Your face reveals nothing. But then, you have had time to practice your deceit. And you laugh because you have me at a distinct disadvantage. I want you for my own, and to betray you would mean losing you forever. Dead women belong to no one. Also, you know I hesitate to ruin my name by admitting I knew your true identity from the beginning. Press me too far,

Valentina, and you will force me to kill you." Paxon lowered his voice. "Through your death, perhaps, I can be free of you."

"Are you my prisoner?" Valentina asked coyly.

Paxon's face was suffused with rage. "You have killed my people! While you may not have wielded the weapon, you are the driving force behind this battle which goes on and on!"

"So now you equate me with a warrior," Valentina baited dangerously.

"It would seem you have many names, young Valentina. Slut, harlot, whore—how do those names roll off your tongue? How does 'Valentina, killer of men' rest with you?" Paxon asked cruelly.

Valentina's eyes narrowed as she pulled at the riding crop on her saddle. Free of its braces, she lashed out, striking Paxon across the cheek. The Arabian reared on his hind legs and pawed the air. Jerking the reins, Valentina gave the stallion his head and raced out onto the plains. The massive beast needed no second urging, his mane flying in the hot, dry wind. He tore across the open land, a wake of earth spewing out behind him.

Wild with fury, Valentina pressed forward. From the corner of her eye she noted movement as Paxon, atop his black stallion, gained on her.

They rode across the plains, mile after mile eaten by the horses' hooves. The white Arabian was the first to slow as he neared a gently flowing stream near the foothills. Sliding down, Valentina knelt by the clear stream and tasted its coolness. When she looked up, Paxon was staring down at her.

"Valentina, queen's procurer! Slut and whore to *Sheikh al Jebal!*"

Valentina rose to her feet, ignoring him as though he weren't there. Turning away from him, she reached out to gather the reins of the Arabian. Violently he swung her about.

"I can see by the look in those dark eyes of yours that you have but one thing on your mind," she remarked. "Surely you aren't interested in my sullied body."

Paxon's brilliant caftan billowed in the warm wind, making him appear a more formidable figure. "One woman is as good as another," he said mockingly. "They all serve the same purpose."

"Do they, now?" she purred dangerously. "Somehow I can't quite believe that. Every woman is different. It's the man who is the same. The man who thinks this. Never the woman," she hissed. "If you want me, you'll have to fight to take me."

"I've never done battle for a whore," Paxon snarled.

"Then I suggest you climb on your horse and leave me. I wouldn't want you to live with a tarnished vision of yourself. Of course," she mocked, "there is always the first time for everything."

Damnable woman, she was laughing at him. No woman had ever laughed at him. When he was finished with her, she wouldn't be laughing. She would beg for more, and then more.

Startled at the determination she read in his dark eyes, Valentina moved back a step and let her mind race. Too well she remembered the feel of those hands on her body, and too well she remembered how her trembling body had responded to his hard caresses. Menghis, Menghis, her heart cried, and her body ached for him. Yet she knew he was gone from her, no longer a part of her world.

"Do you want to make a game of this?" Paxon asked softly. "For if you do, I must warn you that I always win. I am a man, and at this moment I am in command."

Valentina laughed derisively. "And what is it you command? I see nothing save myself and two horses. I will not do your bidding, so who does that leave for you to command?" She laughed again, the deep throaty laugh which made his pulses race. "You also speak of winning. What is it you will win? Tell me, for I'm interested. Surely not a whore and a slut; that's no fair prize for a sultan. Somehow I would have thought a man, a sultan like yourself, would demand

336

a much richer prize than me. You can't have me, you know. I have found love with Menghis," she said calmly. "Oh, you may ravage my body, but you can't take the one thing that is mine to give. The joy of my womanhood . . . my complete surrender! This you will never have. I have tasted the ecstasies of love in Menghis's arms."

Paxon's eyes burned into her. He knew she spoke the truth. Menghis had been able to evoke her surrender to the pleasures of love, yet he had not. "You're mine if I say it is so," he snarled.

"Never."

"I say you are mine. I claim you as my own!"

Paxon licked dry lips and advanced a step, reaching out a long arm and grasping at her caftan, ripping it from her shoulder and exposing a creamy, coral-tipped breast.

Valentina brought up her foot in defense and kicked out, jarring him off balance. The light of battle in his eye, Paxon advanced again, this time grasping her with both outstretched arms, bringing her slim body against his. His mouth crushed hers in a searing, burning, hurtful kiss. smothering her with his close embrace.

Valentina struggled, seeing his sun-burnished features coming closer. His mouth found hers in another hurting, angry kiss. His arms were locked about her, squeezing off her breath, leaving her gasping. Her hands found his head and she ripped his head gear away, leaving his hair free to blow in the dry wind. Still struggling, she grasped handfuls of his close-cropped wavy mane, pulling, tearing, forcing him away from her. Still he refused to release her. Instead, his kiss became more demanding, deeper, searching.

Valentina's legs buckled under her; she was weak from struggling and from the lack of air. Still he held her in his embrace, compelling her to respond, demanding it. Time lost all meaning, and the winds which blew warm against her body were the winds of centuries. Valentina's heart cried out for love, and her body demanded release.

Paxon's dark hair became Menghis's. His lips, although harsh and demanding as Menghis's had never been, elicited a response. In this breach of time the arms which held her were Menghis's arms, just as the lean hardness which took her to dizzying heights was Menghis.

His mouth released hers to scorch a path to her breasts, and she welcomed him. He pressed her to the ground, falling atop her. His mouth ravaged hers and drank in her sweetness. He relished the feel of her perfectly formed breasts swelling against his chest. The wind blew her long hair around them like a protective cloak, fragrant with spices and flowers. Her legs taunted him, finding their way to lock him against her.

Never had he ever wanted a woman so much! Never had mere flesh and bone delighted him so. The feel of her skin was an aphrodisiac to his senses. And *she* wanted *him!* She was responding to his caresses, pleading for more, opening her body to him. She pressed herself more tightly against him in a glorious offering. She moaned and murmured, "Menghis . . . Menghis!"

Suddenly Valentina's head reeled backward from a sharp blow to her head; her face was aflame where Paxon had slapped her.

"So, it is Menghis to whom you make love! Menghis to whom you respond! You forget yourself, Valentina. You are here with me, Paxon, nevermore Menghis." His voice came in breathless rasps. Rage flooded his face.

Fear gripped Valentina. Gasping for breath, frightened, and hardly comprehending the events of the past few moments, she crawled across the ground, hiding her face in her hands. She felt ashamed because her hungry body so wanted to believe that it was Menghis, her love, who made love to her.

"Tears will not return Menghis to you. I know, just as you do, that my brother has taken the throne of *Sheikh al Jebal* and is no longer a part of our world. You weep for a man who is like the dead. And you still prefer him to me?" Paxon's face was black with rage, and standing above her, framed by the infinite

338

blue of the sky, he appeared like a giant: ruthless and dangerous. "Knowing you can never be with him, do you still prefer him to me? Answer me, Valentina. Your life may depend on it."

"Yes," Valentina whispered breathlessly. "I love him."

"Speak up, woman. I did not hear your answer."

"Yes! Yes! Yes!" She screamed, eyes wild, all control lost. "I will always prefer him to any man. I will always prefer him to you! Don't you understand, Paxon? I love him! All choice has been taken from my hands. Allah decrees it, my God has commanded it, the fates demand it! I love him!"

Paxon's face was incredulous. Even under the threat of death she still professed her love for Menghis. "You have allowed my brother the advantage, Valentina. How can you tell the ripeness of a melon unless you have tasted it?"

"I have tasted it, Paxon, that night on the oasis in the desert, after Saladin placed my hand in yours. It can change nothing. I love Menghis."

"Perhaps another sampling will be more to your liking." Paxon lunged for her, trapping her beneath him. Struggling was useless; he was too powerful.

He tore her garments from her until she was naked. His violence terrified her and left her helpless. She wanted to strike out, to kill, to maim . . . He was too strong, and her fright was heightened because she had feared him for so long.

He took her quickly, brutally, ravaging her with his lips and teeth, tearing at her with his fingers. He left not an inch of her unexplored, disregarding her shame. Through it all she cried, screamed, and unknowingly, because of her fear, begged for Menghis to save her. . . .

Valentina lay quietly beside the Saracen, listening to his soft breathing. Satisfied that he was sleeping deeply, she rose softly and tiptoed to her scattered clothing and the waiting horses. Her caftan was beyond repair, the tatters barely sufficient to cover her nakedness. Only a few feet away were the garments which Paxon had divested himself of before his attack on her.

Deftly she slipped Paxon's tunic over her head and gathered up his boots and all other clothing. Gentling the horses, she lifted herself onto her Arabian's saddle and took the reins of Paxon's horse. Frantically, before he could awaken and stop her, she whipped the Arabian and raced from the oasis, the black stallion tagging behind.

Paxon jumped to his feet when he heard the commotion caused by the mounts and Valentina's loud urgings. He made a vain attempt to stop her, but without boots or clothing he was at a distinct disadvantage. His rantings and obscenities rang loudly in the desert stillness.

All the way back to Napur a pall of despair hung over her. When the walls of the palace were visible in the distance, she stopped her mount and finally was able to shed locked tears of frustration. She felt dead inside. It was as though she had been dead all this time since having seen Menghis on the throne of *Sheikh al Jebal,* and no one had had the decency to bury her. The love of one man and the hatred of another had killed her as surely as if a knife had been plunged into her heart.

Her whole life had gone awry since she had come to this damnable land where war raged and the value of a human life was less than that of a goat. Berengaria's treachery; the French soldier whom she had been forced to kill; the two soldiers of Islam who had defiled her; her pledge to Ramiff; the deceit in which she engaged to help the Crusaders; loving Menghis; losing Menghis; attacked by Paxon; raped, beaten . . .

And she had survived it all! Survived to live another day and bear the brunt of more brutality. She would never give in without a fight; she was determined to survive.

As long as there was breath in her body, there was hope. Paxon was a mere man who could crucify and torture her, but more horrible was the torture of the

340

spirit. Rosalan had taught her this, and so had Menghis.

Paxon's violence had wounded her flesh. He had used her and humiliated her. This she would never forgive. He may one day kill her, she thought, but never would she permit herself to accomplish her own death for him! No, she would live to fight another day!

The more she thought about it, the deeper her convictions became. And when she thought of the mighty warrior trudging across the plains naked as the day he was born, she laughed. She enjoyed the fact that she, a woman, could humiliate a man like Paxon. He had abused her, but she had survived to strike out and by her own determination had gained a small, but pleasing, measure of revenge.

By the time Valentina reached the stable yard, she was in good spirits once again.

"I've always wanted a black stallion," she said loftily to the wide-eyed stableboy. "Brand him as mine with a cross."

The stableboy, frightened out of his wits, hurried to do her bidding. He planned not to be around when the sultan returned. There would be a battle, and he knew he would receive the brunt of it. Servants always did. He would hide in the cellars if he had to. He didn't know whom he feared the most, the sultan with his rages or the long-haired woman whom Ramiff had made the mistress of his palace.

The branding iron hot and ready, the boy flinched as he marked the stallion's flanks with a cross. What had the mistress done to capture the sultan's horse? He knew she must have taken the stallion by some means of trickery. The sultan guarded his mount more closely than he did his purse.

Rage engulfed Paxon as he cursed first in one language and then another. When his curses failed to produce his garments and horse, he drove his huge fist into the softness of the ground. The full enormity

341

of his situation hit him and he began to curse again. He would have to travel across the plains naked, which would take hours. His lean body would be burned to a crisp if he traveled by day, and he would freeze at night. How would he explain his condition when he walked into camp? A man without a horse was one thing, but a naked man without his horse was definitely something else.

He cursed again as his mind raced, and he began the endless trek. How Valentina must be laughing at him! This was the second time she had made him the fool—first with the granaries and now this! No woman would make a fool of him! She would pay for this if it was the last thing he ever did! As the sun rose higher in the desert sky he contemplated if he would live to see his revenge. If he did, and if necessary, that woman would pay with her life!

Valentina had informed Rosalan of the trick she had played on Paxon. After laughing and joking about Paxon's situation, Rosalan left to share the news with Ahmar.

By sundown the palace was buzzing about Valentina's trick on the sultan of Jakard. A naked man walking the plains! The women tittered behind their veils as the men held their garments closer to their bodies. And what was this rumor coming from the stable that the mistress had had the Saracen's stallion branded with a Christian cross? What would happen when the sultan arrived to claim his mount? It was said that the mistress rested in her chambers, a secret smile on her face as she nibbled on figs.

Valentina stirred herself, knowing she had many affairs of state to contend with today. Working helped keep her mind from her heartaches. Her slender hands sorted documents and corrected any errors before she stamped the parchments with the emir's official seal. Where was the Saracen? How much progress had he made?

A rich bubble of laughter erupted from her as she added the last stamp to a stack of documents. So, a woman was good for only one thing, and all women were alike. "You have much to learn, Saracen."

Chapter Twenty-six

Endless days and sleepless nights. With each breath Valentina was conscious that Menghis was lost to her. Her eyes unknowingly searched out the shadows for him. An elusive melody from the minstrels in the marketplace reminded her that her love was gone. A breeze carrying the freshness of the woodlands brought his face to mind. And at night, when all was still and there were no diversions of work to be found, the pillow beneath her head became his shoulder, and the coverlet lightly resting upon her body became his arms. When sleep would come it was only for brief spells, for she would awaken, whispering his name, and tears would stain her cheeks. Her yearning for Menghis became a physical ache, eating away at her, forcing her to remember their times together and renewing her grief.

Even the stars over Napur brought fresh memories, calling to mind the moments of ecstasy she had spent on the grassy knoll in his embrace, where he had covered her with his body and quelled all her fears and thoughts of the world below the Alamut. She ached for his cherishing, needed his love, craved his understanding.

With her memories of ecstasy came the inescapable knowledge that she had failed him. She had turned her back on him and had left Alamut, his pleading for her to stay wringing her heart and his dark, soulful eyes burning through her. Because she had not stayed, had not offered a hope for their future together, he had taken the only path open to him: the throne of *Sheikh al Jebal*. Why hadn't she listened to him? Why hadn't she held out a hope to him? She had put her pledge to Ramiff and her aid to the Christians before him, and he could not forgive her for it. Could never forgive her for it! And now all she had was a searing emptiness.

In vain Valentina wished she had never dared to climb to the Alamut. Had never met Menghis! Had never felt his warm embrace or heard him whisper her name in his sleep. How simple her life would have been if she had never known his love; a love as pure as the mountain streams and as warm as the desert sands. A love which had filled her life—no, she thought, not filled her life, but had given her life.

Until meeting Menghis she had been only a shadow of a woman. Menghis made her complete. Through him she had discovered herself. The bittersweet memories of his caresses warmed her blood, and the gentle yet demanding pressure of his loins against hers when they consummated their love revived in her a throbbing hunger. He haunted her; he was still real to her; his kisses, his embraces, the sound of his voice whispering adoring phrases of love, tormented her.

Torment. Each day, each hour, it was her legacy. Not only from Menghis, whose memory brought her a bitter, blazing torment, but from Paxon, who exacted a different kind. Paxon; even his name was a threat. She knew from Ahmar that Paxon had elected to stay in the vicinity of Napur, reenlisting the Islamic forces who had gathered in the plains nearby. She knew he had spies reporting to him her every move. Waiting, waiting with vengeful eyes for Valentina to make a move.

Paxon had not come to the palace since the day he had followed her out onto the plains and accosted her. His humiliation was too great to risk facing her mockery. Valentina had abandoned the fear that Paxon would report her treachery in aiding the Christians to Saladin. But his threat to her life still plagued her. She knew he would see her dead—not because she sent supplies to Richard, but because he must finally accept the fact that she would never be his.

Paxon had not revealed her true identity and her treachery because his silence throughout would implicate him as an accessory, and he would be forced to admit publicly that he was a fool. Not because he really loved her. She represented a challenge to him, one he was determined to win, else he himself would kill her.

She would never be free. Not from her memories of Menghis, nor from the threat of Paxon as long as she remained in Napur. Her pledge to Ramiff was ended . . . it was impossible to continue aid to Richard . . . Paxon stalking her . . . Menghis unreachable. Solemnly Valentina admitted that she had no other recourse but to leave Napur. She would go back to her own people, back to where she would at least be free of Paxon, even if she would never be able to leave behind the stirring memories of Menghis.

She would leave Napur, escape from the prying eyes of Paxon's spies. Knowing she would never make it across the plains and the desert on her own, Valentina began to devise a plan. The nearest faction of Crusaders was at Beth Nable, led by the Lionheart himself. He would help her return to Acre, from where she could find her way back to Navarre.

For the next few days Valentina spent a good deal of her time with Rosalan. The time was fast approaching when Rosalan would be delivered of her child, and Valentina longed to be with her friend at the most important moment of her life. Yet Valentina was fearful that Richard might decide to withdraw from Beth Nable any day now and widen the distance between her and her only means of returning to her own people. She toyed with the idea of having Ahmar escort her, but she realized how much he wanted to be near Rosalan when the child was born. No, she couldn't deprive him of that; she would try to get to Beth Nable on her own.

345

Fedawi still lingered in and near the palace, offering their silent protection. Menghis still had not withdrawn his men. Their very presence made her feel closer to Menghis; let her know that he still cared enough to be concerned over her. But she would not ask them, either. Before they could agree to her request, they would ask Menghis. In essence it would be the same as asking him herself, and she was determined never to beseech him for anything in her own behalf again. She would do it alone. Always alone.

Moments before she was to climb onto Paxon's black stallion, Valentina walked into the secluded portion of the garden and stood, head bowed beneath the Judas tree. She was distressed because she had found her white Arabian limping when she had slipped into the stable to saddle him. The only other mount she was familiar with and was certain could carry her swiftly across the plains was the black stallion she had had branded with a cross.

"Kadi," she whispered in the soft night air. "How I wish you were here to counsel me. But you rest in Allah's arms, and I must do what I think is best. I leave Napur. I have done my best for you," she said as tears slipped down her pale ivory cheeks. "But I will never forget you. When I return I will see to it that you have a decent burial so your people can mourn you. I'm doing what I must. I have no other choice. I can't stay here any longer. I must return to my own people. I have not forgotten, nor will I ever forget, what you've done for me." She squared her shoulders and quelled the tremor in her voice. "I flaunted myself in the face of my fate. I've lost, and now I must look to my own survival."

Paxon, sultan of Jakard, stomped back and forth in his tent, knocking things over in his wake and muttering obscenities at Cat, his black panther. The black panther snarled in defense of himself and slunk off into a far corner, out of his master's enraged pacing. Everything was going wrong! The whole damn war was awry. Nothing, *nothing* had gone his way since laying eyes on Valentina's lithe beauty. Her eyes haunted him. Those changeable eyes, green with hot anger and sapphire-blue with passion.

His blood grew hot in his veins as he remembered the feel of her in his arms, her fragility, her warmth and her strength and her coldness. That day out on the plains he had tasted both. For the inexplicable moment when he had seen her eyes turn dark as sapphires and felt her response—but it had been for Menghis! It was to Menghis she had offered her soft, pouting lips and slender, graceful body. Never to him, Paxon!

He had been a fool! He pounded his fist into the palm of his other hand. A fool! To think that he had dishonored himself because of her! He had protected her by not revealing her true identity when he discovered she sat as regent for Ramiff's kingdom of Napur. He had been glad she was alive and accessible to him. Fool! To implicate himself this way! And when he discovered she had been sending aid to the Christians, still he had done nothing. Nothing more than threaten! Why couldn't he see then that she was beyond his threats? Menghis, that bastard, had seen to that. Offering her protection, surrounding her with *fedawi*. Keeping her just beyond reach.

He would kill her! Yet . . . yet . . . if her eyes should become sapphires for him, if she would offer herself to him . . . no, he would kill her! She had played him for a fool. And he had allowed it by keeping her secrets.

Paxon halted in his steps. Did he desire her death because she had aided the Christians or because he could not allow her to belong to anyone else?

Paxon shook his dark head, refusing himself the answer to his own question. He had duties to perform. Word had come to him earlier that the yearly caravan from the south was nearing the well of El Khuwielfa; much too close to Beth Nable, where the Lionheart had ensconced himself. "Too close for comfort! He could feed his army for a year with the spoils of that single caravan," Paxon muttered to himself. Word

347

must be gotten to the caravan to make a detour around El Khuwielfa, out of range from Richard's scouts.

Bitterly Paxon realized this was a mission he must perform himself. He alone carried the authority to persuade the caravan leaders to detour.

Two sunsets later Paxon and an escort of fifty men found themselves near the head of the caravan. He spurred his horse and rode to the front, signaling for the leader of the wagons to halt. Quickly he explained the circumstances. The master of the caravan bowed low and spoke haltingly. "We have seen no danger as we crossed the desert. If we leave the trail, as you suggest, where will we find water? The wells are here as we travel. What you suggest will cost us lives as well as our animals. We must arrive at the seaports within the week. Already we have lost several days' travel because of violent sandstorms. We will make camp now, and stay on the road. Tell your Malik en Nasr that we appreciate his warning, but our decision is to stay near the wells."

Frustrated, Paxon could only glare at the old man and his rich wagons of supplies. "You have enough provisions here to feed the Christian armies for a year. Why must you close your ears to what I say? The Crusaders will be at a disadvantage in the desert. At the most you will lose one day, perhaps two. Are the caravans more important to you than all the people who ride with you? What of the women and children?"

"That is the reason we must stay here on the road and be near the wells, because of the women and children," the caravan master said patiently. "The matter is ended. We'll make camp here and start again in the morning."

"Fool," Paxon muttered through clenched teeth. He gave the order to the escort to ride ahead and pitch their tents. The caravan would stay at the well of El Khuwielfa. There they would remain for the next several days, watering their endless line of people and beasts of burden.

Valentina urged her mount on, pity for the animal tugging at her conscience. He had carried her for two days across the plains and onto the burning sands. He was the only living thing she had seen since leaving Napur, and their relationship had solidified into one of mutual trust. He carried the burden of her life and she did not even know his name, or even if Paxon had given him one.

In her saddlebags she carried little food for herself; just a wedge of cheese and dried meat. The balance was grain for the stallion, and slung across the saddle were several goatskins of water. Wisely she had had more concern for her mount's nourishment than for her own. He was the one upon whose strength she depended to carry her to Richard, to her own people.

Her water supply was running low, and she had consulted the crude map she had drawn after referring to the scrolls in Ramiff's library. Soon, now, she would be approaching the well of El Khuwielfa, about a day's journey from Beth Nable.

Onward she rode, careful not to overtire her mount. Several times she dismounted and led him forward, sparing him the burden of her weight. But she would soon tire of walking in the loose sand and climb regretfully on his back once again, apologizing to him for her weakness.

A few hours after sunrise, when the sun was still low on the horizon yet blinding her with its glaring heat, she urged the stallion to the top of the rise, expecting to see the well of El Khuwielfa below her. The stallion needed little urging, for the scent of fresh water came to his nostrils on the wind. Sensing what spurred her horse on, Valentina gave him his head.

Even before they crested the rise Valentina heard the wild braying of camels and the sound of human voices calling and shouting to one another. Forcibly reining in the stallion, she approached the rise with caution. There before her was a caravan of such proportion that it looked like a traveling city. The beasts of burden were countless, as were the herds of sheep and goats and the yokes of oxen pulling sleds of merchandise.

Valentina withdrew back over the rise, tugging at the stallion's bridle, insisting that he come back and keep their presence secret. The stallion seemed to have the same first instincts as she. Fresh water! People! Life in place of desolation! "No, we cannot . . ." she whispered to the animal. "We can trust no one. Only a few hours more and we'll be with the Christian troops."

Reluctantly the stallion obeyed her. Onward they rode, to Beth Nable.

As she rode Valentina negated the thought of telling the Lionheart of the caravan. If his scouts had not discovered it for themselves, she would not tell him. She was finished with interfering in men's business. Under the blazing sun Valentina came to the conclusion that men would always wage war. Not for principles or ideals or even in defense, but simply because they liked the sport of it.

The sun was just about to set and already the air was becoming cooler when Valentina noticed the smoke from cook fires in the nearby foothills. Kicking her heels into the stallion's flanks, she spurred him toward the regiment of soldiers for the Holy Cross.

She passed through a narrow ravine and was halfway up the slope when she was halted by a pair of lookouts. "State your business here," one demanded. The look of shock on his face when she answered in his own language surprised Valentina. She hadn't thought about how she looked, so naturally had she worn Arab garb to protect her from the desert. Now she realized that she was the image of a Moslem. Khalats, cloak, turban, and headgear, and riding an Arabian saddle.

"Take me to the Lionheart. I am a countrywoman to his queen." Whether it was the authority in her voice or her declaration that she was Berengaria's countrywoman, Valentina did not know. But after sending her another quizzical glance, the lookout did as he was instructed.

Down the far side of the slope they rode, the vast campsite looming before her. Thousands of men were camped here, yet it was like a city of the dead. There were no groups of men gaming with cards or dice. Where were the minstrels lifting their voices in song? The men's faces were gaunt from sickness and hunger. Hundreds lay beneath inadequate blankets, listless and ill. Through the camp to the far side where Richard's tent had been raised, Valentina's eyes darted about her. Occasionally eyes would be raised in inquiry, but there was none of the ribaldry that Valentina knew a woman riding through an army camp could expect. Hungry men had no interest in women.

Hungry men! What had happened to the supplies she had sent? Where were the flocks of sheep for meat and the goats for milk and cheese? And the grain! What had happened to the grain? To the sugar and the dried fruits? Her eyes peered through the waning light to the long ditches on the perimeter of the camp from where a foul smell emanated. There lay her answer in rotting, fermenting animal flesh. The supplies had been wasted.

Wasted! No foresight, no planning, simply carelessness, wastefulness, her mind screamed. These Christians—idiots!—had no idea how to preserve food. They had probably killed most of the sheep at one time and glutted themselves. Or else they had used a portion of it for bribes and payment for spies, rather than spend any gold. Didn't they know by now that they couldn't eat gold!

Bitter anger boiled within her, leaving her light-headed with rage. Wasted! She could almost see them eating only the choice parts, fighting over them. Glutting themselves with no thought for the morrow. Disgusted, Valentina thought of how a Moslem could live for half a year on one sheep, utilizing every ounce of the animal right down to the hooves!

The lookout brought her to the large tent bearing the dragon of Richard's standard. He left her outside while he went in to announce her. Valentina rested on an empty keg as she waited for audience with the king. Weary to the point of exhaustion, she could only stare ahead of her with blank, unseeing eyes. She didn't want to see, she couldn't bear to see, the suffering of the men, the waste of life because of stupidity. On her way to Beth Nable she had pondered how much she would tell Richard of her adventures and what had happened to her on the day of the massacre. Up to now she had been undecided, wishing to spare him her problems, wanting only to be returned to Acre. Now she couldn't even think about herself. All these men in the face of death. How had he allowed this to happen?

A knight of the realm who had been inside the tent gently tapped her on the shoulder and bade her enter. She was shocked at the king's appearance. He was thin, almost gaunt, his lush red-gold hair and beard straggly and unkempt. His blue eyes were still brilliant and alive, but in them was no recognition of her.

Curtsying deeply, Valentina said, "My liege, have you no memory of me? I am Lady Valentina, lady-in-waiting to Queen Berengaria."

For a moment Valentina had the horrible impression that Richard didn't know who Berengaria was. Then his eyes lit. "Yes, how are you faring, Lady Valentina?"

Had the man gone mad? How was she faring? Was that all he could say? Didn't he wonder how she had come to be in the middle of the desert, alone and in his camp? These questions blared through Valentina's thoughts, but she reasoned that if he had gone mad, she had better go easy with him. "I am well, my lord. And yourself?" What madness was this? She couldn't believe she was standing here exchanging pleasantries with the king as though he had suddenly come upon her in his castle's garden.

"In grace with the Lord, Lady Valentina." As though coming out of a long sleep, his eyes widened with surprise and puzzlement. "How in God's name did you get yourself here?"

"That is a long story, my liege. Do you have time to listen?"

"Time is the only thing plentiful in this camp," he said sadly. "Sit beside me, Lady Valentina, and perhaps we can share a cup of wine. I believe there is still some left in the medicines."

"I would be honored," Valentina said softly, "but there is one request I have. My horse, can it be arranged to have him watered and fed?"

"Fed!" Richard stormed suddenly, startling her out of her wits. "Fed! Feed a horse while my men lie starving! Women!" he grumbled.

"My mount carries his own rations on his saddle . . ."

From outside the tent came a flurry of excitement and brawling voices. A horse brayed in fear. The stallion! Valentina rushed through the tent flap to find at least ten men fighting each other for the saddlebags. The black stallion screamed in fear as several soldiers handled him roughly in order to steal away his saddle baggage.

Valentina reached for the first available object. Gripping one of Richard's boots, she hurled herself into the melee of men. "Stop! Stop it! Get away from him! Leave him alone!" she screamed, hitting the offenders with the boot, kicking out menacingly.

Amazed, the soldiers fell back, hangdog expressions on their faces.

"Curs! Vipers! Leave the poor animal alone. He's carried me all the way from Napur, and I won't see him treated this way. If one thread of his mane is touched, I swear I will kill the man who does it. Now, slink off into your alleys like the dogs you are and leave him in peace!"

Richard watched from the opening to his tent. He threw his head back and roared with laughter. "Serves you well! You are a pack of cowardly dogs to be so easily put off by a woman!" he blared scornfully at his men. "Else why would the enemy find you such willing targets? Cowards!" The offenders slunk off to lick their wounds, muttering obscenities and cursing horses in general. "Come back and fight!" Richard ordered.

"My liege!" Valentina exclaimed. "Would you have them come back to do me harm?"

Richard suddenly looked enbarrassed. "No, no, Lady Valentina . . . forgive me . . . I wasn't thinking." Then he blustered, "Not that the cowards would even care to do battle with a woman!" He then turned his attention to the black stallion. "You say he carries his own provisions? Fine animal . . ."

"My liege, will you see that my mount is watered? And perhaps he would share his provisions with your own steed, Flavel?" she said craftily. Almost immediately, he called to his guard to see to both horses.

"And see that the rations get to the mounts and not in your own belly!" he admonished.

Valentina thought she was going to be ill. Men attacking a defenseless animal to steal his groats. She knew she must tell Richard about the caravan at El Khuwielfa.

"Now you may have my ear, Lady Valentina. Tell me how you came to be here." He sat across from her on an empty keg which had once held grain and peered at her intently, as though she were about to tell him the most interesting tale he had ever heard.

Valentina had already decided how much she would reveal. She told him of Berengaria's treachery and having been caught up in the massacre, omitting the part about the French soldier. She confessed that she had lived among the Bedouins in Saladin's camp, also omitting that she had been ravaged by two of Saladin's soldiers. She quickly ran through her sale at auction to Emir Ramiff, saying she was bought for the harem but never participated in its policies. Everything concerning Paxon she omitted, even that he had been Berengaria's lover. She simply told the king that his queen had found fault with her. No mention of *Sheikh al Jebal* was made, either. It was not necessary for the king to know about him. When at last she told Richard that she had sent him the supplies, he stood up abruptly, knocking over the empty keg and shouting in outrage.

"You! You sent the supplies? And you took the gold!"

"Of course I took the gold! I had to replace the monies in the treasury. What if Saladin had demanded repayment? How could I steal from the people of Napur?"

"Steal? From those thieves? You call it stealing when you were performing your Christian duty?" His face was crimson, his eyes nearly popping from his head.

"Yes, I call it stealing!" Valentina shouted back. "Those people were good to me! Emir Ramiff trusted me, and I betrayed him as it was by taking that which was not mine to give. Yes, I took the gold! And if you had thought more of the supplies, you would have paid your bribes with the gold rather than with food-stuffs!"

Immediately she knew she had hit a sore point. She knew her speculations were correct. Richard had probably cursed himself a thousand times over for parting with the supplies rather than the gold.

"You made me pay for those supplies!" he accused.

"You only paid in gold. I was paying with my life!"

"You charged twice what the supplies were worth," Richard stormed.

"And how much is a life worth? What did you consider a fair price for the lives of your men? Half? A quarter? Nothing?"

Valentina thought the blood vessels in his neck would burst. "I have never struck a woman, Lady Valentina, but you sorely tempt me."

Valentina stumbled backward, not from fear, but from disgust. Self-disgust. To think she gave up Menghis for this . . . this stupidity. It was almost too much to be borne! It had come down to this and she saw now she had been the fool.

"You are not the only one between us who is tempted, my lord," she spat back. "When I think of the number of caravans that were sent out to you, and still your men lie starving! What did you do with it all? Did you think that those supplies were manna from

355

heaven and they would never cease? Bah! Men make me sick!"

Richard watched her, astonished. There was only one other woman who had dared to speak this way to him: Queen Eleanor, his mother. A slow smile of appreciation crept across his face as he eyed Valentina.

"I fear we sound like two fishwives, Lady Valentina. Forgive me. Will you join me in that cup of wine now? Tell me more of this kingdom—Napur, was it?"

In spite of herself, Valentina sat with her king, marveling at the sudden change in him from hostile warrior to gentle friend.

When he finished his wine, Valentina broached the subject of the caravan. "I have information which would be most useful to you, my liege. Once a year a great caravan leaves Cairo for the seaports. This year the caravan goes to Jaffa, seaport for Jerusalem. At this moment it is at the well of El Khuwielfa."

"You are certain of this?" Richard asked sharply, eyeing her suspiciously.

"Quite certain. It was only this morning that I passed it. They appeared to be camped for at least a few more days, else they would have been on the move many hours before I happened to come upon them."

"And they didn't notice you?"

"No, my liege. I went unnoticed."

"How can I be certain of that? Women are foolish, and if they had seen you, they would have broken camp and could be many miles from the well by now."

Somehow his logic escaped her. There were times this evening that she had thought herself in the company of old Mohab just before his death. "I am certain they did not see me."

"If they had, you know, they might have thought you a scout and broken camp and fled into the desert."

"If they broke camp, it was not because of me. Also, a caravan of that proportion cannot travel very fast. What difference would a few miles make? You need food! You need horses!"

"I know what I need, Lady Valentina. What I don't

356

need is a woman telling me how to command my army. My men are starving, sick . . . a few miles could mean life or death!"

"There must be some men who are able to make the journey," Valentina persisted.

"Only those damned Turcoples. The bastard soldiers of fortune. They are well fed, they've seen to it. Although how they do it is a mystery to me!"

Valentina could not suppress a smile. The Turcoples were men of the desert. They could teach the wasteful Christians how to make every morsel of food last for a week.

"What will you do, my lord?"

Richard's eyes blazed with fervor. "I know the well you speak of; it is not far from here. I will take the Turcoples with me. We will be disguised as Arabs, and we'll ride into the caravan camp and see the situation for ourselves. We'll ride in boldly. Who of all those people will know we do not belong?"

After Richard rode out with his band of men, looking ridiculous with his red-gold beard beneath an Arab headdress, Valentina worked tirelessly by dressing wounds and offering the comforting touch of a woman to the wounded.

Her arms ached and her spirit was low as she looked into the men's lifeless eyes. Perhaps now they would have something to live for: restored faith in their king.

Her tiring chores completed, Valentina sat down and spoke to one of the men. "What is this the men are working on?"

"They are building siege engines," the soldier told her. "Our armies are making preparations to march into Jerusalem. We quartered here in Beth Nable because the town rests at the mouth of the ravine. It will make our march easier."

Valentina's eyes were thoughtful as she watched the men working. "And the Moslems, they are quartered inside the walls, is that it?" The soldier nodded.

Shortly before dawn Richard and the Turcoples rode into camp, their mood triumphant. King Richard

357

dismounted, his Arab caftan billowing around him in the cool morning breeze. He motioned Valentina to follow him into his tent.

"We rode into the caravan after we hobbled our horses and ate with the Arabs," Richard said. "We fed our horses and no one was the wiser. We'll ride out at noon, and by nightfall we'll have captured the entire caravan. My armies will once again be the armies of yesterday. Nothing can stand in our way!"

Her heart heavy in her breast, Valentina couldn't understand the vague feeling of doom that was settling over her as she watched the soldiers prepare for the ride they would make with their king at the noon hour. She walked through the camp, listening to the renewed hope in the voices of the men as they saddled their horses. Litters of the wounded and ailing lined one of the larger tents, and Valentina walked through them, gazing down at the young faces. From time to time she mouthed soft words of comfort or touched one of the soldiers with a gentle hand. Soon, she told them, compassion in her voice, they would return to their families. Those who could smile at her did so, and reached out emaciated hands for her to grasp. The turmoil within her subsided as she continued her walk. She hadn't done wrong. There would be no more remorse, no more self-reproach, no more anything. From this point on, Richard could command his armies with full bellies and enough medicines to treat his men as they should be treated.

Settling herself under a tree, she waited for Richard to make his exit from the tent in full battle dress. The soldiers were lined up four deep, awaiting the order of their king. Richard thrust aside the flap of the tent and stood in his mail, his shield clutched in front of him, the red-gold hair gleaming in the bright sunlight. He raised his spear in the sign of victory and gave the order to mount.

His eyes found Valentina and he walked over to her. His brilliant blue eyes were humble as he gazed at her. "I wish to ask one more favor of you," he said quietly. "I know of your intention to return to Acre,

358

but will you give me and my men the pleasure of your company when we return victorious? I wish you to share what you have helped us to do."

Valentina nodded. What did a few more hours matter? She could ride by the light of the moon. "God go with you, my liege," she said softly.

Richard gave no sign that he heard her words as he mounted Flavel, his golden war horse. With the lance raised high he led the column of soldiers from the camp. Valentina watched the French troops follow Richard and the foot soldiers follow the knights. It was indeed an impressive sight with the sunlight sparkling on the glinting armor and weapons. She watched till they were out of sight and then sat back in the shade of the tree. Soon she slept. As always, dark-haired, dark-eyed Menghis walked through her fitful dreams.

At a harsh cry from one of his men, Paxon shielded his eyes and looked to where the man was pointing, a look of horror on his face. Paxon saw a sea of soldiers, led by King Richard, surging forward at a rapid pace. The caravan with its people wouldn't have a chance; it would be a slaughter. He and his men could do little to stave off this massive attack. He had barely an instant to make a decision, and he hoped fervently that it was the right one. Quickly he ordered a contingent of men to ride out toward the Holy City, while he headed toward the caravan with his main body of men. "Fill every well from here to Jerusalem! Leave not one drop of water!"

Richard charged headlong into the caravan. Frightened, laden camels roared and balked as the army descended on them. Women and children went down as they raced from the caravans into the open desert. The sands became blood-red as the foot soldiers showed no leniency for those in their path. Pleas of mercy went unheeded as Richard bore down on the frightened, kneeling people who were being defended by Paxon's inadequate company of men. Despite the fact that they were cruelly outnumbered, they fought valiantly under Paxon's brave leadership. The desert was loud with the sound of the battle. In three hours the fray was over, and Richard shouted to all that he was the victor. With five hundred prisoners to lead the laden animals, Richard gave the order to take everything.

On their return from battle the remaining men greeted them jubilantly, their faces joyous. Valentina watched from her position under the tree as the prisoners, their heads bowed, staggered into the camp. Why didn't she feel as joyous and jubilant as the men? Richard, his voice triumphant, his bearded face victorious, shouted for all to hear. "We have confiscated gold and silver, brocades and stands of weapons and medicines. And," he roared, "the most precious of all—barley, grain, sugar, and meat!" A roar of approval rang across the plains as the prisoners lifted their heads, their faces filled with sadness.

A lone rider descended on the jubilant camp, his expression ominous as he bade Richard to enter the tent. Valentina followed and listened in horror as she heard him tell the king that the Moslem warriors had begun to block up the wells. There would be no water.

"My liege," Valentina said quickly, "go now, send your men. They are filled with good food; their morale is high; there is nothing they cannot do at this moment. You must move quickly. You can still save some of the wells." Her shoulders slumped as she saw the indecision in Richard's eyes as he glanced around at his officers.

"What should I do?" he asked hesitantly.

"You must send your best men on the best horses to save the wells. You must do it quickly, else you are lost," Valentina persisted, seeing that Richard's officers had become mute.

Richard correctly read the look in her eyes and lowered his own.

The feelings of exultation and exhilaration caused by the raid upon the caravan rapidly deserted Richard. Here he was, surrounded by his men who pleaded to be led on to Jerusalem, while the Moslems destroyed the springs and filled the wells leading to the Holy City. What was he to do? His mood blackened as through

360

the long night he watched the moon rise above the distant mountains and felt the air become cool. He knew that hidden eyes observed him from the shadows and that death reached out its evil arms. There was no water. The distant mountains rose like giant monoliths and, in his mind, became battlements.

Valentina, disgusted by Richard's lack of leadership, had stolen away from camp unnoticed. How could Richard help her get to Acre when he couldn't help himself? She had packed enough provisions for herself and her horse and then headed northwest toward Acre and home.

Chapter Twenty-seven

Paxon paced the area outside his tent, kicking up the sand and glowering off into the distance. He was seething from his inability to persuade the caravan to turn into the desert. Richard's scouts had had an easy job of spotting the milling throngs at the well as they watered their beasts. Paxon had failed, and now the Christians would have food in abundance. He squinted into the sunset, feeling a small sense of satisfaction from the fact that Richard would have great difficulty in finding water. The one commodity that Paxon had been able to deny the Lionheart. Paxon kicked up the sand again when he thought of the disgrace he had brought on himself. Saladin, Al Adil . . . all of them would keep their opinions to themselves, but he knew what they would be thinking. They would all know that he had not used all of his persuasion to force the caravan into the desert, away from the well. He knew he should have brought more than fifty of his men here. Why had he been in such a hurry to leave the camp outside Napur? After Richard's raid on the caravan, he now had less than eleven men left. What use had fifty men and the civilians from the caravan been against the Lionheart's army? This, too, would be noted by Saladin, who deplored the waste of one human life.

Stamping back into his tent, he threw himself down on the meager pallet which served as his bed. He, too, deplored wasted life, and that was what had happened at the well. Lives had been wasted because Richard had been able to overtake the caravan. Wasted!

How had this disgrace happened to him? All his life he knew he was to be the sultan of Jakard, and where was he now? Somewhere in the desert with eleven men to his account, and bearing the knowledge that because he had not been more forceful with the caravan master, he had helped supply the starving Christian army. An image of Menghis flashed through his mind. Menghis, who had what he himself had wanted. Only through an accident of birth had Paxon been left with the responsibility of Jakard and the responsibility to serve the Islamic nation. Menghis, the illegitimate son, was enjoying that which Paxon desired most—power! Menghis ruled a society of men, the *fedawi*, and sat remote on Alamut, while he, Paxon, was roasting in the desert. Menghis was known the world over as *Sheikh al Jebal*, the feared Old Man of the Mountain. Feared and, through fear, respected. Menghis, Menghis, always Menghis. He had always been their father's favorite. Even Valentina professed her love for him. "But only for now, Brother," Paxon intoned menacingly. "If the woman will not be mine, then she will not belong to anyone!"

Outside his tent was a flurry of excitement as three men rode into camp. Hastily Paxon rose to his feet and went outside. Perhaps some of his men had returned with news of the Lionheart. As the riders uncovered their faces by throwing back the long tail of their headgear, Paxon saw at once that they were the men he had left to watch the palace and report on Valentina.

"What are you doing here? You were to stay in Napur and report the woman's actions to me."

"That is why we are here," one of the men hastened to explain. "The woman left the palace—"

"When?" Paxon interrupted, a scowl on his face.

"We have no idea. But we think it was several days ago."

"You think! Fools, how did you discover this?"

"When she was not in evidence for several days we began to investigate. We found she had taken . . . er . . . your black stallion. Also, on our way out here we noticed riders in the foothills. We are not certain, but we think they are *fedawi*. You once said the *fedawi* watched her . . ."

Paxon wasn't listening. His mind was racing. Valentina gone from the palace . . . several days, his man had said. The *fedawi* riding the foothills. Evidently she was not with them; she had slipped past their vigilance also. The caravan! Instinct told him that it was not the Lionheart's scouts who had spotted the caravan, but Valentina. She had taken the news to Richard!

"Mount up and find the woman. She is somewhere near here, she must be. Find her!" he shouted. "Find her before the *fedawi* find her and circle her with their silent protection! I want that woman!"

While the three men rode out into the desert, another of his soldiers scurried about saddling Paxon's mount. While he waited, Paxon prepared himself for several days in the wilderness. Gathering together his essentials, he raged inwardly. Valentina . . . Valentina . . . she was the reason for his failure to protect the caravan. She was the reason for many things, but this last, this blot against his name, was the ultimate.

Prepared for his trek across the sands, Paxon leaped into the saddle. If he found her, and he would, he would kill her! Grasping the reins in his hands, Paxon suffered one brief moment of truth. A truth that rocked his very soul. He would kill Valentina because he would rather see her dead than know she belonged to Menghis. Heart and soul she was Menghis's! Every breath she took, every moment until her death, she would belong to Menghis!

His lids lowered like hoods over his night-dark eyes, and his expression hardened and became predatory. Spurring his horse's flanks, Paxon broke out of camp in search of Valentina. The predator was in search of its prey.

The moon was high in the heavens when Valentina reined in the stallion for a brief rest. The sands were silvery in the bright moonlight, and she let her fingers trail over them listlessly, making random patterns. She felt alone, desperately alone and frightened. She rebuked herself for refusing to ask King Richard for an escort to Acre. He would have given it to her; he would have given her anything when he first returned from pillaging the caravan. She should go back and ask for his aid. She was just thinking of how far she had traveled from the camp when she was jolted by a familiar voice.

"I'm pleased to see you've decided to return my horse," Paxon said coldly.

Angry with herself for lowering her defenses and allowing him to come upon her unnoticed, Valentina snapped, "I am pleased you are pleased. Take him and leave me alone!"

"And what would happen to you, alone and at the mercies of the desert? What would your mighty King Richard, killer of innocent people, think?" he mocked. "And Menghis, what would Menghis think?"

"I don't care what anyone thinks, least of all you!" Valentina's face mirrored her bitterness. "Get out of my life, Paxon, and leave me be."

"You'd like that, would you not? To be free of me," he said resentfully. "However, you will never be free of me, Valentina, never." His tone was ominous and held a barely concealed threat. "I could leave you out here to die, but it would be too easy a death for you. I have something else in mind. Mount up. I'm going to take you to see what you and your man of peace have done."

"Leave Menghis out of this. He had nothing to do with Richard taking the caravan. It was me! I told the Lionheart that the caravan was at the well of El Khuwielfa!"

"I suspected it was you who informed the English king. Now I have it from your own lips." His features were black with fury. "Wherever you are is death for my people. Mount up!"

"And if I refuse?"

"Then I will force you. Now!" he ordered.

Valentina looked at Paxon for a long moment, then she spoke. "I think I am beginning to see something that I only suspected before, but now I am certain. You use the threat of my death against me. You want me to believe you would put me to death because I aided the Christians and am guilty of treachery against Islam. But now I know that is merely your excuse. You want my death because I will never be yours and you would rather see me dead than have me love another." The blazing rage in Paxon's eyes told her she had hit the mark.

"Mount up," he snarled.

"You are pathetic, Paxon. I could almost forgive you if you loved me, but even this is not so. You love no one. You merely want me, want to see me grovel to you, declaring my love for you. And then you will have won and your self-respect will have been restored. At that point you would cast me aside, another victory you have won, and go on to new fields of battle."

"You are mistaken. Now, mount up." His voice was coldly controlled.

"Perhaps I am mistaken. Perhaps my surrender to you is only so important because of Menghis. Menghis has something you can never have."

"Mount up!" he raged, seizing her by the arm and forcing her to climb atop the stallion.

Having no other choice open to her, Valentina settled herself in the saddle and followed Paxon's lead. They rode in silence, and from the stiffness of his back she knew she had spoken the truth. He wanted her because she belonged to Menghis, and the sadness of it was that he couldn't even admit this to himself.

Reining in his steed, Paxon ordered her to dismount, then asked, "Would you like a drink of water?" Valentina nodded gratefully. Paxon dismounted, holding the whip which had been affixed to a strap on his horse's saddle. The whip clasped in his hand, he pushed Valentina a short way to a little spring which fed fresh water into an outcropping of rocks. "I see that your mouth is parched and dry. Fill the spring, and don't stop until the chore is completed!"

"But you asked if I would like a drink."

"And you said you would. Just as your people are going to ask for water. There will be none. Richard's army will never get to Jerusalem because very soon they will die of thirst. Now get yourself to the task! And should one drop of water touch your lips, you will feel the crack of this whip across your back. You remember what a whip feels like, don't you, Valentina, queen's procurer?"

Ignoring his insult, Valentina protested, "I have no idea how to go about filling the spring. It will take . . ."

"Yes, it will take a long time," Paxon answered, taking a drink from the water skin hanging from his belt. "As for the method, that is up to yourself. I suggest you begin by blocking off the flow of water from where it springs. When you have changed its course, it will filter into the sand and be absorbed. Anyone passing through here would have to know where to look in order to find any water. Now begin—there are many wells and springs from here to Jerusalem!"

Falling to her knees, Valentina scooped sand endlessly, carried rocks, and blocked off the trickle of water from the underground spring. She would not beg. Never! When her tongue became thick and swollen, she would not beg. She would die first.

Valentina clenched her teeth and scooped sand as fast as she could. She worked diligently for two more hours.

"Mount up. We have many wells and springs to fill before we make camp." Valentina's mouth was so dry she couldn't answer. She mounted the horse and followed Paxon. By now the sun was reaching its zenith and beat down unmercifully on her back as she trailed behind. How much longer could she remain on the horse's back before she fell off? Another hour passed and then another before Paxon halted, a well in full view.

"We'll rest here and continue after the sun sets." Valentina slid from the horse and staggered to the nearest tree and fell against it. Would he allow her water? She had to have a drink. Never in her life had she desired anything more than wanting to put her face in the cool water and drink forever.

"You'll be no good to me if you're dead," he said cruelly. "Just wet your lips, but don't drink the water."

Ignoring him, Valentina rushed to the spring and lowered her head into the cool water. She drank thirstily. She would never get enough. She drank more as Paxon stood watching her, laughing. Withdrawing her head from the spring, she wiped her mouth with the back of her hand. Her eyes bulged suddenly as she leaned over and retched violently. Spasm after spasm rocked her body till she fell to the ground.

"I told you not to drink the water. If you insist on acting like a camel, then you deserve what you get," he said mockingly. "Rest and then sip at the water."

"You're inhuman!" Valentina gasped as she held her stomach.

"We will see who is inhuman after I show you the remains of the caravan. Then tell me who is inhuman. Here," he said, tossing her a ripe fig. Valentina looked at the fig in her hand and then at Paxon. With her last ounce of strength she threw the fig into the desert.

"I want nothing from you," she said bitterly. "Leave me alone. Why do you insist on taking me to the caravan?"

"I want you to see what your . . . generosity to the Christians has done to my people." Valentina closed her eyes. Paxon spoke harshly. "I could almost forgive you the wagonloads of supplies that you sent out, they were at best . . . ineffectual, but your informing Malik Ric of the caravan from Cairo was the last thing I could tolerate."

"Ineffectual? Perhaps in your eyes. To my own it was saving a few so they could return to their families. If I saved just one, then it was worth it. I would do it again if I had to do it over. To know that one mother will see her son again is all I need to know. And don't pretend to be so sanctimonious. You are only making excuses 'to yourself. I know what you really want, Paxon, but it is not in my power to give it to you. My heart, my soul, and yes, that which you most want, my surrender, belong to Menghis."

"You spin a fine tale," Paxon said harshly. "Since you have been so generous to my brother, I wonder if he will be so kind in return. When I hang you on a cross in Jerusalem, as befitting a traitor and a spy, will he come down from his lofty throne to save you?"

"You will have a long wait, my friend," Valentina said softly, "for no one will come to my aid. I will hang on your cross till the vultures pick the flesh from my bones and my eyes from their sockets, and still no one will come. And when I stand in my heaven, I will pray for your soul and that of every Moslem in your command. But," she said in warning, "only after I pray for Menghis."

"Spare me your prayers," Paxon said coldly. "Right now, at this moment, the only person standing between you and your death is me. I'm the only one who can save you."

Valentina answered quietly, "If I'm to pay for what I've done, then so be it. If you think I'm going to beg, you are mistaken. I'll beg from no one."

"Then you will continue to fill the springs on our ride to camp. You will undo what you have done." He laughed suddenly. "What good is all the barley and the grain without the water to make the bread and the broth? They will look upon their bounty till their eyes fall from their heads, and then they'll die. When you get to that heaven you speak of, what will they say, those saints you pray to? Will they forgive you for giving with one hand and taking with the other? It would seem to me that when you arrive at this heavenly palace in the sky, you will have many things to answer for. Mount up! We ride on!"

Just as the moon moved from behind a cloud, Paxon halted the horses and spoke quietly. "This is what your Christian armies have done. Look at the torn, butchered bodies; look at the babies who lie without their mothers; look at the old people who had one hope, to get their wares to the sea. Even in the moonlight you can see the blood-soaked sands. There are thousands of dead bodies lying there with no one to bury them. The vultures and the birds will feast for weeks on their rotting flesh. The children will no longer laugh and cry; the babies will have no one to hold them in their arms; the old and the sick will have no one to aid them in their last years. This is what you've done; this is the senseless slaughter you made possible." His voice became savage as he forced her from the horse. "Walk! Walk through the dead and pray to your God to forgive you. Look at their faces so that their image is something you'll never forget!"

Valentina's stomach lurched threateningly. She couldn't move. She was paralyzed by guilt. God in heaven, was he right, would those faces be burned in her mind till the end of her days? God forgive me, for I have sinned, she prayed silently as she looked first at one dead face and then another. God forgive me, for I have sinned. Her eyes dry, a tight line about her mouth, she narrowed her gaze and turned it on Paxon. "I did what I had to do; I could do no less. I, and I alone, will have to live with what I've done, not you, not Saladin, not the Moslem armies. You are right, I will never forget this sight. I will carry it with me to my grave. How much farther to the next well?" she asked calmly.

Paxon watched her through slitted eyes. It wasn't possible, but she seemed to have regained her strength; a new and grim determination seemed to flow out of her.

The next day passed with Valentina doing Paxon's bidding. As each well was filled she died a little. Would those young men ever see their families again? She was taking the one thing from them that they needed most, and then she would die for her efforts. All through the long, backbreaking hours there were always Paxon's eyes boring into her, willing her to beg for mercy, to beg for water, to beg. She would not beg. When she couldn't stand the agony any longer, she would lie down and die in the hot sands. Nothing mattered any more.

From some deep, invisible force Valentina gained the strength to do Paxon's bidding. At last he seemed to tire of the sport and ordered her to mount up. They continued to head north. Valentina glanced questioningly at Paxon.

"Yes," he said, "in a few hours we will reach Jerusalem. You will have a choice to make. Your complete and willing surrender, or your death."

Valentina kept her eyes straight ahead, toward Jerusalem, toward her death.

Three hours later they came upon a solidly constructed Moslem stronghold. Paxon felt something stir in him as he led the exhausted Valentina into a barren, stone-walled cell. His arrogant, speculative expression sent fear coursing through her as she tried to imagine what his next move would be. She knew she looked terrible, her dark hair hanging in strings down her back, her clothing torn and tattered, her skin dry and parched from her hours spent in the withering heat. The idea of a warm bath and clean clothes would be a luxury, a luxury that would be denied if she were to ask, and she would die before she asked. She would ask nothing of this tall, arrogant Saracen, except perhaps a speedy death.

"I see you're trying to determine my next move," Paxon said coolly. Slowly he looped a section of a heavy chain around her neck and snapped it shut. His movements, meant to torment, were just as slow when he attached the other end of the chain to weathered bars in a high, square window. "If you struggle you'll choke to death. You are my prisoner, a prisoner of the Moslems! Your fate will be decided shortly," he said mockingly, his eyes hot and smoldering.

Valentina forced a smile to her lips, her own eyes stormy. "Your mouth tells me I am your prisoner, but your eyes tell another story." Suddenly she laughed throatily as she gazed at him. "Even now you want me—admit it!" she taunted. "You've waited for me to cry and mew, to beg you to set me free, to barter my freedom with my body. You want to be gracious in your refusal. You can't understand why I haven't broken, why I'm still alive. We both know that another would have bent beneath the task you set before me." She advanced a step, only to be pulled backward by the heavy chain collar. She swallowed and remained still, her head held high. "Somehow I will get free of you, and when I do . . ."

"You are hardly in a position to make threats," Paxon said coolly, narrowing his eyes. "When your king meets his ultimate demise, I want you there to see it. Your Lionheart will never set foot in Jerusalem, you have my word."

"And you have my word that I will be free of you! Do you think this damnable chain is going to keep me here? Think again, Saracen. Somewhere, in some place, there are *fedawi* who will help me. This—this—trinket you have holding me here is just that, a trinket!"

She knew her threat was empty. She had slipped out of Napur in the dead of night to be free of Paxon's spies and Menghis's *fedawi*. Her present situation was hopeless.

His laugh was brutal, mocking, as he stared at her. "Perhaps. But by that time your body will be so wasted you'll die. I have no fear of the *fedawi*. They are men, just as I am, and they are flesh, as I am, and they can be killed just as I can be. Remember what I said. If you move you'll strangle yourself. It will be interesting to see how long you can stand on your feet. You will be given water, nothing more."

"Thank you, your majesty," Valentina taunted. "If I could bow to your majestic presence, I would. When you next set eyes on me, I will be standing here, just as I am now. I will be alive while my heart and my mind plot your death. And if for some strange reason I should die, then my spirit will be here, and I promise you that it will follow you through all eternity. It will haunt and torment you for the rest of your days!"

Her low, throaty laugh sent a chill up his back. What kind of woman was she? Shackled as she was, she could look at him with defiance turning her eyes to a glittering green. A few more hours on her feet with the heavy chain around her neck would tell a different story. A story he would see through to the end.

With the sound of the quietly closing door, Valentina's spirits sank. She looked around the empty cell and knew for the first time that she would die. There was no way she could remain on her feet. Was it possible to sleep on one's feet without moving? No, her legs would give out and she would choke to death. Her head reeled sickeningly, her eyes glazed, and she felt herself slumping forward.

A sound in the room pulled her awake. Though her vision was blurred, she noted two figures. She felt herself being raised off the floor and nestled in the strong arms of the two men. A piece of meat and a piece of fruit were thrust into her hands. Tears blinded her eyes as she devoured the succulent meat and the juicy fruit. Only one word was spoken by the two men, a quiet command to "sleep." Valentina needed no second urging. Her heavily fringed eyes closed, and she slept in the arms of the *fedawi.* From time to time she felt her body being shifted from one man to the other, and in her dreams it was Menghis's arms that comforted her.

Suddenly she felt herself shaking violently as she was placed gently on her feet. She blinked in the dimness of the cell and felt, rather than saw, the men leave. Did her eyes deceive her, or had they passed

372

through the thick stone walls? No, it was just a cleverly concealed doorway.

She forced her eyes wide open and stood erect as Paxon entered the room. If he was surprised to see her still on her feet, she could read no sign of it in the semidarkness.

"Good evening, your majesty. Forgive me for not bowing in your presence, but as you can see, I am . . . indisposed. You thought you would find me dead, is that it? I told you I would survive! Ah, I see by the look in your eyes that you aren't sure if I'm real or if this is my spirit talking to you." Her low, amused laugh sent the hackles on Paxon's neck to twanging. "Would you like to touch me to see if I'm real? No?" Again she laughed. "Are you telling me that all desire for me has left you? I see you can't make up your mind, you can't made a decision. Why is that? Ah, I see, you really *do* think this is my spirit talking to you. Actually," she continued to taunt him, "I have died, and now I am an angel. You do know what an angel is, don't you? Those ethereal beings we Christians believe in. We sprout wings in the dead of night and fly through the heavens. When we're tired of flying, we shoot arrows of love into all the Moslems. Then we sit on a cloud and watch all the Crusaders capture the Moslems, who are struck with brotherly love!" The low, husky laugh was so chilling, so barbaric, that Paxon flinched as the sound bounced off the walls and seemed to come to rest in the center of the empty cell.

Blazing anger raced across Paxon's face, and without a second thought he raised one large sun-bronzed hand and struck her sharply across her face, leaving a red imprint.

Tears smarted Valentina's eyes as she laughed. "We angels have long, never-ending memories. You'll rue the day you did that," she said quietly. "And the day will come when I'll loop this collar around your neck, and when I do I'll lead you through Jerusalem like a pet on a leash. Remember that."

"Perhaps I should write down all these things that

I'm to remember. The list continues to grow and I might become confused."

"It would amaze me if you knew how to write," Valentina baited him.

Paxon was not amused, and his voice was heavy with malice. "I can write well enough to sign your death warrant. I brought you water, but since you seem so well and hale and hearty, I see there is no need for it. The night will be long and cold, rest well."

"And I wish *you* well, Paxon, sultan of Jakard. Sleep well this night, for there may not be many nights left to you. Sleep, and dream of your walk through Jerusalem on a leash."

Paxon closed the heavy door behind him and strode over to the two burly guards who barred the entrance to the cell. His face a mask of fury, he lashed fiercely into the two men. "Who entered the cell?" he demanded.

"No one," the burlier of the two men said quickly. "No one was admitted to this cell."

"If the girl is still on her feet in the morning, you'll meet your death at the noon hour," he snarled unreasonably.

His mood murderous, Paxon strode down the hall to his quarters, his face cold and hard. She couldn't be an angel, could she? Why did he allow her to stir his emotions like this? She couldn't be human. No man or woman could stand for five hours shackled as she was and survive. Her body had to be weak from lack of food and water. Was that God of hers protecting her . . . or was it the *fedawi?* How had she done it? And she could still laugh at him! What was it that ran in her blood? Weariness overtook him as he lay down on his bed. Tired as he was, sleep would not come. Instead, his arms took on an ache that demanded attention. His body craved the flesh of the woman he held prisoner. His dark eyes hungered for the sight of her naked flesh.

He suddenly thrust his long legs over the side of the bed and was halfway to the door before he stopped. That was what she wanted, to see him come to her and remove the chain. Then she would laugh with abandon. His dark eyes narrowed, and he knew in his gut that no matter how many days he kept her locked in the cell, in spite of how many hours he kept her on her feet, no matter if she had neither food nor water, she would be standing there when he next entered the cell. She would win. She would survive whatever he inflicted. She would survive everything save her death.

His heart pounded in his chest as he paced the room, trying to quench the desire threatening to engulf him. In his frenzy he smashed a ewer of water and then smacked first one large fist and then the other against the stone wall. The pain was a welcome release to his tortured emotions.

Daylight arrived, and the sun blessed the walled city of Jerusalem with a clear brightness. Rising above the walls surrounding the city, the sun reflected its glory in the pools of the markets and illuminated the reliefs on the eastern walls of the Holy Sepulchre, leaving the western edifice in deep shadow. People had been teeming into the marketplace for hours before sunrise. The Jews of the city were frantically setting up their stalls and displaying their merchandise. It was Friday, and they had only until a few hours before sunset when, according to their custom, all trade would halt in celebration of the Sabbath.

Red-eyed and weary from lack of sleep, Paxon prepared himself for the day. Earlier a missive had come to him from Saladin, requesting his presence at a council meeting to be held in his pavilion outside the gate of Magharib. Paxon was loath to attend the meeting. All present would know of his disgrace concerning the Egyptian caravan. As the hour neared, his mood became blacker and his thoughts focused on Valentina. Deliberately he tarried with his morning ablutions, sparing no time to look in on her. Pulling on one boot and stamping his foot forcefully on the tiled floor to seat its heel, he hoped she had died during the night. Lashing his belt around his hips and positioning his scimitar properly, he prayed she still lived. Disgusted with his vacillation, Paxon stalked out of his chamber, his thoughts murderous, dreading the moment when he would face Saladin.

Saladin called his council. As the leader of the Islamic forces, he would decide on the plan of defense. Into the pavilion the men thronged, seating themselves and exchanging whispered greetings. Many familiar faces were missing from the circle. Al Adil, Saladin's shrewd brother, had been sent to stifle a revolt in the land beyond the Euphrates, and Taki ad Din, who had been Saladin's right-hand man, had been laid to rest in a lonely grave on the eastern frontier.

When Paxon entered the pavilion, all voices were stilled. His discomfort was evident in the set lines of his face and by the moisture accumulating on his brow.

Instead of reproaching him, as everyone expected, Saladin rose from his seat and took Paxon into his arms. "You are a mighty soldier, and your failure is for all of us here to bear. The small amount of men with you would not have been enough to quell a village of nagging women. Sit among us, Paxon. You are not in disgrace in this camp."

Paxon felt an overwhelming gratitude as he moved to take the place beside Saladin which the general had indicated.

Then Saladin gestured to Baha ad Din, the learned chronicler who was his aide and companion. "Speak to us of the war. We will benefit from your knowledge." While Baha ad Din spoke, Saladin struggled with his thoughts, knowing that the mood of his chieftains shifted between zealousness and dread. They feared that a siege upon Jerusalem would be another Acre, and they wanted to keep to the open plains.

When Baha ad Din ended his talk, Saladin turned to face his chieftains. "In my hand I hold a missive from Aboul Heidja. The *mamlūks* and his officers have reached a conclusion. They blame us for wishing to shut ourselves away in the city of Jerusalem. They fear it will be Acre for the second time and that our country will fall into the hands of our enemy. They feel we would do better with a range battle. Only then, if Allah shows his mercy, would we be the masters. If we were defeated we would lose Jerusalem, but our armies would be saved."

Saladin knew that the missive also reflected the opinions of the chieftains who graced his pavilion. He was grieving at heart because he had a deep attachment for this city of Jerusalem, a true love. "Another missive has also reached me. It states that the armies of the enemy are less than two days from where we now sit. They are divided in their intent. There are those who wish to descend on the city and others who intend to return to their own territory. While they are divided, we have our greatest opportunity. We must leave Jerusalem to the mercy of Allah, and we will march on to Jaffa and meet the 'Unbeliever' there."

Sage heads nodded in agreement. After the inertia of a year's defensive caution, Saladin would lead his armies from Jerusalem to Jaffa.

An hour before sunset the two *fedawi* lowered Valentina to her feet and gave her a drink of water. "Will you return to the mountain?" she asked softly. Receiving no response, she sighed heavily. And then she was alone in the quiet cell, the last streaks of daylight creeping through the high window. Paxon would be here soon, and then she would see what he was going to do. What would he say this time? How would he react to her still being alive? Would he finally set her free? What would he do with her? Her fate rested with him.

Paxon thrust open the door, knowing full well that she would be standing erect, her eyes mocking and defiant. He wasn't disappointed. Quickly, before he could change his mind, he released her from the chain. Dark eyes looked into hers, and he took her by the arm and led her out into the twilight. He waited, his face expressionless, as she mounted the horse he assigned her.

Two of the guards rode alongside her as Paxon spurred his horse and galloped to the head of the line with Saladin. Paxon grinned, his teeth gleaming. "I made my decision," he said arrogantly.

From time to time Paxon would shield his eyes and stare into the desert. He knew the *fedawi* were out there somewhere, doing whatever it was they did in the desert. They would protect the girl with their last breath. Would he get her to Jaffa, and if he did, what would he do with her then?

Chapter Twenty-eight

R ichard the Lionheart had made his decision. The Christian army broke into fragments and turned back from the hills of Jerusalem. The French were unforgiving of Richard's hesitation and left him to take to the north, while other factions of his army wandered off toward Jaffa. Richard himself scurried off to Acre to lick his wounds and find some honorable reason to leave behind the fiasco of the Crusade and return to England. He had only lingered this long in the Holy Land because of his promise to take Jerusalem. Now this task seemed impossible. He accepted his failure bitterly and started toward the sea.

As Valentina rode among the gathering army of Saracens, which now numbered twenty thousand mounted men, her fearful gaze noted the hundreds of siege engines. The machines were packed on the backs of camels and mules. The throng of Moslems who clung to the flanks of Saladin's ranks exulted in songs and tales predicting that soon the "Unbeliever" would be driven out of their land. At last!

While Saladin's enormous column of men-at-arms snaked toward Jaffa, Paxon rode back to where Valentina was riding under close guard. His black eyes gleamed with the prospect of victory and his smile was broad and mocking. "Soon now, Valentina," he said confidently while he watched for her reaction, "you will see how efficiently our army moves. With your own eyes you will watch the Christians be driven into the walls of Jaffa where we will trap them like rats!"

Valentina's face remained unreadable and she regarded him unflinchingly. Her eyes were a deep and murky green and gave Paxon little satisfaction. "Not a tear shed for your countrymen, Valentina?" he scorned.

"Not for my countrymen, nor for you. I've done what I could do; the rest is in the hands of my God."

"And who is your God? The Lionheart?" He laughed, a deep, roaring laugh which held no humor.

"Is it possible you're not as certain of victory as you would have me believe?" she asked softly, her voice deep and husky and ringing through the core of him.

"I am as certain of this victory as I am of your death," Paxon snarled. How could she remain so calm in the face of her people's destruction? In the face of her own destruction? Was she truly in his blood, and even if he did put her to death, would she ever really die as long as her memory would haunt him? As long as he would yearn to hold her in his arms? Suddenly his face darkened. If this was truth, then Valentina would live as long as he himself would live. She would be immortal as long as his body still possessed life. He would always want her, always desire her!

Valentina gazed steadily into Paxon's eyes. She knew this! he realized. She was aware of her hold over him! She knew that her death would not be the end for him, but only the beginning. The beginning of a long life in which he sought her in the arms of other women, in their voices, in their beds. By the fury of Allah, what had gone wrong?!

Paxon left her, his steed tearing up great clumps of earth as he charged to the head of the column.

Onward they rode, Valentina's gaze finding familiar faces among the men in the column. *Fedawi!* Would they seek to gain her release? No, she thought, all hope ebbing. If her release was their goal, it would have been accomplished while Paxon had her chained to the wall. Menghis must have sent them to watch over her and later report to him what fate she had met.

The sun was bright and beat down upon her, and yet it could not warm her. There was a coldness in her soul which presaged her very own death.

Valentina stayed with the main body of Moslems while raiding parties took to the field in search of wandering Christians. The reports which filtered back heartened the men of Islam. The first contingent of Saladin's men had reached the walls of Jaffa and driven Crusaders from the field into the city and behind the newly reconstructed walls, to beg their God's mercy and protection. More than five thousand Christian soldiers were penned behind the walls as Saladin launched his main attack. The battle raged for three days. The Moslems gained the advantage and pierced the heavy gates of Jaffa.

From the hills outside the city, Valentina watched the horror of war. The Moslems had erected their engines and were bent on taking the walls. Mangonels, or catapults, were severely punishing the Christians. The solid beams creaked and groaned with the heavy weights that were loaded into the spoonlike bowls which then hurled their contents at the walls. The counterweights gave the propelling force and crashed down in a deafening thunder.

Heedless of the raining arrows showering down upon them, the Moslems worked over the bodies of the fallen. Swung from ropes attached to a framework of beams, and covered by stretched goatskins which acted as a shield to protect the men working it, the battering ram pummeled the gates with the sound of splintering wood.

Valentina had heard the order given to sap beneath the walls at the far end of the city, which faced the sea. Tunneling beneath the thick walls was a last resort, Valentina knew, but Saladin was not allowing chance to defeat him. He would be prepared, no matter what the outcome. This was merely a precautionary measure. There was no doubt of the outcome of this battle.

Even now the belfries were positioned at the high walls. These tall wooden structures were mounted on wheels and pushed up to the walls. Armed men flocked beneath the covering of arched shields to climb the inner ladders, and from where Valentina stood, they looked like a phalanx of armed ants scurrying over the walls.

Cries of the dying reached her ears as she watched the outnumbered Christians meet the Moslem attack with longswords drawn. Bowmen and javelin throwers braved the onslaught. Valentina's eyes kept traveling to the Christian standard waving over Jaffa. Endlessly the melee continued and still the Christian banner waved, until the mournful sound of the chieftain's horn was heard. Before her tearful eyes the Christian banner was lowered, and rising in the waning light of dusk was the yellow and black standard of Saladin.

Hope died. The Moslems had broken into Jaffa, and although they were victorious in their immediate success, the ultimate defeat would come at a later stage in the war. Valentina knew her people. The Christians would never relinquish the right to the home of their faith. They would continue to fight. Another army would be recruited; more gold would find its way to the weapon makers and armor fitters. Defeat at the hands of the Moslems would never be tolerated.

Richard was weary with the Crusade; his interests were centered upon protecting his throne in England. Saladin was also weary of the war, which demolished his homeland and slaughtered his people; but if this siege he waged on Jaffa proved successful, he would once again taste victory and have no desire for a truce. *In order for peace to reign, Saladin must lose Jaffa!*

While the battle still raged, Valentina witnessed three men storm over the walls and drop down into the midst of the Moslem warriors. The bravery of these Christians swelled her heart. As she watched they seized three mounts from the attacking Moslems and rode out.

Instinctively Valentina knew that their mission was to ride to Acre for reinforcements. Silently she cheered them on until one by one, each man fell beneath the blade of a Saracen scimitar. Crestfallen, Valentina shed tears of hopelessness. Acre, reinforcements, King Richard, her heart cried. Suddenly she came to life again. The Christian envoys never had a chance, but she, sitting outside the walls, did!

Frantically her eyes searched for the familiar faces of the *fedawi*. At last she saw them, looking down upon Jaffa, mesmerized by the scene taking place below. Seizing the opportunity, Valentina slipped away from her guards to the *fedawi*. Hurriedly she whispered her orders before the ensuing guardsmen could recapture her. The *fedawi* looked at her questioningly, but when she whispered the name of *Sheikh al Jebal,* they scurried to do her bidding.

Paxon found Valentina where he had left her with the guardsmen. He assumed that she would be as defeated as the Christians behind the walls, and he was surprised to find this stalwart young woman who gazed directly into his eyes, seeking the answers to questions her lips would not ask. "Victory is ours, Valentina. See how ineffectual your scheming has been? Your efforts to aid your Christians had little effect on the final outcome."

"Yes, victory is yours," Valentina whispered. "You have won."

"If you were to plead for your life, perhaps I would listen," Paxon said. "I'm feeling most charitable at this moment." His eyes searched hers, pleading with her, begging her to say the words which would free him from his promise to issue her death warrant.

Valentina's silence blazed through him. She would prefer death to belonging to him! Nothing could make her say the words he demanded to hear. "We ride into Jaffa. Prepare yourself," he said gruffly.

Wordlessly she turned away, feeling his glaring eyes. What he wanted to hear she found impossible to say.

Down the hills and over the plains leading to the broken gates of Jaffa, Valentina rode with the long column of victorious Moslems. Spirits were high, and little attention was paid to her. Paxon rode with Saladin at the head of the ranks. Through the battlefield she rode, averting her eyes from the bodies of the fallen. The stench of the battlefield filled her nostrils, and the harsh cries of the circling vultures churned her soul. Would these same scavengers of the desert soon tear morsels of flesh from her own body?

Paxon had given orders to have Valentina taken to the *sikhara,* a miniature watchtower topped with a minaret, which rested upon the rocky slope above the sandy shore. "You'll be safe there," he explained. "Spirits ride high in the men, and the rich plunder of Jaffa is very tempting."

"Do you care so much for my safety?" Valentina asked challengingly.

"I care only that *I* be the one to command your death! I have no wish to find that you have robbed me of that satisfaction by meeting your death at the hands of a crazed soldier."

"Are all the men of Mohammed crazed, then?" Valentina retorted.

Fury rose in Paxon. "You are the most contrary woman I ever had the misfortune to meet!" he roared, grabbing her shoulders and shaking her hard. "You will accept my protection just as you will accept my punishment!" She was flung away from him, and her eyes blazed—not with hate, but with a sadness that cut into his heart.

Paxon's men led Valentina through the back

streets of Jaffa. Crazed with its victory, Saladin's army was beyond its general's control. Shops and dwelling places were looted, the Moslems set their torches to a monastery, and before Valentina's revolted eyes they ransacked and destroyed a church. Smoke permeated the air and dreadful sounds of butchery poured from the alleys.

Thankfully, the far end of the city was quiet, the noise of madness behind her. Here, where the tang of the sea and the gentle lapping of surf could be heard, Valentina was ensconced in the turret.

Before the hordes of invading Moslems, the Christians retreated. Some tried to escape into boats, while Alberic of Rheims, the commander of Jaffa, tried to quit the city in one of the vessels. But his knights pulled him back and led him to a tower within a quarter of the city that was still held by Crusaders. Less than two thousand men had survived the Moslem attack, and now they were in a most precarious situation. The walls of the citadel in which they stationed themselves had not been entirely rebuilt, and the cowardly Alberic held little hope for their survival.

Valentina rested in safety, yet her mind traveled the journey to Acre, to King Richard, and she prayed he would not tarry with his assistance.

Saladin fought to restore order among his ranks and to launch a new attack upon the citadel in which the remainder of the Christian army took refuge. His soldiers refused to obey him. Defeated, Malik en Nasr retired to his tent, which was pitched near the baggage trains, and he was joined by his officers. There was nothing the general could do but allow his men to run themselves out and come to their senses.

Valentina lay in her bed, but sleep would not come. She counted the hours minute by minute, judging the length of the journey Richard would make from Acre. Turning over and over in her troubled mind what she could do to help him gain access to the city. In her loneliness, visions of Menghis filtered through her thoughts. She lay beside him deep in the woods on a grassy knoll where the stars blessed their love. Menghis! her heart cried in anguish. Is this how it will end for me—never to see him or love him again? Oh, Menghis!

King Richard had placed himself in command of the galleys which drifted soundlessly beyond the surf of the Jaffa beach. News of the Moslem attack on Jaffa had reached him while he was making the last of his preparations for embarking upon his journey to Europe. The strange men who brought the message for his ears alone had cried out that Jaffa was taken. Unless help reached the city at once, all would be lost. If it struck Richard as strange that the messengers were Moslems, he did not say so. He only knew that he was needed and that this was his one chance to restore his honor.

Richard boarded his galley, accompanied by the Earl of Leicester and Andrew of Chavigny. Hundreds of men-at-arms and volunteers put out to sea, sailing along the coast, just beyond the horizon. They reached the Jaffa beach in the dead of night and harbored there till dawn, when they would launch their attack.

When the first light of day arrived, there was nothing to cheer the Christian hearts. The beach was overflowing with Moslems and Turks, and above the strip of sand smoke billowed from the low gray wall of the city, half a mile away. Moslem banners flew over the fortress that stood on a low headland above the sand.

Slowly the galleys moved closer, Richard standing with his knights beneath the red awning on the stern while he scanned the shoreline. To attempt to force their way across the beach in the face of Saladin's army would be suicide. To all appearances they were too late. It was the consensus that all the Christians within the walls of Jaffa were dead.

Valentina watched the horizon for signs of King Richard. She had always believed that he would come by way of sea, as the journey was so much shorter. There, in the first light of day, she saw Richard's galleys! King Richard and reinforcements! Her heart beat in her breast as she waited for some sign that he would make his move to help the trapped Crusaders, praying that he would not fail to assert his command, as in Beth Nable.

Her attention was caught by a black-garbed figure as he dropped over the wall beneath her window. He fell heavily to the sand below, and she held her breath as she waited for him to regain his feet. Fearlessly the figure raced through the camps of Moslems and dove into the cool green sea. She followed his progress over the swells and saw him swim toward the nearest galley. Someone on the galley must have witnessed his daring plunge into the water, for the ship lifted sail and was drifting toward the swimmer.

Richard, too, had seen the man swim toward the galley. He ordered that the man be picked up. The swimmer proved to be a priest of the garrison. Breathless and dripping sea water, he dropped to his knees before the English king. "Mighty king, the Christians await you. All is lost to them without your aid."

"Christians!" Richard bellowed. "Alive! We thought them all dead! Where are they?"

"Shut within the citadel on the eastern side of the city."

Richard took his first assertive action since directing the galleys to Jaffa. "Damnation to all who hang back!" he swore at his commanders.

Ordering his vessel to row in, he took his place at the bow. The long oars dipped and rose, and the red galley with its dragon's head slipped into the line of the swell, followed by the fleet.

The men armed themselves for battle, fastening their longswords and shields about themselves. Richard's galley was the first to grate upon the sand. It rolled in the swell while the Moslems ashore shouted their war cries and waited for the Christians to touch land.

Mesmerized, Valentina watched the pageant below. She couldn't just stand there! There must be something she could do! She thought of Richard's armed men trying to scale the walls of Jaffa. It would be suicide!

The Moslems would take the advantage. With the Christians hampered by their heavy armor, their losses would be uncountable.

Valentina thrust open her window and leaned far out over the sill. There, just below her, she could see the overhanging keystone of a gate. If only that gate could be opened, it would save countless lives. But how? Paxon had seen to it that she was under guard every moment. Even now two of his men stood outside her locked door. The drop from her window to the sand below was too far a fall. What use would she be if she lay there dead?

There was only one hope. Quickly, before she could reconsider, Valentina ran to the locked door and pounded upon it with her fists, shouting loudly to the guards and hurling insults.

"Moslem sons of dogs! Plague-ridden curs! Followers of the Koran, the recitation of idiots and madmen!" On and on she raved, each epithet worse than the one before it. She cursed Mohammed, the Koran, Allah himself!

"Shut your mouth, woman," one of the guards threatened, "else we'll shut it for you!"

"You! You are less than the dogs of the alley! Less than the flies of the desert! You are weak like children! Only the believers of the 'True Cross' are men! You are less, you are lice!" she shouted, baiting them. At last she heard the key being inserted in the lock. She ran to the far side of the room and shrieked, at the same time flinging herself beneath the low bedstead.

The guards burst into the room, scimitars drawn, their faces set in hard, murderous lines. They hesitated for a moment when they did not see her. The breeze from the sea caught the window and banged it against the side of the turret. Thinking she had leaped to her death, the guards hurried to look out. Valentina seized her chance. Scrambling from beneath the bedstead on the side opposite the window, she raced for the doorway, slamming the stout wooden door behind her and turning the key in the lock. The astonished guards banged on the door, their curses following her down the corridor.

Outside, Richard waded through the swell. For armor he wore only a mail shirt and a steel cap. On his shoulder he carried a crossbow, and his longsword clanked at his side. Shooting bolts at the Moslems, Richard gained the shore. His sword drawn, he slashed at the opposition, covered by the arrows that the shipmen plied from the prows.

The Moslems recognized the English king and drew back, incredulous. The knights of the realm circled about Richard, offering the protection of their bodies. Several other galleys were beached by this time, and equipment was tossed onto the sandy strip. Stools, benches, bedding, and beams were caught up by men and lugged ashore to form a barricade from which they could fight.

Richard was fraught with the frenzy of the battle. He refused to take a stand behind the barricades. Holding a shield before him, he ran across the beach to the gray wall of Jaffa. As he came closer he spied the postern gate that was just below the room in which Valentina had been held prisoner. He intended to scale the wall and find his way to that gate and open it. He was just about to attempt the wall when the postern gate flew open and he heard a low, throaty voice. "Sire!"

"Lady Valentina! Angel in my need!"

There was little time for more than a look of gratitude from the Lionheart as he pushed Valentina away from the gate and up the flight of stairs leading to the courtyard. "Find safety, Lady Valentina," he cautioned as his knights clanked up the stairs in his wake. "When I have regained the city, you'll travel back to Acre with me. Hold fast now," he warned. "The worst is yet to come."

The Lionheart clattered into the streets of Jaffa. The Moslem looters yelled in amazement at the sight of his dripping figure as he led his knights in battle. Back, back, the Lionheart pushed the Moslems till he gained the quarter of Jaffa which housed the trapped Christians.

By this time his galleys held the beach front and his banner was raised. The knights of the garrison took heart at his coming and sallied forth, driving the Moslems toward the outer city.

By his quick action, Richard brought about something of a miracle. The men from his galleys took the waterfront of Jaffa before Saladin's main body of men could come to oppose them. The disorganized Moslems in the streets fell beneath Richard's sword. The element of surprise caused Saladin to withdraw his men to the nearest hills to review the situation.

The news of Malik Ric's arrival spread over the countryside. And when evening came and Jaffa was quiet, some of the Saracen chieftains went to the Christian lines, curious to see this king who dared to land in the face of an entire army.

They came in peace and Richard admitted them. They found the Lionheart still in his mail shirt, surrounded by his knights. Nothing could have pleased Richard more than these dark Moslem chieftains in their ceremonious caftans. Saladin had already sent word that he was willing to discuss peace.

Ruddy-faced and victorious, Richard let it be known that he was ready for a truce.

Chapter Twenty-nine

Menghis sat quietly, his mind whirling as the thick, odious incense swirled about his head. He shouldn't be having these thoughts now that he was *Sheikh al Jebal*. There was no room in his mind for thoughts such as he was having. He had renounced the world below when he climbed the mountain for the first time. His life was over the moment he assumed his position on the throne. For now, for always, for-evermore, he was *Sheikh al Jebal,* and *Sheikh al Jebal* had no life, no meaning, beyond that of the Alamut.

He felt his chest constrict when he sensed the presence of the *fedawi* in the citadel. For a moment he thought his chest would explode when the men knelt at his feet and spoke to him reverently. "The woman rides toward Jaffa with the Saracen, the sultan of Jakard. At first he was intent on killing her, but now she is well and the *fedawi* ride unseen with her. Malik en Nasr will fight the Lionheart's armies at Jaffa." They told Menghis about Paxon's treatment of Valentina in the cell. "The woman asked if we were returning to the mountain. We gave her no answer." Menghis nodded slightly to indicate he had heard the words spoken, and the *fedawi* left his presence, bowing low.

The white panther, full-grown now, snarled and sprang to her feet, her teeth bared. Menghis laid a gentle hand on the cat's head but made no move to get up from his seat near the billowing incense pot.

Paxon with Valentina. How he must be gloating that he was keeping the promise he had made to Menghis on that stormy night so long ago. Was it really so long ago, or did it just seem that way to him in his solitary state? Everything seemed so long ago. Even his love and his remembrances of Valentina.

Valentina in Paxon's arms. Paxon's lips on hers. His brother's words came back to haunt him. Valentina belonged to Paxon now. Now that Menghis was *Sheikh al Jebal,* he had no claim on the beautiful dark-haired woman he had come to love so dearly. Now she belonged to Paxon. He said he would win. But Paxon could only win if he, Menghis, allowed him to. It wasn't too late. He could stand up and walk away from the Alamut; he could descend the mountain and claim Valentina. Then Paxon's prophecy would never come true. All he had to do was stand up and walk away. Leave the Alamut and the *fedawi* behind. When he started down the mountain he would no longer be *Sheikh al Jebal.* He would be Menghis.

The white panther stirred fretfully and opened one slanted, sleepy eye. Seeing nothing to upset her, she slept again, her long tail swishing and slapping on the tile floor.

Could he get up and turn his back on the Alamut? Could he give up what was meant to be his life? Could he do it for the love of a woman? The words of his father rang in his ears from a time long ago. They had been sitting in the garden, and the old man had been in frail health even then. He had been in a sorrowful mood that day and spoke lovingly and longingly of his dear dead wife. The words Menghis recalled were exact and precise. "Some men are fortunate to love only one woman in a whole lifetime. If a man is fortunate enough to find such a woman, he needs nothing more. A man could move mountains with his love."

Shadjar got to her feet, waiting quietly, gently nuzzling Menghis's hand.

"Yes, Shadjar, I too am ready," Menghis said, getting to his feet. "I might not be able to move a mountain, but I can descend one to find my love."

The *fedawi* looked at Menghis in awe as he shed his white garb and dove into the crystal-clear spring. He shook his head to clear it and climbed from the pool, all odor of the smoldering incense gone. "Now I can think," he said to Shadjar. "A few small matters to attend to, and then we will leave this mountain."

Dressed in his doeskin garb, Menghis walked one last time around the Alamut, his face smooth and unreadable. From time to time he made a sign to a few of the *fedawi*. One last walk near the area where the deer fed, and then he was ready to leave.

In the citadel he scrawled a message to the council:

> "I, known by you as *Sheikh al Jebal,*
> find the lures of the world too
> tempting. I am unworthy to be
> Master of the Alamut.
>
> "Menghis."

He was at the edge of the grassy knoll, ready to descend the mountain, when he remembered something. He literally raced back to the women's quarters and gathered the wide-eyed Aloe Bud to him. "I'm going to take you to a new home," he said softly. This time you will have no desire to return to Alamut. This time I promise you happiness." The child asked no questions, seeing safety and concern for her in his dark eyes. She held his big hand in hers as they walked to the edge of the knoll. Neither looked back. He lifted her to the saddle to sit before him, her head resting trustingly against his chest. Behind them came a sound of someone or something crashing through the underbrush. Menghis stiffened, ready for action. He never thought they would try to stop him. From out of the shrubbery leaped a white form. Shadjar! "So you miss her, too, you feline fury. Come along, then. We all go back to the world of the living."

When they reached the foot of the mountain, Menghis looked around for his loyal *fedawi* and then remembered. The *fedawi* were no more. They would serve a new master. He was no longer *Sheikh al Jebal*. He was Menghis. A horrible thought struck him as he made his way along the dusty road to Napur with Aloe Bud at his side. If the *fedawi* no longer guarded and protected him, they would no longer guard Valentina and keep her safe. Pray to Allah he could travel faster than the word of his abdication. Else she would be at Paxon's mercy! And she was alone. She was as alone as he was.

For hours they rode along the dusty road, skirting the foothills until they came in sight of Napur and Ramiff's palace. Menghis marched the tired child up the wide gates and asked for an audience with the palace guard named Ahmar. He requested a fresh horse and safekeeping for the child, telling Ahmar that sometime soon he would return to the palace with Valentina.

Ahmar nodded. "Perhaps you would be so kind as to give the mistress a message from me," he said hesitantly.

"I will deliver the message. I cannot promise you when, but it will be delivered."

"Tell the mistress that Rosalan has given birth to a male child."

Menghis's eyes darkened. "When did the birth occur? Does the sultan of Jakard know of the birth?"

"Five days ago the small miracle happened. No, the sultan is not aware of the birth. From the moment the child uttered his first cries, he became my son," Ahmar said humbly. "I beg of you, do not tell the sultan. Neither Rosalan nor myself could bear it if he were to come here and claim the child, as is his right. Will you give me your word? I wish to place Rosalan's mind at ease." Ahmar smiled. "I tell you our secrets and I don't even know your name. Perhaps it is enough for me to see anxiety in your eyes for Mistress Valentina to know you can be trusted."

"I am Menghis."

Ahmar's eyes lit up and a wide smile creased his face. "Bring her back where she belongs . . . Menghis."

"Yes, I will bring her back where she belongs. May your son have a long and happy life."

Menghis's eyes dropped to the child at his side. "Aloe Bud, give your word to me that you will not run away from here and go back to the mountain. Stay here and care for Shadjar. She longs to hear her mistress's voice, just as we do. Soon I will return here with Valentina, and when I do I will want to rest my eyes on your beautiful little face. Your promise to me, give it to me now, I want to hear it."

"I will stay," Aloe Bud said happily. "As long as you give me your promise to return for me." She tugged on Menghis's arm so that he would lower his head. She whispered in his ear, and he smiled down at her and nodded. "I think it can be arranged, little one."

Ahmar looked at the giggling child and the smiling man who held her tiny hand so protectively. Menghis turned to him and said, "Aloe Bud wishes to know if she can see your son and if you will permit her to sing to the infant. I can personally vouch for her singing voice. It is as true as a bell."

Ahmar handed Aloe Bud over to one of the servants with instructions before he went to fetch a horse for Menghis. He stood for a long time with his feet spread slightly apart, his arms crossed over his broad chest. When the lone rider and horse were gone from sight, he returned to the palace, to Rosalan and his son.

He stood quietly outside the door watching Aloe Bud gaze down into the wicker basket holding the infant. She was crooning something soft and heart-warming. There was a smile on Rosalan's face as she looked at the child and then at her son. How beautiful they were. Like a family. His family. It made no difference to Ahmar that he had not fathered the child. If it was of Rosalan's blood, that was enough for him to love the tiny bundle of flesh.

Her song finished, Aloe Bud looked at Rosalan expectantly. "I never saw a baby before," she said shyly. "He is not pretty. He looks like a newly hatched bird with no feathers."

Rosalan pretended anger. "What is this you say, my child is not pretty? For now he looks as if he had been left in the sun too long. Soon he will thrive and be beautiful. One day he will be a king. I know this as surely as I know that you are standing next to me. A mighty king. He will rule his people fairly and justly. He will be full of kindness and compassion, and he will love all his brothers."

"Like Menghis," the child smiled. "He will be like Menghis."

Rosalan smiled at Aloe Bud. "Yes, like Menghis, and like the man who stands behind the door listening to us. Come here, Ahmar, and see how the baby improves. Do you agree that his cheeks look like they have filled out a little? He is not so red, and look how peacefully he sleeps. He must like Aloe Bud's tunes."

Ahmar bent down to stare at the sleeping baby, a fierce look of protectiveness in his eyes. His long arms circled Rosalan and Aloe Bud. "Together we will rear a mighty king," he said huskily.

Tears glistened in Rosalan's eyes, and Aloe Bud squirmed in the hard circle of his arms. She liked it here, and she decided she would stay and wait for Menghis to return. Without Menghis on the mountain she had no desire to go back there. She would wait with these happy people who were also Valentina's friends.

Menghis dug his heels into the sleek flanks of Valentina's white Arabian. The eager stallion reared his head and sprinted forward. Menghis's laughter rang in the bright sunlight as he raced the long-legged animal.

While the Lionheart basked in his victory and Saladin retired to his tent to contemplate the plans of truce, Paxon, sultan of Jakard, was scouting the city for Valentina. His spies had infiltrated the Christian camps in search of news of her. As he had expected, there was nothing to be learned. As though the earth had swallowed her, she had disappeared. If she was beneath the protective cloak of the *fedawi,* he knew his search would be pointless. Yet he would not give up!

What was left for her to do? His men had told him of the trick she had played to gain her freedom from the turret. They had also told him that it was she who had opened the postern gate to admit the Lionheart. Where could she be? If she were with Richard, Paxon would know it. The Lionheart would have held her up to acclaim for her courage and quick-wittedness. No, he would not find her among the Christians. Then where? What would drive her? Where would she go? Suddenly he thought of Napur. Ramiff! She would be on her way to Napur!

Swiftly Paxon commandeered a horse and rode south out of the city.

Onward Valentina rode. She skirted her way around the Moslem camps to gain the byways to the plains. To Napur, to Ramiff's grave. The kindly old emir deserved to have his people mourn for him and show the proper grief. Homed, the son Ramiff had detested, was no longer a threat to Napur. Soon a truce would be signed between Moslem and Christian, and Saladin would have time to oversee the emir's kingdom. Onward she rode. Behind her Jaffa lay in the debris of war. Thousands of lives had been lost, Moslem and Christian alike, and in her heart she did not know which she mourned more.

The sky lightened in the east and found Valentina still within sight of the city. From over her shoulder she saw a lone rider gaining on her. Paxon! She let her glance travel off into the horizon, seeing a wide expanse of nothingness. He would capture her, he would take her. There was nothing to impede his doing so. There was no hope.

Paxon raced toward her and saw her glance back. She had seen him, he knew she had. Yet she wasn't racing off into the plains. Why was she just sitting there, waiting for him? It was as though the fight had gone out of her and she was ready to accept the inevitable.

Closer and closer, he bridged the distance between them.

Valentina steeled herself and waited. It seemed that all her life she waited for one thing or another.

Paxon reined in his emotions as he reined in his horse. His face was dark with rage. "It is well you waited," he said softly in a voice which belied his emotions. "I would have followed you to the ends of the earth."

Valentina merely nodded. There was no escaping the inevitable. "I knew you would come for me," she whispered huskily. "There is no escaping you."

He studied her face and found it unreadable.

The short ride back to Jaffa was an eternity for both of them. Valentina wordlessly allowed him to lead her back, knowing full well his intent. He would kill her.

Valentina's silence preyed on Paxon's mind. If only she would say something . . . anything! It was as though she were already dead. He had seen that look on the faces of men about to go into battle. The frightening resolve, the acceptance of the inevitable, the embracing of the fates. And the men who had worn this look had marched valiantly into battle, bravely facing the end. And it was always the end. They had never returned. . . . Or had she planned a trick? Trickery was second nature to her.

Back at Jaffa, Paxon dismounted and helped Valentina to her feet. When he lifted her down from the saddle, he resisted the impulse to crush her to him. To taste the sweetness of her mouth upon his. His eyes searched for hers, but she would not return his gaze. She expected death . . . but whose, his or her own?

The city was quiet in the early dawn. No one came to relieve him of the horses; he would have to see to them himself. "Wait for me here," he ordered her, knowing somehow that she would not try to escape.

Paxon turned to lead the horses to the watering trough. He heard her light step and swung about, to see her stumbling up the stone steps leading to a side tower overlooking an inner courtyard. This quadrant of the city had been allotted to the Moslems. The dungeons below the tower were now empty of prisoners, but outside, in the courtyard, there remained the grisly reminders of the executions that had taken place. The chopping block which had seen heads severed from bodies bore the stains of death. The pikes from which the severed heads were hung held skulls that had been picked clean by the vultures. Instruments of torture and rusty manacles still clung to the gray stone walls. And in the center of the courtyard stood the crucifix.

If it was Paxon's hope that Valentina would be frightened into hysteria at the sight of these things, all hope died. She had refused to ask him for her life! She would never ask him! He would be forced to wrestle with his sense of justice and his desire for this woman. Rage boiled in him when he realized her intent. Three days earlier, when the Moslem army had

397

swooped down upon Jaffa, the Christian flag had been torn down and Saladin's colors raised. Now she was going to raise the Lionheart's banner!

Paxon choked back a bellow as he watched her raise the Lionheart's banner atop the parapet in place of Malik en Nasr's golden dragon. Damn her soul, how did she manage that? All thoughts of battle forgotten, Paxon leaped over the hard stone steps and reached for Valentina, pulling at her and dragging her down. "I'll kill you for that!" he snarled. "My thoughts were to spare you and take you to Jakard with me. Now I see that I was in error. Your banner may fly in the wind, but you'll die for raising it. Now!"

He knew now that she would never belong to him, never give herself willingly. She belonged to Menghis. She had to die so that he could be free of her. It was the only way that he, Paxon, could continue with his life.

With no wasted motion, the boiling rage driving him, he thrust her against the hard wooden cross, not caring if the sharp splinters gouged at her flesh. Cruelly he stretched her arms out and bound them to the cross, and then her legs. Valentina uttered not a sound. His task finished, Paxon stood back and looked into her eyes, his jaw tense, his dark eyes smoldering. He had done it. Now he could allow her to hang there and die. Now to take that damnable banner of the Lionheart down so that it wouldn't be the last thing she would see.

"Paxon!" The sound of his name jarred him from his thoughts. The voice was low and throaty, almost a whisper. It was so faint he had to strain to hear what she was saying. He looked up at her, the blue of the sky a backdrop which matched her eyes. He knew her eyes to turn a peculiar shade of green in times of trouble and anxiety. But now her eyes were blue—deep sapphire-blue! Did she seek death? Perhaps in atonement for the guilt Paxon had forced upon her by making her walk through the dead after Richard had taken the caravan at El Khuwielfa.

"Paxon, even you aren't fool enough to ride off and

leave me here. The *fedawi* will cut me down the moment you are gone. If you want to be assured of my death, then you will have to stay. You will have to watch me die. You'll see my eyes burn in their sockets, you'll see my tongue become thick and swollen as it chokes me. I beg of you, don't cheat yourself of the pleasure of my exquisite death. Stay and . . . observe, please, if you can."

Paxon looked up at her as he gave the rope around her ankles a vicious twist. His eyes were narrowed, almost closed against the glare of the sun. His tone, when he spoke, was nonchalant, almost conversational. "The sun has blinded you. Your *fedawi* left long ago. Do you think for one moment that I did not know they would free you? But you're wrong. They would have attacked me the moment I strung you to the cross. They would not wait for me to leave. They're gone, Valentina! You and I are the only ones left. And I'll be leaving in a few moments. Even my stomach is not strong enough to watch the vultures pick the flesh from your bones."

"You lie!" Valentina whispered hoarsely. "The *fedawi* would never leave me to die here like this." In her heart she knew the black-eyed Saracen spoke the truth. Even now she could not give him the pleasure of allowing her to think she believed him. "If they've gone, they'll come back," she said bravely.

"You'll be dead," Paxon said heartlessly. "Two more hours in this boiling sun and the spirit will leave your body. No, Valentina, the only one who can save you is me."

Valentina tried to force her numb brain to think. Why did the *fedawi* leave? Tears scorched her eyes and her throat constricted. Did they go to warn Menghis? What could Menghis do? Suddenly her head jerked upright. Of course! Why hadn't she thought of it? The *fedawi* only protected her as long as Menghis was *Sheikh al Jebal*.

Menghis was coming for her! Did Paxon realize what the absence of the *fedawi* meant? Not likely, for if he did he would never leave her alone and ride off.

"You're wrong, Paxon," Valentina said, her face alight with happiness. "Menghis will save me."

"Pray for that to happen, Valentina," Paxon said coldly. "I have one more thing to do before I ride off. I'll pray that you don't suffer too much."

The laughter, when it came, shocked him. "It is well that I can go to my death and know you had at least one good quality. If you should ever have cause to think of me, remember that I forgave you for my death. As I pass into eternity I will think of you riding across the desert. Good-bye, Paxon. Leave me now, keep your eyes straight ahead, do not look back, for if you do I may weaken and plead for my life."

Atop the parapet, Paxon removed the Lionheart's banner and stood for a moment looking down at the beautiful Valentina. His emotions churned. Could he allow her to die on that cross? Would he be able to leave for Jakard knowing that he had left her there to die and for the vultures to pick at her flesh? He tossed out the colorful banner and watched it flutter to the ground and come to rest near the foot of the cross. Valentina gave no sign that she was aware of it.

She felt the vibration of hoofbeats and raised her head just as Paxon climbed down from the parapet. Pray to God it was Menghis. It had to be Menghis.

A loud roar of anger came from the base of the watchtower. Paxon led his horse to a spot near the cross and waited, a murderous look in his dark eyes. "It would seem that you were right. Your savior approaches."

Valentina smiled and whispered, "I knew he would come. I prayed with all my heart that he would come. Now tell me, Paxon, that the God I pray to does not hear me."

Chapter Thirty

Menghis rode into the courtyard, his eyes on Valentina as he spoke to Paxon. "It would appear, from the bodies that line the desert, that you have been busy."

"Your eyesight is accurate, Brother. Let us not add one more body to the growing number."

"The decision is yours, Paxon. Cut her down!" came the harsh command.

"What you ask is impossible. Ask me for my life, it is yours. Ask me to challenge your *fedawi,* and I will do it. Ask me for all the wealth of Jakard, and I will place it at your feet. Do not make the mistake of asking me to cut her down again. She deserves to die for what she did. And you, Menghis, you were a party to her conspiracy and you deserve to die with her. Because you are my brother, I will do nothing. If you persist, it will be you against me, brother against brother! Your *fedawi* are gone! On the other hand, my men wait for me just on the other side of that wall. They've been garrisoned there since the fighting ended, waiting to hear that they can return to their homes. Look!"

Menghis turned and saw that Paxon told the truth. A guardsman stood in the archway with a puzzled look on his face. Even while Menghis watched, two more guards joined him, and still two more.

"The choice is yours," Paxon said.

"So, my brother refuses my request. I'll cut her down myself! But," Menghis admonished, "you will watch me do it." Before Paxon could make a move, Menghis was off his horse and hacking at the rope that held Valentina to the cross. She collapsed against him, sobbing and clinging to him with every ounce of strength left in her body.

Paxon's chiseled features were consumed with rage as he watched Menghis lay his cheek against Valentina's hair. He almost choked on his own saliva as Menghis murmured low, soothing words near her ear and she relaxed against him, burrowing her head into his chest.

Paxon's tone was bitter when he spoke. "You gave up the Alamut for a treacherous whore. Our father would turn over in his grave if he could see you now. Tell me that what my eyes see is not true."

Menghis lifted his head from Valentina's dark tresses and looked at Paxon. "I came to claim that which is mine. But you're right about one thing, I did renounce the Alamut and the *fedawi*. Our father would be the first to understand why I did it. She belongs to me, Pax, and I'll kill you if I have to!"

"Those are brave words from a man who stands alone," Paxon said coldly.

"Brave, perhaps, but true, Pax."

"Seize him!" Paxon shouted. The waiting guardsmen raced toward Menghis and literally ripped him from Valentina's grasp, flinging him to the side of the cross. Stunned with the impact, Menghis shook his head to clear it, hearing Valentina protest as the guards dragged her behind them like a sack of flour.

Paxon tossed Menghis a longsword and moved back out of his brother's reach. Menghis was groggy and unsteady on his feet. He blinked his eyes, trying to bring Paxon's muscular body into his line of vision.

"We end it now, Menghis, and to the winner go the spoils!"

Menghis shook his head again. He saw the blow coming and tried to move out of the way. He took the force of the low blow to his shoulder and staggered backward. Paxon advanced, a look of fury in his eyes as he drove him backward, farther and farther, until Menghis was forced against the courtyard wall.

Menghis retaliated by dancing out of the way and

bringing up his arm and landing a hard blow to Paxon's right leg. Paxon stumbled, and Menghis pressed his advantage by lashing out with the longsword and striking at Paxon's low-flung arm. Metal clashed against metal as brother attacked brother.

Valentina let loose a high-pitched, bloodcurdling scream that made Menghis lurch to the side, the longsword coming against the side of his head. Paxon watched with wide eyes as blood spurted from the wound and Menghis fell to the ground. He made no movement at all. Paxon leaned over his brother, his eyes unreadable, his breathing ragged.

Valentina screamed again and beat at the guards who held her prisoner. "Let me go!" she cried. "Let me go! Murderer!" she screamed at Paxon. Kill me now, for you've just taken the only meaning to my life!"

His eyes narrowed as he brought up his hand and gave her cheek a stinging blow. "If there's one thing I cannot abide, it's a babbling woman," Paxon snarled. "Any more of it and I'll have you gagged. Use your breath to pray for your dead lover."

Valentina's eyes spewed fire as she said in a low, controlled voice, "For now I'll be quiet, but don't ever make the mistake of turning your back on me, because the moment you do I'll kill you. I have no reason to live now, so your threats of taking my life mean nothing to me. At this moment I welcome death so that I can be with Menghis."

Paxon began to force Valentina out of the courtyard, his touch punishing and cruel. "Unhand me! You mad dog!" she cried, struggling to free herself from his grasp. "I have to go to him—let me go!"

Paxon snarled, "He needs no one. There's nothing you can do for him. He's dead!"

"No, no!" she sobbed. "He can't be, he mustn't be! Please, please, let me go to him!"

Still he held her, steering her across the courtyard to the waiting mounts.

"Where are you taking me? Leave me alone!"

"To Jakard!"

Valentina turned in the saddle to see the spot where Menghis had fallen. Tears streamed down her cheeks as she silently made the sign of the cross and bowed her head. "Ramiff, Mohab, if it is possible, look after him till I can join you," she whispered.

When Paxon stopped to water the horses, Valentina slid from her horse and immediately attacked him, her nails raking and gouging his face. Blood oozed from a deep scratch in his cheek, and one eye began to swell alarmingly.

"Bitch," he snarled, grabbing her long flowing hair. "You'll pay for this," he said, flinging her to the ground, his hand pressed to his cheek.

"Murdering pig!" Valentina spat. "I'll do it again, and again, until you kill me."

"You're too eager for death. First you'll suffer. And let's understand one thing. My reasons do not concern your body. You're going to suffer for what you did to my people." Then he added cruelly, "You will die."

"You're a fool, an arrogant, insane fool," Valentina hissed as she staggered to her feet.

"Enough." Brutally he grasped her arm and flung her to the ground again. "It would be wise if you remained quiet, for if you do not, you may find yourself sprawling in the sands. Or," he continued thoughtfully, "I could take a page from your book and remove your clothes and make you walk through the desert as you made me do!"

"You would not dare!" Valentina snapped.

"Would I not?"

Valentina pressed her lips tightly together. She would not utter another word if he killed her. There was no doubt in her mind that he would do what he pleased, and so would she.

Paxon mounted behind her. Out of the city and into the desert they rode, at the beginning of a long, arduous journey.

Eventually she slept, her dark silken head pressed into the crook of her arm. She was awakened suddenly when she felt herself being dumped unceremoniously into the grass of an oasis near a sparkling spring. The ebony eyes stared down at her. Suddenly she was frightened for the first time, frightened of him, and frightened of the harsh, brutal power he exuded. This dark, hulking, smoldering-eyed man had killed Menghis, and he would kill her . . . when he was ready. God in heaven, what was he going to do to her now?

"I see by your eyes that you're frightened of me. That's the first sensible emotion I've known you to display. Menghis is dead, his *fedawi* are gone. There are just you and I in this vast desert. It would be wise for you to sleep with one eye open. I might take it into my head to murder you here and now!"

Valentina was like a wildcat. She attacked him again with her outstretched hands, scratching and clawing at his face. Paxon brought up his arm to ward off her feeble blows. "You're an inhuman beast and you don't deserve to live," she spat as she continued to pommel his chest with clenched fists.

"Your efforts are those of a flea against a wild mountain goat," Paxon said, grasping her thin wrists in a viselike grip.

"You're right, a goat," Valentina hissed, "a dirty, smelly mountain goat!" Licking her lips, she struggled in his grasp. The more she struggled the tighter his grasp became. She was thrown from him suddenly and landed sprawled at his feet. Before she could blink he tore her clothes from her body. They fought like wild animals and suddenly she was standing erect, her breathing ragged.

With a violent thrust of his hand, he threw her into the small spring. His own clothing discarded, he charged after her. Scrambling, she tried to elude him. Time and again he reached for her with an iron grasp and pulled her back into the water. Her body was bruised and sore. She felt herself slide backward in the sand, only to find his body come crashing down on her. His hands were everywhere, rough and demanding, demanding something she would not, could not, give him. Struggling, she kicked out and stratched his back till she felt the warm stickiness of blood trickle beneath her fingers. She screamed as her hair was pulled from her head, her face only inches away from Paxon's arrogant, triumphant smile. Her head was then forced back at an awkward angle. Clasping her long hair in his fists, he played with her, bringing her face to within inches of his and then thrusting her backward till she thought her neck would snap.

His mouth on hers, his strong, muscular legs twined around hers, making her incapable of movement, and he entered her.

Her struggles stopped, her mouth became passive, as she waited for him to take his pleasure. He then pushed her violently aside.

"Christian bitch," Paxon snarled through clenched teeth.

"Pagan bastard," Valentina hissed.

"Tell me about Menghis—I want to know," Paxon said hoarsely.

"That is for me to know and for you to wonder about. Cut out my tongue and I still won't tell you. If you ever do to me again what you just did, I'll gouge your eyes from their sockets and scratch your face to tatters; and when you look like the devil himself, I'll deprive you of your manhood! If you use the brains God gave you, you will never sleep again for fear I'll keep my promise to you!"

Paxon watched her through narrowed eyes as she settled herself against a palm tree, gathering the shreds of her clothing about her in a pathetic, childlike manner. From where he sat he could see tears stream down her cheeks. They weren't tears of anger for the abuse he gave her, they were tears shed for Menghis. Rage roared through him at the tears, and he wanted to kill her, now, to make her suffer. He wanted to hear her beg for her life, beg him so that he could deny her the one thing she wanted. Now this was denied him. Now she wanted to die so that she could be with Menghis.

It was always Menghis. It was Menghis who had the power. It was Menghis who had been chosen to go to the Alamut. There was no need to concern himself with Menghis any longer, Paxon thought savagely. Menghis was dead! Menghis would never haunt him again. He watched as Valentina wiped at her eyes, her face sorrowful as she sighed deeply. What was she thinking now that Menghis was dead? His gut churned at what he knew she was thinking and feeling. He knew there was nothing he could do but sit here and watch her and suffer with her. He would suffer as long as she was alive, and he would suffer when she died. He would never win. He couldn't win. Not now, not ever. And it was all because of Menghis! Even in death he had won. "Bastard!" he said through clenched teeth. "Bastard!"

Valentina, her eyes dry, gulped back a threatened sob. Menghis was dead and she was alive. How unjust, how unfair. She raised her eyes and pleaded silently: I don't understand. Menghis was the man of peace; why did he have to die? What is to become of me? How can I live without Menghis? He was my life, my reason for living. I've never asked for much, and all I ever wanted was for Menghis to love me as I love him. I wanted him to comfort me and hold me close. I wanted to bear his children. I wanted to be able to look into his eyes and see a mirror of my love. Take me, please. Let Paxon kill me. I do not want to live.

Paxon stood and flexed his arms, the muscles in his broad chest bunching beneath his bronze skin. His gaze was mocking and arrogant as he watched her eyes travel over his chest and come to rest on his face. He wanted her suddenly, more than he ever wanted anything. He wanted to hold her in his arms, to whisper all the words that men whisper to their women. He wanted to feel her mouth respond to his and he wanted her body to match his in desire and passion. He forced himself to resist the urge to grasp her arm and bring her to him.

Would she ever come to him willingly, of her own accord, and let him make love to her as a man should, or would he have to continue to take her with his brute force? When had she become so important to him? When had he decided that he could no longer live his life unless she was part of it? Did he love her? Or was it because she belonged to Menghis? What was there about this slender girl with her low, throaty voice that could make his blood run cold and then hot? Right now, right at this moment, his blood was near the boiling point. She belonged to him!

Valentina watched him out of the corner of her eye and felt like a trapped animal with a hunter stalking its trail. Licking dry lips, she continued to watch him as he stretched luxuriously, the sinewy hardness of his muscular thighs rippling beneath the skin. Her breath quickened as she watched him, fascinated with his nakedness. It would be so easy to surrender to his arms, to forget everything for the moment and give herself to him and pretend he was Menghis. So easy, so very easy. She must think of other things, not those hard, muscular legs, not the broad chest, not the hot, smoldering eyes. She had to do something, say something, anything. She had to get away. Panic gripped her as she realized she had nowhere to go. The only thing visible as far as the eye could see was sand and more sand. She was lost.

Paxon noticed the angry look in her eyes and thought that she would never come willingly, not now. "Sleep," he said curtly. "I won't bother you."

"You lie through your teeth," Valentina hissed. "The moment my eyes close you will be atop me. Save your lies. I am not tired."

"Please yourself. My body is already more bruised than I want from your sharp bones. It will take me days to recover from your playful nudges."

"Loathsome desert rat!" Valentina spat as she seated herself near the spring, her eyes wary as she watched him dress. He must be tiring; sooner or later he would have to sleep, and when he did . . .

Paxon stared at her. "Your thoughts are obvious. As you know, a camel can go days without water. I am like that. I can go days without sleep. You cannot get away, so do not attempt anything." Valentina ignored him until exhaustion overcame her and she slept.

Paxon watched her, a frown settling on his face. What was he going to do with her when he got her back to Jakard?

The remainder of the seven-day journey to Jakard was spent in suspicious watchfulness. Paxon would watch Valentina with a speculative look in his eye, which she returned with hate and loathing.

It was night when they at last arrived in Jakard. The city was asleep and few lamps were burning. The palace sat just outside the city, surrounded by vast, sweet-smelling lawns and carefully tended shrubs and trees. Although it was not as large as Ramiff's palace in Napur, it was no less impressive. Against the starlit sky Valentina could see that the watchtowers were topped by minarets, their spires stabbing the velvety darkness. The fragrance of jasmine floated to her on a gentle breeze, reminding her of the flowers on Menghis's grassy knoll. The remembrance brought a stab of pain.

A manservant swung open the main doors, bowing low and offering the Moslem salute to his master. "Have the lamp lit," Paxon commanded, ignoring his servant's obvious pleasure to have him home.

On noiseless slippered feet the manservant scurried off to obey. Valentina looked about the great entrance hall, which rose about three stories to the stained-glass rotunda that was its roof. Now the glass was dark, black as the sky, but in daylight it would throw its dancing jewel colors into the interior. By most Moslem standards the palace was pristine, devoid of frescoes or statuary, having as its only decoration the wide expanse of mosaic floor and bowls of fresh flowers.

In spite of the lavishness of his palace, Valentina gave no sign of being impressed. Paxon brought her to a separate wing on the ground floor with doors leading out to splendid gardens. He watched her face carefully, hoping to see pleasure there, but Valentina's features remained inscrutable.

"There are no locks in my house," Paxon said quietly. "You may come and go as you please, but you must not try to leave the palace grounds, for if you do, you will be brought back. If you see anything you want changed in the palace, you have only to ask."

Valentina turned her back and gazed out at the lush desert garden, tears burning her eyes. Her eyes were wild when she looked at Paxon. "Yes, give me back Menghis's life! I want only Menghis. If you can't give me Menghis, then you can give me nothing. I loathe you, I detest you. You killed him!" she shrilled. "You killed your brother! And you have driven every emotion save hatred from me by your actions. You can keep me here, but you can never make me love you. You can never make me give myself to you. Every day, every hour, every minute I will compare you to Menghis, each time you will measure up a little less. When I can no longer tolerate it, I will either kill you or lay down and die. And then what will you have? This fine palace, women in a harem? May God have mercy on your soul," she whispered.

One day was like another as Valentina rose in the morning and struggled through the timeless hours. She was amazed that Paxon had kept his word to her and had not entered her rooms or demanded anything of her. The change in the dark-eyed man frightened her more than his old arrogant, mocking self. This new Paxon, this quiet, considerate man, was a complete stranger.

One night when the evening meal was completed, Paxon bowed low and spoke quietly. "I plan to leave on a hunt in the morning. I will return in three days' time. I only tell you this so you will not expect me at the evening meal. Remember what I told you about leaving here."

Valentina's voice was flat and devoid of any emotion. "I'll make you no promises. I owe you nothing."

"And I owe you even less," Paxon said harshly.

"You owe me Menghis's life. That is a debt you will

410

carry for the rest of your life, and one you can never repay. You hated him, you always hated him. I saw it in your eyes the night on the mountain. I saw it then and I see it now. You fooled Menghis, but you did not fool me. He never suspected, did he, Paxon? All this talk of Menghis helping me aid the Christians really meant nothing to you. That trip up the mountain was just to bait him in the hope that he would come down off the mountain so you could trick him somehow and kill him. When that did not work, you captured me in the hope that he would come for me. You knew if he left the mountain the *fedawi* would guard him no more, and then it would be just you and Menghis. What I say is the truth, is it not? Deny it if you will. And that day at the tourney in Messina, if the sun hadn't been in your eyes you would have killed him, would you not? Answer me, damn you. Tell me what I say is true. Tell me what kind of man plots and kills his brother. No answers, Paxon? I thought not. Then I will tell you. You, Paxon, were the legitimate heir to Jakard. Menghis, in your eyes, was the bastard son. But the bastard son got what you wanted, did he not? He got the Alamut, he got the power, he got the *fedawi!* You wanted it all. You always wanted what Menghis had. And when you couldn't get it any other way, you killed for it. Now you have nothing. What an empty victory you have achieved. Menghis is dead; the heir to the Alamut is another. Not you, never you. You have me prisoner in your palace. You have my body, but that is all you have. My mind and my heart will never be yours. Never!"

"Vicious woman!" Paxon exclaimed, lashing out at her with a clenched fist. Valentina took the blow to her shoulder and staggered backward.

"The truth is hard to bear," she whispered hoarsely. "Live with it, sultan of Jakard; live with your victory!"

Paxon stormed from the room, leaving her before he killed her on the spot. Her words burned into him, searing him with their truth. Cat, the black panther that had been brought to Jakard from the camp outside Napur, pushed against his thigh, eager for the hunt. "So, old friend," Paxon soothed, "are you still angry for having been left behind? A battleground is not a pleasant place to be, and at least you were spared witnessing my defeat."

Cat rubbed against him again, bright yellow eyes winking questioningly.

Chapter Thirty-one

The prone figure at the foot of the wall in the Jaffa courtyard stirred slightly, and a low groan sounded in the stillness. A savage pain ripped through his head, and the man beat a clenched fist into the sand. He thought he heard a voice, but the unbearable pain prevented him from moving.

Two nomads of the desert looked at each other and then down at the wounded man. One of them shrugged, and the other dropped to his knees and held a skin of water to the man's lips. Menghis drank greedily. The second nomad slid from his horse and opened a pouch tied to his saddle. He worked slowly and deftly and then placed a rolled blanket beneath Menghis's head. Satisfied with what he had done, the nomad then broke off a piece of root and forced it between Menghis's lips. "For the pain," he said simply. Menghis's dark eyes thanked the man. Gently the nomads picked him up and carried him out of the boiling sun.

"You must not move"—the nomad looked heavenward—"until the sun sets for the third time. It is a savage wound you carry," he said harshly. "We will leave you food and water. Pray to Allah for a horse or a camel, for we have none to spare."

Menghis watched the two nomads climb on their horses and ride from the enclosed courtyard. His eyes were blank and puzzled. Who were they and what was he doing in this place? He felt drowsy and disoriented. How had he gotten here? How had he come by the wound on his head? How long had he lain here? Father would be worried, and Paxon, where was Paxon? The thoughts were too much. He closed his eyes and slept.

When he awoke hours later, he knew no more than before he had drifted off to sleep. Was Paxon looking for him? Was Father worried? There must have been some sort of battle. Did Paxon get killed? He tried to raise himself on one elbow to look around, but he fell backward, jarring his head. Pain exploded, and he stuck the piece of root into his mouth and began to chew. He slept again.

At the end of the third day Menghis managed to stagger to his feet and walk around the courtyard. The stench of the dead bodies on the other side of the wall facing the desert was nauseating, and he retched. He had to get out of here. But first he had to check the bodies to be sure one of them was not Paxon. How was he going to explain to Father where he had been, when he could remember nothing? The last thing he remembered was riding out of Jakard with Paxon, the black panther cub running behind them. They were going hunting. Somewhere, somehow, something had happened along the way, but he knew he had not been dressed in the strange doeskin costume he now wore. "Paxon," he shouted hoarsely as he made his way among the dead bodies. Satisfied that the body of his brother was not among the dead, he staggered out to the desert and began his long trek to Jakard.

He roamed aimlessly for days, stopping from time to time for a drink from the skin or when the pain in his head became unbearable. All he knew was that he had to get back to Jakard and find out what happened to Paxon.

A band of camel-riding nomads spotted him several

413

days later, collapsed in a heap, too weary to go on. They held a whispered conversation, and one of the men pointed a dirty finger at his clothing. The name Menghis was mentioned, and then *Sheikh al Jebal*. They shook their heads and made as if to ride off. One of the men argued vehemently and motioned to Menghis's head with his hand. The word *fedawi* was was said in hushed tones. All eyes scanned the desert for some sign of the fearsome assassins. They shook their heads and then rode down to the fallen man. Again they whispered and then picked him up and carried him to a waiting camel.

When the moon crept from behind the clouds, they rode into their encampment. A call was raised, and an old woman walked over to the injured man. Her gnarled hands were gentle as she twisted his face this way and that. Gently her fingers probed the wound on his temple. She nodded, and Menghis was carried into her tent. She made him comfortable and then began to wash the sand and grime from his face. She crooned softly as she cleaned the vicious wound and picked the desert bugs from the clotted blood. Satisfied with her job, she liberally smeared a thick paste onto the wound and then covered it with a clean dressing. She knew who he was. Tales of this fearsome man were rampant across the desert. It wasn't his doeskin attire but his finely chiseled features and raven hair that made him recognizable to the old woman. She had seen him many times when he was a boy riding across the desert with his brother in pursuit.

.She crooned softly to the sleeping man and from time to time wiped at his feverish brow. Before the night was over, Allah would decide if he was to go or not. The old woman prayed that Allah would let him stay a while longer.

Menghis's fever raged throughout the night and into the morning. By the time the sun was high in the sky, it leveled off and then abated. His face was flushed and his body weak. When he forced his eyes open, he tried to smile at the old woman bending over him. She laid a finger against his lips and motioned him to be quiet. She explained where he was and how he came to be there. "It will be many days before you can travel," she said. "You have had no food and water for many days. You must stay here and gain your strength before you can go on. Our people will provide a horse for you when you are ready. For now you must sleep."

Menghis sighed and slept.

The days he spent in the encampment when his mind was lucid were spent talking with the old woman and some of the men. They told him strange things, things he could not believe. They told him he was Menghis of Jakard, who had been selected to sit on the Alamut and reign over the *fedawi*. The Alamut! When Menghis questioned how they knew this, they nodded sagely and said there was nothing in the desert that was unknown to the nomad. They told him of Saladin and King Richard. They spoke of his brother, Paxon, and said that he was a mighty warrior. When Menghis looked at them blankly, not understanding what they said, they told him the fever had eaten his brain and that was why he could not remember. When he told them he didn't understand what they were saying, they looked at him in puzzlement and then tapped their heads again. They offered to take him to the foot of the mountain, where the *fedawi* would see to his welfare. Stubbornly he shook his head and repeated over and over that he had to go to Jakard. The more he said it, the more convinced he was that something, someone, was waiting for him in Jakard.

When it was time for him to leave, he tied the skin of water and the sack of provisions to his horse and looked around at the people who had helped him survive. It was the old woman who grasped his shoulders in her old gnarled hands and looked deeply into his eyes. "Believe what you want, but it was your brother who did this to you. The sand reader saw this, and he is to be believed. The sands do not lie. Remember my words if you remember nothing else. Happiness does not wait for you in Jakard, as you may think. Only evil and misery. You must be wary and wise and look for the deceit and lies that await you. I prayed for many long nights to Allah to spare you, and he has granted my prayers. You must not let the prayers of an old woman be in vain." Menghis felt chilled at her words as he stood in the hot sun.

"I'll remember your words." Without a backward look he rode off to Jakard, his thoughts in a turmoil.

Another few hours and he would reach Jakard. Menghis took his time while his horse watered at the small spring. He drank slowly, savoring the cool wetness in his throat. He let the horse graze on the short, cropped grass of the oasis as he leaned back to get his bearings. He knew now that there was something wrong with his memory. If he was to believe the nomads, and there was no reason not to, then a portion of his life was missing. Perhaps in Jakard he would remember. Paxon would help him remember. The words of the old woman rang in his ears. Be wary, she had said. Be wary of Paxon, his brother. She said it was Paxon who had inflicted the wound to his head. If only he could remember. Why would Paxon strike him so brutally and so viciously and leave him to die? Every time he started to think about it, his head pounded. In Jakard, in familiar surroundings, he would remember, he was sure of it.

The hot sun felt warm and comforting, and he dozed contentedly, knowing he would be in Jakard within hours. For now all he wanted was for this contented feeling to last. Something teased at his memory as he tried to remember another time when he had felt like this, so at peace. The picture, for some reason, was not complete; something was missing. He shrugged and continued to doze. He felt, rather than heard, the hoofbeats approaching and opened one eye to observe the oncoming rider. He didn't move but remained still, watching the rider dismount to water his horse.

"Hello, Pax," he said softly.

Paxon whirled, his face drained of all color. Menghis opened his other eye and knew instinctively that what the old woman had said was true. He would have to be careful about how he acted and what he said. One wound in his head was all he could take.

"Menghis! How did you get here?" Paxon asked incredulously.

Menghis pointed to his horse. "The same way you did," he said lazily.

"Where . . . where are you going?" Paxon asked coldly.

"I think it is safe to assume we are going to the same place," Menghis drawled.

There was something wrong, Paxon could sense it. Menghis wasn't acting as if he . . . "How long have you been here?" Paxon demanded.

"An hour, two, three. Who keeps a record of time in the desert? Where are you coming from, Brother?"

"Hunting," Pax said curtly.

"I see no game. Was it four-legged or two-legged?" He laughed.

Paxon scowled. "What is it you want?"

"Nothing. Should I be wanting something?" Menghis asked quietly.

"Why are you here? Why are you traveling to Jakard? Answer me, damn it, and stop this riddle-talking!" Paxon was anxious to hear Menghis's reply.

"Is there something wrong with a son paying his father a visit? If so, Brother, tell me what it is."

"Father! Our father has been dead for many long years. What are you up to, Menghis?"

"I have no memory of anything of late. It seems I suffered a blow to my head, and the last thing I remember is you and a ride we were taking. Nomads tended to me and helped me regain my strength, and I thought I would come back to Jakard and talk with you. I thought familiar surroundings and my brother would help me to remember."

"I don't believe a word of what you're saying. It will not work, Menghis."

"Are you telling me I am not welcome in my father's house?"

"Prove to me that what you say is true," Paxon demanded.

"How can I do that? I never lied to you, Pax. Why would I lie to you about a thing like my memory? Is there something wrong in Jakard that you don't want me to know about?"

"There is nothing wrong in Jakard." Paxon's mind raced. If what Menghis said was true, it was the perfect solution to everything. He lowered himself and sat down next to Menghis. His manner and tone changed, and he became affable and friendly. "It's just that I'm tired after the battles and I recently returned to Jakard. I'm weary, Menghis. War does that. But," he said, smiling broadly, "things have changed a little. I'm to be married shortly. My bride-to-be awaits me in Jakard. Now the wedding will be perfect with my brother in attendance." He slapped Menghis soundly on the back and watched for his reaction.

"Is she beautiful, Pax?"

"I think you will say, when you see her, that she is the most beautiful woman in the world. Her name is Valentina."

Menghis frowned slightly as he repeated the name. "I've heard the name before," he said.

"I doubt it; the name is rare. I myself never heard of it until I met this beautiful lady."

"When does the wedding take place?" Menghis asked uncomfortably.

"Soon, now that you are here. In fact, I think I will arrange it for sometime within the week. It will be a festive occasion, and we will all be happy. You are happy for me, are you not, Menghis?"

"I do not know," Menghis answered honestly. "Perhaps it is just a surprise. I must get used to the idea."

"Let us be on our way," Paxon said jovially, a dark, brooding look in his eye that was not lost on Menghis.

Menghis got to his feet. "An excellent idea. I have a wild passion to sleep in a bed." The frown never left his face as he mounted his horse and followed Paxon from the oasis. The uneasiness inside him became more pronounced the closer they came to Jakard.

This wasn't the Paxon he knew, not this brooding, hulking, wary-eyed Paxon. Something was wrong. His own uneasiness increased as they rode into the palace grounds. Both men dismounted, and Paxon led Menghis around to the side entrance and took him into the palace through the kitchens. He summoned one of the burly guards who posed as a servant and issued orders for him to fetch clean clothes and bath water for his brother. He ordered a bath for himself and then watched as Menghis was escorted to the quarters that were provided for him.

His eyes narrowed, his stride long-limbed and purposeful, he headed for Valentina's rooms. Roughly he grasped her by the arm and dragged her down the corridor to a door, motioning for a guard to hold her. "There is someone in this room I want you to see and hear, Valentina. If she says one word, slit her throat," Paxon said harshly to the guard. "You will look and listen, do you understand?" Petrified, Valentina could only nod.

Paxon thrust open the door and Menghis whirled to face him. Paxon suppressed a smile when Valentina slid to the floor in a dead faint.

Chapter Thirty-two

"Women," Paxon sighed. "Be gentle," he said to the guard as he bent to pick up Valentina. "I couldn't wait for you to see my new bride. I think those ridiculous clothes frightened her. Well, what do you think of her?"

"Who? I barely caught a glimpse of her. Somehow I didn't think the woman of your choice would be one

419

who swooned and fainted at the sight of unfamiliar garb."

"She's worth her weight in gold," Paxon laughed.

"Then you will never get rich." Menghis laughed, "She looked rather scrawny to my eye."

"I thought you said you didn't see her." Paxon's tone was chilly.

"I said I didn't see her face. However, when a woman faints, she is all arms and legs. That is what I saw. Why are you so defensive?" Menghis asked thoughtfully.

"I'll see you at the dinner hour. Then you shall be properly introduced to my bride-to-be," Paxon said, ignoring his question.

He closed the door quietly and walked to Valentina's rooms. He entered just as she was sitting up in bed, her eyes wild and terrified. "What a dastardly trick to play on me! You're inhuman!" She shivered.

"It was no trick. It was Menghis, and as you can see, he is not dead." He wanted to kill her the moment he saw the joy leap into her eyes. He held himself in check when he added, "He has no memory of what happened. The last thing he remembers is when he lived here with me and our father. He has no memory of the Alamut or of you."

"You lie! What sort of trick is this?"

"You are the daughter of a physician; you must have heard of things like this. Rare, I understand, but they do happen. At first I, too, thought it was a trick when I saw him in the desert, but I am sorry to say that it is the truth. He does not remember you. When he looks at you he will see his brother's prospective bride. I told him we are to be married. He is happy for me, or so he said."

"Never! I told you I want nothing to do with you. I loathe you, I detest you. Your very presence makes my skin crawl!"

"Your feelings will change; if not, your love will die, and this time I will be certain that he is dead, not just wounded. I will never make that mistake again. At the dinner hour you will see if I lie or not when he looks upon you with strange eyes. His life rests in your hands, Valentina. You have several hours to think on it. Pray that your decision is the right one."

When the door closed behind him, Valentina dropped to the floor, her shoulders shaking with sobs. It couldn't be. Perhaps Menghis was playing a trick on Paxon. He was alive! God, he was alive! He was alive, and that was all that mattered. Menghis was alive! Paxon was right when he said she must have heard of such things when she lived with her father. Not for the world would she tell him that the two cases she had heard her father speak of had completely recovered. True, it took time and patience, but they had recovered. She would pray that the same thing happened to Menghis. But the other matter . . . How could she agree to what he asked of her? No, it was wrong, what he demanded of her. She couldn't marry him and live in this palace with Menghis so close; to see him, to want him, to be able to reach out and touch him. An inner voice whispered that she could do whatever had to be done to spare Menghis's life. Would Paxon keep his promise so that no harm came to Menghis? Not likely. At the first opportunity he would kill him, she was sure of it. For now she would wait and watch. All she needed was the knowledge that Menghis was alive. That, and that alone, would sustain her and enable her to do whatever it was that had to be done. Menghis was alive!

Valentina took extra pains with her toilette that day. She donned a colorful gown of rich apricot and wove a strand of pearls through her hair. She knew she looked well, more beautiful than she had in months. Her eyes glowed and her cheeks were flushed at the prospect of seeing Menghis. She still couldn't believe that he was alive and that in moments she would see him and look into his eyes. She offered up a small prayer of thanks and sat down to wait patiently for Paxon to take her to Menghis.

When he came, his manner was arrogant and insolent as he grasped her arm and pulled her from the room. "Remember what I told you: no mistakes and no tricks. You can feast your eyes on my brother all you want, but you will be civil and attentive to me. We understand each other, do we not?"

Valentina nodded. At that moment she would have promised anything just to see Menghis.

When they entered the vast dining hall, Menghis was waiting. Valentina's breath caught in her throat as she stared at him. How handsome and virile he was. How commanding his presence. He had shed his customary doeskin and was now wearing a caftan the color of the sky on a bright summer day. He eyed her appreciatively when Paxon introduced her to him. His dark eyes narrowed slightly when he stared at her and then at his brother. There was something familiar about her, someone she reminded him of. Whatever it was, it would come to him sooner or later. For now it was Paxon's attitude that was confusing him. He was strung as tight as a drum skin. Why? He was right, the woman was quite the most beautiful he had ever seen. Why did she keep staring at him? Was she comparing him with Paxon, and was he measuring up short? For some reason the thought annoyed him.

The dinner was excellent, but Valentina barely noticed what she ate. Her eyes were on Menghis, her heart thumping madly in her chest. Paxon had been right. He didn't remember her. There was no awareness in his eyes. But still, when she looked at him he returned her gaze. He looked puzzled. Was he wondering why she stared at him, why she couldn't tear her eyes away from his? So far she had not uttered a word. Paxon was saying something and waiting for an answer. What had he asked her? She moistened her lips and stared at Menghis, willing him to help her.

He read the fright in her eyes and leaned back in the chair. "Paxon," he drawled, "what would Valentina know of harems? I find your humor in poor taste. You're upsetting her. See how her eyes grow cloudy. Enough of this conversation." He rose and walked around to Paxon and laid a hand on his brother's shoulder. "I congratulate you on your choice of a woman. I envy you. You were right, she is quite

422

the most beautiful woman I've ever seen." He stood next to Valentina, gazing down into her eyes. He saw her tears and was perplexed. And what else was he seeing? Whatever, it was gone, and he bowed low.

Valentina raised her head and said softly, huskily, "Menghis." The sound of his own name jarred him so much that he almost stumbled as he left the table. Why was he having these feelings? Why was he drawn to this beautiful woman who was soon to be his brother's wife? Something teased at his memory but would not surface. It would come, he was sure of it, now that he was back at Jakard.

He stood for a moment outside the door and was startled to hear his brother speaking in a harsh tone.

"So, you couldn't let it be. You had to say his name. Even a fool would have heard the torment in your voice. Don't make that mistake again. He doesn't remember you. He is an honorable man, and he knows you belong to me. Put your memories behind you and we will have a full, rich life. I promise that to you. Forget Menghis."

"Why don't you ask me to cut out my heart? Why don't you ask me to cut out my tongue? I could do those things! I cannot cut him from my mind or my heart. What you ask is impossible. I will do what you say because I know you will kill him if I refuse. I'm no fool, Paxon. The first chance you get and he is unprepared, you plan to kill him. I want your word he will not be harmed. Your word, Paxon. I will accept nothing less."

"You have no right to make demands of me. No right at all. I will do what I see fit. Your concern for my brother touches me deeply. It is a pity he cannot understand what it is you're doing for him."

"If you harm him, I swear I'll kill you," Valentina said huskily, her voice full of emotion.

Menghis left his position at the closed door, his heart pounding in his chest. What did it mean? It was obvious, even Paxon knew it, that the woman had known him before. Why couldn't he remember? How could he forget a woman as beautiful as Valentina?

What had she meant to him? Why was she marrying Paxon if she loved *him?* So he wouldn't be killed. That, too, was obvious from the conversation. Now all he had to do was figure out why Paxon wanted to kill him. The woman didn't trust him. I don't trust him, either, he muttered to himself as he lay down on the low divan. The nomad woman's words again rang in his ears. "Your brother is the one who inflicted the wound you carry." Why did Paxon want him dead?

The palace buzzed with activity for the approaching wedding. Valentina tried to stay out of Paxon's way, for wherever he was, Menghis was, and she could not bear to look at the two of them together. Her eyes would travel to Menghis and then well with tears. His name was always on her lips. She had to clench her hands to her sides to force herself from reaching out to touch him.

Her eyes grew haunted and her cheeks sunken and she merely picked at the food placed before her. She prayed constantly as she paced her room, willing Menghis to come to her and tell her he remembered.

Two days before her wedding, she stood on the balcony watching Menghis and Paxon ride out to a hunt. Her heart pounded in her chest as she fought back the words she wanted to call out.

Paxon and Menghis rode out, each busy with his own thoughts. It was while they sat together waiting for a wild pheasant to appear that Menghis questioned for the first time the obviously unhappy state of Paxon's prospective bride. For days he had pondered the words he had heard on his first night back in the palace. And for days he had stared into tear-filled eyes, and each time he felt more puzzled and unhappy. There was no joy in him for his brother's coming marriage, and this troubled him. If Paxon would just show his hand and get whatever it was out in the open, perhaps they could resolve the matter. This constant blind baiting and the banter of words having a double meaning were beginning to play on his nerves.

A pheasant took wing and soared overhead as both

men raised their eyes to gauge the distance. "She's mine. I spotted her first. She's mine," Paxon shouted triumphantly.

Menghis closed his eyes as Paxon brought up his arm. Mine . . . mine . . . mine . . . He swallowed hard as he opened his eyes to see the pheasant fall to the ground.

"She's a beauty, and I bagged her myself. She's mine, Menghis."

Mine . . . mine . . . mine . . . Menghis. Where had he heard those words before? His heart thundered in his chest and his breathing became ragged and harsh. Paxon, seeing nothing save Menghis's closed eyes, laughed. "You never could stand to see a dead animal. Don't worry, Brother. She's mine!"

In a blinding flash Menghis saw himself upon a mountain, Valentina at his side. And Paxon, his face threatening and alive with malice. "Leave here, Brother, and leave me with what is mine!"

Mine . . . mine . . . mine . . . When he opened his eyes they were cold, dark, and fathomless. "Until you devour it, and then you'll have nothing left," he said quietly.

Paxon's head jerked upright as he looked at Menghis. "And what is that supposed to mean?"

"Whatever you want it to mean," Menghis drawled nonchalantly. "The hour grows late; we had better return."

Chapter Thirty-three

Dinner that evening consisted of the pheasant Paxon had bagged. He bragged about how Menghis had sat with his eyes closed during the entire event. Valentina looked at Paxon and said coolly,

"There are some people who love wild animals and would not kill them for all the gold in the world, much less eat them."

She stared at Menghis, willing him, compelling him, to look at her and remember. He met her gaze and stared deeply into her eyes. "I once had a deer I called Aloe Bud," he said quietly. "Do you remember, Pax?"

"No," Paxon said shortly, his eyes going from one to the other. "You always surrounded yourself with a forest of animals."

Menghis shrugged. "I thought you might remember. It's of no matter now."

Valentina's blood raced through her veins like a flood as she picked at her food, not daring to raise her eyes for fear that Paxon would read what was written for Menghis to see. He remembered, she knew he did! Finally unable to bear it another moment, she raised her eyes, her heart in them, and said softly, "I have never heard anything more beautiful."

Menghis smiled to show he understood, then stood up and asked to be excused, pleading tiredness. Paxon watched his retreating back, a wary look in his eyes.

Again Valentina forced herself to raise her eyes, this time to stare at Paxon as wave after wave of pure hatred emanated from her. She was convinced that, as soon as the wedding was over, he would kill Menghis while he slept. He wanted the supreme pleasure of having Menghis there to witness his marriage to Valentina. It made no difference to him whether or not Menghis remembered. What mattered was that he, not Menghis, would have Valentina.

Valentina stood on her balcony, tears streaming down her cheeks. Her heart was in her throat as she watched Menghis skirt the parapet from one balcony to the other and descend to the secluded garden outside her chamber. She prayed the moon would stay behind the clouds just a while longer. Just another moment and he would be next to her. Her love!

He raced to her, crushing her in his arms, his hand

426

supporting her head as he pressed his lips to hers in a frenzy. At last he released her and stared deeply into her eyes. "I could never forget you," he whispered huskily. "From the moment I returned I knew that somehow you were entwined in my life. You *are* my life. Without you there is no meaning to anything. Later we will talk. Now we must escape this damnable prison we both find ourselves in. Paxon is sleeping off the wine from the evening meal. At best we will have four hours' head start."

Valentina watched as he fashioned a rope from the heavy draperies. He talked while he worked. "I have a message for you from Ahmar and Rosalan. They have a male child they are dying to show off. I left Aloe Bud at the palace with your Ahmar. I believe she sings to the new child." Valentina laughed happily.

Together they ran across the garden to the high wall. "Come, you first. I'll follow you. Make no sound, now," he warned quietly, "or neither of us will live to see that male child."

Safe on the ground, they raced to the stables, careful to stay in the shadows of the gardens. Quietly Menghis led two horses from the stable, the black Arabian and a white stallion. "A perfect match," he whispered. "They both ride like the wind. Valentina, there will be no saddles, and we must walk them to the edge of the desert so that their hoofbeats will not be heard. We will have to ride hard and fast, with no stops for water or food. Can you do it?"

"Of course I can do it. I can do anything if you are with me."

Menghis gathered her close to him as he helped her mount the white stallion. The desert lay before them like a vast, untouched canvas without color.

"Where are we going?" Valentina asked. "Not that I care, as long as I am with you."

Menghis grinned. "To a place Pax will never think to look, at least not right away. To Baghdad, where Saladin keeps an emergency storehouse. He has them near all the major cities. He keeps them well stocked for anyone making a hasty escape from the Christians. Tell me, can you think of a better place?"

"I don't care, Menghis."

He reached out and clasped her hand before he spurred the horse beneath him. The black Arabian raced off, sand spurting up from his heels. Valentina's mount followed closely behind him.

They rode till noon of the following day, and then they stopped for a few moments till Menghis got his bearings. They stopped only once more, to snatch a few hours of much-needed sleep. Valentina lay cradled in his strong arms, her cheek resting in the hollow of his neck. This then, was heaven, she thought as she drifted off to sleep.

Menghis shook her gently and kissed her lightly as he drew her to her feet. "I sense hoofbeats in the distance. We must ride. Somehow Pax has managed to pick up our trail."

Valentina mounted and raced from the cavelike enclosure in which they had rested. Menghis's horse pounded after her.

They rode fast and hard for another day till they came to a small oasis. "Baghdad is not far from here," Menghis said. "In the caves are stores and weapons if we should need them. Not so much water, Valentina," he cautioned. "Later you can gorge yourself. Two more hours and we'll be safe, for the moment. Valentina," he said quietly, "you know what will happen if Paxon finds us, don't you?" She nodded.

"I'll have to kill him. If I don't, he'll kill us both."

"I know that, Menghis."

They continued with their ride, skirting the city of Baghdad, and eventually worked their way to the banks of the Tigris River, where the terrain was rocky and barren, except for a few sparse clumps of windswept trees. The low cliffs along the riverbanks were dotted with caves. Menghis went from one cave to another till he found the one he wanted. Once inside, the horses safe in the darkness, Menghis led her further into the cavern depths. After disguising the entrance once again with saplings and shrubs, he lit several candles and then prepared some food.

Valentina looked around in awe. "And Saladin said he was short of provisions!" she marveled.

"Men of war always lie. Saladin is no different than your king. That is no longer important. The only thing important is that we are safe for now. We can eat and sleep in peace until tomorrow. And then we will sit here and wait for Paxon to arrive, because we cannot run forever. We must meet what must be met. We have a better chance here, without the ranks of Paxon's guards."

They gorged themselves on dried figs and ripe cheeses. They found a bottle of wine and emptied it and then slept entwined in each other's arms. Valentina squirmed contentedly and murmured his name over and over in her sleep. Menghis smiled in his sleep, his arms tight about Valentina. There was no lovemaking, no mingling of long, searching kisses. The heat of their bodies nestled closely, and the overwhelming feeling of their love, brought contentment and peace.

They woke the following day and breakfasted on dried figs and cheese. They drank another bottle of wine and sat back to wait for Paxon. They sat close together in silence. Words were no longer necessary.

A few hours after noon they were startled out of their thoughts by the sound of a voice. "Menghis! You bastard! Come out and fight like a man! Or are you going to plead you're a man of peace and prove you're afraid of a fair fight?"

Menghis rose from his place near Valentina, his eyes expressing his sorrow. She knew the pain that this battle with his brother caused him. Taking up his lance, Menghis walked out into the bright sunshine, leading his horse behind him. Down on the sandy beach, near the water's edge, he mounted. Only then did his eyes seek his brother.

"Pax, the truth. What does the woman mean to you? The truth to your brother."

"She has betrayed those who gave her life when she was about to die. She lies and steals, and she would die for the Christians. Does that answer your question?" Paxon asked coolly.

"To a point. One more question, Brother. Remember now, the truth. Would you have let her die on that damnable cross?"

"You ask many questions that are none of your concern. However, since you are my brother, I can do no less than give you an answer. Yes, I would have let her die."

Menghis looked deeply into the dark eyes of his brother and nodded.

"It's time," Paxon agreed. "No games, Menghis. To the death!"

The ebony eyes were solemn. "You have only to ask, Brother, and I will oblige." Gently he flicked the reins, and the horse danced his way across the sands.

Paxon inched his way to take his position in front of Menghis. The fight to the death had begun. Paxon's eyes measured the length of the sandy strip of beach, the sun directly in his eyes. Menghis's snorting, pawing steed seemed jittery as he tried to quiet it. Paxon's mount waited patiently, almost docile.

Paxon hefted the lance in his hand, positioned his shield, and was satisfied. The horse jolted forward. Both riders crossed lances in the middle of the field. The clank of metal against metal was loud in the stillness. Both riders retained their seats as they galloped back to their positions to repeat the charge. This time the sun was in Menghis's eyes. The Arabian had a mind of his own as Menghis spurred him onward. Just as Paxon's lance shot out, Menghis slid under the horse's belly, his own lance grazing the steed beneath Paxon.

"Bastard," Paxon shouted to his brother. "I said no tricks."

"So you did, Brother. Forgive me, I forgot."

Three more times they charged, neither brother unseating the other.

On the seventh charge, Paxon again had the sun in

his eyes. The lance gripped securely, he waited for Menghis's call to charge. He was a split second off in his timing as he took to the sandy strip, his lance held high, dark eyes full of hate, white teeth gleaming. The lance shot forward at the exact moment Menghis was abreast of him. His aim was accurate, but the effort of the toss made him slide sideways on his mount, and Menghis's lance found its mark. His body jolted backward as blood spurted from the wound, and then he slumped forward.

Menghis reined in his horse and galloped after his brother, grinding to a halt. "Fool!" he shouted. "Why did you do it? You had the advantage. Why?" he cried in a tormented voice.

A bubble of blood stained Paxon's mouth. "The sun was in my eyes," he gasped.

"You lie," Menghis said gently as he eased Paxon from the horse and held him in his arms.

"How bad is my wound, Menghis? Can I be taken back to Jakard? No lies, Brother."

"No lies, Pax." Menghis's voice was husky with emotion. "You could not survive the ride even if there was a litter."

"Menghis." Paxon grasped his brother's arm imploringly. "How did it happen? Where did it all go wrong?" he asked, his voice a hoarse rasp. "Was it because I never learned to love? Was that my mistake? Was it because I was so taken with fighting wars that I had no time for life? How did I allow my jealousy of you to get such a stranglehold on me? Tell me, Menghis, before I die, how did it happen?"

"I have no answers, Pax. If I could bleed for you, I would," he said in a tormented voice, watching life slip away from his brother.

"I know that now." Paxon coughed, blood dribbling from the corner of his mouth. "You have everything, and I can leave nothing behind me. There will be no one save you to mourn me and no one to take care of Jakard, as I promised our father."

"You're wrong, Pax. You are leaving behind the greatest thing a man can leave when he goes to his other world. The woman Rosalan has given birth to a male child. Your child, Pax. You leave behind an heir to Jakard."

Paxon's eyes were glazed with pain. "I said no lies, Brother. How can it be . . ." he demanded, his breath shallow and irregular. "Who is this woman, the one you call Rosalan?"

Menghis felt unspeakably sad for his brother because he did not even know the woman who bore his child. He spoke softly, thinking how lucky he was that it would be Valentina who would bear his children. "Her name is Rosalan. She was in the palace of Napur with Valentina. Her background is Bedouin, like our own forefathers."

"If you speak the truth, fetch the child so I may see him before I die," Paxon gasped weakly.

Menghis's anguished eyes sought those of Valentina. Her eyes pleaded as great tears rolled down her cheeks.

"Pax, the ride will take hours, and I don't . . ."

"I'll live till I see the child. Do it, Menghis."

"Pax, I can't lie to you. Another hour, two at the most. I could never ride to Napur and fetch the child and be back before you . . ."

"Damn your eyes, Menghis, I said I would live and I will." The words cost him dearly and he fell back, his breathing harsh, ragged gasps.

At the sight of the gushing blood Menghis tried to quiet his brother. "Don't talk, Pax, lie still."

"Call the *fedawi,* they will bring my son. Did you forget . . . they will serve you till the end of your days. You have only to ask. Do it, for there isn't much time."

Menghis's mind raced. Paxon was right. How could he have forgotten something so important? While the *fedawi* might not guard him any more, they would do as he asked. All he had to do was make his request known, and the men would race across the desert and bring back the child.

"Take care of him, Valentina," Menghis said as

he turned and sped toward the sandy strip of beach at the far end of the caves.

Valentina dropped to her knees, tears streaming down her cheeks as she clasped Paxon's hand in hers. "And he calls me a fool," Paxon gasped as Menghis's call to the *fedawi* shattered the quiet beach. "He is so in love with you he can think of nothing else." At the sight of her tears he spoke sorrowfully. "Do you weep for me, Valentina?

"Yes, Paxon, I weep for you. Perhaps you think you fooled Menghis, like the time on the mountain, but I saw what you did. The sun was not in your eyes. You could have killed Menghis at that moment, but you didn't. Once I cursed you for killing him. Now I thank you for sparing him."

"Once I heard my father . . ." A violent fit of coughing overtook Paxon, and he clutched at his chest, his breathing very shallow.

"Don't try to speak, Paxon. Save your strength for when you see your son. Please, lie still," Valentina cried in a tortured voice.

"I must tell you something. Once, when I was a boy . . . I heard our father speak to Menghis, and he told him that he loved his mother dearly, that love such as his could move mountains. I always remembered that, for it was Menghis's mother he spoke of, not mine. I could never have moved a mountain for you . . . Valentina . . . but I would have tried if you had . . I would have tried to move the mountain . . ."

"I know that, Paxon." Valentina cried with abandon. Paxon held out a trembling hand to comfort her.

"Save your tears, Valentina. I am not worthy of them. I caused you to shed many tears, and for that I am truly sorry. Has the sun gone beyond the clouds?"

Valentina raised her tearful eyes at the bright golden sun, and her heart sank. "Yes, it is getting dark," she said sorrowfully.

Paxon groped for her hand and tried to speak. "There isn't much time, Valentina."

433

"You must hold on, Paxon; fight like the warrior you are. The *fedawi* will not let you down. I know they won't," Valentina whispered hoarsely. "Fight, Paxon, fight like you never fought before. This time you will be fighting for your son. Your son, Paxon. Rest a moment, and I will see if they are approaching."

Valentina scrambled to her feet and raced to the edge of the sandy beach where Menghis was standing, his hands cupped to his eyes to ward off the bright glare. "They're coming," he said hoarsely.

"There isn't much time, Menghis," she whispered. "Dear God, make them ride faster," she begged.

A patrol of *fedawi* rode the desert, one rider in the lead, his arms encircling a small bundle. Menghis's eyes lit up as the rider handed down the small, tightly wrapped bundle. Menghis gave the child to Valentina and turned to speak softly to the men. Within moments they rode off, their mission completed.

Valentina raced back to Paxon and dropped to her knees, her hands busily unwrapping the tiny infant. "Your son, Paxon," she said tearfully. Gently she laid the baby on his chest and watched as his hand tenderly cupped the tiny head.

"Menghis, it is so dark, I can barely see. Light the lantern and hold up my head. Hurry, there is so little time."

"He is so beautiful, so very beautiful, Paxon. He will be a remarkable child, a magnificent man. And when he is grown, we will tell him of his father." Valentina was crying openly now, and Paxon smiled happily as he cradled the small child to his face.

"Menghis, your promise, Brother . . ." He coughed, his lips dark with blood. "I have no right to ask, but look after my son for me. Tell him if I had known, if I had been as wise as you . . . tell him . . ."

"I'll tell him. Pax. You have my word that he will grow to be as mighty a man as his father." Menghis handed the child to Valentina and clasped his brother to him.

"Mine, the one thing that is really . . . mine."

Silent tears coursed down Menghis's face. His brother. Paxon. Warrior. Paxon. As he looked down on Paxon's chiseled features he saw on them a peace that had been denied Paxon in life.

Menghis buried his brother in the deep recesses of Saladin's cave while Valentina cradled Paxon's son, Mehemet Cenghiz. The warrior was laid to rest. He had joined Allah.

"How beautiful you look holding the child," Menghis said softly.

"I feel beautiful. I only wish it were our son I was holding. Menghis, we must go to Napur so that Rosalan can have her child returned to her. Your *fedawi* would not have taken the time for explanations but would merely sweep him out of the cradle. She will be out of her mind with worry."

Menghis smiled. "You forget Aloe Bud is there. She would have said something reassuring to Rosalan when she saw the *fedawi*. But you are right, my love, we must return to Napur."

The ride to Napur was a quiet one. Valentina held the infant and crooned soft, soothing words while Menghis watched, a smile of contentment, mingled with sorrow, on his face.

As they approached the gates to the palace it was Aloe Bud who greeted them with shrill cries of happiness, clutching first at Menghis and then at Valentina. "I knew it was you who sent for the baby. I told Rosalan not to worry. I told her Menghis would bring him back safely. Oh, I'm so happy," she continued to squeal. "Valentina, do you think that Cenghiz looks like a hatched bird with no feathers? Rosalan says all babies look like that. Oh, I'm so happy to see you!" she squealed happily.

"Where is Rosalan? And where is Ahmar?" Valentina asked as she entered the palace.

"They pray beneath the Judas tree. I told them there was no need, but they would not listen. See, here comes Rosalan now."

Rosalan stared and stopped in her tracks at the

sight of Valentina and Menghis. It was to her baby she ran, arms outstretched, Ahmar close behind her.

"So, steal my child, will you? I should have listened to the child," Rosalan cried happily, tears streaming down her cheeks. "Oh, Valentina, I never thought I would see you again," she said, hugging her friend. "Now we're all together. I thought I would die when those men swept the child from his cradle. You were gone and so was my baby. You must tell me what has happened since you left. Come, we will have tea and cakes."

Menghis and Ahmar stood watching the two women as they laughed and hugged each other, tears streaming down their cheeks. The expressions on both men's faces clearly said, "Foolish women."

"Rosalan, I have such news for you that you will never believe in your wildest dreams. Such news," Valentina repeated happily, her voice girlish and young.

"Tell me. Don't keep me waiting," Rosalan demanded. "What is it?" she cried, hopping first on one foot and then on the other. "Valentina, tell me this minute!" She stamped her foot.

"You and Ahmar are to go with Cenghiz to Jakard and rule the palace and keep it intact for your son. It was his father's last request. You were right, Rosalan, your son was born to rule. For now it is you and Ahmar who will shape and guide his future in Jakard."

Rosalan was speechless. Ahmar wore a silly grin on his face, and Aloe Bud was dancing with glee. Menghis smiled happily as he put his arm around Valentina.

"Can I go with them, Menghis?" Aloe Bud squealed.

"But of course you may go. What in the world would Cenghiz do without you to sing to him at night? What would I do? I cannot sing," Rosalan laughed. "When are we to leave, Valentina?"

"A week or two. Cenghiz should be in his new home as soon as possible. Take with you whatever you need. All Menghis wants is for you to be happy."

Menghis drew Valentina aside in the shadows of the garden. "Valentina," he said quietly, not knowing how to continue, at a loss for words.

Valentina read his meaning in his night-dark eyes, which were swimming with unshed tears. "Go, Menghis. I understand there is a time in each man's life when he must be alone. For you that time is now. Hurry back to me, Menghis. I will be waiting." She smiled gently, showing him with her eyes that she would wait forever if necessary.

Menghis took her in his arms. "And where have you learned so much of the ways of men? How do you read my needs before I know them myself?" He gazed into her eyes, seeing their clear sapphire brightness which bespoke her happiness. "If only Allah will help me to make you as happy as you are at this moment."

"All that is necessary is for Allah to place me in your arms and keep me there forever. My happiness will be complete when my love returns. Hurry back to me, Menghis."

He kissed her deeply, meaningfully, his lips silently telling her that his life had no meaning without her at his side. He would return. He would always return.

Valentina passed the next few days catching up on the news of Napur, which Rosalan and Ahmar excitedly shared. Even while they spoke, Valentina's thoughts were on Menghis, listening for the sound of his mount's hooves on the garden path or his voice when he entered the palace.

Ahmar had seen to it that Ramiff was given the proper Moslem burial befitting a much-loved emir. Mohab was placed beside his old friend, just as he had wished. Master and servant were equal now in an eternal friendship.

Saladin had appointed Menghis and Valentina to rule the kingdom of Napur under his direct supervision. While they spoke, Aloe Bud ran in from the garden, squealing excitedly. "His first tooth—little Cenghiz has his first tooth!" They all laughed and said they would follow her to the garden to see for themselves. Valentina lagged behind.

Aloe Bud put her arms around Valentina's neck, hugging her tightly. "We miss him, don't we?" she said shyly.

"Yes, little one, we miss him." Valentina's voice was warm and deep, as it always was when she spoke of Menghis.

"He will be home soon now, I think," Aloe Bud reassured her.

"I think so, too." Valentina smiled. "Come, now, I must see Cenghiz's first tooth."

Valentina awakened to the pressure of lips covering hers in a kiss as warm and penetrating as the desert sun. Menghis! Happiness glowed in her eyes as she threw herself into his arms, holding him as though she would never let him leave her again.

There was no time for words as their lips came together, carrying them to a blissful place of ecstasy. Menghis's lips became more urgent, demanding, exploring, claiming her for his own. Deeply, scorchingly, his lips caressed hers, then became demanding again, urgent, imperative.

His lips exacted a response of passion, tasting, teasing, bringing her to unknown heights. He blazed a path to her throat, to her breasts, caressingly, then demandingly, urgently. He whispered her name over and over, as though he could not believe she was at last in his arms. Their lovemaking was as wild as the surf and as rhythmic as the seas.

Hungrily she answered his kisses, touching him with her cool fingers, exciting his passion to a crescendo. His sun-darkened hands moved over her, seeking, searching, drawing her closer, always closer.

And always he whispered her name.

Their bodies demanded release as they strained toward each other, and low sounds of ecstasy and passion heightened their love.

The soft cries of her name beckoned to her, called

to her, summoning her to join him at the zenith and culmination of their flaming desire. "Valentina!"

Afterward he lay beside her, her dark head resting upon his shoulder. She sighed contentedly, feeling his arm tighten imperceptibly around her, nestling closer, whispering soft words of endearment. Her man of peace. Her man of love. His lips caressed her warm bare shoulder as he breathed her name.

"Shh," she whispered, placing tender fingertips against his lips. He turned his head, pressing his mouth against her smooth wrist, loving her sweetness and seeking the warmth of her.

"I am here, I'll always be here," she whispered. "You are my life. I will cherish you and our love for all time."